The Shadow of This World

PubRight

PubRight
New Tripoli, PA 18066 USA

The Shadow of This World

Print ISBN: 978-1499341607

Cover by Sessha Batto

This is a work of fiction. Names, characters, places and incidents either are the product of the author's imagination or are used fictitiously and any resemblance to actual persons, living or dead, business establishments, events or locales is entirely coincidental.

Second PubRight electronic publication: May 2014
Second PubRight print publication: May 2014

Published in the United States of America with international distribution.

Dedication

To Denysé Bridger
For inspiring this tale

Chapter One

Veluria followed the echoes of water slapping ancient pilings. The cobblestoned passage lay cast in shadows, dank and spiritless, yawning ahead with a dim pinpoint of light to guide her path. She wished she could have ignored the message but her instincts—and traitorous sentimentality—refused to acknowledge the danger. Had Stefano indeed summoned her? And for what purpose? It seemed out of character, this young man hardly adept at the subterfuge that came so easily to others of his family, the Medicis. The name, whispered down long corridors, brought chills and loathing, intermixed with respect and awe. A heady concoction. One she found exhilarating, and all too enticing.

"Before the game is afoot, thou still let'st slip," she whispered into the dank enclosure. Frowning, she mentally cautioned herself against dipping into arcane pockets of knowledge, though no one of this time would know the quote or its source. Or rather … they shouldn't. And that bothered her, sending icy prickles cascading over her skin in stark contrast to the cloying warmth and humidity trapped in the passageway.

She moved with stealth bought at a price, her senses on high alert, attuned to whispers and soft shushings. Scent and sound engulfed her as she floated toward the distant opening, her skirts fanned out about her slight figure, the rustling of heavy silk lost to the thrumming in her ears.

Pausing, she closed her eyes, extending her senses in search of a presence—felt, not seen—as the mists from the canal seeped through the underground corridor. A cool breeze drifted past, a wraith, a hint of something. Or someone.

1

Stefano? She whispered in her mind, a question. She didn't like questions, not when her senses should have locked onto his presence. She fingered the velum and the masculine scrawl that hinted at a mysterious tryst, one that made little sense. For nearly a month she'd been carefully building rapport and currying confidences, using her relationship with Stefano to open doors, building on the young man's standing at court. This summons had the ring of ominous despite the pretty phrases and sentiment.

Carissima Veluria,
Mio fiore più preziosa... Cuore del mio cuore...
È urgente incontriamo segretamente...

Unfortunately, with Stefano, everything was 'urgent', including his *ardeur*, so much so that her not inconsiderable skills struggled to keep up. The small entertainments, as her mentor had so coyly referred to the terse instructions issued for the execution of her mission, had surprised and delighted her. She could get used to being someone's 'precious flower'. But not at the cost of losing perspective. Far too easy to do when a naïve young courtier seduced so prettily.

This time ... this place: Venice. The name itself reeked of the seductive, amongst other things. Stefano, of all the Medici brood, was the adept, the one who navigated the tricky passions so unique to the halls of power in the city. Papàl, civil ... the handsome boy-man managed indulgences without incurring costs. Something her sisters would examine with interest if she ever managed to return to her own dimension.

Mother Superior may have been correct to question her choice, but the young Stefano, for all his naiveté and courtly mannerisms, still provided a relatively safe ingress into the centers of influence and corruption. Had she tried for one of the other, more elusive—and eminently more powerful—brothers, the inevitable suspicion and distrust would have denied her the access she required. For now she was nothing more than one of a long line of Stefano's infatuations, of little consequence, dismissed as yet another vacuous courtesan. And, as such, virtually invisible.

That kind of anonymity could not be bought at any price.

The heavy skirts dragged at her waist, the need for authenticity far outweighing what common sense dictated was unsuitable when mission parameters went askew. She stared at the brightening opening leading to the canal, debating her next move.

Damn. This makes no sense. Why am I here?

The answer came in a blinding rush—a searing white hot pain assaulting her brain, catapulting her against an ornate beam supporting the passageway. Veluria gasped for air, desperate to thrust the filthy presence out and away before it discovered the hidden vaults guarding her own secrets. She fought the rising bile and vertigo but the drilling intrusion refused to release her, robbing her of all thought. She slumped against the beam and slid boneless onto the wet stone.

Zoning in and out of consciousness, she felt rather than heard the staccato rhythm of booted feet. The attacker—or a rescuer? She could not discern from whence the presence came. Gathering what energy she could, she lay supine, waiting. She would need every nuance and control her long years of training afforded her. But the stab of fear penetrated like a battering ram, turning her gut inside out, perception upside down.

"Veluria, take care, there may be other interested parties," Mother Superior had warned. *"Prepare yourself, child, for we must not interfere, though your need be manifest. Use the gifts available."* She paused, hands clasped about her tora, the clacking beads suddenly silent.

Veluria interjected, before the Mother could continue, anxious to assure, though she, of all of them, had less need to do so, "I am not inexperienced with the Council. They will not disrespect our hegemony so easily next time."

"I hope you are right, but..."

"But what, Blessed Mother?"

Shaking her head, she waved Veluria toward the door. Before she could exit, the Order's Elder said, so softly Veluria nearly missed the words, though the import seared itself into her soul, "I fear the Dark One, child."

****

Andreas hesitated. The thud of flesh impacting a hard surface reverberated through his chest, the frantic susurrations of lungs

3

screaming silent pleas, her fear, hard fear, and then nothing. He'd been following at a safe distance, watchful. The opportunity to probe while she hesitated for a mere instant was too much to pass up.

The penetration into her psyche had been easy, far too easy. He should have known better. Instead of identifying pathways, he'd simply alerted her to his presence, awakening her pain receptors.

You idiot!

The Council had tasked him. He was not off to a good start.

"Seguire questa donna, Padre Andreas. Osservare. Riferire a me. Solo a me. Lei è una minaccia per tutti noi." The Monsignor had tapped a carefully manicured blunt nail on the walnut desk, emphasizing each point: *follow, observe, report ... His Eyes Only.*

"Monsignor sì, ho capito," Andreas replied, though he did not understand. None of this made any sense. His Holiness considered this woman to be a threat to the Papacy. He was more right than he could possibly know. But how *they* had come to that conclusion rested on false logic. They looked to her dubious French connections and the kind of missteps pillow talk afforded, though how such a light weight as Stefano de' Medici could be a source of concern afforded the young gallant far too much import in the larger scheme of political machinations. At least in *his* opinion.

Gods be damned, he loved and hated this time. The simplicity and austerity of his upbringing nearly imploded upon the vipers' nests of competing interests, the plots within plots within plots, in an endless round of intrigue and backstabbing that contaminated his homeland and all he held sacred.

That he did not belong here was a given, yet he had been the logical choice given his ... unusual proclivities and abilities. Serving two masters was seldom a problem, though often a condition of his trade. He would best remember to whom he owed absolute fealty. That was a calculus with a zero sum outcome if he were not careful ... at least as careful as the alleged 'French woman'.

With no small amount of admiration, he had to admit that the woman's behavior, her demeanor, was spot-on. Skillfully played, so much so even *he* had developed doubts. However, in the absence of any other leads, following the Monsignor's directive afforded him purpose, until opportunity presented itself.

4

The woman, Veluria, had an agenda, of that he was certain. That his probe slammed into an impenetrable defense system told him volumes about her abilities. What remained unclear was the *when*, that crucial element of time ... and place. Was she like him, Venetian? He suspected it was so—she had that classical grace, the sultry earthiness and stark sensuality he hungered for. Dark on dark, ebon-kissed, eyes black as his soul.

He smiled at the fanciful turn his thoughts had taken him. That brief foray into her mind had been intoxicating, inexplicably so. There was something there ... something forbidden. As hard as she tried to mask it, the stink of modernity rested as a distant echo. No, she was no French seductress sent to spy on the royal court. For now he would store that piece of knowledge and let the Council calculate a new paradigm. Keeping the statisticians busy and off his back served his purposes well.

Andreas crouched on the cobblestoned pathway, his robes splayed about his slim form. The temptation to try one more time overcame caution. She already knew he was there. She was vulnerable, for how long was anyone's guess. Accepting a stalemate was not an option. That was not why he'd been selected.

He laid a hand on a damp stone for balance and shut his senses down, one at a time: eyes, ears, smell, touch, all forced to the background. He slowed his breathing, allowing her energy to envelop him—misting, swirling, penetrating his consciousness. He probed cautiously, peeling away the layers, mindful of her pain and her watchfulness. Loins burning, he writhed with need, desiring nothing more than a violent mind rape, preparing himself for the sharp edges and metallic smoothness of resistance. Instead she fed him a confection, delectable, so soft he wallowed in its luxurious feel as his veins throbbed wildly, the heat pooling in his groin.

Gods, she was good. A true master of her craft.

But I am better. More evolved. Because I come prepared...

Caressing her gently, he moved aside the fibrous barrier to take a peek, to indulge in a taste only. He needed her whole, not parsed into fragments, useless to his needs. She would not willingly serve him or the Council, but she could advance his objectives by being his eyes and ears where clerics dared not tread.

All I need is a clue. Let me in, *mia puttana deliziosa*. There. A single thought, hidden—*Stefano, message.*

5

The Medici brat? *Caro dio. This* is what she shelters? Why him? The boy-man was an idiot, his family beyond dangerous. Surely Cosimo's youngest was not more than he seemed—a court wastrel, destined to be married off to cement the family lineage in whatever propitious manner the Papacy and the trade mogul determined.

What if he, and the Council, were wrong? What if the Monsignor was right, for all the wrong reasons? He did not believe in co-incidence. The woman, Veluria, had calculated the probabilities, just as he had. Obviously her answer had a different solution. *That* was a metric worth investigating. Now, more than ever, he needed her talents. Withdrawing, he argued with his inner desires, urging control and patience. As enticing as penetrating her mental defenses was, it was nothing compared to the promise of burying himself in her slick tight core. That thought alone was worth a few Hail Marys. He grinned mirthlessly.

The shuffle of boots on cold stone reverbed down the tunnel— solid, confident and long-strided. Andreas melted into the shadows, drawing his cloak over the energy shield, annoyed that he'd failed to pay attention to his surroundings. Buffered from outside stimuli, he had felt secure enough to wander through the woman's inner thoughts, but the journey had so captivated him that he'd lost his awareness of everything but for the sensual caress of her mind.

Stupid. Dangerously so.

The huge figure passed, brushing lightly against him with stray fingers of energy probing, then spinning off into nothingness. Cautious, and not a little spooked by the fleeting encounter, he reached out for some recognition, some sense of familiarity.

That was more than odd. The stranger gave him nothing. A blank, impenetrable, nameless *nothing*.

What in God's name was going on?

The man paused at the crumpled heap and glanced about quickly before scooping the woman into his arms as if she weighed nothing at all. So tall he had to bend away from the curved ceiling, he staggered slightly as he carried his burden toward the dimly lit opening.

Andreas shifted awkwardly, his gut roiling. Of one thing he was certain, no matter that the woman stalked the serpentine passage

6

expecting to meet her paramour, this creature was *not* Stefano. Nor did she recognize him—her audible intake of breath and stab of dismay betrayed her inner awareness of the otherness of the creature. Fear, soul-numbing fear followed. An urge to coddle and sooth her distress rose unbidden.

Sweet Mother, but she was delectable.

Why had the Monsignor failed to apprise him of other potential interests in the woman? Or did he even know? He doubted it. His Holiness was hampered by an antiquated surveillance system and lack of resources. Unlike others of his ilk, he harbored boundless ambition without having familial ties with the Medicis. That simple quirk of fate set him permanently outside the ring of influence—something that aggravated and made the man amenable to manipulation.

Andreas smiled grimly. Now was not the time to dwell on the petty concerns of the age. The stranger approached the opening to the canal at a leisurely pace, hesitating now and then, listening. Andreas feathered his breathing, fearful the man would realize he was being observed. It made him lightheaded but sensitive to energies bubbling along the damp conduits.

The woman, Veluria, controlled her own energies, of this he was certain. Yet when he stole through her defenses, her mind had screamed out, a pulse-pounding screech of pure terror that had cut him, nay seared him, and branded his soul, binding him to her. She could reach out if she willed it. Reach out for help … reach out to him.

And he would have her for himself…

He keyed on the softer shuffling now, movement receding, as if the stranger had foregone his leather boots in favor of soft slippers. His burden was a slip of a woman, but richly gowned, layers upon layers of lush silk fabrics that had swished along the uneven mosaic tiles in her heedless attempt to evade detection. Though the giant's silhouette implied brute strength, her boneless form and bulky togs made transit through the low-ceilinged tunnel difficult and slow.

The man's bulky frame blocked out the weak light coming from the entrance to the docks. With obvious relief he stretched to his full height and turned right, the faint shush of fabric the only sound marking his passage.

This nameless stranger—how had he known to come to her rescue? Had he somehow heard her silent scream of terror? Andreas had savaged her with that first clarion blast, ramming against her defenses. He shook at the shared memory and phantom aural ache and rued his lack of finesse and control. She had finally opened to him long enough for him to know that the only one she stole to meet was the Medici fop, Stefano.

Andreas whispered, "No, this makes no sense." She'd been summoned by the Medici boy clearly for a clandestine meeting. The *why* echoed in his head.

He'd sensed only himself and the woman, certainly not that foolish boy. And where had the stranger hidden? Why had he not intuited that presence? He stroked his Crucifix, then slid a finger along the hilt of the stiletto, assuring himself of God's protection and his own resolve.

Silently he slipped through shadows, keying on her energies, now restful, as if she felt safe. He knew that to be a lie.

"*Dammi la forza, mio Dio.* I do not understand the face of this evil." Andreas prayed his God would reveal the nature of the forces allayed against the Council, against him. He feared only that which claimed no name.

He hastened toward the canal, anxious not to lose her energy signature, then stopped abruptly. Panicked, he scanned in every direction. The fetid waters lapped rhythmically with the creak of gondolas; his pulse pounded until the sound became a roar, drowning out all but his fury and despair—her essence severed.

Gone.

Chapter Two

Stay back, Brother. She is fine." The tall man carefully shouldered his way into the narrow cubicle, mindful of his burden. He set the woman on a makeshift cot and turned to his sibling.

"Tonio," Stefano whispered, "she should not be here. This was a mistake. I never would have written that note," he paused, his face a mask of fear and concern, "had I realized how much danger..."

Tonio glowered at his brother, cutting him off. The young man had no idea of the stakes in this particular game. As always, his infatuations and conquests occupied him to the exclusion of all other considerations, a fact he and Nico secretly admired but their father no longer found amusing.

Whatever Cosimo had divined from his spies, the woman's elevation to person of interest had been swift and surprising, brooking no hesitation on Tonio's part when tasked with drawing the woman away from the court, forcing her into a vulnerable position. His father's preternatural instincts, bordering on prescience, had so far fueled considerable success in manipulating events in the family's favor. If this woman, and her supposed French connections, had merit in the old man's plans ... well, who was he to argue the point. Politics seldom concerned him. Exercising directives did. This one had gotten interesting the minute he'd detected the interplay of energies in the tunnel.

As did the fact they had apparently picked up what amounted to a parade of stalkers. He'd lost the shadowy figure in the tunnel, but apparently not the hive of frustrated Papàl Guards who'd been dogging his heels for days. He tolerated their interference most times. This was not going to be one of them.

9

Stefano continued to fuss over the prone woman, mindlessly adjusting her gown until the tiny cubicle filled with an irritating high pitched rustle as the lengthwise grain of the silk resisted his frantic strokes.

Tonio hissed, "Uncle Giovanni's guards approach. Be quiet. It would be best if they did not discover all of us together. I have made other arrangements that do not include the family's incessant meddling."

His younger brother whined, "But why are they here?"

"Because Father or Uncle could not be sure you would follow through." His thoughts skipped a beat, logic dictating that there might be some question about his own commitment in this matter. His fondness for Stefano was no secret. Ignoring the implied complication he assured the young man, "You have nothing to fear, little brother, nothing but your unseemly attachment to this strange woman."

Stefano hissed, "I fear nothing, Brother, and I don't give a damn about unseemly. Do you think having the Papàl Guards parading about in all their finery will insure that I will—as you put it—'follow through'? If you do, you are a bigger fool than our dearest uncle."

Tonio advanced toward his younger brother, shoulders tense, long, elegant fingers fondling the jeweled hilt of his cinquedea.

"I think perhaps, dear Stefano, you should have more respect for Pope Leo. Father worked his particular form of magic to ensure our family's right to the succession. It would not do for anyone to think we are not united in this matter."

Stefano sneered at the older man, "Always the apologist, Brother. Whatever the old man says, you are there to kiss his..."

Tonio moved with uncanny speed, pinning his brother against the ancient frescoed wall, his right arm pressed against the young man's windpipe, his left gripping the short sword. Stefano's pupils narrowed to slits as he succumbed to his brother's brief show of mastery. Tonio recognized the capitulation with a brief nod, taking a fractional step back to put some space between them. The young man's slight intake of breath assured him he had his undivided attention.

Tonio felt the woman's mind probing, not yet fully functional. They had no time for this useless bickering. If they did not leave soon, the bigger threat would trail his, and the woman's, residual energies, leading the unknown observer directly to this warren ... and the courtesan his besotted brother loved to distraction.

Disgusted, Tonio released the smaller man, murmuring, "Go, now. Check the corridor. We will take her to the palazzo. If it is as Father suspects, we..." He let his words slide away, echoing after Stefano's retreating form.

Tonio whispered, "Don't worry, Brother. Your paramour will be safe. You have my word on that."

The tall man paced quietly to the unconscious form. He traced an index finger over her full lips, surprisingly soft, yielding to his touch, an inviting pout. He bent to inhale her subtle fragrance, floral—and something more...

Dangerous, this one. No wonder the man in the tunnel had followed so closely, all of them like moths to the flame. She was compelling, unique—a true adept. They would divine her secrets and if it were as Cosimo suspected, he would take her back to Florence where he and his family could protect their political investment.

Tonio placed a hand over Veluria's brow and intoned, "Sleep, my Lady. You are safe. *Dormire il sonno dei morti per Dio ti ha scelto per fare il nostro lavoro.*"

Stefano came up behind his brother and whispered, "The man who followed you still lurks, just inside the corridor. How he evades the Guards perplexes me."

Tonio shrugged and murmured to himself, "I think I know..."

****

Andreas cast about the interior of the passageway but no energy signatures lingered. How had they vanished so quickly? Where had the man and his burden gotten to?

His gut clenched at the remembered sweetness as she'd reeled in pain from his probing. He should have slipped seamlessly through her mind but there had been defenses and layers—barriers that undisciplined minds should not be privy to. He'd launched an assault that had unexpected consequences for both of them.

The channel lay open, breeched with a chorus of yearnings and sensations long cast aside. The Council must never know of this corruption for they would cleanse and purify and leech his desires,

11

removing this delicious agony. Now, once tasted, he could not bear the loss.

He slid the stiletto from its leather sheath and drew a thin slice across his palm. Satisfied, he watched the beads form and dribble, lava-thick, as time and motion stilled. The wound closed as he licked the thick droplets, savoring the iron-rich tang of his essence. His tongue tingled as a familiar sensation seeped through the layers of his awareness.

Ah, there. He had her. Somewhere close, within reach. Whoever she was—whatever she was— her essence, her energies, sank deeper into his consciousness. She was quiet now, pain free, but that was not of his doing.

Something had changed, altered the pattern. Had he the choice, he would have her ache, her discomfort and anxiety as testament to his own painful longing. For now he must determine how and why she floated in stasis. That was a gift unique to their kind, not one he would have expected from the undisciplined minds of this era.

To his knowledge no one could voluntarily attain that state—it required the assistance of another adept. In this time, in this place, only one potentially had that skill—so said the Council researchers. His adversary had a name, a fearsome name—*Antonio de' Medici.*

Despite the man's deserved reputation, and the potential for his thwarting the Council's purposes, Andreas' plans could be better served now that all the actors took their rightful places. However, the Monsignor would not be pleased that the man known as the Dark One, the Demon de' Medici, had insinuated his presence, though that was of little consequence to Andreas' real mission. He would obey the directive His Holiness so succinctly placed in his care for it serviced both masters…

Follow. Observe. Report.

****

Stefano and Tonio pressed their backs against the rough walls inside the room. The din of chatter outside their hiding place was maddening. Footsteps and scrapes complimented the whooshing and whirling of robes and capes beyond the sturdy door as the two brothers shallowed their breathing. Veluria began to stir on the

12

makeshift cot. The Guards' return could not have happened at a worse time.

"She mustn't wake now!" Tonio growled in his brother's ear. "I have no wish to confront our Uncle's guardians with only a half-assed explanation for why we are here."

Tonio asked himself, *How the hell is she coming out of it? That shouldn't be possible.*

The brothers watched her stir restlessly. Stefano knelt beside the tiny woman, gently pressing his hand against her mouth lest she cry out. She twisted her head away from Stefano's hand as the voices grew louder just outside the door. Someone tested the door's handle, yanking forcefully.

"La porta è chiusa, il capitano."

Tonio recognized the Corporal's voice. The soldier gave a desultory shove to prove that the door remained firmly locked, then backed away as his Commandant ordered him off. Pressing an ear to the door, Tonio breathed a sigh of relief as hurried footsteps receded toward the canal. Someone had instilled the fear of God in the Guard. They were not known for having this much persistence.

"This place is not safe, Tonio," Stefano hissed.

"I fear you are correct, in more ways than one." Tonio frowned as he still sensed a presence, one that had tickled that space in his gut that warned him of danger. "We still have that stalker, and I am certain he is not one of ours. We must proceed with care."

Drawing a bit of black velvet out of the pouch at his waist, Tonio handed it to his brother and directed, "Tie this over her eyes. She will stay under longer if she cannot detect light." He let the *I hope that is the case* remain unspoken.

Tonio scooped the semi-conscious woman in his arms and strode to the door. They were out of time and he had insufficient energy to place her further under. And he tired of the cat-and-mouse game. He needed to take control and secure the prize, for prize it surely was. The woman had gifts, he could feel that as clearly as he knew his own capabilities. His father's instincts were seldom misdirected.

Stefano slowly pressed down on the latch and cracked the ancient door enough to determine if the corridor was indeed free of prying eyes. Sensing nothing, he opened the door a bit more as it groaned on its rusty hinges.

****

Veluria braced against the strong arms of her captor, her equilibrium severely compromised from the onslaught of mental and physical intrusion. Fighting the waves of disorientation and confusion, she catalogued what little she did know: she was being transported somewhere at speed, carried by … who? Not Stefano. No, this one had a scent she didn't recognize, and it managed to overwhelm her with its sheer maleness. She risked opening her eyes only to find them bound in soft velvet.

Before she could reach outward with her compromised senses, motion abruptly ceased, followed by a sensation of falling, then swaying. She wished she could hear but the buzzing in her ears as she struggled against whatever had trapped her into a state of unconsciousness impaired her abilities, even her extrasensory gifts. Damn, what had they … what had *he* done to her?

This, this… thing that ensnared her with unforgiving strength, was he the one who'd invaded her mind like a battering ram, inflicting such excruciating pain she'd been hard pressed to defend herself? Like a residual limb, the regret and dismay lingered, leaving her nearly enraptured with the whiplash change of emotions. When he'd come stealing once more, ever so sweetly, she'd allowed a boon, knowing full well the intruder would already know, or have guessed, her intentions.

He'd danced with her psyche, the steps mimicking a macabre courtship—a sultry rumba to a background rhythm of fear, desire and intense curiosity. Such delicious enticements—she'd almost forgotten herself in the rush of temptation to explore. Her last encounter with a Council operative had been far less engaging, his brute force approach and unrelenting machismo had proven no match for her training … and very special gifts.

But her intruder had power, power *and* control, and perhaps something more… One thing she knew for certain: the man was unique, and dangerous. Someone of her time and place.

But the man who held her so carelessly, with such casual strength, he *was* of this time, of that she was certain, but as to how she could not say.

The man spoke, his voice a deep rumble against her breasts, "Get the lines, Stefano," then with his breath fanning across her cheeks, he murmured, "and let me make you a little more comfortable, M'lady." He chuckled deep in his throat, "No point pretending. You're awake. Mostly."

"Tonio," Stefano's voice came from her right and forward of their position. "Where do we go from here? That stalker of yours ... he'll be watching for us. If he is not alone it is possible that every route will be closely monitored."

Stalker? That's interesting. So the intruder and this man are not one and the same. Relief seemed foolish, given her current circumstances, but there it was.

Fumbling with the knot, the man adjusted the cloth to sit firmly against her eyes and said to Stefano, "Not to fear, *il mio fratellino*. The Papàl Guards will clear the way. They will unwittingly be our accomplices this night."

Keeping her face secured to his massive chest, all she could feel on her overheated skin was a leather jerkin and a few stray laces that gouged her cheek.

Odd. He'd called Stefano 'il mio fratellino', a surprising endearment. Could he be...?

The man continued issuing instructions to Stefano. "Head us to the Grand Canal. We will take the traghetto to St. Mark's, just three tourists seeking the pleasures of Venezia on this fine evening."

Stefano clearly did not like the plan, judging from his muttered curses, but apparently he complied to her captor's satisfaction.

"I wish to sit up," Veluria hissed into the leather jerkin, unsure if her words were clear enough to understand.

Without a word, the man released her from his grip, lifting and settling her on the seat next to him. From habit she tucked the voluminous folds of her gown about her legs, smoothing the rumpled fabric down and away from the uncomfortable corseted bodice.

Damn, I hate corsets.

The gondola bobbed through a light chop, leaving her to guess they had exited one of the narrow feeder canals onto the Grand Canal proper. From the heat and angle of the sun on her exposed flesh, she knew she'd lost an entire day to this misadventure. Sweat beaded on her forehead, the gown far too hot for day wear. It would be a ruin in no time, if it wasn't already.

Sweet Mother, if you can hear my thoughts, please do not let my sisters know this thing about me. Allow my vanity to remain unremarked, our little secret.

Veluria choked back a cough as acrid scents of refuse, smoldering lamps and the unmentionable stench of too many humans packed into too tight a space assaulted her sensitive nostrils. From the hubbub off to her right, they'd be approaching one of the many protruding docks, busy with commerce and Venetian citizens going about the evening's activities.

The man cautioned, "Shush, M'lady. We will be at our destination soon." His voice reeked of menace and determination. "You will do as I say, otherwise I *will* bind and gag you."

Veluria nodded she understood. She was in enough discomfort already that incurring additional did not seem prudent. The more she learned about her situation, the better her ability to react when the time came.

She wondered about Stefano but from the sounds, the young man was busy securing the gondola to the dock. Since she'd awoken from that bizarre state, he'd been nothing but acquiescent to the stranger sitting next to her, his shoulder brushing against the bare skin on her forearm whenever the gondola rocked side-to-side. The sensation was not unpleasant.

If this man was Stefano's brother, then which one? What little intel Mother Superior had ferreted from historical records was comprised of confusing rumor and supposition—and allegations of dark magic. Nicolo was the middle son, skilled in diplomacy. The other, the eldest, was Cosimo's right hand... and a merciless enforcer of the Medici's will. Private Papàl correspondence referred to that one as the Demon de' Medici. If *this* was that man...

Damn her luck.

Tonio stared at the rigid set to the woman's face, her lips pursed in intense concentration, a telltale tic in a prominent vein on her temple giving away her desperate attempt to make sense of her situation. That she didn't panic was to her credit. She was definitely trained, but in what exactly had yet to be determined.

16

On a whim he stroked her cheek, willing soothing energy to flow through his fingers. He understood the nature of her confusion. It pleased him no end that he could keep one such as this off-balance. Unlike his hapless younger brother, he was not without skills.

Idly he traced the curve of her chin and the long, swan-like neck, palest of pale flesh, soft and inviting. The woman sank into the cushions, arching away from his touch, quivering ... though not from fear. Fascinated, he followed the line of her bodice, cut straight across and corseted to present soft bulbous mounds for his appreciative gaze. He licked his lips, the action unconscious as sound receded, replaced by his ragged breathing and the blood pumping hot and needy in his veins.

Veluria—he would think of her by name now—feathered her breaths to long, slow inhalations, exaggerating the line of her breasts. Whether deliberate or not the effect was enticing. Her flesh glowed with inner luminescence, drawing his face and hands inexorably closer.

Damn it to hell. She was good. No wonder Stefano was smitten. It would take a far better man than his hapless younger brother to resist the charms of a French courtesan, especially this one.

Tonio rose awkwardly from the cushioned seat and leaned to fend off the dock, his jerkin rubbing seductively across her small breasts. She tensed, her small hands fisted in the silken folds of her skirt.

Two can play that game, M'Lady.

Smokey oil lamps spewed dank, choking fumes over the still water. They would make their way across the Grand Canal to where night promised a brief surcease as Venezia's citizens sought relief from the stifling heat in the great square, all the better to mask their passage.

"Over there, Brother." Tonio pointed to the waiting ferry. He breathed a sigh of relief that the Papàl Guard were not about, broadcasting to the citizens that a person of importance was expected. Though the Medicis had learned long ago that hiding in plain sight was often the safer of many unsafe options in these troubled times, tonight Tonio required anonymity.

"M'lady, I will remove your blindfold." With a sweep of his hand, Tonio whisked the soft cloth off the woman's delicate face.

Wisely she kept her eyes hooded, not allowing too much light in at once, as that would blind her.

"Tonio, we must hurry. Vel—" He choked off the word as Tonio gave him a sharp look and made a slashing movement across his throat.

Tonio stepped onto the dock and extended a hand to assist the woman as she carefully gathered the rich fabric into a bundle, leaping nimbly onto the creaky dock. Stefano followed quickly, tied the gondola off and hastened to speak with the owner of the ferry.

Veluria whispered, her voice subtly accented, "You are Antonio, then. My cousin, Charles, speaks well of your abilities, Monsieur de' Medici. He will be most … appreciative if you and I manage an accord in this matter."

Tonio nodded, a slight smile playing about his full lips. At half his imposing height, she forced him to bend as if in supplication when he breathed a reply, "Oh, I assure you Mademoiselle, an accord has already been reached, about which you will have little input." To his surprise she ignored his implied threat. Interesting.

Veluria glanced at Stefano impatiently waiting on the ferry. It was a look of concern, and perhaps genuine fondness. When she turned back to stare at him, slivers of ice tickled his spine. Whoever she was, *whatever* she was, she'd just thrown down the gauntlet. If she expected to control him the way she did his younger brother, she was in for the shock of her life.

He hoped she enjoyed a challenge.

Chapter Three

Andreas pressed further into the alcove where he'd sheltered away from the stomping antics of the Papàl Guard. With infinite patience he waited until he heard the old creaky door groan on its hinges, followed by the quick shuffle of feet, at least two pair, heading swiftly toward the canal.

Remaining cloaked, he followed at a distance, pausing at the entrance to the narrow walkway lining the canal. To the left he glimpsed the men boarding a gondola. The taller man held the woman in his arms, her body still and unresisting. A frisson of concern creased his brow—his incursion through her defenses would have drained her to some extent, but certainly not for that amount of time.

If the Medici's interference and continued control was sufficient to override his own considerable talents, even temporarily, he would need to keep that from the Council. For surely they would either recall him, or worse yet, provide their version of backup—something he wished to avoid at all costs.

Failure was unacceptable—the costs to his world and the sanctity of his mission catastrophically high. He simply would not allow history to relegate the brotherhood to a shadow existence should the prognostications of the statisticians pan out. Everything pointed to here and now: the dissolution of peace in his world, the threat of yet another apocalypse, all resting on fragile links with a past so distant as to be almost ludicrous. How history would judge their interference rested on outcomes they could only guess at.

Nervously fingering his Crucifix, he watched with interest as the younger man—whom he assumed was the paramour, Stefano—

expertly oared the craft through the narrow confines of the canal. He had no such skill. He crept along the nearly deserted dock until he found a willing gondolier just setting down to eat his dinner. He could guess the trio's destination, but he dared not lose sight of them, for once in St. Mark's Square, he would be hard pressed to track them through the crush of evening revelers. Andreas knew that if he lost them, he would be subject to an uncomfortable interrogation by the Council that would make the Monsignor's petty complaints and threats pale in comparison. The phantom pain in the palm of his hand reminded him of his ultimate purpose and to whom he owed his allegiance.

Follow. Observe. Report.

****

Tonio urged the woman toward Stefano and the waiting ferry. They had little time before the stalker would arrive. Whatever the man's intentions and abilities, it would be best to be in the crowded square amongst the evening partiers to mask their passage. His younger brother took a seat at the prow, followed by the woman. She sat daintily, seemingly at ease. He took his place at the stern where he could keep an eye on any pursuers, difficult though that was given the dense water traffic.

His eyes strayed periodically toward the woman, backlit from the setting sun with her features in shadow. She was a difficult read, more than normal. The sad fact was that most women tasked his powers with unnecessary emotion and volatile temperaments. He preferred the company of his squad and the simplicity of their camaraderie and shared missions.

The woman—*Veluria*...

Why did he have such difficulty calling her by name? Because names had power as his father so often reminded him? Names—her name— made it personal, intimate. But connecting with her on any level was beyond stupid, a thing he recognized, yet seemed powerless to avoid.

Tonio shifted in his seat and allowed his fingers to trail through the warm waters, thinking back to discussions with his brother, Nico, when they'd had far too much to drink and way too much time on their hands.

Nico had said, *To intimidate and instill terror requires detachment, Tonio—a calculated neutrality that denies your victims hope and bends them to your will. And when they refuse to bend, there are other, more permanent solutions. Are you willing to step down that path, my brother? Are you so willing to sacrifice your soul in service to the family? Will you become as a statue, sightless and remote?*

If thrusting my blade deep into an opponent's gut isn't the ultimate act of intimacy, what is?

That's not intimacy, Tonio, that's ... indifference. Would you sell your soul so cheaply?

I have no soul, Nico. I never did. And you are not one to talk. You use that golden tongue of yours the way I use my blade. Often with the same results.

Touché, Brother. You may be right. May God have mercy on us. I fear mercy is not what He has in mind...

With an effort Tonio roused himself from his self-indulgent musings and refocused his attention on the French woman. She sat gazing out over the expanse of water, outwardly calm and composed despite the inner turmoil roiling just below the surface. That kind of self-control was admirable. Though slight of build she conveyed a haughty demeanor, clearly the result of her reputed years in the French court.

A few tendrils of silky blue-black hair escaped the intricate braids, the wisps framing a heart-shaped face. He could see how his impressionable younger brother would be enraptured of such a siren. It was forever the young man's curse to follow his cock after every piece of attractive ass.

Tonio knew without a doubt that Stefano had bitten off more than he could chew, a sentiment shared with their father. How the family managed this potential new resource was none of his business. His only task was to see the woman to the palazzo where Cosimo would determine the next steps, that and try to protect his brother as best he could. The state of the boy's heart was the least of his worries. There were other matters afoot that would reveal themselves all in good time.

A French courtesan with Charles' ear ... and unspecified 'abilities'? With events unfolding at breakneck speed across the

21

continent, her presence at their court could be no accident. That she had selected Stefano for her particular attentions was both an easy solution, and a brilliant choice. The problem lay in determining exactly how she planned to move her chess pieces. He had faith in his family, in Cosimo and Pope Leo, but what if they were not the ones pulling the strings? What if...?

Damn, I just want to go home to Florence and leave this wretched city to wallow in its endless drama.

Veluria gathered every stray bit of energy, willing it contained and at her command, not an easy task given the fractured state of her psyche. The episode in the tunnel had caught her by surprise and she still had no firm grasp as to why a Council operative would take such risks when engagement offered nothing in return. Whatever had transpired also seemed unrelated to her current situation. Her mind raced through probabilities and possible scenarios, with *wait and see* an unavoidable solution.

With the Council and the Sisterhood seeking the same answers, it should have come as no surprise that their mutual interests would cross paths. That fate chose that particular moment to thrust a new player onto the stage, the Demon de' Medici no less, might be fortuitous and just the opening she needed.

The Council operative was the devil she knew ... but *this* devil? From what their historians catalogued, he was a born assassin, with a black heart and an even blacker soul. History painted him as the penultimate blackguard, a gross injustice. He was more, much more. A frisson of fear tickled at her spine.

Stefano's knees, pressed hard against the small of her back, were a small reassurance, though she would not rely on him should her situation become untenable. She sensed she had an opportunity to shortcuts heretofore unavailable in this time and place. Lies and intrigue and fanciful phrases had gotten her an entrée into the right circles but not to the prize. She'd been sidetracked, delightfully so, with Stefano but that did little to forward her pursuit of answers to the vexing perturbations the Sisterhood had detected. What little time remained must not be spent in idle dalliance.

She chuckled to herself, *As if being kidnapped and swept away to parts unknown counted as a dalliance.*

She was losing discipline and focus. She should be asking what purpose kidnapping her served? Claiming kinship with Charles—the heir to the major houses of the Habsburgs, Castile-Aragon and Burgundy—would hardly suffice as a reason, hell ... everyone was related to everyone else in this timeline. Her connection, alleged of course, to the French court would be the likely source of their interest. That was the line she needed to pursue for it might lead to the clues she sought.

If history intended to derail and knock their timeline askew, the Medicis and their damnable interferences had to be at the center of that looming event. With most of the potential players in one basket, so to speak, she was in a unique position to calculate the probabilities ... and to predict probable outcomes.

She glanced away from the fearsome giant staring her down. This one seemed immune to her wiles, a disquieting thought as she had been selected for this mission based on a very particular skill set. She would do well to remember her limitations in this matter. But notwithstanding certain shortcomings, she was not without resources.

Tonio turned his attention to the receding dock, watching with interest as a robed figure awkwardly boarded a smaller ferry. Their stalker would bear watching, but for now they had position and the approaching square—and his men—to provide a sufficient distraction. He rose as the ferry bumped against a piling.

His brother hopped onto the dock and helped secure the lines, then turned and reached for Veluria as Tonio easily lifted the woman into his waiting arms. The brief contact, with his hands wrapped securely about her diminutive frame, had sent a powerful surge of heat to his loins, though this time it seemed a transient event, not one she directed consciously.

Had it been a mistake to use his powers on her? With so little understanding of what guided his abilities, he generally exercised extreme caution in their execution. He could ill afford to allow an open conduit between them. No, he must avoid contact at all costs from now on until Cosimo determined just what she was.

With a final glance to the darkening eastern skies, he launched himself out of the ferry and strode quickly into the milling crowd.

Tonio glanced around St. Mark's Square, already crowded with early evening pleasure seekers, pickpockets and others on more deadly assignments. He nodded once, a bare tilt, to acknowledge his men spaced about the huge square in a carefully controlled octagon of protection. A tap on his sword alerted his men and as one the group strode lazily over the cobbled stones, stopping here and there to exchange banter or stare with admiration at the finery on display all about them.

Veluria took Stefano's proffered arm, impressed at her captors' attention to detail, the guards deployed discretely, yet within reach should they need assistance.

Their group made a pretty picture: the tall, dangerous man, dark of visage, and her attentive escort, wrapping her in an air of refinement and gaiety. She surreptitiously arranged her gown to allow access to the small totems sewn in the seams. Not that she needed them, but Reverend Mother was ever insistent on certain … assurances.

Veluria tittered at an imagined jest, allowing her body to brush alluringly against Stefano who responded with a quick hug. His older brother tensed but ignored them, though she could sense his curiosity and suspicion. Unlike Stefano, he would understand that her co-operation came at a price.

Keeping the man off-balance would not be easy.

Stefano wrapped an arm about her waist and pulled her toward a gaggle of well-wishers with Tonio hissing, "Stefano, no…"

She was inclined to agree with Tonio, they needed to move this charade along. Her young lover seemed in no hurry to reach whatever was their ultimate destination, whether out of fear for her safety or something else wasn't clear.

While Stefano engaged in light-hearted banter, Veluria took a moment to assess the man standing reluctant guard over them. At nearly six-foot-four and powerfully muscled he towered over his contemporaries, a mountain of a man, dark and menacing. A line bred Medici by all counts, he sported the same aquiline nose and sculpted jawline, square and unforgiving. Full lips set into a permanent grimace and piercing dark eyes would put the fear of God into all who crossed paths with him.

For someone his size he moved with surprising grace. That he was a fearsome warrior and accomplished with a blade was well-established. But her real interest lay in abilities she could only sense. He had done something to her, something that should not be possible, not here, not now.

Why can't I remember?

Stefano bent over a gloved hand, his lips brushing the soft cloth with a coy wink at the tittering older woman. Moving off to whisper an endearment or tease, he abandoned her to a quick stab of jealousy and anger that jabbed like a knife-prick, sharp and insistent.

Tonio? No, not him.

Who then? Where?

Using the banter as an excuse, she spun, her arm sweeping toward the Cathedral, her words, "Isn't it a lovely…!" ringing out as she swept in a half-circle, desperate to pinpoint the location of the attacker. The residual energy would dissipate quickly as the festival of masked, bejeweled revelers undulated in waves all about her. All intent on their own pursuits. *Where was he?* The crush of bodies parted briefly as she stared toward the docks.

There!

Instinct dictated she turn and move away from the assailant, yet she felt strangely sympathetic and curious. This incursion was less adversarial, yet the fact he was able to penetrate her defenses so easily spoke volumes of the operative's abilities and put her in a tenuous position.

Without thinking, she moved away from the group, only to be blocked as Tonio moved into her path.

"I have him, M'lady," Tonio muttered. He reached for his brother's arm and jerked him back, his voice cold and stern, brooking no argument, "Stefano, now."

With a wink, Stefano said, *"Scuse mio fratello rozzo..."* and bowing at the waist, he swept an imaginary hat low to the cobblestoned surface. "We have a most urgent appointment."

If Tonio objected to being called boorish, he gave no indication. Instead he instructed his brother to take her arm and follow him as he pushed through the crowd.

Veluria was happy enough for once to follow the Demon de' Medici's lead and to accept his dubious protection. Through a quirk of fate, she'd been placed in the hands of a man who had the potential to step beyond the confines of his father's vast game of shifting political alliances. Granted, with Antonio, the apple fell not far from that tree—he and Cosimo were two of a kind, both dangerous men with unusual capabilities, or so the rumors intimated. Her assessment of the man was that he would act in the service of family as long as it suited.

However, the fate that awaited Stefano, with his preferred bloodlines and courtly mannerisms, teetered on the whims of a prelate with considerable influence in matters of state, and on Cosimo de' Medici, the ruler behind the throne. How Antonio de' Medici handled the outcome of Cosimo's negotiations with the Habsburgs could be the key to unraveling the mysterious forces threatening her world. Perhaps Mother Superior had been right about her reservations at using Stefano as her entrée into this vaulted inner circle of power, but there was no debating the fortuitous outcome of finally securing the services of one who *could* lead her to the ultimate solution.

How fate choreographed the next steps would go a long way in determining if the man everyone feared would be her willing accomplice … or the destroyer of all she held dear.

As the phalanx of partiers made their steady procession across the square, Andreas followed, once more deploring his rashness and the ungodly compulsion to feel her—Veluria's—essence. Yes, he'd alerted her to his presence. But it could not be helped now. That small taste had sent his senses reeling, his blood sluicing red hot through his veins.

Her guard dog notwithstanding, he could access her core at his choosing, allowing her to lead him to the ultimate solution to their mutual dilemma.

Invisible to the masses, his cowl pulled over his head, he slipped through the throng, rosary beads clacking in a simple, devout rhythm. His presence went unremarked, just another cleric out for evening vespers.

Chapter Four

Veluria's gaze was drawn repeatedly to Antonio, his uncommon bulk parting the sea of people with ease. She'd lost sight of the phalanx guarding their passage across the square but there was no question they were close and ready to intervene when necessary. She wondered what it might be like ... serving under such a master. Did they do it out of fear, or out of respect?

He wore power effortlessly, the threat of violence barely below the surface, not so much concealed as simply ... available. But there was more to him than that. Others would see it as something discomfiting, a matter of dominance and an utter lack of compassion, a being who was nothing more than a cold impervious shell.

Defenses. Like her own carefully constructed barricades, his walls radiated like a beacon to her heightened senses. What interested her was that he made no effort to conceal the fact that he possessed rather extraordinary abilities. What others saw was a mere shadow of his true existence. For lesser men to be called *Demon* would have led to the torture chamber and a slow agonizing death. For him, it'd become the currency that allowed him to function without drawing undue attention.

Damn. I've been too long in this world, walking in shadows. Shadows that keep me from seeing clearly.

She'd already drawn 'undue attention', first from the Council operative—unavoidable and not unexpected, though the nature of the man's abilities was unclear. The contact—the assault—had held an element of voyeurism, perhaps even obsession. If there were a description for what she'd suffered when he'd probed her, *rape* was the only word that came to mind. And it had hurt. It still did.

Antonio de' Medici then made a surprise entrance onto this damnable stage, acting at the behest of, by implication, the redoubtable *pater familias,* Cosimo. That was a potential complication she hadn't counted on. To make matters worse, she suspected Tonio of fostering intensely protective instincts toward his younger brother. Those instincts radiated disapproval of her and her influence over the young man's emotions and position in the court. Whether or not he divined her true purpose had yet to be determined.

Mother Superior was either smiling benignly at her stroke of good fortune or suffering apoplexy at the potential for out-of-control mayhem.

Mother Superior paced the sanctuary, her robes in angry agitation about her ample figure.

"My dear, we must restore the balance of power to the rightful rulers of our world, a balance that slips away, each day closer to disintegration of all the principles we revere."

The older woman stopped abruptly and drew in a breath, then spoke so softly Veluria had to lean close so as not to miss her next words. "You will find that the politics of court and war dominate that shadow Venezia, unlike our enlightened times. History tells us much of that period," she shrugged and pursed her lips in a grim line, "but not everything. What you, we, seek might be an object of power that has the potential, in the wrong hands, to effect the changes we only now detect."

Veluria understood that 'object of power' might be a thing, a person, an unspecified congruency of events, even deliberate interference. The statisticians could only guess and add euphemism after euphemism to mask their own lack of understanding of the processes.

Fingering the tora, her face creased with concern, the woman said, "The probabilities are not ... favorable."

Veluria sighed, "I understand, Reverend Mother."

"Do you, my child?"

"The gateways may be unstable, difficult to locate. I-I..." she hesitated, regretting the hitch in her voice, the misgivings too readily apparent, "...might be stranded there." She mentally chided herself for the weakness and stated, this time her voice strong and filled with conviction, "I do thy bidding, thy Word is mine, so shall it be."

"So shall it be..." Mother Superior intoned. "Now. Particulars. We will lend assistance but it will depend on those damnable bolt holes being in the right place at the right time. Think of yourself as the Lone Gunman, use whatever resources come to hand. You will not be faulted..." the woman grinned wickedly, "...for thinking outside the box."

Veluria followed her Orders' Head of Operations into a large room filled with storage containers, racks of clothing and mannequins in obscene parodies of human stances.

"My dear, allow me to introduce you to that most heinous of all devices. The distaff answer to the Council's perversion: the hair shirt." With a flourish, she held up a lovely bit of stiff fabric, lace and satin ribbons. "I give you ... the corset."

The Medici family: Cosimo, Antonio, Stefano—these were known historical figures. Yet the reality of dealing with men who so deftly exercised influence and control over not just a city and a religious institution, but a continent as well—none of that had been anticipated when she had been tasked with journeying through the portal between their cities, their shadow worlds. She had never suspected there would be someone on this side who could match, let alone possibly defeat her gifts, if he chose to be her enemy.

She felt the weight of a stare upon her and looked up, her gaze locking with Antonio's deep-set eyes. No expression could be read in their endless depths, but he smiled and in that moment she realized that he had likely calculated the probabilities—and now he might be closer to knowing what she was and why she had come.

He would rightly guess that she was not what she claimed, but he could not possibly understand the nature of her mission, or what she truly was—a being out of time and out of place. She could feel his black eyes boring into her with a knowing that frightened and titillated, setting every nerve ending ablaze.

Fear. That would be the little death that training and belief could defeat. *But this—this was something else.*

Stefano hissed, "Are you all right?" and placed his arm protectively about her shoulders. She settled against him, his compact body warm and comforting. This innocent she could handle. It was the taller, cold demon stalking ahead of her that gave her pause.

Her fingertips tingled as she smoothed her gown, the hair on her arms standing up at the familiar, and most welcome, sensation. Off to her right she spied a stairwell, rough-hewn and hemmed in by ancient stone edifices, leading to an upper floor or the roof. In the dim light, it appeared wrapped in a smoky blue haze. Her captors paid it little mind. She was sure this led to a portal, as it had that feel of other-worldliness, a homing beacon to her own time and place. She risked a nonchalant glance at the stairwell again, marking its location in relation to the square.

A fleeting thought of flight caressed her mind. She knew where the stairs were now, the link mathematically encoded, accessible only to her. She could return later, if she needed an emergency bolt hole. Assuming it would still be there. No one had informed her about how to discriminate between naturally-occurring gateways and the constructs held in place by the scientists of her own generation.

The other, more vexing, problem was, even if she did flee, she suspected that both Antonio and the Council's operative had the ability to track her. Both men seemed keyed onto her energy signature, an unfortunate and annoying development when she lacked the means to slam a virtual door shut against any pursuit.

She needed some damn shields—even now the Medici *demon* probed, sending tendrils of energy to snake her neural pathways. *Does he think I don't notice?* His powers had an unschooled, neophyte's feel, rough around the edges but for all that ... insistent. *I wonder if he realizes what he's doing.* Unfortunately, once he figured it out he would learn quickly.

Confusion and determination wrestled for dominance and, for a moment, it controlled her mind. She couldn't help but turn her eyes to him. If she weren't careful, he could steal her very thoughts, look into her soul like a voyeur and rape her most private self.

That word again ... *rape*. But this was not the same as the full scale invasion she'd suffered in the tunnel. This was curiosity, tinged with admiration. If she didn't know better, she'd say it was naïve, coy, perhaps even flirtatious.

Flirtatious? Merciful Mother, that did not compute.

Her hands trembled. She would need to find a way to counteract his growing abilities before they subsumed her very essence.

Or I could give in, submit.

For a frightening moment, that thought gained dominance, hurtling through her veins in a hot rush of sensuous pleasure fueled by unbidden, forbidden desire. The intensity startled and rocked her back on her heels. She stumbled and fell heavily onto the uneven cobbled path. Stefano's gentle touch and gasp of concern brought her back to her senses.

Mon dieu, what had just happened?

****

"Hai fatto bene, Padre Andreas," the Monsignor intoned. He repeated, "Well done indeed."

Andreas kept his eyes lowered, fingers twitching with irritation as he kept them buried in the folds of his robes. Despite His Holiness' pleased tone, he had *not* done well at all. He had failed to divine the location of the woman, despite his link. The mob in the Square, the Demon's men effectively blocking his every attempt to approach, all had conspired to defeat his purpose.

So much for Follow, Observe.

During his report he'd noted the Monsignor's almost giddy excitement at learning what should have been self-evident facts. The Medicis continued to exercise nearly absolute control over events, the French woman was not who she seemed... He found it difficult to care about the import of such mundane particulars, not when he had other, more urgent, concerns.

Thoughts racing nearly out of control, he longed to succumb to the compulsive urges that her link provided. Sweat beaded on his brow as he pushed the Monsignor's monotone discourse to the background. Opening to the ambient energies, he sought the one who promised completion, fulfillment, undeniable ecstasy.

She held him in thrall and he yielded to her, inviting her formless essence to brush his soul.

There. Like a second heartbeat. Feel the rich red heat coursing, my desire, yours ... as one.

In false supplication Andreas bent to hide his lust and his throbbing erection, nodding at uneven intervals as the Monsignor uttered meaningless directions to the scribe at his left.

"Andreas. You will continue with your task. Report only to me. Do you understand the gravity of what we face?"

"Yes, I understand." Andreas smiled inwardly for he doubted the dim-witted prelate had a clue. The Monsignor would play this close to his vestments, hording his bits of intelligence against the day when he prayed for opportunity and fortune to align in his favor.

He risked standing upright, relieved at his ability to control his wanton body's functions once again, and approached the desk.

"I will report to you alone, M'Lord. If I divine their intent, shall I...?" Andreas left the question hanging as he bent to kiss the proffered ring, then backed away carefully.

The Monsignor gave a careless wave of his hand and murmured, "No need, Father. We will decide the best course of action when the time is right."

"*Come vi piace.*" Andreas touched the crucifix to his lips and paced slowly from the chamber. The fool might think he need only hide his plans from the Papàl Legate. He thinks me his creature. He thinks me of this time and place, as do they all.

Andreas strode slowly along the narrow corridor, perpetually damp, perpetually intense with the fervor and gleeful adherence to the petty concerns of this time. He allowed himself the brief respite from maintaining the dual links, allowing his hand to trail along the rough stucco, fingers bouncing in slow staccato rhythm over ridged designs and swirls. The architects of this world were truly masters of the art. He admired the primitiveness, the attention to detail, so unlike...

"*Mio Dio,*" he gasped, staggering against the wall, thrown as by an invisible adversary, powerful, lifting him, crushing him. He sobbed in agony.

Oh dear God. Why can it not be me?

****

Nearly prostrate, her voluminous gown cushioning her petite form, Veluria desperately collected her thoughts, emptying stray images, flooding her eyes and ears with the sensations and brilliant auras of the revelers wheeling in splendor, shadow to light to shadow, winking in and out until they filled her. She allowed the wash of joy and intrigue and mindless pursuit of pleasure to swamp her, hoping to flood the link. Better yet, to sever it.

That had been no naïve expression of interest—that had been full-on lust and the shock of that desire had been mutual, of that she was certain. That he had shut it down so abruptly indicated it came as a surprise. That saved her, just barely, from reciprocating … what? What *did* she feel?

Stefano set her to rights and wrapped a protective arm about her waist. He seemed oblivious to what had just happened. Not so his older brother. Though Tonio still stalked ahead of them, clearing their path, she could tell from the set of his shoulders and the mindless way he rubbed the back of his neck that he'd been as thoroughly blindsided as she.

When Reverend Mother eventually debriefed her, *that* was going to be an interesting discussion.

In any case, knowledge of the gateway would remain safe for a time, but for how long she was uncertain. The phalanx of Antonio's guards closed ranks as they approached a narrow alley leading off the main square. She had not been this way and disliked the uncertainty, searching frantically through her resources to pinpoint the general direction. She might need that mental roadmap should her link to the bolt hole be severed, even temporarily.

Thanks to Stefano's assistance she negotiated the rough stones leading to the narrow alley without further mishap, the connection with his brother severed. The young man pressed close, his hand teasing her breast, the fullness cupped gently in his right hand as he nuzzled her ear. She barely heard the whispered, suggestive endearments, her head still buzzing from the near orgasmic experience.

Now did not seem the time for Stefano's *ardeur* to kick in. Could he have sensed the wash of energies that consumed her, and his damned brother? Fortunately Antonio kept his back to them, concentrating on the task at hand which was to get them out of the Square and to whatever destination he had in mind.

No matter how much he loved and wished to protect his younger brother, when it came to that much unbridled passion, she would not want to be in Stefano's shoes should Tonio glimpse him fondling her breasts so openly. She had grown to care about her young lover, the dalliance a calculated risk with sometimes satisfying outcomes. Pitting the brothers against each other ran counter to her objectives and was not a legacy she cared to leave when she exited this dimension.

However, engaging Antonio de' Medici in a contest of wills? That was an intriguing proposition, but a risk with consequences she could not predict. The uncertainty about how much he knew and understood about his own powers must guide her now. If she could control that budding promise of self-awareness—partition and parlay the devious Medici mindset to her advantage—she might redirect his interest. If he ever decided to act on it, would she be strong enough to deny him? *Would she even want to?*

"Veluria, are you...?"

"I am fine, Stefano." She brushed her gown, aligning the layers, spinning in a slow circle to fan the folds over the rigid hoops.

"If you are quite finished, Madame? We have an appointment to keep." Antonio spoke with disdain and motioned his men forward through the narrow opening. "Stefano, go on ahead and make sure there are no unwelcome surprises. We shall be there shortly."

Stefano nodded and strode off with two of the guards. Tonio filled the space left by his brother, pressing Veluria against the wall, forcing her to brace her left hand against the ever-damp stone. What she wanted was to press her hands against his massive chest, to get him to back off her personal space ... and using that excuse to explore what lay beneath the leather jerkin, the hard muscles and a heart thudding like a bass drum.

Damn him.

A small smile played about Tonio's full lips, dark eyes glinting even in the dim light. Bending down, his hot breath brushed past her ear as he whispered, "You may fool my besotted brother but you do not fool me, M'Lady. I know who you are. I know what you want. Best keep that in mind."

Veluria kept her head down and face carefully blank. Let the Demon enjoy his moment of intimidation. She would have been disappointed had he not seen through at least one or two veils of her disguise. What he did not know was ... *what* she was. That piece of knowledge she tucked away in the private space the Sisters had so diligently fashioned, a honeycomb of safety, each space, each construct, to serve her higher purpose.

When she finally lifted her chin to stare directly at the domineering force trapping her, she settled her features into mask of anguish and acquiescence. Would he buy the artifice? The false fluttering of eyelashes, the … oh dear Mother, dare she say it? The heaving bosom?

Before she could ask herself how far she could push his buttons, the demon pressed her hard against the wall, his hot breath tantalizing against her cool cheek. With shocking gentleness, he brushed her mouth, his tongue trailing wet warmth as he eased her lips apart for the briefest taste, leaving her light-headed with her blood pounding through her veins.

Mercy, what was that? I thought I was the seductress.

With a sneer, he said, "Shall we?" and pointed down the alleyway, inviting her to go first. His withdrawal was like an ice bath on overheated skin, a sensation open to interpretation.

With as much dignity as she could muster, Veluria moved in the direction he indicated, acutely conscious of the gush of wetness flooding her engorged private place. The man chuckled, deep in his throat, and she wondered if he knew this thing…this physical reaction to his unexpected show of affection.

As she gathered her skirts, she felt the dark giant's presence as he moved in close.

Then pain, sharp searing pain stabbing through her chest.

Need. Desperate need.

Not him, I would know if it were him.

Then who?

Bewildered, Veluria staggered ahead of the man who would be her captor and her master.

Chapter Five

Stefano stood at a non-descript door that, under other circumstances, would likely have passed for an entrance to a simple artisan's shop. No light escaped the door's bottom. Shutters stood diligent guard over the windows, yet a faint sound of music could be heard from within. Stefano knocked on the rough door in an arrhythmic cadence. In mere moments a similar knock came from the far side. Stefano answered the call, and the door creaked open. The guardsmen formed a veritable tunnel as Stefano beckoned Veluria and his brother to the doorway.

"We don't have time for this," Antonio growled but his younger brother had already whisked the woman into a room crowded with masked, bejeweled figures swirling in a riot of color and movement.

Stefano grinned and waved at the throng of party-goers, just a young man intent on an evening's entertainment. He beckoned Tonio and Veluria toward a far wall so they could speak in private.

"The Papàl Guards are positioned about the palazzo. Obviously one of our dear uncle's lackeys decided to exercise some initiative after losing the scent earlier." He spun Veluria in a circle, her gown flaring and shimmering in the candle light. She afforded him the briefest nod of understanding.

Tonio scowled and cursed, "Damn them, the interfering fools."

Stefano laughed out loud as Veluria squealed, but his eyes were cold and sharp as he said through clenched teeth, "My thoughts exactly. Fortunately Father has business dealings with the Cigogna family so I was able to invite myself to these festivities." He slapped the taller man's forearm and said, "Problem solved, dear Brother."

36

Antonio muttered, "Fuck this..." but Stefano had gripped Veluria's arm, pulling her into the joyous throng.

"*Una maschera mia signora*. Here. You'll need this." Stefano produced a feathery, red and black mask. With coquettish charm she brushed stiff stays and soft flesh across his arm as she spun to allow him to place the confection over her head.

Momentarily forgetting their precarious position, Stefano flushed with pleasure and anticipation. Antonio's scowl should have been a warning signal that he trod on shaky ground, despite his quick thinking.

Antonio leaned close and whispered in Stefano's ear, "Keep your focus. We, you, can't afford to have you thinking with your cock and losing control with this piece of..."

Stefano frowned at the implied criticism, stung by his older brother's lack of faith. "I am in control, Tonio. Give me some credit. Your eyes see what they wish to see."

"Or maybe my eyes see what really is, eh? In any case, do not lose her in here, or you will answer to Father on your own!"

While the guards stood silent sentinel in the alleyway, the host for the evening gala, the eldest son of Signor Cigogna, led the trio through two archways into an intimate space reserved for special guests. A chamber orchestra competed with a din of chatter that enveloped them as they entered a long, narrow room filled with garish masked figures, awash in feathers and sequins, giddy with wine and the promise of debauchery.

Veluria bobbed and ducked past a small group engaged in a card game, incongruous amidst the sea of noise and movement. She waved to a stout woman across the dance floor, tittered coyly then blended smoothly into a swirl of dancers. With her petite size she vanished, leaving Stefano to swivel in dismay as he realized she'd slipped away.

"Veluria? Wh—?" Stefano choked on rising bile as he desperately searched the jammed room.

Tonio grabbed his brother's arm with a death grip. "I told you, imbecile!" His eyes flashed with naked fury. "Go find her. I'll alert my men in case she tries to escape."

Stefano silently cursed himself for his mishandling of their simple mission. He plowed into the middle of the swirling sea of partiers.

"Red and black mask," he muttered," I'm looking for a red and black mask." A server pressed a wine goblet into his hand as he carved a torturous path through the crush of bodies. He downed that goblet, then another, while scanning the room through the smoky haze. The heat and wine—combined with the prospect of facing his brother with yet another of his failures—gave him a splitting headache. Feeling woozy, he backed against a wall and clenched his fists in despair, swaying unsteadily.

The orchestra paused to polite applause as a petite frame brushed against his hip. Her silvery-white mask glimmered in the pale light, the upper edges adorned with extravagant ostrich plumes. It hid her entire face with sculpted alabaster cheeks and full ruby lips, the eye slits revealing nothing. She moved temptingly close to him, slowly backing him up to a wall until she had him pinned, pressing hard against his groin. He moaned with anticipation but hesitated. The mask was different though this vixen was the same height, the gown similar … but not. He tried to focus on a familiar floral fragrance from the vixen's hair.

Bemused, curious, Stefano pulled the woman closer until he could fondle the edge of the mask. The woman dodged away with a giggle. She sauntered to an alcove, dimly lit, and paused as if waiting for something … or someone. He followed close behind, still unsure. There were highborn families amongst the throng and he dare not make an error that would compound the mess he'd already made of the evening. With a flourish the woman released the mask's binding, then turned and grinned devilishly, her sea-green eyes crinkled in mirth.

Stefano sputtered, "But you aren't…"

He found it difficult to focus on the woman's features, so similar to Veluria's that if he tilted his head just so he could convince himself it was her.

She giggled and pulled him toward the rear of the building. Placing a finger to his lips, she teased in a breathy voice, "I found a place where we can be alone."

That did not seem like a good idea. But on the other hand, it wasn't a bad idea either. He swayed, bracing his hands on the flirt's waist to keep from falling over.

Confused, he croaked, "But what about...?" *What about what?* some inner voice whispered. Since he had no answer to that question, he allowed her next words to over-ride his better judgment.

"Never mind all that. You and I have better things to do with our evening." The woman giggled and climbed the stairs without a backward glance.

Stefano staggered after the woman.

****

Veluria paused at the rear entrance to the baccaro. The courtesan had done her part well. The Sisterhood had traced her movements with their usual precision and had anticipated such an opportunity once the parameters became apparent. Still, she stood in awe at the speed with which they had placed her doppelganger, the whore a most satisfying short term solution. The probabilities calculated to a very favorable eight-five percent success rate.

Moving swiftly past the cluttered tables in the servant's quarters, she took care to leave no trace of her passage. The solid oak door stood slightly ajar. She could hear the faint sloshing from the canal, mere meters distant and reeking of decay, and worse.

Silently she gathered the remains of her gown, now devoid of several layers, as the courtesan had cleverly removed sufficient material to refashion a dress remarkably similar to the original. The only drawback was the bodice—and the woman's ampler gifts— though Veluria doubted Stefano would take note when the object of his desire presented him with such largesse, especially in his drugged state.

Veluria had urged the woman to keep her own mask, given that it encompassed her face completely, unlike hers which covered the eyes only. Under the influence of the aphrodisiac, Stefano would easily be led astray, his mind focused on the coming pleasures to the exclusion of all else. And once in the heat of passion she was certain he would acquit himself with his usual fervor. Veluria was almost jealous of the woman's opportunity to enjoy the young one's special talents, especially with the 'enhancements' flooding his system.

She eased onto a narrow ledge that skirted the brackish canal. Glancing left, then right, she determined that her most likely location was on the Canale Della Giudecca. To the left she could follow it eventually to the Lido, to the right the Piazzali Roma. Somewhere along this route there would be a gondola to take her out of range of the Dark One, the Demon de' Medici who, even now, was scanning the narrow streets waiting for her to bolt to freedom. Before she'd encountered this man, such awareness and near constant surveillance would have been unthinkable.

She sighed, vexed at the unrelenting barrage on her senses. There had to be a way to neutralize his abilities, or at least redirect them away from her before he forced her off task. Too much was at stake in her world to risk this kind of interference.

She murmured, sotto voce, "Help me Reverend Mother, your daughter accedes to your everlasting goodness, lead me to the light, bestow upon me the gifts of my womanhood that we may serve thee through time and space for all eternity."

Despite the lingering heat, and damp, cloying air, Veluria shivered. She rubbed her bare shoulders and arms vigorously, hoping to speed the blood flow and dispel the residual essence of Antonio. Where he had touched her, brief though it had been, she still tingled with energies familiar and disturbing, though not all of it his. On this matter she remained confused and not a little concerned.

Her senses bled softly into the stygian darkness. To the left, she pulsed energy, testing and evaluating. That way led back toward St. Mark's Square and potential complications with the Papàl Guard— and who knew what all pursued her this foul night. Her better chance lay away from the crowds and away from the faint source of energy that could only come from the Council operative.

She'd wanted to ask the whore if she had any information from the Sisterhood but the woman had been tasked with one job only— and that did not include a dossier on the man who so baldly breached her defenses. She spun right and tiptoed gingerly along the rough stone walkway, ghosting silently toward her destination.

****

Tonio leaned against the bacarro's front entrance door, concerned that his instincts, for once, might have led him astray. He was unused to indecision, to not knowing. He'd not been surprised that his idiot younger brother, a witless, charming ass, would be the one to lose their quarry. That it was he who had laid the scenario for

40

that eventuality would mean hell to pay when he reported to Papà. The old man was not so infirm that he couldn't do damage should he choose to punish his oldest son and most trusted advisor.

Kicking the door in irritation he bellowed, "Fuck this! Eduardo, find my ass of a brother. Now."

Eduardo, the nearest guardsman, drew his short sword and pushed the heavy door open. He turned to Tonio with a questioning look. "My Lord, what if he's with…?"

Antonio glared at his man. "I don't care how many he's fucking. Bring him to me. Naked if need be."

"*Sì, mio Signore. Immediatamente.*"

Tonio rubbed his temples, the old pain resurfacing as it always did when he probed for too long. He'd been at it for hours, nibbling at her edges, only to be rebuffed, shut out when penetration seemed assured. He remembered the taste of her lips, soft and quivering with anticipation, prepared to yield, albeit reluctantly. He'd taken great delight in drawing her in, seizing control, then withdrawing. Such simple satisfaction, to have her press upward, ever so slightly—curious and oh so willing.

If he were honest with himself, it had taken every ounce of his considerable will-power to not ravish her on the spot. Her scent, so delicately kissed with lavender and a fragrance he didn't recognize, had intoxicated him. As had the taste of her lips and the warmth of her tongue briefly tangling with his own.

He'd gotten her off-balance, tweaked her interest.

Dammit, I can't afford to let her get under my skin. She's nothing but trouble.

Tonio wished with all his heart his beloved, dim-witted brother had not taken her fancy. The man-boy was ill-equipped for the machinations of the court ladies, let alone one such as this. That his House, his family, the very structure of his culture was in desperate disarray because of these evil influences pulling strings gnawed at his gut. Something, someone, was forcing them all to dance like marionettes. He had enemies all around, but the one he feared most passed beyond the realm of words, a realm to which he was convinced *she* held the key.

"My Lord." Eduardo pushed through the door with Stefano and another in tow. "I found him with this … woman. He claims she is the one you seek."

Tonio waved Eduardo aside and stared at his hapless brother with distaste. The young man was virtually naked, and clearly still in a state of arousal, a fact the thin bit of cloth draped about his waist and nether regions failed to hide. The woman in question bore a faint resemblance to Veluria—height, facial features, hair color—but she was far too voluptuous, reeking of whore instead of the refined sensuality of the alleged Frenchwoman.

Stefano giggled and wrapped his arm about the woman. "See, Brother, I did not lose her after all." He parted her pale rose-coloured silk robe, stroking the gentle rise of her belly and nuzzling a plump breast.

Tonio balled his fists, fighting for control, strung tight. He felt the air about him disappear, sucking his lungs dry, until a red haze coated his eyes and his anger and fear erupted in a startling display of sheer power. With breathtaking speed he drew his stiletto and flicked it through the thin cloth protecting his brother's manhood. With a roar he slammed the smaller man against the stone wall, pressing his left hand against Stefano's throat, his right holding the stiletto perilously close to the young man's cock.

"Why you?" he hissed. "Why is this…" he pricked soft flesh "… so much more valuable than mine or Nicolo's?"

Stefano gurgled in blind panic, writhing in pain as sensitive tissue responded to the rapid knicks and pricks. Tonio emphasized each word in blood, taking no small amount of joy from his brother's acute pain and paralyzing fear.

"I should cut it off and save us all from the misery of watching you fuck everything up."

"Tonio. Please." Stefano gurgled, his face contorted in agony. "I'm going to be sick…"

Antonio released his brother in disgust. He motioned to Eduardo to bring the woman over. After a cursory examination he determined she had nothing to offer him, though his men could certainly use some entertainment for the night's aborted mission.

"See that she fulfills her obligation to my dearest brother."

Wild-eyed, Stefano choked out, "But I can't, not like this. Tonio, please."

Tonio barked to his man, "She is yours after."

"*Gracie*, M'Lord." Eduardo thrust the woman onto the cobbled stone, her silence strange and foreboding. He was sure that nothing

42

good would come from this but his fear of the Demon de' Medici overrode any other concerns.

Antonio turned to go. A black mist coagulated about his soul, driving him into despair and self-loathing. He needed to find her, though not for reasons he understood. As the pain ramped to excruciating hammer blows to his temples, he prepared his senses to once again seek the thing that eluded him so cleverly.

"M'Lord? Where are you going? Don't you wish protection? The night grows long and there is an ill feel in the breeze."

"*Caccia, il mio vecchio amico.* I go hunting.

Chapter Six

Veluria stole quietly through the night, ever aware of competing energies demanding their due. She had avoided a potential derailment of her plans, such as they were. Meeting the pater familias of the Medici clan had an appeal, to be sure, but she preferred it be in a more public, less adversarial venue where she could make use of any competing loyalties, jealousies and ill-will garnered through Cosimo's sometimes heavy-handed plotting.

And she would like to understand his oldest son's capabilities before tackling the old man. Rumor had it that he was an order of magnitude more powerful than his offspring—something to mull over and give one pause. Going one-on-one with Antonio had been stressful enough. With two of them probing her at the same time? She was not a fan of suicide missions.

Leaving the party, escaping to regroup and reassess her options, had seemed prudent, especially when the Sisterhood had so conveniently provided the means. She had taken that as a sign. Now she worried that she had perhaps miscalculated and jumped at the chance for an easy out. Had her judgment been that clouded by the psychic assaults coming from two fronts?

Stealing through the night, sans her benefactor and raison d'etre for gathering information, put her in an untenable position. Though she had curried favor amongst the lower elite and was not without other options, those pathways would be less effective, and infinitely slower to utilize. Almost like starting over.

And what were the odds that Stefano, or his damnable brother, would simply let her vanish into the background? How had *she* suddenly become a 'person of interest'? She wasn't *the key*—her term for the elusive clue that would allow their scientists to understand and rectify the threat to her own civilization.

This all felt like one monumental mistake. Mother Superior chose her because she wasn't prone to errors.

Why can't I see clearly?

Why did she see only him, the Demon de' Medici, so aptly named for he compelled her undivided attention with devilish ease? Intermixed with dominance and control, she perceived a strange passion driving him. Lust she was used to, it was after all her preferred method of control, one of her very special gifts, that translating of *want* to *need*.

That one kiss, barely a touch, had somehow developed an import, a significance blown so out of all proportion that she had panicked, rushed into making hasty decisions. His reaction had been as perplexing: withdrawal, confusion, even anger but whether at himself, her or his brother was difficult to say.

What she did know was that they were inextricably linked at some level that went beyond even her understanding of the complex interplay of energies.

That she was vulnerable around the elder brother was undisputed. She would need to take care for she risked more than the mission, more than the fates of their worlds. She had a soul and forces only dimly perceived seemed intent on robbing her of her very essence. She was tethered by competing enmities, both laying claim to her emotions, both ready and willing to inflict pain to bring her to heel.

The assault in the tunnel had left residual disquiet, not because the Council operative stood to access information but because there had been an unexplained psychotic edge to the episode, an unnerving neediness not easily dismissed. It had left her feeling ... unclean.

For the foreseeable future she lacked the dubious luxury of choice. Events were now in motion and, not for the first time, she wondered just how much her mere presence here affected history and the timeline. She left the theorizing to those who specialized in such studies. Her job was to find out, if at all possible, exactly what or who had altered or interfered with the normal course of events.

The pathway along the canal ended abruptly, forcing her through a narrow alley onto the empty street fronted with merchant quarters and modest townhomes. Feeling vulnerable she sought to occupy her mind with something other than the endless loops of unanswered questions. The state of her gown, the fact that she wandered the empty streets in the middle of the night unescorted, that she'd abandoned Stefano to the certain wrath of his volatile brother…

That thought brought her up short, so much so she stumbled and nearly went down on the rough stones. Curious, she risked seeking Stefano's energy signature, a passive activity and unlikely to draw the operative's attention. She ducked into an alley and leaned against the stone wall, cursing the corset and its restrictions. With an effort she calmed herself with several shallow breaths, shutting out as much of the night sounds and scents as possible.

Whether or not she was successful depended more on the strength of the emotional attachment than on proximity to the person. Since she'd developed an inordinate fondness for the young man, the odds were in her favor that she could establish a feel for his current mental state.

She was unprepared for the wash of pain spearing her gut. She bent over, retching, aware only of agony and anger and a gush of emotions she could barely comprehend. The brothers' essences intermingled in a tsunami of fear and panic and self-loathing.

How was that even possible? She'd established no such link, nothing so powerful that could conceivably allow Antonio's energy such easy access.

The Demon de' Medici caused her young lover's suffering, as well as his own. Stefano's distress rapidly faded into the background, replaced by a complex sea of emotion that defied description, dominated by the demon's, Tonio's, hate … and regret.

How could she be drawn to such a man? How could she not?

Staggering, she fled down the empty streets knowing one thing for certain. Antonio de' Medici was on the hunt. For her.

****

Antonio attacked the night the way he approached everything, full frontal assault, without guile or finesse. He had little patience for fools and tonight his brother had stretched that patience to the breaking point. His shame and regret was a palpable thing but he must not let it interfere with the execution of his duties to his family.

Duty? Is that what drove him?

The simple mission had devolved into a disaster, partially of his own making. The woman was a formidable adversary with remarkable skills, certainly worthy of Cosimo's attention. What he couldn't fathom was why or how she'd managed to insinuate herself into his thoughts, planting seeds of an emotion he reserved only for his brothers.

If desire had a rhythm it was a staccato beat, not the faint flutterings of the merely smitten, but the steady thrum of senses on full alert, blood pounding hot and strong through his veins. Heat flooded his face, a burning, like ice, like fire, like nothing he'd ever sensed or experienced in his long, troubled life. He thought himself immune, protected from the vulnerabilities of emotions that served no purpose.

His father had taught him well and for years he'd banked those fires, taking his pleasure on his terms. But this ... *this* was out of control, a wildfire racing through conduits long idle, now ablaze. He felt the panic and the bile rise in his throat and the delicious assault on his groin, hurtling him into readiness.

With a gasp, he collapsed against a fractured surface, rough and pitted, harsh on hands that knew little gentleness. What was wrong with him? It could not be her alone—this was too strong, coming from separate directions, beating at him like a storm gone wild, wind and hail and rain surrounding him from every quarter. He wanted, needed escape and knew there was none. Papà and his uncles would see to that. He would take back the control of the Demon, the Dark One. His gifts must not be squandered, his training forsaken, his attention splintered, fractured like a mirror hurled into space from the highest parapet.

His priority remained the same but the reasons behind it had shifted dramatically. He now understood he must find the woman before the other did, that nameless stalker who was but a wraith, vague in shape, indistinct— a darkness from which no light could enter or leave. He silently cursed his ability to feel other's thoughts ... to peer even into their souls. It was a constant reminder that he had none of his own.

The distant sound of revelers, the strange shushing of cloth and soft-soled feet, lapping wavelets and creaking docks swayed to a symphony that was uniquely Venezia. Florence, his home, had nothing like this, this ever-present danger clothed in soft hues, vengeful nights and a sea that hungered for the soul of the city with a voraciousness not even he could match.

He ached for relief, for freedom from the pressure in his skull, and pain that threatened to drive him to his knees. The best he could hope for was to have cool logic replace the jumble of emotions consuming him from within: fear, longing, desire, need. None of that served his purpose.

He allowed a frisson of shame to remain. What he had done to his brother was inexcusable. Stefano was one of the few things in this world he truly cared about. The young one needed his guidance and protection. Instead he'd reverted to the monster all knew him to be.

With a sigh he straightened and forced all extraneous sensation to the background, willing the pain in his head to retreat. Logic dictated that she'd lose herself in a crowd, perhaps retreating back toward St. Mark's Square. Yet from that direction he sensed the stalker, the man's presence like icy fingers of dread racing up and down his spine. If he were in her position he'd try to put as much distance between them as possible. And that included himself.

With no way to know for sure he decided to go with his gut instincts. Turning to the right, he hastened toward the Piazzali Roma.

Were he a betting man, he'd lay odds he'd find Veluria first. Perhaps when Cosimo was done with her, he could indulge his fevered imagination…

****

Andreas paused at the steep stairwell, the stone stairs slippery and canted to the left. The tunnel had been carved by hand in a time beyond memory, using the natural grottoes alternately as tombs, then hiding places when the time of troubles visited the city, spreading hideous death and destruction until only the weak-minded and foolhardy chose to remain and guard a once glorious culture.

Andreas felt the reverence for and the residual fears of the ancient ghosts who inhabited all spaces where god and man fought for jurisdiction and pre-eminence.

A flicker at the end of the long tunnel indicated a candle or torch. Few, other than brigands and the destitute chose to inhabit the underground warrens. The rest of the populace avoided the caverns out of superstition and fear. Curious he extended his senses, realizing it was too much to hope that his quarry would so conveniently await his pleasure.

What swamped him was a perplexing mix of pain and terror, someone—a woman—in considerable distress, but alone. He would have turned away, left her to her misery, except for one thing … a residual trace of the woman he sought. Veluria?

No, not her, though without seeing for himself, he could not be sure.

Shivering with anticipation he plunged with abandon down the steep tunnel, stopping only when he reached the small alcove from which a weak light winked as from a stray breeze.

The stench of blood and sweat and sex pummeled his nostrils. He blinked against the sudden light, eyes drawn to something huddled in the corner. "Veluria?" he whispered.

The small form moaned and struggled to stand. The woman was a mass of bruises, her eyes blackened, nose bloodied, face filthy, arms and legs stained with unmentionable substances. Her generous breasts hung like savaged globes, scarred, reddish-purple splotches a roadmap of lustful mouths hungering for a feast. She carried the remains of her gown over her left arm, unconcerned about her nakedness and vulnerability.

"Padre," she croaked weakly. "Have you come to save me?"

Andreas hesitated, unsure how to proceed. The resemblance to Veluria was uncanny. And there was no mistaking that this pitiful creature had been in contact with her, and not that long ago.

Remembering the role he played, he said with false kindness and concern, "Of course, my daughter." When he asked if she wished him to call the authorities, he was not surprised the creature objected strongly. "Then tell me your name and explain what has brought you to this heinous state."

"Giovanna, Father." Trembling she sank to the stone floor and attempted to cover herself with the wisp of fabric.

With difficulty he managed to prise sufficient details to piece together the evening's chain of events. He stared at the whore with interest. Apparently with her help, Veluria had shaken off the

49

Demon de' Medici and his fop of a brother. How or why that had transpired was of little consequence.

"Father?"

The woman had finally turned her ravaged face toward him with a look that pleaded for ... what? Comfort, absolution?

He murmured the first words that came to mind, "You have done well. The Lord will reward you in the next life, most generously."

Through swollen lips, she hasped, "I want what is due me now. I have no use for eternity."

He admired her defiance, her understanding that eternity, and the empty promises thereof, had little to do with the here and now. She was wise beyond her station. Payment now, let the Church and its God worry about the hereafter. He had just the solution.

"Capisco, figlia." Andreas held his growing excitement in check, but barely. "But I must ask you to do one thing for me."

"No. I have done enough," she pointed to hideous, angry welts along the inside of her thighs, "I can do no more."

Andreas purred in soothing intonations as he advanced slowly, fearful he might spook her into bolting. Carefully removing the remains of the dress, he set it aside, then stroked her hair, letting his fingers tangle in the dark strands. She cringed and drew away from his touch.

"Bend over," he husked, parting his robe.

"*Vi prego, per favore, no.*"

Andreas lifted her hips to receive his offering, his cock thick and eager to dive into her depths. It had been an eternity since he'd availed himself of such pleasure. That this vessel carried the essence of the one thing he desired above all others made it that much sweeter. He drove deep, to the hilt, then withdrew slowly, savoring the sensation. Slow, loving thrusts—each accompanied by a throaty moan of 'no, no, no' echoing weakly off the stone walls.

"*Tranquillo, figlia. Sono quasi.* You will soon receive your just reward."

As the tide released his passion, he grasped her hair and roughly jerked her head back, driving deeper and coming on a single swell and a rasping moan of "Veluria" as he smoothly drew the blade across the whore's throat.

50

"*Riposa in pace, figlia.*" Andreas lowered the limp body carefully to the stone floor and adjusted his robes. He saluted the still figure with the crucifix, intoning last rites, then backed away and began the long climb up the torturous tunnel.

Pausing at the entrance, he quickly scanned the dark street, his senses at full alert. His beloved would be on the run from the Medicis. In her shoes, he might have done the same thing, given what powerful adversaries they were. Their training, the careful adherence to bloodlines, uncommon intelligence combined with luck and a devotion to family unmatched by any of the Great Houses of the time—all that and more made them formidable indeed.

But the Demon was something else entirely. His powers, and his alone, could terminate his mission with dire consequences for his Order, his culture and even time itself. The operative, Veluria, was also an unexpected complication in that she had awakened unholy desires he'd denied himself for far too long. He craved her and her alone. How ironic, he was a man with a banquet of sin to be sampled and treasured and savored—but instead he succumbed to her wiles, yearning for nothing more than the black comfort of her soul.

Like a bloodhound on a scent, he snapped his head around and sighed, "Ah, there." Adjusting the link, he allowed the energy to flow through and around him, accentuating the signal. "And the Demon de' Medici. Interesting."

With the Council suspecting the Medicis being at the nexus of the historical perturbations, having all the players in one spot would serve his purpose better than divide and conquer. The Demon would secure his quarry soon enough so he need do nothing more than wait.

Veluria had no idea how deep his hooks went into her psyche. Everything she did, everyone she touched would be an open book to him.

And when the time came, he would finally have his heart's desire…

Chapter Seven

No, Papà, I do not know where Tonio has gone."

Stefano hung his head in misery. He ached in places no man should bear, far beyond the physical discomfort his enraged brother had inflicted, justifiably so. It was shame, a deep abiding black hole that ate at his soul, not in small nibbles but with ravenous bites, tearing, ripping and shredding until he could barely stand against the assault on what he once considered his greatest strength—purity of spirit.

Tonio had tried, so very hard had he fought for him, but time and circumstances, and this vexing miasma of intrigue and unknowable confluence of fate had finally broken the walls of protection his possessed sibling had erected. Protected no longer, Stefano could not help but feel abandoned. He blamed Antonio, for that was the easy way and he was always about ease of passage.

'Tonight could be different. Tonight could be when you become the man you were meant to be.' Antonio's deep voice husked softly in his mind, as ever, his spirit-guide.

"… and I assume you took care of your little problem?" Cosimo de' Medici glared at his youngest son, everyone's court favorite, the handsomest of the three he'd sired legitimately.

Stefano gulped audibly, having paid little attention to the incessant tirade about his shortcomings on this matter. "Yes sir. The Guards took care of the … matter."

Cosimo huffed, "Well, then. Come, my boy, let us sit. I have much to discuss about your prospects."

"Prospects?"

Stefano's gut clenched, knowing full well what his father had in mind, none of it good for his future wants or desires. He would be auctioned off like a prize stallion to the highest bidder, likely to one of the hideous Habsburg bitches, of which dozens seemed to come out the narrow parapets so favored by the Duchys and their prideful inhabitants.

He whispered, "I wish you had cut it off, Brother. You would have saved me from a lifetime of agony."

"What?"

"Nothing, Papà."

Cosimo, short and deceptively stout, guided his taller son to a small alcove off his main meeting room. A fire burned cozily against the far wall, driving away the ever-present damp and chill, even in the heat of high summer. Plump cushions, burgundy velvet and tasseled at the corners, lay close at hand. A flagon of red wine and a plate of cured meats and cheeses sat invitingly between the cushions.

With a sigh, Cosimo sank onto the nearest pillow. Stefano followed, lowering himself slowly as the brush of cloth against his cock opened and irritated the small knicks and cuts. Phantom pain, and a strange remembered pleasure from his public coupling with the whore, left him feeling twisted and oddly curious about his unexpected arousal and feelings of satisfaction as the men had goaded and cheered him on. They'd chided, then commiserated, when he could not perform a second time, the blood and angry marks a testament to his brother's well-deserved reputation as a cruel and violent man, one to be feared and respected.

What threatened to consume Stefano's soul was the knowledge that he had wanted it, desperately, the pain, then the slick, smooth feel as he commanded her body and drove his own relentlessly to explode with a roar, an ecstasy of release even his beloved Veluria had only begun to awaken in him. He recognized it for what it was, a perversion, and he desperately wanted to embrace it, own it, to call it up at his every whim. The stray wisps of memories set his blood boiling and his cock aching with need.

In the deepest recesses of his mind he pleaded, *Antonio, help me before I am lost.*

Cosimo chewed idly on a piece of meat and observed the play of emotions on the young man's face. Tonio's man, Eduardo, had apprised the capo della famiglia of events as he had observed them, leaving no detail, however small, unmentioned.

"*Hai fatto bene, figlio mio.*"

"*Gracie,* Papà." Stefano mumbled. In another time, another place, such praise, a simple 'you did well,' would have burst his heart with pride. Now a cauldron of doubt and shame and desire threatened to bury him in darkness from which there was no escape. A darkness Antonio knew all too well. He did not wish to join his brother in the living hell he dwelt in every day of his tortured life.

Stefano bent close to his father, concentrating hard on the old man's intonation of events unfolding on the continent. Carlos had inherited Burgundy and Castile-León and stood next in line to inherit Aragon from the ailing Ferdinand, placing the young man in the enviable position as effective ruler of all of the area known as Spagna.

"You understand what this means, do you not?" Cosimo queried his son.

"I think so, Papà. When Carlos' father, Phillip, died ten years ago..." Cosimo nodded encouragingly, "...that left Maximillian with no direct heirs other than Carlos."

Stefano sat up straighter and rubbed his left hand over his brow, the implications now clear. No wonder his father worked so diligently to secure the favor of the man who would rule Spagna, and eventually most of the continent.

Cosimo continued, "Carlos has indicated a certain ... willingness to consider my, and Leo's, proposal in exchange for our support when the time is right."

"But the French..."

"Will not be a factor, of this I am assured from a trusted source." Cosimo grinned and patted his son's knee. "You, my boy, will have an integral part to play, never fear."

Stefano cringed inwardly. That was *exactly* what he feared.

Cosimo interpreted his son's discomfort to the injuries his increasingly out-of-control older brother had inflicted. He opted not to pursue the matter of the woman, Veluria, as he was assured by Eduardo that Antonio was 'on the hunt' and Cosimo knew exactly what that meant. The woman would be in their custody soon enough. They could make the proper determinations and proceed as planned whatever the outcome of his interrogation.

"Rest, my boy. We will talk more on this later."

"*Gracie*, Papà, sleep well."

Stefano lunged to his feet, willing the pain away. With mincing steps he hastened from the small room and made for the stairs to his quarters. Once in the safety of his private chambers, he stripped quickly and gazed with horror at the purplish bruising and oozing cuts on his cock. He wished for nothing more than a soft pillow and the pliant flesh of his beloved, his Veluria.

Where was she? Why could he no longer feel her tender presence?

In silent supplication, he began his evening prayers for salvation of his soul.

****

Andreas allowed his shadow-self to mold onto the stained gray stones. Distracted by the powerful energies channeling through his aura, he failed to triangulate the respective locations of the woman and her pursuer. The sound of footfalls striding relentlessly toward him startled him into breaking the connection. As he pressed against the solid foundation, bits of loose mortar shifted and rolled with annoying clarity. Andreas willed the sounds to mute, masking their inexorable path to the cobbled street with his aura.

The entrance to the tunnel lay off to the south. He'd taken shelter in a narrow alleyway leading to the canal. The overarching structures leaned inwards, blocking the night sky, leaving all in utter blackness. He'd adjusted his shadow self to allow for the implants to work at full power. He offered a small prayer of thanks to his Order for their foresight.

The woman had been close, her confusion and distress masking her location. He could only surmise that she'd been consumed with the need to avoid her pursuer. He was unconcerned. Her location was of little consequence. What mattered was that the Demon find her. Once together, he could manipulate circumstances, and them, so that the answers he sought would be revealed.

Bemused, he listened as the now familiar stride announced the approach of the Dark One.

"Antonio de' Medici," he murmured with derision, "on the hunt."

Andreas locked onto Antonio's essence, the unique energy signature that made this one man, above all others, the most dangerous entity in the known universe. The key to all their survivals … or their destruction.

He waited a moment for the tall figure to pass, then peeled his shadow-self from the rough stones, rounded the corner and carefully pursued his quarry. The Dark One's stride took him toward the Piazzali Roma, a section of the city housing the highborn and court favorites. Following the scent. He murmured, "Curious that she would head that way."

Furtively Andreas ghosted behind his quarry, intent only on the wavering energies. He stumbled on the uneven footing, wrenching his leg and bringing him to a halt, gasping with pain.

"*Porca miseria!*" he swore. The last thing he needed was to reawaken old injuries. He had no wish to repeat the months of rehabilitation after this very same ankle had suffered a debilitating injury when a Gateway had shifted and collapsed unexpectedly on his leg, leaving the left ankle almost beyond repair. Until then no one knew the passageways capable of inflicting so much damage on corporeal forms.

He hesitated to expend his resources in restructuring his neural pathways, as time and circumstance continued to erode his options. The Demon advanced too quickly and would soon be out of his range. Andreas slipped past the entrance to the tunnel. He paused for a moment, satisfied by the mingling energy signatures.

"*Dammi la forza,*" he intoned, as he would require strength as well as cunning. He would need to find another vessel, and soon. The whore had been too spent to be of much use. He smiled at the remembered pleasure as his essence bled and blended, shadow on shadow, just out of range of the Demon.

Antonio hurtled through the darkened streets, obviously familiar with the area. Though still narrow, the road now passed by elegant domiciles with ornately carved finials over imposing entryways. The Demon suddenly ceased his headlong rush, backed up a pace and swiveled his head left and right as if listening for something. Fingering his cinquedea, he turned to his left. Without knocking, he pushed the solid door open and entered into a furious din of many voices raised in anger.

Andreas followed Antonio, but before the link was swallowed in a well of competing energies, he felt the Dark One's tide of assurance, the swell of smug disdain for his quarry, then a strange tickling of anxiety, perhaps even fear.

Andreas knew and understood this fear, felt it in his groin, in that deep space he'd reserved for himself alone. Like an invading army, she'd commandeered all of them to her will.

"*La mia puttana, puttana la nostra ... siamo tutti persi,*" he moaned to the night. Lost to the whore, all of them.

"You poor fuck," he spat, though whether he meant himself or the Medici puppets was unclear.

****

"Idiota! "Your cousin bleeds us dry with his commissions and his fucking extravagance!"

Cardinal Guilio de' Medici smiled sagely at the man going nose-to-nose with him, his arrogance and intensity masking a small stature and portly frame. Voices erupted about the cluttered space, appalled that one as powerful as the Cardinal should suffer the deprecations of a lowly mathematician.

Several men advanced menacingly toward the peacock preening and preaching a message of fiscal restraint. Not a few fingered cinquedeas, prepared to defend the good Cardinal's honor, if not his unique position as the cousin of the current Pope. Favor could be bought, or it could be won at the pricking end of a stiletto. The Cardinal was no stranger to either approach.

His Eminence held up a hand to stay the advance of his would-be rescuers.

"Benedetto, you task me as always." He smoothed his rich Cardinal's robes, making sure his own weapons remained within easy reach. He believed in the power of prayer, backed with the instruments of the Lord and the position of his family. His distant cousin huffed a refrain of responsibility that the good Cardinal understood in principal, if not in practice. He stood convinced that the glory of his God, his Church and his Family would be writ in the sanctity and beauty of the towering edifices for which he and his cousin Leo actively commissioned, not only for the Vatican, but for their home city of Florence.

His Eminence knew one's enemies must never forget that the family had access to almost limitless resources, when pressure was applied correctly. The Cardinal removed his hat and set it on the small table by his side. He waved to Benedetto to sit next to him. The small man thankfully slid onto the uncomfortable seat and continued his diatribe as if the interruption had not occurred.

Antonio stood quietly by the doorway, cataloguing and evaluating each guest, some of whom he did not recognize. His cousins, Guilio and Benedetto, and several of the managers of the various mills from his father's vast holdings in Florence and the nearby Duchy of Modena to the north and the Republic of Siena bordering the southern reaches, made up the bulk of the assemblage. He was uncomfortable that so many of his father's supporters should risk being in one spot without suitable protection, although he discerned the presence of several of the Papàl Guards stationed surreptitiously both inside and at several points behind the *domicilio elegante*. Protection from invasion by way of the canal seemed well in hand.

"It is good to see you, Brother," a deep voice whispered in his right ear. Antonio nodded his head once, his body vibrating with excitement. This was an unexpected pleasure.

"Nico," Tonio grunted roughly, "what the hell are you doing here? Didn't you get your fill of boot licking at Maximillian's court?"

Nico smiled and moved close to his taller brother. "It's not boots I'm licking these days, big brother. I am after bigger prey than that petty despot."

Antonio swung to embrace Nico, pounding him on the back with so much enthusiasm the smaller man grunted and pulled away.

"It's been too long, Nico. Are you staying with Father? When did you get in? And why…?" Tonio's questions exploded in a rush of affection. As much as he loved his younger brother, his middle brother, only five years his junior, had earned his undying respect and admiration. Like Stefano, the man was canny in the ways of the court, using the Medicis' gifts, and their own special shared lineage of powers, to ferret out intrigue with such astonishing clarity that their father has assigned him to permanent residence on both the Spanish and the Habsburg courts without the yoke of marriage to constrain his movement and shifting loyalties.

"I'm not staying, Tonio. In fact I must hie to the docks and pick up passage to Castile. I leave soonest." He drew his brother deep into the recesses of an alcove. "There is someone here of interest, Tonio. Be wary, for there is great power, power I do not understand."

Tonio looked sharply at his brother. "Where?"

Nico glanced to the ornately carved banister and the elegant stairway leading to the living quarters of the Courtesan whose house had been conscripted by the Cardinal and his retinue.

"Upstairs, Brother." Tonio tried to brush past his muscular sibling but Nico grabbed his arm and restrained him. "I am not joking, Tonio. Be careful."

"*Sono sempre attento, fratello*, you can trust me to take care."

"Then I must be off. Give Father my regards. I shall report when I have the details I need."

"Travel safely, Nico."

"*Ciao*. And Tonio?"

"Now what?"

"If you hurt him again, I will not tolerate it, do you understand?"

Antonio's face flamed with shame. He had hoped his brother would not get wind of his indiscretion but there had never been secrets between them. Their actions, feelings, intentions—all an open book, like a single mind sharing two different bodies.

"I promise on my life, Nico," Tonio murmured as his brother strode through the door. It was a vow he would keep, no matter what the cost.

In his heart he felt the faint stirrings of Stefano's dismay and something else ... disturbing. To find his brother's sensitivities intruding unbidden was unusual and worrisome but he had no time to analyze that now. The woman he sought was close, though her energies dissipated in the cacophony of power blasting him: men of fervor, religious and otherwise, men of acumen and political savvy, men of corruption and men of violence. Too many men with too much power in too small a space. He felt claustrophobic and short of breath.

How did Stefano and Nico put up with it, the incessant din, the bickering and backstabbing?

Though counterintuitive, he deliberately sought the calm amidst the familiar discord, seeking to pinpoint Veluria's exact location, and to determine if she were alone. Backing into the wall, he lost himself in the shadows. Once more admiration colored his perception of the woman. It took a certain amount of *insolenza* to enter a known lair of Medici power and influence—an all-male one at that—without incurring curiosity and discussion. Apparently only Nico had noted and remarked her passage to the upper reaches of the house.

He squinted against the smoky haze, willing himself to focus. With a start he felt the familiar tingling in his groin, the unwarranted desire and quickening pulse. He tried to control his breathing but it came shallow and fast, making him lightheaded. The headache that had nearly disabled him early in the evening came back with a full-on rush of pain.

"*Sì, vi sono ora, strega,*" he whispered. He had her now. But *what* he had he could not be sure. Was she a witch, a siren, or someone like him—an anomaly, a mistake? He would find out soon enough.

The hunter crept quietly up the marble stairs, cloaked in shadow, unremarked.

Chapter Eight

Andreas pressed against the stone wall. He grew weary of cold, damp stone and narrow alleys leading to water, always to water. The 'pearls' the poets waxed bucolic over were nothing more than stinking, fetid channels of refuse. He longed for his own time, though not what he knew would be a trying interrogation with the Council. He was not exactly keeping 'on message' as their scribe would say.

He'd also gone far beyond the Monsignor's simple exhortation to follow, observe and report, though probably not far enough in the Council's estimation with the timeline in jeopardy and the key poised to wreak havoc on all their futures.

He'd stolen the idea of 'the key' from Veluria's subconscious. The Council had suggested the presence of a magic totem, inadvertently discovered and its powers released with a cascade effect that impacted their own time and place. That reeked of an overactive imagination. He didn't believe in magic but he did believe in the power of greed and self-interest. Like Veluria he would keep his options open, and like her, he was betting that the key they both sought was a *someone*, not a something.

While he managed to redefine the parameters of his mission into terms that had logical consistency, he had yet to factor how to use the woman's powers. All he 'felt' was some congruence between the Demon de' Medici and this puzzle that was Veluria, and it tweaked a deep well of lust and longing in his groin.

He must seek out another vessel soon or risk losing himself to her allure. That fortuitous encounter with the whore had been like a small unsatisfying appetizer for a starving man. The main course lay just within reach, so close he could taste it, smell it, feel it. A tortured moan escaped his lips as he pictured her writhing under him until he lost himself in her pale flesh. His ears rang with the pounding of blood coursing through his system, gasping at the dank mist in choking pleas for surcease from the beast gnawing at his innards.

He could deal with the competing demands of the Church in this dimension, and the far more dangerous Council in his own time, but he paled at the insistent demands on his body, a body too eager to respond to whatever 'she' insinuated into his psyche.

Andreas came on a gurgled moan, humming her name, and pleading to his God, "What is she, my Lord? I need to know if I am to serve you well." Weak-limbed he crept out of the shadows and drew the stiletto from within the folds of the tunic. With irritation he drew the blade along the inside of his forearm, watching the rich red flow trickle past his wrist. As her hold on him grew stronger he feared what might be necessary to shock his system into severing the bond.

He knew that the real fear was that he would succumb to that bond and be corrupted, lost forever, the impossible made manifest … and strangely desirable.

"You are lost," he muttered, aware that this mantra rose unbidden to his lips with increasing frequency.

The slamming of a door to Andreas' left startled him into leaping back into the safety of the shadows. He risked peering around the corner of the building to confirm that the Demon, the Dark One, had exited the building in haste and was proceeding quickly in the direction of the city docks. His long strides soon carried him out of his line of sight.

Furious at the distractions wreaking havoc with his senses, he worked through the limited possibilities: either the woman was on the move and the Hunter grew bold enough to pursue her openly, or they had all been wrong about her location and Antonio had been forced to cast his net in a wider circle.

Andreas glanced at the slowly healing slice on his arm, mildly curious that it was taking longer than normal for the pink flesh to knit. His groin ached and his cock already felt the irritation of the rough wool, slick with his seed. He hated this place. If he didn't leave soon, he would never feel clean again. In any case, he was running out of options.

"Find her for me, you bastard," he growled.

Without thinking, Andreas pushed off on his damaged ankle and hissed at the shooting pain. Bracing a hand against the cold stone to keep himself steady, he waited impatiently for the ache to subside. He knew better than to blame fate, yet it did seem that his luck had taken a decided turn for the worse. If he lost Antonio, and by implication, Veluria, his chances of infiltrating the halls of power would be slim to none. The Monsignor simply did not have the political clout to ease his passage to the power mongers of the time.

Grumbling irritably, he followed the retreating figure as best he could.

****

"Hold your arms out, child. I do not wish to bind you overly tight. The talisman must remain accessible."

"*Gracie*, Marie. It was good of you to take the risk. But hurry. I feel him approaching."

"There, the Reverend Mother would approve." The tall woman spun Veluria in a small circle, the rich satins in a waterfall of palest blue, ballooning over the stays.

Veluria minced to the mirror over the vanity and leaned forward, adjusting the laced bodice to accentuate her small breasts. The small pearl on its black satin ribbon hung suspended above her cleavage. She inhaled softly, testing the limits of her corset, satisfied that Marie had left just enough slack so if she had to move quickly she would not be constricted by the insane fashions of this time. She would never again complain about her order's ceremonial habit.

She glanced at her cohort in the mirror and hissed, "You must go Marie. You, uh, stand out and he must not see you."

The woman chuckled. "What, shrimp? Just because I'm six-feet tall and...?"

"Marie, please, he is almost here. I must compose myself. This one is not easy."

"All right, but take care, child. We will track you as best we can. Be safe."

Veluria thought, '*that may not be so easy,*' as she pivoted toward the door, hands clasped white-knuckle tight as she poured her energy into the gateway to ease her sister's passage. When she felt the last puff of energy fold into itself, she exhaled slowly and waited.

Veluria had been drawn to the house, not because of the vaulted company within, but because she'd sensed the energy signature of a gateway … and not a naturally occurring portal. It was too good an opportunity to bypass.

What she'd discovered, after surreptitiously sneaking past the card players and drunken sots passed out about the spacious room, was an upper floor and Marie, anxiously awaiting her arrival. That was bold, even by Mother Superior's standards. Although, so long as Marie stayed close to the gateway and did not interact with anyone else, the perturbations in the present timeline would be unaffected.

That was the theory.

Marie had quickly replaced Veluria's ruined gown with a lighter weight garment into which they'd cleverly inserted several talismans in case she needed backup of a magical and not-so-magical nature. One such was a stiletto with a jeweled hilt and poison embedded in the steel.

At that point, with both the Council operative and Antonio de 'Medici in hot pursuit, she would have enjoyed the security of a large caliber composite handgun. But of course, *that* was forbidden.

Instead she leaned against the bedpost and awaited the pleasure of the Demon on stealth approach in the hall, armed with nothing more than her feminine wiles and not a small amount of anticipation.

****

Antonio hesitated at the top of the stairs. The landing off to his left opened to another, narrow set of stairs leading up to servants' quarters and storage areas. The small rooms to his right, accessed by a hallway dimly lit by candles spaced unevenly down its length, beckoned with a familiar energy, and something more. Cautious now, he stole quietly toward the rear of the house, keeping to the floral patterned rugs to mute his passage.

Laughter and the scuffle of chairs and tables being re-arranged for more evening entertainments wafted from the salon below, the sound soon lost to a background buzz as he extended his senses, trying to pinpoint Veluria's location. What had seemed like two wells of energy evaporated to a single powerful source, then everything extinguished to flutter like weak embers.

The cat-and-mouse game grew tiresome. He was hungry, thirsty and tired, his nerves raw and his head pounding so hard he could barely hear. The more he tried to avoid thinking about Veluria, the more he became obsessed with how she'd felt when he kissed her, how she *could* feel in his arms.

Antonio wished for his brother, Nico's, presence to help him sort out the barrage of conflicting signals and the strange effect it had on his ability to concentrate. He allowed the familiar flood of cleansing anger to wash over him, nervously fingering the hilt of his cinquedea as his system prepared for a conflict that never seemed to materialize. He yearned for a physical opponent, someone he could pound to a bloody pulp.

Shutting his eyes against the pain hammering his temples, he tried to fight the whirls of confusing thoughts and sensations assaulting him: Stefano in her arms, awash in passion, lost to her exquisite heat, his cock commanding her pleasure, then twisting in pain, blood dripping, pleading ... Antonio staggered against the brocaded corridor, his back pressed against the wainscoting, the harsh wood a comfort, a piece of reality in a world gone topsy-turvy. He desperately needed something he could use to focus.

He whispered, "*Mio Dio*, what is happening to me?"

He had to get control of himself for he knew with certainty that the woman owned his thoughts, if only for a brief moment, yet a moment too long, for it released his own lust and intense shame. He could not allow this thing, this creature of power, to tread like an advancing army through his being. If he could not control her, her power, he could lose his besotted, beloved younger brother. If it wasn't too late already. That 'thing' he'd felt, for a fleeting instant, held the sulfurous essence of evil and corruption.

Antonio straightened to his full height, nearly brushing the ceiling, and slid the dagger into its sheath. The weapons he must bring to bear would require a different form of steel. This *thing* he faced would require cunning for he must harness its power. Only then could he protect his people, his family, and himself. He unlatched the bedroom door to swing inward, the dim yellow light from candles scattered about the room revealing a tiny figure, waiting patiently with hands folded demurely. Antonio ducked as he entered the cluttered sleeping chambers, eyes sweeping the space to assure himself they were alone.

She—Veluria—looked serene and in control. He had expected a doe, startled and in blind terror of her pursuer, but this petite visage kept her counsel wrapped in quiet, regal assurance. She was not the typical beauty of the French Court, bejeweled and powdered and stayed within an inch of her life. Instead, she had an easy grace, poised, almost battle-ready. Despite her tiny frame, she displayed a handsomeness of spirit that commanded his attention. Truly, this woman was a force to be reckoned with.

"*Madame, je vois que vous souvenez de moi.*" Antonio stumbled over the phrasing, French never being his strong suit. Of course she'd remember him.

With a small uptick to her mouth, she said, "I make a point to remember my kidnappers so that I may later report them to the authorities."

Her voice still had that odd timber, vaguely accented in an unfamiliar way he could not pin down.

She must have interpreted his expression correctly for she said wryly, "And to save you asking the question, no, I am not French, although Charles is my cousin by marriage." He'd already figured that out but it still begged the question—where was she from?

Since the woman seemed uninclined to share any additional information, Tonio lounged against the doorframe, blocking her exit with his sheer bulk and using the silence to study his brother's paramour with undisguised interest. Stefano indeed had exquisite taste. The blue silk of her voluminous gown accented skin so pale it appeared translucent, her face heart-shaped with a pointed chin, lashes thick and dark, shadowing intense eyes mirroring the color of the Aegean when storms threatened, flashing silver-black like a breaking sea.

By some miracle the blue-black braids remained relatively intact after the frenetic activity of the day and evening. However, more tendrils now curled about her face and down the back of her swan-like neck—he found the effect oddly pleasing and wondered, not for the first time, how long her hair would be once he freed the strands from their tight bonds. The thought of running his fingers through the silken strands left him dry-mouthed and his throat constricting.

Instead of lowering her eyes away from his bold stare and concentrating on her hands, she held his with a steady gaze and simply denied him access to her thoughts.

Damn.

He could leave the finer points of divining the woman's capabilities to Cosimo or he could assess the mettle of the adversary facing him. What he needed and what he wanted seemed strangely at odds.

Of course, she could say no in as many ways as she pleased—he did not need to ask permission—yet he hesitated, acutely aware that the answers he sought might not be to his liking. Yet he had no choice. And why he needed to talk himself into what came naturally, aggressively so, perplexed and annoyed him.

With an effort he attempted a neutral stare, but felt his features forming around the more natural glower that caused strong men to grow weak in the knees, or so he was told.

It made no difference—she held firm, sufficiently content to allow the silence between them to waver like a brocaded curtain, sold and tangible with implications neither would acknowledge.

Finally growing claustrophobic in the confined space, Antonio dislodged himself, speaking dismissively, "My brother hardly qualifies as a kidnapper, Madame. He and I have only your best interests, and your honor to defend. Forgive us, forgive *me*, if we seemed to behave in an unseemly fashion."

That clumsy little speech would have left Nico rolling on the floor.

The woman brushed a stray tendril that had fallen out of place behind her ear, an unconscious gesture, perhaps indicative of some level of anxiety? Small movements like that often spoke volumes about a person's inner turmoil. Or it was clever misdirection.

He doubted she knew he could sense the energy enveloping her like a living breathing organism. Her posture spoke to careful control, the energy contained, her defenses in place. He had her at a disadvantage, yet she yielded no quarter—an ability he demanded in himself and admired in others.

Yes, Stefano had chosen well. But why she should chose 'him' was another matter altogether. He was a mere boy compared to her worldliness. Though he could not pinpoint her age, she was not as young as she seemed.

"If you have seen quite enough, signore, perhaps we could retire to the drawing room and discuss how you will compensate me for my … inconvenience."

Compensate? What the fu—?

Veluria moved past Antonio, pausing slightly to allow him to bend away from her so that she could maneuver her unwieldy skirts through the entryway. She lifted her chin and shifted a shoulder coquettishly to draw attention to her bosom and the soft, rosy flesh straining against the silken material. She smiled at the ever-so-slight intake of breath.

So, I have you guessing now, my Demon?

Satisfied the balance had shifted back in her favor, she swept down the hall to the left, following the darkening corridor to the rear of the building. Most of the houses in this section of the city had the same basic layout. Since she hadn't the time to investigate, given the haste with which Marie had been forced to dress her and arrange the few weapons at her disposal, she relied on guesswork and luck find an excuse to move out of the bedroom and away from his smoking hot stare that had undressed her in more ways than she could catalog.

At the end of the corridor she turned left again, this time into an arched doorway that led to a long, narrow space overlooking the canal two floors below. Several tall windows, some with fanciful stained glass, allowed ambient light from a pre-dawn sky to filter through, laying down intricate patterns on the mosaic flooring. Several portraits and a moderately-sized religious landscape dominated the plain paneled wall.

Veluria waved to a divan barely discernible in the dim light. Antonio shook his head no and strolled to the large painting, feigning curiosity about its unusual treatment of the Madonna.

"Bellini," she murmured.

"That is not Jacopo's style." Tonio frowned and waved his right hand over the muted grays and browns of the background that gave the figures such monumental proportions and sense of place.

Well, that was unexpected. The man continued to surprise her. Prevaricating, she asked, "His brother?" in hopes of allowing herself some time before the real test of wills began.

"Ah, Giovanni. Well, then…" Tonio let the words trail off as he continued to stare at the painting, his back to her, not yet ready to engage.

Veluria arranged the skirts ballooning about her, almost consuming her petite frame in a cloud of blue fabric. Annoyed she tamped the offending material down as best she could, utilizing time honored delaying tactics to avoid the coming confrontation.

By some common consent or acknowledgment of the inevitable, they seemed to come to an unvoiced agreement. He turned toward her, allowing her the luxury of finally taking the measure of the man standing with careless disregard before her.

The strengthening dawn cast shadows over his huge frame, not just tall but massively built, his shoulders broad and muscular under the dark leather doublet and stained white shirt with billowing sleeves, worn but serviceable. He had well-shaped legs with muscular thighs bulging through the nondescript brownish wool hose. Leather boots in desperate need of oiling came to mid-calf. When he turned toward her, she glanced surreptitiously at the codpiece and wondered with a sneer if it were padded.

No one would call this man handsome. Imposing, yes. Terrifying, definitely. Faint scars jigsawed across the dark stubble that accentuated a strong jaw and an unforgiving set to his mouth. Full lips offset the fierce demeanor, giving him a compellingly sensuous aura. She knew what those lips, that tongue, could do…

Except for the eyes, he and Stefano looked nothing alike, though with Tonio they achieved unfathomable depths and a glint of cruelty. If she hadn't experienced the tenderness, sensed the guilt and pain, seen for herself the unyielding devotion to his brother, she might have bought into the soul-less devil persona. But the chink in his armor was there, though he might not be aware of it.

Stay on target, Veluria. If the man wants to stay a sociopath, leave him to it. His inner demons have nothing to do with you.

Thank you, Mother Superior. She resisted the urge to brush at her shoulder, shooing her imaginary spirit guide away.

"If you have had your fill, Madame?" he mimicked her former tone and faced her squarely, this time with menace and a clear intent to arrive at answers satisfactory only to him.

On the low divan, with her eyes drawn first to his sheathed weapon, then to the object of her curiosity, she realized with a start that the codpiece indeed was not padded, a fact becoming more evident the longer the giant glared at her. She found it interesting as she had carefully tamped back her energies so he was reacting to her, as a woman, not as a 'device' as the Reverend Mother was so found of calling her flock's special abilities.

Harshly he spat at her, "What are your intentions?"

"*Signore*, I have no idea what you mean. You have no right..."

"I have every right, Madame. He is my brother and it is my duty to protect him from the wiles of such as yourself."

Veluria bristled. The beast might as well have called her a whore. Clearly he baited her. Why, she was not sure. She would need to think carefully on his train of thought for it might reveal much about the man, and hopefully the secret she must prise out of him.

"Hmm, Stefano is your brother? Then you must be...?" She entered into the pretty phrasing and accepted forms. Each knew the other—and all relationships, tangential or otherwise. The well-rehearsed steps would allow for certain variations later on.

He looked ready to strangle her as he spit out, "Antonio de' Medici."

Tonio crouched, bringing himself eye-level with her. They had done this dance before and she was well-aware of who he was. His face flushed with his growing fury and frustration. He might not mean to harm her but she wouldn't place any bets on that when he teetered on the brink of giving in to well-schooled violent behaviors.

She steered the interrogation in a less dangerous direction. "Well, *signore*, I still do not understand why you chose to abduct me." The lilt at the end of the sentence held the hint of a question ... and perhaps mirth.

Tonio's gut quivered, his groin aching as he crouched before her in a desperate attempt to remove her gaze from his growing arousal. He felt the heat steal up his neck, setting his ear tips on fire. If his choice was to wring her neck or fuck her senseless ... well, that was no contest.

With relief, he realized she had steered them to safer ground.

He explained, "That was no abduction, woman, but a rescue. You were out cold and someone advanced from the inner reaches of the passageway. I watched the tableau play out and knew that my brother would not be able to defend both of you against that kind of mischief."

"So you stepped in to save the day?"

Tonio growled, "Something like that, yes."

"And that frantic flight across the Grand Plaza and dragging me down alleys and into that, that ... den of iniquity."

"That 'den of iniquity' is owned by a business associate of my family, one who would take great offense at having his establishment so maligned."

Tonio failed to wipe the puzzlement off his own face as he remembered clearly tasking his dim-witted sibling with alerting the pallazzo's staff to their imminent arrival, only to be detoured into the raucous party. The ultimate escape of their captive had been a vexing consequence of his brother's poor improvisational skills.

He despised being vexed. And the last thing he wanted to be reminded of was his subsequent action, taking Stefano to task in front of his men, inflicting such cruel and humiliating injuries that he wouldn't blame his brother if he never spoke to him again. Cosimo would care little about the incident, leaving the brothers to deal with each other in their own way, but Nico's simple '*If you hurt him again, I will not tolerate it, do you understand?*' cut him to the bone.

Can you feel my pain, M'lady? Do you even care?

Veluria boldly stared into the dangerous man's deep-set eyes. In the dim light of pre-dawn they were the darkest brown, almost black, and glinted with gold flecks. Like daggers they sliced and diced across her flesh, setting her nerve endings on fire and her nipples hardening to stiff peaks against the stays. Fortunately, *her* state of arousal was not so obvious.

The frown lines between his eyes bespoke a lifetime of care, displeasure and violence. She could sense him a man who would give no quarter, who could kill without a second thought, whose sole purpose in life was protecting his family and his people.

"They call you Demon de' Medici, don't they? The Dark One. I think perhaps it is 'you' whom I must fear, not this mystery stranger. I have no enemies. I am but a simple ward of my cousin's sent on a diplomatic mission of goodwill between my sovereign and the Papàl Legate." She dismissed him with a toss of her head. "You, indeed, have no such standing here in Venice."

Antonio smiled wolfishly. "I think, my dear, that you are quite wrong on many counts." With a small groan he rose to standing position and extended his hand.

"It grows light enough to tread the streets. Is there a back way that we might exit this building without disturbing my cousin's guests and business associates?"

Veluria wondered, *'now what does he have in mind?'* but replied, keeping the concern out of her voice, "We can go through that door to the servants' stairs and then out through the kitchen."

"Fine. Then let's away, Madame. Time grows short for all of us, I fear."

Confused by his cryptic statement, Veluria gathered the folds of her skirt and attempted to lunge to her feet but the hem caught under the divan and drew her back with a lurch. Antonio placed his hands around her waist, almost entirely encircling her slender form, and lifted her effortlessly. He held her suspended, weightless, drawing her close to his chest until fabric brushed fabric, teasing slick satin against smooth leather.

Veluria barely contained a gasp as every square inch of her body responded to the brief contact, sending a wave of heat through her belly and the unwelcome gush of wetness to coat her clenched thighs. Without thinking, she braced her hands against the leather jerkin, not so much to push away but simply to steady her quaking frame. Even through the leather she felt the thrumming of his heart, rapid staccato beats synched in time to her own unsteady rhythm.

She whispered, "*Gracie, signore.*"

Antonio stared, entranced, at the frail pheasant trapped in his embrace, feeling only throbbing sensation beyond anything he'd ever experienced. Was this the power Nico had alluded to? He didn't think so. He and Nico beat as one heart, one mind. This was a thing he knew and understood—that confluence of powers and sharing of energies.

But with this woman—her name, *Veluria*, whispered through the corridors of his mind where even he feared to tread—it was as if he had a hole in his most private self, buried in the deepest well of his soul and she had the means to fill it, to fill him.

If only I had a soul ... would you fill it, could you?

With palpable relief he set her down and watched hungrily as she arranged her skirts, dissembling. Could she have felt it also?

Huskily, Veluria asked, "Where, M'Lord?"

"What?"

"Where are we bound?"

Relieved to think about something concrete, Antonio muttered, "To my father's. Stefano has made a mess of this and Cosimo will have answers from all of us."

At the mention of his father, Veluria trembled with barely contained excitement. Cosimo de' Medici, the prime mover in all games of intrigue. Whatever she was up to, whatever information she desired, his father would be her next target. He wished her luck.

He had gained nothing but a stiff cock and a hunger he was hard-pressed to explain. He would be a fool to think she harbored the same interest in him, but still…

With elegant strides Veluria exited through a narrow doorway and felt her way down the curving staircase, her skirts billowing behind her. Antonio followed but paused at the door and thought, *who are you, what are you?*

He mindlessly adjusted the codpiece to take the pressure off his straining cock and allowed his thoughts a moment to explore the possibilities.

Chapter Nine

Shadows danced on the still waters, the mist heavy against the pilings jutting away from the narrow walkway bordering the elegant abodes. This was a newer section, built to house court favorites, and strung along a narrow waterway ajumble with gondolas and other small craft. Despite the attempt to impart a feeling of richness and importance, the confines of the space gave it a claustrophobic feel.

Veluria emerged from the narrow door and angled carefully along the slippery edge, thankful for the weak morning light that reflected off the upper windows along the tunnel of homes. She lifted her skirts, praying for balance, as one misstep could send her plummeting into the murky waters, an entertainment she did not wish to provide for her so-called rescuer.

Idly, Veluria wondered about Stefano. Where was he? Why had he not been the one to pursue her? Why could she not detect his essence, his spirit? Too many questions, too few answers, and the Dark One loomed with overwhelming intensity over all. She felt, then heard, him treading lightly behind her, mere steps away. For all his size, the man moved like the softest summer breeze, with a grace few could match, even men half his imposing stature. It was no surprise that he used that unusual height to intimidate and instill fear in his opponents. Even she, at times, trembled slightly when he approached too close, too intimately, despite years of training, learning discipline, discovering how to use her petite frame to its best advantage.

Veluria smoothed the soft fabric about the talisman, masking its energy from the real or imagined probing by the Medici Demon. Unlike the larger version, with the cleverly embedded poison in the blade, the miniature stiletto was fashioned for a female hand and sized to fit into a silk purse. In her case, it lay craftily hidden just under the hem of her tight corset. She knew she needn't concern herself overmuch at its discovery. Women of means all carried such a device, even in the company of trusted servants and companions. One should never underestimate the dangers lurking on the city pathways.

This instrument, however, had a dual purpose which would be of inordinate interest to her quarry. It contained within its ornately carved bone handle the means to fashion a portal from thin air. The Reverend Mother's researchers had cleverly disguised the electronic device using the most advanced science of miniaturization of the day.

"This way, Madame."

Startled, Veluria jumped at the briefest touch on her left elbow as Antonio indicated their way down the narrow alley separating blocks of attached domiciles. How uncharacteristic of her to be lost in her own musings. She must take care, diligent care. Too much rested on successfully finding the key and preventing its use. The future loomed, both in the here and now, and in her linked world.

Antonio pricked at her elbow and muttered, "Wait here." She dutifully backed against the stone wall to allow him passage toward the brightly lit opening. Coming from such dim light into the glare would put them at a disadvantage, a fact she should have recognized at once. Perhaps this was more of a rescue than she had first envisioned, grateful that Antonio de' Medici had his wits about him.

A figure loomed in the opening but Antonio strode toward the unknown presence with authority. He had words, spoken quickly but in tones too low for her to catch. When finished he nodded once and indicated she should advance. The figure disappeared briefly, then three more arrived to form a human tunnel leading onto the narrow cobble-stoned street.

"The Papàl Guards shall accompany us to the Grand Plaza, at which point my men shall join us for our journey to my father's residence."

Veluria had the good grace to look astounded at that. The Papàl Guards answered only to His Holiness and a few of his most trusted advisors. That this man obviously commanded their respect, but more importantly answered to his direct orders, made her worry that the Order had not fully examined the political clout of this particular branch of the Medici family. From their vantage point of history, having a pope and a cardinal in the immediate family had seemed an interesting bit of religious trivia. Apparently, they had been wrong. What else they might have missed could have serious consequences.

Antonio watched the play of emotions, and some consternation, on the woman's face. Though she managed a careful mask most times, he could use his ability to read his enemies and connect the inner turmoil with small indications, muscle twitches, tilt of chin, or creased brow to discern intent and other things.

It made him a daunting adversary, yet by choice he refused to apply his gifts to court intrigues and shifting alliances, having little to no patience for the pretty posturing and deft words required to navigate that battlefield. He much preferred his way, behind the scenes, a clean strike, leaving nothing to chance. He did not believe in luck, even less in friendship or alliances.

He did believe in family and pledged his skills and his life to the few who mattered most in his world. His beloved, though dim-witted youngest brother, Stefano, and Nico, the one man in the all the world he would choose to have at his back, formed the core of his heart. Without them, without the need to protect and support them, he would be nothing and no one. Not even his father commanded that level of devotion, a fact Cosimo understood and utilized at every opportunity.

Without looking back Antonio moved quickly onto the street and turned right, heading back the way he had come in the wee hours of the morning. Still too early for the privileged to be up and about, the party made their way without incident through the newer sections of the city. Antonio set a blistering pace, taking shortcuts through litter-strewn alleys until emerging finally onto the Grand Square. Six of his men waited impatiently, each positioned for maximum advantage as they anticipated from which quadrant their leader might emerge.

"Marco," Antonio barked at the man standing closest, "if you would." The man glanced once at Tonio and proceeded quickly to meet with the Papàl Guards. He discretely handed each of them a small leather pouch, then spun on his heel and resumed his position to the right of his *capo della squadra.*

"Madame, we must make haste."

"I grow weary from your haste, *signore*. If you have not noticed before now, I am in no way prepared for an extensive journey on foot through the heart of the city. And where exactly are we bound, if I may inquire?"

"My father's temporary residence is near his business interests."

"And that would be...?"

Annoyed at the delay, Tonio barked, "Sestieri de San Polo."

"The docks?" Veluria asked, now confused about their ultimate destination.

"Not the shipyards. No. Cosimo rents a fondaco from the Ferrera's. Trust me, it will meet with your approval, I am sure," Antonio sneered. "Now, if you don't mind, M'lady."

Antonio waved his men into formation and proceeded to the northeast across the square, all the while scanning for possible trouble. That all the trouble he could ever handle trailed reluctantly in his wake gave him no small measure of concern. The confusion she felt had coincided with something disturbing, something that should not be possible. Again, the question arose—who and what was she?

Veluria steeled herself for a taxing rush headlong through the Square. She'd had a strong flash, a premonition almost, that they were to board a sailing vessel. In point of fact, the swell of the Adriatic and the swaying of the vessel had nearly rocked her off balance, so strong had the sensation been. And she was almost certain that had emanated from the tall man, but how and why was a mystery.

If she let her nerves get the best of her she would be useless, and appearing vulnerable was the last thing she could afford now that a meeting with the fabled Cosimo de' Medici seemed imminent. She was less concerned about Tonio. The potential existed for drawing on his strength and power to bolster her reserves despite the conflicting interplay of energies that had both of them unbalanced and confused.

She'd never had anyone, here or in her world, touch her in quite the same way—psychically or otherwise. The longer she was near him, the more ... aware she became, aware of the shadows retreating as the sun bulged above the Campanile, aware of vendors and

77

passersby, aware of the prickly feel of the lace against her breasts, of the slide of silk along her calves, aware of an exquisite pressure in her groin and labored breathing having nothing to do with their fast pace and threatening destination. That awareness bled outward, drawn inexorably toward the Dark One, toward his broad shoulders and narrow hips, toward his arrogance and assurance and domineering attitude.

Being around that man was definitely not a hardship.

As a distraction, Veluria filled her inner vision with images of Stefano—his stocky frame and lovely hands, dancing dark eyes and square, dimpled chin, a man-boy with courtly manners and a way about him that made her laugh and blush and long for his youthful touch and incomparable endurance. As she swept into yet another alleyway of domiciles of indeterminate origin or use, that image morphed into a dark stranger with demanding hands wrapping round her throat and pressing into the soft flesh, lifting her chin to meet a hungry mouth, gripped in an embrace impossible to break.

Veluria stared wide-eyed at the man ahead of her, recognizing shared destiny when she saw it. Unfortunately that kind of destiny could very well compromise her mission and that would not do at all. She watched, curious, as the Demon hitched his shoulder and rolled his head, as if he too felt something unusual. She would expect that response if she had used her powers to broadcast sensations like some aural aphrodisiac. But she hadn't, at least not consciously, and she was too well-schooled not to know the difference between dormant and active. No. This was something else and she feared that which she could not understand.

The small company darted down a short alleyway and emerged onto a moderately sized piazza. To the right and south, the canal bordered a line of boxy warehouse structures, at first seemingly nondescript until closer inspection revealed tasteful additions to entryways and tall, narrow windows.

Antonio anticipated her question, "Converted storage facilities. My father, and others with similar interests, use these as needed when business dictates a more personal presence." He waved to the imposing edifice off to their left. "My father fancies this one." He turned her attention to the north end of the quay, "The loading docks are there, as is Cosimo's fleet."

Veluria smiled at the measure of pride in his voice—unexpected for he favored disdain and disinterest much of the time. She also noted that he used 'Father' and 'Cosimo' interchangeably, a measure of their relationship that would bear watching. The Sisterhood never let even the smallest nuance slip past.

Although the passage of time had been marked primarily with footfalls, she became aware of the nearness of noon, the air heavy with moisture as the sun climbed above the looming structures. Through the thin haze, the Adriatic Sea sparkled with intense light, mirror smooth and placid, imprisoning the galleys until wind and tide granted favor.

Antonio dispensed his men to the left and right, then indicated that the woman should follow him through the teak door. He pushed into a veritable sea of robed men milling about the spacious rotunda—clerics, tradesmen, scholars—all engaged in the single-minded pursuit of Cosimo's attention, if not his particular favor. His father would be holding court, if it suited, in the upper reaches of the gallery that encircled the cavernous open area.

He guided the woman to a seat near the stairs. "Please wait here. I shall return shortly."

Veluria sighed with relief as she sank onto the stone bench. Her feet ached and her back screamed with the effort to maintain a rigid posture. *Damn these stays. I can barely breathe!* She watched with interest at the peacock array strung about the huge room, all engaged in subtle—and not-so-subtle—machinations, intrigues and 'offers too good to refuse'. She smiled at that phrasing. Though from well before her own time, it had etched its way into her popular culture, something this time and place would also appreciate and embrace.

The Demon stood off to the side, just beyond the curving stairs, speaking rapidly with a harried-looking man carrying what looked like parchments. A roughly dressed scarecrow edged past her, reeking of the sea and rum. Clerics clustered like gaggles of cheeky crows, assured of their importance and salvation, not so sure of their rank amidst the supplicants to a higher power—commerce.

The Demon glanced her way, sending frissons of energy racing up and down her spine, only to lodge inexorably in her nether regions, her body responding to his challenge with sweet pressure and welcoming heat. Slick moisture coated her inner thighs.

79

Damn it, enough already!

For once she was glad to have the voluminous skirts to hide her arousal. Heat, flushing rosy-pink, overspread her cheeks, racing past her slender neck, settling temptingly on the soft mounds pressed above the tight silk bodice.

There were the inevitable admiring glances, even from the clerics. She bent her head to hide a smile.

It started as a tingle along her spine, then morphed into a cascade of frigid, icy needles flash-freezing her nerve endings. Then pain, inexplicable pain ... and hot, burning desire. Fire and ice.

What the hell? Antonio?

The Demon had turned away, his attentions directed elsewhere. There was a familiarity to the near physical sensations, something she'd felt before. Feeling bloated and overrun with discomfort, she leaned against the cool marble wainscoting, willing the sensations to pass. It didn't take long to dredge up the source. It could only be from the *other*, the Council operative, and he had to be close for the energies were nearly overwhelming.

Before she could think further on the odd confluence of sensations, Antonio returned and beckoned her to follow him up the stairs. He rudely strode up the steps, taking them two at a time, leaving her to follow awkwardly, gathering her skirts and cursing once again the fashions of that time. The small man with whom the Demon had been conferencing appeared magically at her elbow, offering a hand to assist. She gratefully accepted.

Destiny dwelled in those upper reaches, the chessboard pieces aligned, awaiting the first move.

Chapter Ten

Andreas grimaced in annoyance, forced to dodge from shadow to shadow, still hampered with fleeting pain. Dark eyes flaring in the dim light of emerging dawn, he scanned the frantic activity on the dock. The sky yawned its last gasp as dark stole away, no longer in control of its destiny. Andreas felt the tide, felt the sway of the unwieldy scow laden with barrels of wine and oil and unmarked cargo, bouncing against thick pilings and rough-edged planks.

He touched his brow with the silver crucifix as if in silent supplication or thankful prayer for the rise of a new day. Silently he cursed the discomfort and awkwardness of his injury, the ankle commanding far too many of his body's resources as it went through the painful healing process.

Pain to heal pain. On any other day he could accept the trade-off, but this day it had interfered with his tracking, leaving him with far too many questions and a mystery that required solving before his quarry sailed off into the dawn.

What the hell are you doing on a goddamn BOAT!?

A passing journeyman carrying a small wooden box dodged perilously close to the edge of the dock. The startled man realized his mistake and glanced nervously to his left before moving on. Andreas cringed. He needed to avoid that kind of unspoken broadcast. It wouldn't do to draw attention to himself.

Besides, the real question was: where was Veluria and why couldn't he sense her presence?

With an effort of will Andreas continued to lounge carelessly against a stack of crates. With his slight frame and robes proclaiming him a simple cleric, he'd be no threat to those busy with the matters

81

of commerce. The docks swam with deckhands and passengers, a babel of tongues shot through with urgency, the tide waiting for no man.

Andreas released a small burst of energy, casting about in a broad band to avoid having the Demon pinpoint his location. He'd taken enough risks exposing himself like this—his shadow self was less effective in the brighter light of day with no comforting walls to shield him.

She's not here.

That left the matter of the Demon's presence on the docks as a nagging concern. Quickly he calculated probabilities but found no satisfactory resolution.

"Damn it. Why are *you* here?"

Disgruntled, he had no recourse but to expose himself. As casually as he could muster, he backed away from the shielding tower of crates and angled toward the furthest ship, the one commanding a final spurt of activity as thick hemp ropes flew in graceful arcs to land on deck. Two swarthy deckhands pulled at the companionway, securing it, then spun away to tend to the task of pushing off from the pier.

Well forward, almost to the bow of the vessel, a tall figure bent over the rail, his head and face obscured by the hood of his cape. Andreas risked a closer look as the ship slipped its moorings. The figure was clearly recognizable—few carried that height and bulk, that commanding presence that so marked the Demon de' Medici as unique amongst his peers. Yet the energy, the man's essence, seemed … not quite right, a bit off.

Muttering, "Who are you?" Andreas dropped all pretense and aggressively sought out the man's identity. Fists clenched he stood perched at the end of the pier watching the ship slowly ease into the waning tide. The fluttering and tickling sensation in his gut mimicked the slow roll of the vessel as sails snapped into place on a freshening breeze.

As if he felt the probe, the man on deck raised his head and stared directly at Andreas. With a smooth sweep of his arm he dislodged the hood, revealing unkempt sandy blond hair framing a stern face. Intense blue eyes shot arrow straight onto Andreas' open-mouthed stare. A small smile played at the stranger's mouth as his gaze lingered, his eyes knowing. With a slight nod, he swept the hood over his head, spun away from the rail and stalked regally toward the aft cabin, leaving Andreas to gasp in consternation and bewilderment.

"Mio Dio, how did this one escape the Council? *Fanculo a lui*!" Andreas swore out loud, heedless of his audience who gazed at him, curious and somewhat taken aback at the cleric's anger and harsh language.

Andreas ignored the ache in his leg and stomped the length of the pier, thinking hard and fast about this new intelligence. Another chess piece, another knight on the board, when he'd thought them all safely dispatched. This was unconscionable. His handlers would hear of this. That they would fail to inform him, their most valued field agent, of another with such power, how could...?

Andreas ground to a stop, the thought taking root mid-flight. Only one other could possibly replicate the Demon's energy signature so closely. Not a perfect match to be sure, but close enough to fool him, especially in his weakened condition.

What was needed was a dose of logic and rational judgment, not a racing mind and unproductive anger. With effort he calmed himself, muttering a mantra of soothing phrases as he clacked his beads rhythmically. Slowing his heart rate, he once again mastered his inner turmoil, sorting through what he knew and what they had but surmised.

So there was another. Genetics would dictate not but they had been wrong before, his most esteemed colleagues with their research and prognostications and smug assurances.

Andreas raked his hands through his hair, his mouth set in a thin line, veins bulging dangerously on his slim neck. "Nicolo," he breathed, "the second most dangerous man in this cluster fuck of a game those idiots dumped me into. With no warning, no intel. How was I to know he could...?" Andreas' voice trailed off, once more aware of his surroundings and the untoward interest of passersby.

His thoughts still racing, Andreas settled on the two most likely explanations: Nicolo either had a genetically similar energy as his brother Antonio, or he had the capability to alter it to match the Dark One.

The former was cause enough for concern, and thought to be unlikely given that the men were all half-brothers. Cosimo's genetic legacy would surely have suffered dilution, though not so much with

Antonio, who was line bred through a close cousin reputed to be the love of the elder's life. Nicolo was the result of a brief liaison with a Habsburg beauty who died in childbirth. Cosimo had dipped into Florence's merchant class for his final marriage, the result being the brainless idiot, Stefano, whose powers—other than his good looks and charming manner—had yet to manifest.

The latter possibility, the one that suggested this Nicolo had that kind of command over his psychic abilities, would send the statisticians into an orgy of research as that capability could only be engineered and controlled with implants in his own dimension.

Whatever the explanation, Andreas knew he'd blown his plan to bring his quarry and the woman together. His only chance to avoid the ire of the Council, and even of the good Monsignor to whom he'd be giving an abbreviated report as soon as he recouped his strength, was to start over. He'd keep his musings about the middle brother to himself for the time being. There was no rush as the man would be off stage for the foreseeable future and no threat to the current mission.

Right now he had to reacquire his targets. The Demon was still his best option for finding Veluria. And *she* was his best option for solving the equations and understanding the predictions that had motivated the Council to violate their guardianship of the gateways.

"Where would you go, I wonder?" Andreas murmured and smiled slyly. "Perhaps to Papà?"

He would need best speed and walking on his still aching ankle did not appeal. Andreas moved to the dock jetting into the shallow bay in search of transport. A young man looked up expectantly, waving his hand to indicate he was for hire. Andreas grunted his assent and climbed down into the small skiff, settling onto the rough wooden bench seat.

"Padre?"

Andreas stared blindly at the oarsman, trying to recall the exact location of Cosimo's current residence. The man kept several palazzos scattered about the city but given the time of day and the demands of his business, there was only one choice.

He muttered, "*Sestieri de Polo, e rendere veloce. La residenza Ferrara*, do you know it?"

"*Sì.*"

Andreas scowled at the wide-eyed youth and turned to stare at the greasy water slipping past the small craft. Unconsciously he fingered his beads, the movement on the string registering one click at a time. The shape and texture of the cold alabaster, the repetitive motion, helped him focus. Time, he was running out of that commodity at a fearsome rate. He would lay odds that the next move on the chessboard would be Cosimo's. But how the chess pieces in the game would align themselves was anyone's guess. He'd made enough moves already, despite the missteps, to come close to taking the Queen and neutralizing her.

That thought sent a frisson of lust to his groin. 'Neutralize' wasn't exactly his intent, though it was a necessary prelude to the release from his obsession. *She* was going to pay dearly for his indiscretions. His fall from grace would not end on a whimper.

Embracing the ancient adage, *better to ask for forgiveness than permission,* brought a small smile and reminded him that he needed more analysis before engaging in any further moves.

The piece that would be king, the 'key'? That piece had yet to reveal its identity, let alone the nature of the opponent manipulating the supporting assets. He'd had the Demon son pegged as an annoying guardian of the clan, the knight as it were—expendable. Not anymore. There was more at work here, more probabilities to calculate.

Shadows within shadows. Plots within plots. He stroked the blade hidden in the folds of his robe, remembering the heat and sweet gush of blood...

****

The harried man glued to her side prodded Veluria toward an ornate walnut door at the far end of a hallway carpeted with a thick Persian rug. Antonio stood impatiently as her guide abruptly released her elbow and scurried into the room. She brushed past the Demon and entered a richly appointed, tall-ceiling space with a wall of narrow windows overlooking the canal. Walnut wainscoting and palest cream stucco gave the space dimension and intimacy. A heavy walnut desk occupied pride of place at the far end, but in the middle a cozy seating area invited conversation ... and plotting.

Antonio indicated a settee so she once more arranged her skirts while she took the measure of the players arrayed about the room. Antonio muttered something to the man who had accompanied them into the salon. He hastily lay his burden of parchments onto the desk and retreated quickly. Other footsteps followed, clearing the room. That left her to face her newest adversary, known only by reputation, and her Demon about whom she feared she knew far too much already.

Well, this should be interesting…

Cosimo settled onto the chair opposite, waving his tall son to stand by the petite woman in a show of dominance and power. He fully appreciated how daunting Antonio could be without even trying. It gave him great enjoyment to use his eldest as a weapon of intimidation, particularly when it brought rosy coloring to the cheeks of an especially attractive woman. He would have said 'girl' upon initial examination, but this one had a world of experience in her demeanor and a hard set to her eyes.

He would not err on the side of frivolous disregard of certain feminine wiles as had his youngest. He fully intended to plumb her depths before allowing any further missteps. She and Stefano might make a pretty couple, but he had plans for the silly young man that did not include mystery French whores and their petty court intrigues.

"Monsieur, it is my understanding that your son has effected a rescue … of sorts. For that I am, of course, grateful, as will be my cousin, François."

Tonio, standing behind Veluria, raised his brows in surprise and motioned to his father to continue the questioning. Cosimo twitched a finger imperceptibly, their code for shared knowledge and a need for further interrogation.

"Yes, and my salutations and best wishes to him and his new bride. Claude? Of Brittany I believe." A manservant approached with goblets and a plate of meats. Cosimo waved him off and leaned forward intently. François stood in line to inherit the French throne, sooner rather than later if the rumors from Nico were correct, and Nico seldom steered them wrong.

He had sent his son packing to Spagna only hours after his arrival from France based on the hints about Carlos the woman had dropped in Stefano's ear. Carlos, the heir to the continent, and one with whom he would curry favor.

Settling his bulk on the edge of the chair, he waited to see what direction this most interesting conversation was headed.

Veluria was impressed. Her world's modern communications often seemed clunky and slow compared with the nuanced intelligence that spread like wildfire through the court gossip network. While Stefano had accepted her subterfuge as emissary from the French court, his father did not. He was too smart by half and she'd best be on her toes around him.

Veluria raised her eyebrows and said, "*Si, signore,*" pausing with classic Gallic disdain, "Claude." She had no idea whether or not it was a good match, but expressing an opinion gave her an edge and the aura of having insider's information.

While Cosimo waited expectantly, she prevaricated to gain a measure of control over the competing energies washing through and around her. The Demon and his father formed a straight line broadcast path aimed directly at her core—the effect was uncommonly intense and uncomfortable. Because the two men seemed to be doing it unconsciously reinforced her appreciation of the raw, undisciplined nature of their abilities. It was far easier to control a disciplined mind once she'd determined the architecture of the neural pathways than one with such an organic nature that its complexities were not easily identified, let alone amenable to statistical analysis.

Off to her left she felt the faint stirring of a weaker signal, most likely Stefano. Having him close gave her a measure of relief. In the back of her mind she'd been concerned about him, about his mental state. Tonio gave no indication that he knew his brother was in the same house. She'd love to be a fly on the wall if and when the brothers came together to work out whatever had caused Tonio so much guilt and shame.

Keeping her face a mask of pleasant acquiescence to the Capo's hospitality, Veluria selected a goblet of wine and sipped daintily, allowing the drama to play out while she examined probabilities. Lost in thought, she didn't hear the door opening.

Cosimo shifted in his seat, exclaiming, "Ah, Stefano! Come and see who graces our presence this fair morning."

Stefano?

She twisted slightly to get a better look but halted mid-turn when Antonio's hand gripped her shoulder so tightly she hissed in pain.

He murmured, "I'm sorry," and released her but moved in close enough she could feel the heat from his huge frame.

She listened to Stefano's steps moving around his brother and realized the young man could not see her with Tonio hovering so close. Cosimo waved his youngest forward with a genuine smile of affection, then gestured in her direction, his grin now sly. For Tonio he leveled a pointed glare and a warning.

With all eyes on her, the air left the room and she could have cut the silence with a knife. From a constant ambient hum of energy it was like being dumped into a sensory deprivation chamber. Not even the sound of her heartbeat registered.

Stefano broke the trance with a hesitant question, "Veluria?" He breathed a sigh of relief and said, "Thank God, you are safe."

Sensation rushed back with a roar: Tonio moving away, leaving her back exposed—in more ways than one; Cosimo shifting in his seat, a calculating expression on his face; Stefano approaching with an air of relief and anticipation tempered with reluctance. Was that because his brother still loomed near?

Or is it me?

The young man bent to brush his lips lightly on her brow, but withdrew quickly when he detected a less than wholehearted welcome. Her miniscule cringe had caught not only him by surprise, but also Antonio whose satisfaction rolled in waves over her.

Cosimo smiled benignly, clearly entertained by the interplay and jealousies. He waved to his manservant, "I believe I will have some wine after all." Cosimo tilted his goblet and gave her a toast. "To you, my dear, and to *all* your many interests."

Chapter Eleven

Antonio, why don't you take our guest for a tour of the Palazzo while I have a word with our layabout here." Cosimo grinned but no one in the room misconstrued it for less than the veiled threat it was. From paternal indulgence to angry displeasure, Cosimo's mercurial changes of mood were legendary.

Stefano shuddered, then squared his shoulders, approaching his father cautiously as one would a lion guarding his kill.

Antonio held out a hand but Veluria managed a graceful exit off the hard cushion and waited patiently for the Dark One to lead her from the room. The Demon, *her* Demon, swept the contingent of servants and guards hovering outside the door in the hallway out of their way before quietly closing the double doors with a perceptible snick.

"Sit."

"Papà, it was not my fault…"

"Quiet, my son. This matter is of little consequence at this time. We shall let your brother work his particular charms. Whatever mysteries she shelters will not last long in his expert hands."

Cosimo chuckled, fully aware of his son's unique talents in extracting the minutest piece of information from both enemy and ally.

"I don't want her hurt, Papà." Stefano tried to hide his dismay and fear by appealing to cold logic. "She is, after all, a ward of the French court, and as such is a valuable asset if, and when, Francis succeeds to the throne."

"An asset how?"

"As our guest," Stefano emphasized the word 'guest', "she brings a measure of respect to our house, having sought us out to deliver a personal message of goodwill, rather than to the Duke and his flunkies. She pays homage to Florence in this matter, rather than Venice. A good thing, no?"

Cosimo barely avoided barking out a laugh. "May I remind you that she did not seek us out? I seem to recall your brother mentioning allegations of kidnapping." He chuckled at that. The woman had cleverly avoided an unpleasant accusation in favor of reworking the episode into a negotiable commodity. How kind of her to place a non-existent family obligation on the bargaining table.

I do admire a woman with wit and intelligence.

He continued to press the issue, determined to instruct his youngest by pointing out his failures in seeing through the obvious subterfuge. "Is it not apparent that her so-called message of goodwill is as genuine as the vapors on the canals in the early morn?"

Stefano squirmed and appeared ready to debate that point. Surely the boy did not still believe her a ward of the French court!

He was poised to give his son a good tongue lashing when the young man interrupted. "Even if she isn't all she claims, Papà, so long as others think of her in that light, is it not still useful to us?" He rubbed his chin, one of his few nervous gestures, generally allowed only when with family.

Cosimo clapped his hands with delight. "Excellent, my boy. And what else…?"

Stefano thought hard for a moment. "She makes a useful, uh, item for trade?"

"Yes, well." Cosimo knew better than to push his youngest beyond his limited capabilities. Analysis would never be his strong suit, but at least he had the manners and the trite phrases down pat. More importantly he would follow directions to the letter when properly motivated.

"Papà? As my consort should she not also be accorded a measure of respect?"

"Consort?"

Cosimo tapped a finger on his thigh. The boy's obsession with the woman ran deep, perhaps deeper than he had realized. He'd turned the discussion from usefulness to the family to his own selfish desires, something neither of his older brothers would ever consider.

It wasn't unexpected but still, he was not happy with the turn the discussion had taken.

Stefano stood and paced the room. He had difficulty framing his next words. "I-I … she's different, not like other women."

"How so?"

"She c-can sense things. She, uh…"

"And you discovered this how?"

"It was when we were…" Stefano flushed bright red "… uh, when I was, we, uh…"

Cosimo laughed out loud. "When you were fucking her? And exactly what epiphany did you have at that most propitious moment, my son?"

Stefano collapsed back on the seat vacated by Veluria. He stroked the cushion, as if he could almost feel her residual energy through his loins, his face relaxing as he drew comfort from the phantom contact.

"She is like Tonio and Nico, Papà. Not exactly the same, but close. That bridge we all feel, one to the other, the one Nico and Tonio share the strongest, that knowing. She has it."

Perhaps the boy isn't as clueless as I thought.

He continued, "Yes, I know, my boy. I felt it also, though she hid it well. That one is wise beyond her years, I fear. Or she has had some training, though God only knows who at the French court…" He held up a hand and muttered, "…or wherever she's from." He continued with his train of thought, "None of them has sufficient intelligence to make use of such gifts, or even to recognize them for what they are."

Stefano's voice took on an edge of pleading. "We can use that can we not, Papà? If she were bound to me, it would be a most useful pairing. Strength, Papà. Just what we need now."

And there it was. He would give the pup credit, he managed to twist the family's fortunes with his own desires. Unfortunately it was past time for the boy to assume the mantle of his responsibilities.

No matter how diplomatic, how politic he couched his next words, Stefano would not yield without considerable resistance. He girded himself for the certain conflict.

"Hmmm, the other day you might have convinced me of the merit of that evaluation, but today the situation is different. Our priorities must change to suit circumstances."

"But…" Stefano half rose from his seat but Cosimo waved him back.

"I do not dispute the value of a *possible* favorable outcome from such a match." Out of the blue he asked, "Is she by any chance carrying your child?" It was a valid question, given the circumstances. He sneered, "It wouldn't be the first time."

Stefano blushed and mumbled, "I don't think so."

His escapades from an early age had alternately vexed and delighted his brothers, leading Cosimo to expend a substantial portion of his youngest's inheritance on buying off or seeing to the dispatch of unwanted offspring. Of them all he seemed blessed with potency that went beyond all normal expectations. Tonio had laughed and patted him on the shoulder and told him to be happy for his gifts and not have to rue the unfortunate curse he and Nico bore in the service of family.

"Then we shall proceed as planned. The woman stays here for further evaluation." He quickly added, "…as our guest." He stood and approached Stefano, his face set in a hard line. "You, however, will have a somewhat different role to play."

His son blanched and croaked, "Role to play?"

"In light of what Nicolo has brought to my attention regarding matters in the French court and with Carlos' succession, it has been our singular good fortune to arrive at an arrangement with a distant cousin of the Gorizia's."

"But I thought that portion of the Tyrol had been bequeathed to Maximilian and was no longer of interest."

"Yes, that was the case." And that situation lasted less than a week as alliances shifted. He went on, "But let us, for a moment, consider a most fortuitous bonding with the Habsburg lineage. This distant cousin has three daughters, most fair of face, I am assured. One of them will suit you. I am in negotiations with Duke Friedrich as we speak."

"Bonding? You mean marriage?"

Cosimo glared at his youngest. They had been having a verbal sparring match for months over Stefano's obligations to the family. Placing him in an advantageous position within range of the power mongers surrounding Maximilian would not only strengthen Florence's position vis-à-vis her neighboring states and republics, but would also facilitate the delicate negotiations his middle son conducted on the family's behalf in Seville. And it would help fashion a measure of peace with the Venezian contingent for whom war was simply commerce by other means. That Florence had suffered from that ill-advised business tactic on more than one occasion was forever etched into Cosimo's memory. He needed peace to grow his interests, a commodity increasingly difficult to fashion with so many players waiting in the wings—almost all with drawn swords and cinquedeas.

Before his youngest could offer up additional complaints, Cosimo stood and stalked from the room. As he exited, he pronounced with finality, "Get used to the idea, Stefano. This will happen in the very near future. Best to prepare yourself as have your brothers. They each know their roles and accept what must be done. As will you."

Cosimo left the room with a heavy heart. Of all his sons, this one was still a child in many ways, trusting to a fault, of good heart and cheerful disposition. How unfortunate that God had graced him with the talents so valued by the idiots at the Habsburg and French courts. He had no choice but to send his son into what might prove to be a lion's den. Clasping his hands behind his back, Cosimo paced the long hallway leading to a salon at the rear of the Palazzo, brow furrowed with worry.

He murmured, "I hope Nicolo was wrong for once. If what he hints about Friedrich..." One thing Cosimo knew. He must not let Antonio learn anything about the rumors and innuendo circulating about the Duke. If he did, and if even half of what Nico reported were true, he would not want to be the one standing in his oldest son's way.

****

"Madame, this way, if you will." Antonio held out a hand but Veluria brushed past him into the small walled garden. Faint echoes of waves slapping the stone abutment and the occasional skritching sound as pilings and piers groaned in unison led her to peer over the smooth granite cap lining the top of the barricade.

"This is lovely," Veluria sighed, and truly meant it. Such retreats in the heart of the city were indeed rare and precious, and most unexpected in this, the center of the commercial and shipping district. The Grand Canal commanded her attention off to the southeast, and in the distance the stunning visage of the Rialto Bridge gleamed in the mid-afternoon sun. A slight breeze brought relief from the building heat. She felt a trickle of sweat along her spine and twisted uncomfortably against the stays.

"Is something amiss?" Antonio edged next to her, like a phantom morphing from the shadows.

She would never get used to the man's ability to materialize without warning into her very personal space. Such closeness bespoke an intimacy she feared and desired. She reached out for Stefano, seeking a measure of comfort to ground herself and restrain her developing attraction to the huge man who might hold the key for them all. Unfortunately her connection continued to degrade and she no longer commanded access to his thoughts or feelings. Why … she couldn't be sure.

"No, *signore*, I am quite well, *gracie*. Such beauty," Veluria waved a hand to encompass the vista spread before them, "gives me chills."

What gave her greater chills was the brush of flesh against flesh as the Demon moved in close. He'd rolled up his sleeves in deference to the growing heat of the day, revealing deeply tanned muscular forearms. The brief touch seemed more deliberate than incidental.

"My father's interests lay to the north." Tonio pointed to a mass of imposing warehouses where the canal opened out onto a bay that fed eventually into the Adriatic. The sway of masts heralded the fleet of ships awaiting cargo. "Our mills in Florence require that we maintain a presence here in Venice."

Veluria nodded with interest. She well understood the intricate interweaving of commerce, politics and war that dominated the fabric of the city and its denizens. The tall man, and his threatening visage, should have made him a natural fit in this theatre of avaricious pursuit of power, but somehow Veluria detected a depth to his character, something off-kilter, that had nothing to do with his heritage or the unusual 'gifts' he and his brothers wielded so adeptly.

"And exactly what is your role in all this?" Veluria decided to begin the inevitable interrogation on her own terms. She needed to define this man's position, determine exactly how and why his energy so swamped her own abilities, before she could mine him for the location of the key, whatever 'the key' was. Euphemisms, the Holy Mother gloried in them.

Find the key, daughter, and save us all.

Well, she was convinced she had found the one who could lead her to the object of power, but what she would or could do with it remained to be seen.

Antonio's gaze followed the petite woman's, taking in the wall of algae coated stone across the canal. He drifted closer, drawn by the set of her shoulders and the graceful curve of her neck as it flowed like peach satin into the square-cut bodice. He approved of her lack of pretension, eschewing the bouffant sleeves and exaggerated skirts so common to Venezia. Unlike his brothers who seemed inordinately well-versed in fashion, Antonio preferred simplicity and elegance to the frippery and extravagance of his peers, male and female. He liked the cut of her gown, clinging to a narrow waist with just enough flare to accentuate her slim figure.

Without a thought he fingered the leather lacing on her bodice, his mind racing as he imagined pulling the narrow thongs through the eyelets, slowly, enjoying the exquisite feel and the soft shushing sound—the promise of what lay beneath the smooth fabric. He imagined releasing her breasts into his hands, slipping the ribbed fabric away to drop carelessly to the ceramic tiled floor. Imagined undoing the braid that circled her beautifully shaped head, freeing the blue-black tresses to fall about her rosy-hued shoulders. Imagined cupping her chin in his rough hands, dark against light, pressing into the flesh until she bent back to receive his mouth.

The memory of their brief kiss still taunted him. That anyone could taste so sweet defied explanation.

As he reached to pull a strand of hair off her neck, Antonio caught himself, appalled at what he was about to do.

Mio dio, what is this? Where has my mind gone? This is insanity.

Insane indeed. This was his brother's woman, as much as Cosimo might dispute that fact. Antonio had seen the looks exchanged between his brother and this woman. He didn't need special skills to detect the connection they had with each other. That his beloved brother was entirely besotted by her concerned him, but he would do everything in his power to make sure that Stefano would have all that he desired. If this woman proved beyond a shadow of a doubt that she was worthy of Stefano's trust and love, Antonio swore to himself that he would personally thwart his father's grandiose schemes to see the lovers pulled asunder.

He owed Stefano that. It might be the only thing he could do to make amends for his rash and vicious attack on the boy.

"*Perdonatemi, mio signore*, your father wants a word with you." Cosimo's manservant approached circumspectly, as if intruding on an intimate moment. That would surely give the man pause since in his long years of service he'd probably never once seen him so much as look at a woman, let alone engage in polite conversation on the terrace.

"*Gracie*, Paulo. Please stay with Madame until I return."

"M'Lord, your father wishes for me to bring," Paulo stumbled as he had not been accorded the woman's surname and feared using her given name in a gesture of disrespect, "Madame to your brother." He hastened to add, "A light lunch awaits once your discussion is completed." Breathing an obvious sigh of relief that the mercurial elder would find little fault with his delivery, Paulo held an arm out for Veluria.

Tonio held back, his gut in a knot. It was one thing to resolve to see to his brother's happiness, even if that meant supporting a potentially unsuitable match. It was quite another when the debilitating headache returned at the mere thought of Veluria and Stefano together.

He watched Veluria disappear into the palazzo, his face a grim mask of displeasure.

Veluria gathered her skirts, reflexively touching the nape of her neck, reveling in the shadow play that left her senses on high alert. She had all but swooned as the tall man had loomed over her, invading her space with transient touches. Did he think she couldn't feel the gentle tug on the laces, couldn't imagine him stripping her bare and teasing her flesh with soft caresses?

How easily she would have shed the armor she'd carefully installed against such a sweet assault. It was as if he'd never asked for anything for himself, had never before acknowledged he might have needs or desires. There was a naiveté, a coltishness, about the hardened warrior that brooked her defenses. Somehow he had unconsciously unlocked the door that guarded her heart, ensnaring them both. Had it not been for the fortuitous interruption, she suspected things might have spun out of control.

What was it about this Demon that had her thinking the fates had aligned to bring them together? She surmised, no—at some deeper level—she *knew* that he let few in, that in fact she might be the first to plumb the secrets of the man behind the mask of violence and disdain for his fellow man.

But then he tried to slam the door shut, but not before she glimpsed the heartache and shame, the agony and guilt. Again, the guilt. What in God's name had he done?

Perhaps Stefano would finally give her answers to the vexing questions.

Reluctantly she swept past him, allowing her skirts to sweep across his legs, fabric on fabric, a hint that left a nervous surge racing up her thighs to settle with delicious intensity in her private space.

She needed to find answers and soon. All the emotional turmoil served no end and kept her from achieving her goal.

Damn it, Reverend Mother. You prepared me for everything else. Why did you not prepare me for this?

Antonio watched Veluria exit the patio. Again he marveled at how something so tiny could turn him into a towering volcano of heat and lust, the visions of her in his arms consuming him. He could sense her long after she swept through the patio doorway and disappeared into the dim light of the atrium.

Curious at the odd summons from his father, he quickly made his way to Cosimo's private apartments on the third floor of the palazzo. He would need a moment before confronting the old lion. The man was canny to a fault, and it would not do to allow him any awareness of the unusual dynamics that Veluria's and his powers manifested in the garden. Taking the stairs two at a time, he permitted one small memory, then shut her out of his consciousness until he was ready to once again sample the flavor and bouquet only hinted at that day.

****

Cosimo leaned against the stone balustrade, his hands braced against the smooth granite, rocking slightly on his heels. He had watched his eldest and the mysterious French woman with interest and had noted Tonio's unusual willingness to be close to her. His 'enforcer' seldom allowed contact with another unless it was to administer his particular form of persuasion to unwitting victims. Of all his sons, this one had mastered the arts of interrogation and intimidation with an ease and enthusiasm that had delighted and frightened his many instructors. That he had learned to temper his aggressive nature when it came to his younger brothers spoke to his ability to control and channel his gifts. Cosimo appreciated and applauded Tonio's restraint but was in no way lulled into believing that the man was anything more than a smoldering volcano, ready to erupt without notice.

"You wish to see me?"

Cosimo smiled and turned toward his son, amused at the studied, placid expression. He could allow this little masquerade for now. What he had seen and sensed from afar could play out in the family's favor since Antonio would likely not take the news at all well, too imbued with his younger brother's well-being for his, and the family's, own good.

"Yes. I have just received a most favorable response from the Duke. He has expressed, shall we say, a certain level of enthusiasm for the proposition. So much so that he wrote…" Cosimo tapped his forehead as if trying to remember the exact words, "…you have three sons, I have three daughters."

Antonio's small intake of breath betrayed his feelings on the matter. This was exactly what he feared. His father would go ahead with the match in one way or another, and it wasn't just Stefano on the auction block. His gut clenched with the possibilities opening for his future. That the family would even entertain such a thought…

"Don't look so concerned, my boy. You and Nico serve me well in other capacities. But Stefano has unique gifts which, for this match, I will exploit to the fullest." Cosimo moved off the balcony and turned toward the writing desk. The bank of tall windows filtered the late afternoon light through a filmy gauze covering. He reached for a square of parchment and extended it to Antonio. "Read for yourself."

Antonio scowled at the tiny lettering then threw it onto the desk. His voice thick with scorn, he stated, "Still trying to impress, I see."

Cosimo laughed out loud. "I thought you might agree with me. Remember, the Duke has several cloisters he maintains with the Duchy's funds. He attempts to elevate his rank to ours."

Antonio sneered, "But a Pope and a Cardinal will trump his monks any day of the week."

"Quite right. But we can use that ambition to our advantage. The Habsburg court stands to change in some significant ways in the near future. We need to be part of that change or it will consume us. Stefano will be our instrument to assure our interests." He held up a hand to stay Antonio's next words. "And my decision is final on this matter."

Antonio murmured, "I understand," though for the briefest moment his face belied his feelings until the mask settled once more. "If that's all, Papà? I have matters to attend to. I shall leave you to break the news. Your guest also awaits your pleasure."

"Tend to your duties, Antonio. I will let you know when it is time for me to explore exactly what our guest has to offer." He gave his son a crafty stare. "I have a feeling it could prove entertaining."

Antonio stalked from the room leaving Cosimo to ponder what his eldest planned to do next. That he did not back this decision—considering the marriage not in his brother's best interest—was quite clear. His son also had his gut in a knot over the woman, setting up an interesting conflict of interests.

But however it played out, ultimately Tonio would protect that which mattered most—the family. And perhaps he might also see how his clever father had opened a new possibility, a new opportunity to serve. His attraction to the woman, and her potential as an ally in the always shifting loyalties of the continental courts—whichever one she actually served—offered intriguing possibilities.

Cosimo wandered over to a small leather-topped table flanked with burgundy brocaded stools. He examined the chess pieces with interest. The rooks he'd dispatched early, with Nico moved into striking distance at C5. He'd yet to call his knights into service. Nodding sagely, he picked up the heavy marble piece and moved G1 to F3. Sliding onto a stool, Cosimo pondered the disposition of the pieces, frowning at the black Bishop at C8. This was the imponderable, the thing he'd been feeling for several days. A new player graced the stage, with similar abilities to the woman, perhaps even stronger. Most certainly dangerous. Cosimo had him blocked by Nico, but perhaps that move would not have the outcome he anticipated. His gut told him the threat was closer than Spagna, very close indeed.

****

Andreas grew weary as the heat of the day drained his meager resources. He was hungry and thirsty and had not slept in days. He had desperate need of a vessel to restore his flagging energies and to take his mind off the passion that threatened to consume him when in such close proximity to *her*.

He moved surreptitiously along the narrow pathways jutting in several directions off the Ferrara estate. Though unremarkable in outline from its near neighbors, the imposing edifice broke the dullness of gray granite with ornate finials and over-sized windows. He admired the beautiful leaded cut glass and recalled that it was Venice that controlled the secret process and had been a center for glass-making for almost four hundred years. He grumpily latched onto his vast store of trivia to occupy his mind when his patience for his beads grew thin.

He gave thought to abandoning his watch and seeking audience with the Monsignor, if for no other reason than to entertain himself with the righteous fool's concern and unending need for gossip. His games with the Papàl envoy, the good Cardinal, were of no interest to his mission, yet they formed a convenient excuse for him to maintain his cover and to secure access to areas a normal citizen would be unlikely to breach.

He rather enjoyed playing the role of cleric. Venetians were, if nothing else, agnostics at heart—the citizens' lack of religious zeal spoke volumes of their shaky relationship with the Vatican. Over the years, the city had been subject to interdicts by the Holy See, the most recent imposed during the War of the Holy League under Pope Julius. Those shifting alliances had been of the neck-snapping variety with Venice entering into an unholy pact with Henry and Maximilian against the French.

Having the woman represent herself as a ward of the French court was an interesting, though odd, ploy. Political games aside, what mattered were that her peculiar abilities to set his training to naught over-rode the Monsignor's petty concerns. That she might wreak havoc on the man's ill-conceived politicking with competing interests in the church amounted to a mere sideshow as far as Andreas was concerned.

The sound of a door slamming brought Andreas to full alert. He peered around the corner to find the Demon de' Medici standing only yards away, his face a study in irritation. Andreas faded against the rough stone, drawing on his remaining reserves to cloak himself in the shadow of the alleyway. He felt rather than heard the dangerous man passing, a whirlpool of anger, tightly coiled and spinning so fast it would consume all who ventured in his path. Andreas knew that someone would pay dearly tonight. He preferred it not be him, but he knew he must follow the Dark One. There were answers with him, and the woman was not going anywhere. At least not for a while. Of that he was pathetically sure.

Chapter Twelve

In here, Madame, if you would..." Paulo held the door as Veluria swept into a well-appointed salon. Unlike the ornate, thickly brocaded wall-coverings on the lowest level, this room was spare in ornamentation. The walls sported walnut wainscoting topped with cream-colored stucco artfully applied in random swirls that caught and reflected the light streaming in the south-facing bank of windows.

She muttered, "Gracie," but the manservant had already left, closing the door quietly. Veluria paced about the room, willing herself to stay calm and not dwell on the disturbing interplay of powers that had almost entrapped her in a game of ... what? Exactly what had happened in the garden? Who had tempted whom? It had been such an intense exchange, almost like two lovers rutting on a forest floor, heedless of their surroundings, aware only of each other. She reached out gingerly, seeking the Demon, testing her resolve and ability to contain her energies. With a sigh of relief, she felt his awareness drift away, like clouds dissipating after a storm, the air fresher, though still fragrant with a lingering scent of musk and animal wildness.

To distract herself, she cataloged the furnishings, memorizing every detail, including the pattern of the rug—octagonal, with a deep burgundy floral pattern so favored by the ruling elite. With its political and economic interests still firmly in place in the Middle Eastern regions, Venice lay claim to that rich cultural heritage which the fair city adopted as its own. The textiles, of a nubby linen weave in a variety of patterns, adorned not only the floors but also doubled as wall coverings, though in this salon the large rug occupied single pride of place in the center of the room.

The space had a very male feel to it. She wondered who occupied the suite and if she were in fact a detainee rather than a guest. To her surprise a wave of exhaustion swept over her, almost staggering in its intensity.

How much time had passed since she'd responded to Stefano's request for a clandestine meeting? Days, weeks? It felt that way, though in truth the string of episodes, the engagements with enemies and allies alike, could be measured in mere hours, hours that had been productive in unexpected ways.

She collapsed onto a settee hoping to alleviate the strain of the tight bodice constricting her midsection only to have the voluminous folds of the skirt and the hooped stays preclude her achieving any kind of supine position.

"Can I help?"

"Stefano," she gasped, mildly annoyed that she'd neither heard nor sensed his presence. She must be more tired than she thought.

The young man fussed with her skirts as she struggled to sit upright, feeling more than a little foolish with the state of her disarray. But she had more problems that a simple wardrobe malfunction. She needed to get her head back in the game. Antonio de' Medici had effectively derailed her, forcing her down pathways over which neither of them seemed to have much control.

Whatever attraction, feelings, she'd developed for Stefano's older brother had to be set aside. If she didn't resume her role she would miss an opportunity to insinuate herself into the one arena that mattered. Cosimo was known as the kingmaker, though it was a misnomer. The fractured politics that divided city-states and the Papacy from each other—and the rest of the continent—functioned on the shoulders of commerce and the waning threat of eternal damnation.

The Medici family played a pivotal role in the building of a new empire that had changed the face of the continent and the course of history. Her history.

Stefano interrupted her train of thought. "Does this remind you of anything?"

He leered at her in his old lecherous way but the good humor failed to extend to his eyes. It seemed she was not the only one playing a role. With an effort she resumed the mantle of the courtesan, rearranging her face into the familiar coquettish mask.

"If you mean when we, in that Count's ... what was his name?"

Stefano muttered, "Gustaf," as Veluria recalled what should have been a mortifying situation.

"That sitting room with the hideous Moorish pillows he'd imported to impress Carlos ... who never did come to visit."

"I believe we were the first to, uh, make use of them, no?" Stefano carelessly rearranged her skirts so he could slide next to her on the narrow seat. His actions seemed stilted and awkward.

"You are such a wicked one." Veluria summoned a warm rush of pleasure, hoping to steer the young man back to lighter sparring and teasing while she re-established her persona.

A shadow passed over Stefano's face. "I may be more wicked than you know."

"Whatever do you mean? Surely that night we..." she sputtered to a halt when his face turned pale, his breathing labored.

The young man choked back a sob, his agony palpable. "You don't know me, Veluria. Not anymore. I am not the person I was just two days ago."

Antonio's overwhelming presence intruded, almost as if he were in the room with them. He'd been the source of Stefano's and his own distress, of that she was certain. Perhaps now she would learn what had transpired and so traumatized both brothers to the point where they'd buried it beyond her ability to divine even the smallest hint.

"Explain this to me. What has happened? Who has done this thing to you? Tell me, now!"

Veluria did not have to feign anxiety for she sensed the agony, the barrenness of his soul. The sensation was akin to falling down a well without a bottom, a spiritual rush through cold, clammy air—so real it raised the hairs on her arms.

A few of her sisters were mediums, graced with the ability to 'see' into the realm of the spirit world. She was not so blessed, yet the connection had such a three-dimensional quality she could swear she saw his spirit circling about the cavity that had once been a vibrant boy-man.

She murmured softly, "Stefano, please?" but he stuttered, "I, I can't."

"Stefano. You can trust me." She poured sincerity into her voice, willing him to believe. "I would never betray you."

Stefano grimaced, making no effort to hide the emotions warring for predominance, his fists clenching and unclenching as he battled some inner demon. A demon who would be his brother.

She took his face in her hands and rubbed her thumbs along his jaw, allowing her energy to open to whatever tortured his spirit. She hissed in dismay as a frisson of fear and something she could not identify flowed through her. Such pain, such agony, such...

Pleasure? What in the name of the Holy Mother?

Fighting through the confusion was akin to swimming upriver in a full flood. Channeling it was simply out of the question, although that worked in her favor as it avoided what she liked to call 'blowback'—a reversal of energies that risked initiating awareness in potential adepts. Like Stefano.

"I'm not the fool everyone thinks, Veluria."

She brushed a finger across his lips and said, "I don't think..." but halted when he raised a hand to stay her words. His eyes took on a hard edge, calculating. She could swear she saw Cosimo staring back at her—with recognition and no small amount of satisfaction.

His voice tight, he rasped, "I know you are like us. Like *him*."

Him? Antonio or Cosimo? Did it matter?

Stefano glared at her accusingly. "Don't try to hide it. I've always known." He stood and towered over her. Softly he continued, "I am so very sorry."

"I don't understand. Sorry because someone mistreated you, hurt you?"

He whispered, his voice an agony of emotions, "No, I hurt someone. Someone who didn't deserve it. I started it. I should have stopped it." Stefano grasped Veluria's hands, clinging to them like a lifeline, trembling as with palsy. His next words cut her like a knife, "But I didn't want to."

He didn't want to? Did he mean he didn't want to hurt that person? Or ... he didn't want to stop it? What in God's name...?

Stefano had his lips clamped in a thin tight line, making it clear he was offering no further comment on the subject. Instead she focused on his admission that he recognized her 'gifts'. That was hardly cause for concern. All the Medici men were well aware of their own unique abilities and, in true Florentine fashion, exploited those powers with single-minded cunning and legendary deceit. Even Stefano, the kindest and most fey of the famiglia, had a preternatural understanding of court intrigue. Coupled with a glib tongue and stunning good looks, the boy-man charmed with a savant's guile.

Reverend Mother had factored in the probability that she would be found out, yet the head of their order had assumed she would be able to mask her own abilities when necessary. In light of the Medicis' extraordinary psychic gifts, that amounted to a miscalculation on the woman's part, something she would have to turn to her advantage if at all possible.

For now she was more concerned with Stefano's cryptic confession, though without context she was having trouble understanding why he embraced this soul-searing self-flagellation.

She stated with a conviction she feared might prove groundless, "I cannot believe you would intentionally inflict suffering on anyone."

With a darkness not even his demon older brother could match, he growled, "Believe it."

"Stefano, no…"

He lunged back from the settee, dragging her with him. Still grasping her hands in an ever-tightening grip that nearly crushed the fine bones in her fingers, Stefano raked her with such a hungry stare she felt the first tremor of fear snaking along her spine. He yanked her roughly into his arms, as close as the awkward bodice and heavy silk fabric would allow.

"Damn it," he muttered.

Ignoring her protests, he half dragged her to a door set at the far end of the room. With one hand firmly around her waist, he pushed the door open, revealing a spacious bedchamber beyond. He thrust her through the narrow entryway, his excitement evident as his cock strained the fabric of his wool codpiece.

Veluria took in the dark walnut four-poster bed, several wood benches and an ornate leather-covered Spanish chest at the foot of the towering bed. The coverlet was a rich tapestry of muted browns, greens and russet. It lay rumpled and tossed to one side. The indentation remained where Stefano had tossed restlessly, pulling the fine linen sheet away from the down-filled bolster. A gossamer spill of sheer ecru curtains surrounded the imposing bed on three sides. A

106

small stool lay overturned from where Stefano must have kicked it over when he heard her in the antechamber.

Veluria turned to take the measure of the young man advancing, not aggressively as she had half-expected, but with his heart in his hands, to do with as she will. Under other circumstances he would have what he wanted, whenever he wanted it, so artful were his gifts that he gave back tenfold in pleasure and devotion. But not this day. Not when he'd let her glimpse a capacity for violence ... and the potential to enjoy it beyond anything she could have guessed.

The contrast between Stefano and Antonio hit her like a runaway train—an image unsuitable for the time but it was the only frame of reference she could conjure. Antonio, a man of violence, believing himself devoid of a soul—and, ultimately, redemption— harbored a deep well of tenderness and a capacity to care that belied the demon persona he so carefully nurtured. His youngest brother, on the other hand, beguiled all with a mask of youthful exuberance and innocence.

Even she had bought that image of the shallow dandy, the court favorite with pleasing mannerisms and a decided gift for conquests of the heart. She trembled at the memory of the last time they'd touched and fondled—his scent, his exquisite gentleness that had set every nerve, every synapse on fire. It had been a most pleasant ... entertainment. Clever boy, constructing a magnificent false front and using it so artfully.

Stupid. Stupid. Stupid.

It might have seemed a betrayal of the young man's affections, a violation of trust, when his older brother so possessed her and sent everything in her sensual arsenal into free-fall. At this moment she was less inclined to suffer feelings of remorse. But if she could not rein in her rampaging hormones, she would have to recuse herself from the mission.

No, Reverend Mother would not be happy.

"I've missed you, *amore mia bella*," Stefano husked in her ear. "More than you can ever know. When you were attacked, I feared I would lose you. Had it not been for my brother, all would have been lost."

How convenient for Stefano to overlook the fact that he was the one who summoned her, placing her in peril. Wherever he'd been holed up, he'd chosen to let his brother do the dirty work instead of coming forward to see to her safety and well-being. It would do well for her to remember that.

It became harder and harder to think as Stefano drew her close, bending her slim neck in an exaggerated arc until her artery bulged and pulsed, as if begging for his tongue to taste the heat. He had such a clever tongue, so eager to sample every inch of flesh. Heat and pressure in her private place begged for her to yield, just one more time, to give in to his sweet demands. Sometimes her training and self-control came into serious conflict. With so much at stake, she must yield to the euphemistic greater good and subsume her own needs.

Damn you and your mission. When this is said and done, Reverend Mother, I am going to need serious therapy.

Stefano felt the familiar heat settle in his loins, no longer tempered with a desire for subtle restraint and consideration. All his life, his peers and court toadies had fed his lust with admiration and exhortations to outdo himself. Even his brothers had looked on with sly smiles and unabashed support while working behind the scenes to set to rights the inevitable fall-out from his headlong rush into one infatuation after another. From the age of fourteen he had set a standard amongst his cousins and circle of friends of a randy lad graced with a way with the ladies, young and old alike, to the dismay of his father's business managers whose profits often contributed to salvaging his freedom from demanding fathers or irate, cuckolded husbands.

Veluria was different, exotically so. She offered herself with no expectations beyond the sharing of pleasure, sometimes with the hint that it could be so much more … exciting. Until two nights ago, he'd never allowed his secret yearnings free of the inner space where he concealed his very particular tastes.

Because she knew him in ways no other woman could, he would finally be able to explore all the possibilities that had been denied him for far too long. He could finally set aside matters of propriety— Veluria would understand, and she would not pass judgment.

"Turn around," he whispered into her ear, "and let me loosen those bindings." Veluria complied as she lifted the strands of hair that had fallen from the tight braid and bent forward.

"Beautiful, you are so…" He finished off his thought with a taste of the pale flesh behind her ear, nuzzling with exquisite softness, feather light, using his tongue to moisten and warm, then his breath to chill. He gently removed the lacing, pulling the long strand through the eyelets, slowly drawing out the sensation, letting the sound envelop their senses, building anticipation.

Before Veluria he'd never known how incredibly seductive a slow hand could be. Too often his liaisons were frantic couplings disguised as passion, but gradually he learned to optimize the experience in favor of securing advantage before moving on to the next encounter. Cosimo would chide him on his rash behavior but he would listen attentively to the gossip.

Tonio and Nico were wrong—they weren't the only ones conscripted to serve the family's needs. But unlike his brothers, he chose who and when—at least until now. If his father insisted on his betrothal to one of the horse-faced Habsburg whores, all that would change. It did not proscribe finding comfort elsewhere, it just meant he'd need discretion and subterfuge—traits he found annoying at best. And unlike the freedoms he enjoyed in Venice and at home in Florence, at the court he would become much like a butterfly specimen on black velvet—ever on display and under constant scrutiny.

I don't wish to live my life that way.

Stefano gently maneuvered the stiff corset off Veluria's bodice; but before dropping it onto the bed he held it up, curious at the imbalance, and smiled.

"I see you have protection, M'lady."

"As well I should. You never know what manner of brigand might be about in the late afternoon."

"Brigand." He chuckled, enjoying the analogy, but set the stiff fabric on a bench far away from the bed. He'd prefer she didn't have a stiletto available in case she objected to the activities he had in mind.

Veluria kept her tone light, yet he sensed the faint tinge of concern. "A brigand of the very best sort, I have been assured."

"Then let us see just what such a cad might have in mind, shall we?"

Stefano went light-headed as her small breasts fell into his eager palms, the mounds soft and pliant, fitting exactly as if God had intended her body for him alone. Never had he had such a connection with another human, not even with his brothers for whom he would willingly give his life. This went beyond that, far beyond. For her, and her alone, he would do anything, any act, heinous or otherwise, nothing could ever keep her from him. Not his father and his plans, not the court favorites or his brother's men, or his friends who seemed to live vicariously through his exploits, no one could come between them now. He'd never felt so sure of anything, the rightness of it, the need to claim it and make it his own.

With practiced ease, he slipped the heavy fabric from her body, revealing filmy undergarments that outlined her hips and the sweet rise of her belly. She was so small he had to lean forward to reach the hidden places that she so loved for him to touch, each small stroke, each tease, each small hitch of her breath a stab of sublime pleasure in his groin.

Veluria turned and swiftly removed his doublet and finely-woven shirt. She had to stand on tip-toe to reach his mouth, clasping her delicate hands at his waist to give her leverage. Always the tease, he stayed just out of reach, forcing her to wriggle against him until he yielded for a taste of her full lips, his tongue probing with increasing urgency.

She disengaged only to run her fingers down the length of his torso, stopping to tweak his nipples between her fingers, drawing them out, then digging in with sharp nails until he murmured a small mewl of pain and pleasure.

Yes, you do know what I want. Oh God, yes.

As she followed his contours, she traced a path along the ridge at his hips, then lower to slip the buttons securing the codpiece, allowing the fabric to fall away and release his engorged cock into her hand. She kept her eyes on his chest as he unbraided her hair, allowing the pins to drop soundlessly on the thick carpet. As she stroked him, he focused on the delicious pain and pleasure. She glanced down, then back up, her mouth in an 'O' of consternation and disgust.

"Who did this to you? Tell me and I shall have him destroyed." She pressed, her anger barely contained. "Stefano. Who?"

"It doesn't matter."

110

"You don't mean that. I know you too well. This has scarred you and I will not have it."

"No, it hasn't."

"Stefano, stop with the cryptic remarks. I don't understand." With a moan she looked at the still seeping wounds, now ridged in sharp relief as his cock swelled with need in her hand. "This has to be so painful…"

He whispered, "It is. And that is why I cannot explain…"

Veluria shook her head violently, prepared to argue the night away but one look at his face stayed her tongue.

"Please, *mi donna amata*, just love me now. Let me fill you, I need this, I beg you…"

"*Sì, il mio amante*, come lie with me. Make love to me as if the world is ending."

"Like the world is ending, yes, that is exactly how I feel, my Veluria."

Stefano swept her into his arms and deposited her onto the feather bed, then lay atop her small frame, carefully nudging her thighs apart, mindful that she might change her mind at any moment and unsure that he could pull back now. His pain, and desire, had reached a point of no return. He needed to feed it, to push himself through it, to own it, control it.

Veluria winced as he thrust himself deep, the lacerations and scars rough to her sensitive flesh. But her moans of pleasure-pain as he plumbed her depths drove all thought from his brain as he wrapped his hands about her beautiful neck and squeezed. Her nails raked his back and she bucked wildly beneath him but he held her fast, thrusting his hips and driving deep, brutally deep and silently begging forgiveness and praying Antonio never found out for he would surely end this torment with one swift stoke.

Releasing her throat, he ignored her gagging and flipped her over as if she weighed nothing, hitching her up onto her knees. Spreading the pale cheeks, he ignored her moans and plundered the tight entry with his fingers, stretching until she writhed beneath him.

As he entered her again, he whispered, "We leave tonight, just the two of us. Together. Forever." And then he opened to her as he thrust to the hilt, flooding her with images until she finally understood the who and what and why.

That is who he is. He is the one who showed me the way.

He came on her sweet screams.

****

Andreas watched with interest as the Demon exited yet another private domicile. This was the third in a row and each time the Dark One's temper sank to new depths. One of his men approached cautiously, mumbled some communiqué, then returned to the small knot of soldiers comprising the Medicis' private army. How the Demon had summoned these men eluded him. It seemed they materialized by magic whenever the giant went on the prowl in the city.

Andreas debated following the man as this seemed a useless endeavor. He could spend his time torturing himself while the woman whored with the younger son—not something he fancied, yet of all his options, experiencing her pleasures vicariously had far greater appeal than dealing with the ire and psychotic turmoil of the Dark One.

Andreas bolted down a side alley headed back to Cosimo's domicile. He'd leave the Demon to whatever errand his father had sent him on. He much preferred keeping a proverbial eye on Veluria—her name caressed his mind softly—but with her secured within the palazzo's walls, he would learn no more that evening.

The progress he'd made was of little use to the Monsignor, but keeping the man in the loop and convinced of his utility meant he had continued access to local resources. Now might be the right time to report to His Holiness. After that, he could perhaps reward himself with a visit to Le Vergini and indulge his need for a vessel with one of the many novitiates recently acquired by the convent. He suspected he would need his strength in the coming days.

The prospect of relieving the cloying ache in his groin overrode all other considerations. Andreas headed back toward the Central Square on foot while Antonio proceeded with his men away from San Polo.

Too concerned with trivial tasks, neither man detected the perturbations in energy that heralded their universes' slide into chaos and a world of shadows.

Chapter Thirteen

Cosimo glared at his manservant, then at his eldest son. Moonlight flooded through the bank of tall, narrow windows lining the canal side wall of his small study.

"That will do, Paulo. Leave us."

Paulo lit the last remaining candle on the desk and left the room quickly, closing the heavy walnut door behind him.

"Sit." Cosimo sank onto the plush cushion by the fireplace, and pointed to the one usually favored by his youngest brother. The irony was not lost on him. One fuck-up replaced by another.

Tonio had returned to the palazzo in a foul mood, the afternoon and evening frittered away on meaningless interrogations of petty men with delusions of grandeur. Although he'd instilled a satisfying fear of God in the merchants, seeing to his father's business dealings was not something he enjoyed, nor was he adept at the nuanced negotiations involved. Sending him out that day had been a fool's errand and designed simply to get him off the premises so Cosimo could see to matters that concerned Stefano without his interference.

He felt a headache coming on, one of the debilitating explosions of agony that could send him to his bed for hours, if not days. Only his father suffered the same malady. A result of their special "gift", no doubt. He would need to fight it, keep his wits about him.

"The information you sought..." Antonio began an explanation, then halted as he watched with concern as the waves of pain cascaded across his father's lined face. He recognized the source immediately, having suffered too often himself not to have sympathy for others in the throes of the excruciating agony.

Cosimo croaked, "It is of no consequence now. Too late."

"I can still…"

"No, Tonio. Listen, for I do not have time to debate this issue. Hear me out for it will be in your hands, and I must make it clear what the stakes are for all of us."

Curious now, Antonio settled onto the cushion and awaited what he guessed would not be good news.

"Friedrich has accepted my proposal, with his usual conditions, this you know," Cosimo stared at his son intently, "but what is new is the urgency with which we must proceed."

"Urgency?"

"I am to send Stefano, alone, to the Imperial Court. The Reichstag has been convened yet again and Friedrich wishes to parade his latest coupe in hopes of gaining favor. Bringing our house and his together would do much to convince the Dukes that he is worthy of joining their ranks. Stefano will marry his oldest daughter there. Immediately."

Antonio sat quietly, absorbing the implications. This was not unexpected for Friedrich who, though considered mercurial by his peers, could move decisively when his interests were at stake.

"Alone?" Cosimo nodded. "I don't think so. Stefano must be prepared for facing the Reichstag. His pretty court manners will take him only so far. Those vultures will eat him alive and I will not have it. I will accompany him with a few of my hand-picked men."

Antonio thought, *I will work behind the scenes to assess the implications for this hurried arrangement. Stefano will have a choice, if I have anything to say about it.*

"It matters not. He is gone, that foolish boy."

"Gone? Gone where?"

Cosimo kneaded his eyes. "The candles, please."

Antonio heaved up from the plush cushion and extinguished the candles on the desk. His father had moved into a full blown attack, so much so that the wavering candlelight would be causing shooting stabs of pain into his skull. They had little time left to work out the situation before he'd need to have Cosimo moved to his quarters.

"*Gracie*, Tonio, *gracie*." He kneaded his temples, grimacing. "The fool has run off."

"Dammit. Do you know why…?" Stupid question. The blood pounding through his veins threatened to blow the top of his head off. "So he learned of Friedrich's plan, is that right?"

He wasn't sure who he was more furious with, his father ... or himself. They—no, *he*—should have seen this coming.

"*Sì*, I knew he hesitated but I assumed he would do the right thing for the family."

"And you are so sure this is the right thing? You put family first, Papà. Does it never occur to you that perhaps Stefano's happiness might come first?"

Cosimo looked at him with surprise. He stuttered, "Th-there is no difference, it is about the family. You know this. You have lived by this credo all your life. All that you do, all that you are, is in service to the family. We have made you what you are."

Antonio sneered, "Yes, exactly right. You have made me what I am today."

Antonio pushed off the cushion and rose with difficulty, the pain in his head sending waves of nausea through his gut. In truth it wasn't just his damnable malady causing him such physical distress. After what he'd done to Stefano, the aggravating waste of his time seeing to miniscule details of commerce...

Antonio stalked about the salon, livid with anger. Anger at his father for his absolute control over all their destinies. Anger at Stefano for being such a slave to his damned misguided sensibilities. Anger at the interminable scheming that greased the wheels of politics and commerce. But mostly anger at himself—his gut clenched as he fought against the strange inner stirrings the woman had aroused. Feeling that stood in opposition to his deep well of *famiglia fedeltà*, the loyalty that insinuated his very core and gave him reason for living.

Quietly Cosimo said, "That's not all. Please, Tonio, sit. My head pounds so I cannot think. And I must be clear on this."

Antonio sank back onto the cushion, his mind too agitated to focus clearly. He nearly missed his father's next startling words.

"He has taken her with him."

"Her." Antonio's world tilted dangerously as he had had no warning, no inner alarms to alert him to any of these events. That she could so mask, not only herself, but Stefano as well spoke to a power only hinted at. That troubled him far more than knowing she had run off with his beloved brother. Stefano's feelings for the Frenchwoman were no secret to any of them.

"She's no more French than..." Antonio muttered.

115

"What?"

"French." He paused, aware he was making no sense. He and Cosimo had to work through this dilemma logically. He asked, "Is she French, Papà? What do we even know about her? We have few contacts with François' court, and not even Nico has succeeded in penetrating the layers of protection about the King and his closest advisors."

"So, you suspect as do I ... that she is not who she claims." Cosimo waved his hand dismissively. "That does us no good now. The question remains. Where did he go, where did *they* go? We must bring him back into the fold, Tonio. He is too valuable an asset to risk having him taken."

Antonio clenched his jaw, rose to his feet and stared down at his father. Voice tight, he stated with deadly calm, "An asset."

Is that what the old bastard thought about his youngest son? A fucking *asset*? A prized stallion to be farmed out like valuable breeding stock? He'd accepted his and Nico's standing as mere cogs in the machinery that was the Medici legacy. But for some reason he'd sensed a level of affection for Stefano not accorded him and his brother.

Maybe we're better off, Nico and I. What would either of us be like if the bastard had actually cared about us?

Antonio glared with loathing at the man to whom he'd sworn his loyalty and said, "Yes, I agree. I shall find your asset, Cosimo..." he emphasized the word 'asset' and with undisguised menace warned, "...and then we shall have a discussion, you and I."

Unconcerned at the threat, Cosimo said, "He will not be easy to track, boy. Remember, he has gifts, not as strong as yours, but gifts all the same."

"I only need to loosen a few tongues, Father. Remember, it is what I do best."

As he exited the salon, Antonio resisted the urge to slam the heavy walnut door shut, not so much in deference to Cosimo's distress, but to prove to himself he could control the almost overwhelming need for violence. He curled his fists into tight balls and let the pain wash through him. It was out of Cosimo's hands now.

Now it's my turn.

****

"You have done well, my son." The Monsignor offered his ring as Andreas bent to pay obeisance to His Holiness.

Andreas had expended what few energy reserves he had left in constructing an elaborate web of lies, innuendoes and suppositions that would keep the Monsignor busy chasing down phantoms and off his back. So long as he could continue as a hand-selected operative of the church, his cover would afford him access to channels well-insulated from the public eye. None were as secretive as the minions of the Papacy, especially when in pursuit of political and economic advantage.

His misinformation would stir the pot and give the Monsignor sufficient fuel to stoke the flames of discord within the church hierarchy. Better yet, they could call into question the motivation of the monolith that was the Medici family. He had no qualms about prodding the beehive. The Brotherhood's statisticians might enjoy flipping coins and waiting to see how the probabilities fell out. He was amenable to a more proactive approach.

That would require a few Hail Marys but not nearly so many for what he had planned.

With false modesty he said, "*Gracie, gracie*. If I may, I would like to spend the evening in prayer. I feel the need to restore … my soul."

The Monsignor gave him a sly smile and murmured, "Of course."

Andreas nodded respectfully as he turned to leave, but he paused as the Monsignor called out, "The chapel will have no visitors this evening. Feel free to use it at your leisure."

Andreas hastened through the dark corridors searching for the small entryway into the vestry. He smiled at the bald-faced lie. Yes, he had needs, not for his soul, but needs that pressed heavily on his groin, pressure so great he could barely function, his mind clouded. Perturbations in the energy fields niggled at his consciousness, and he knew he ought to pay attention, but he had priorities. One priority now. Find a vessel and recharge. The Monsignor's offer was more than generous.

Andreas slipped into the small chapel, entering through the side door nearest the altar. Weak light from the votive candles near the

117

statue of the Virgin cast shadows onto the ceramic tile floor. Two elongated shadows, one steady, one wavering, caught his eye. He sighed with relief. The good Monsignor was not without compassion for his flock.

He spoke softly to the kneeling figure. "Come with me, my dear. Your time in prayer has been well-spent. Now you shall reap the rewards for your devotion."

Andreas lifted the small form off her knees, more roughly than he intended, but the demands of his body were great and he had little patience left for the niceties the prioress expected. He led the novitiate out of the chapel and down the hall to a cubicle set aside for contemplation and privacy.

He motioned for the girl to enter. "In here."

When she hesitated, he shoved her roughly inside, then closed and securely latched the door. A single candle burned steadily on a rough-hewn round table. A cot with wood planks normally supporting a mattress lay bare but for a single woolen blanket bunched at the foot of the bed. The stone walls were free of adornment, not even a cross, and would insulate any sound. Satisfied he would be undisturbed, he turned to the novitiate.

"Let me see you."

He tilted her chin so that the veil molded to her face. Andreas pulled at the wimple, sliding it back off her shaved head and exposing a face rapturous in anticipation. He slipped the scapula and wimple off, then grimaced with distaste. A girl, not much more than a child. The prioress had her nerve sending him one so young, and most assuredly a virgin. He had hoped for someone with experience who could pleasure him without the tedious need for instruction.

There was nothing for it. She would have to do since he was out of time and nearly out of energy. Unfortunate for both of them. He pointed to the cot as he parted his robe.

"Bend over and lift your habit. And, girl..." Andreas gave a small concession to her inexperience, "...there will be pain." Her whimper of fear, then expulsion of breath, brought a smile to his face. He fingered the stiletto, then cast it aside. Best not to be tempted. He had the entire night ahead of him to recharge.

****

Antonio finished handing out pouches filled with gold coins to the five men he trusted most in his company.

"You know what to do. I want answers by tonight. The longer we wait, the less chance we have for recovery. Go. Now."

Antonio knew with certainty that his brother and the woman, Veluria, would rush to the safety of France. Even if she were not actually tied to the French court through marriage or blood, the Medici family influence carried sufficient weight that just the mere presence of his youngest brother in those territories would offer innumerable opportunities to exploit a fragile political truce.

The Venetian propensity to instigate hostilities was a never-ending source of irritation for all concerned. François would do most anything to insure a measure of peace, at least in the short term until the matter of the Spanish succession was put to rest. Offering to negotiate the return of his brother in exchange for some as yet unnamed advantage would suit all parties involved.

That was the problem—that his brother would be returned, with or without Veluria. Antonio needed to mediate in such a way that he gained control over Stefano's destiny. If the French woman was what he wanted, then he would have her. If he could mount a retrieval before they crossed the border into French territories, he would be in a position to dictate terms. Once in France he would need additional leverage to extricate the pair. It wasn't a matter of where they were going, it was a matter of how.

Antonio had dispatched his men to seek out which ships had set sail on the tide and which were readying within the next two days. Overland was fraught with dangers, though he knew his brother to be a fine horseman. If it were him, he would opt for keeping a low profile and have the woman masquerade as a boy servant—her petite frame and young features would surely serve her well in that role. He prayed his brother would eschew the inconvenience of an extended trip by horseback, or even by carriage, in favor of a more comfortable voyage on a well-appointed ship.

The violent fluttering in his gut convinced him he was on the right track, though the strange sensations in which he normally placed his utmost trust seemed askew. Dovetail joints just slightly out of plane. He sensed another energy, faint but building in strength—familiar, yet alien. It had a congruence with his own energies that he had felt in the corridor two nights ago when all this had started and he had found his existence complicated, turned upside down, by a petite vixen.

Veluria's intelligence, her beauty, her arrogance and fearlessness—all might have caught his attention on their own merits. But there was something more, something that prodded those private places deep inside, where his heart sheltered from his world of violence and mayhem.

Cosimo had been quite right. The family had made him what he was: soul-less, adept at deception and manipulation, cruel in the pursuit of the higher good—that of the family—and methodical in his application of force to achieve his desired ends. He understood power above all else. But until he had met Veluria, with her peculiar hold on him, he had not permitted anyone, leastways a woman, to gain a foothold into the one thing he most feared—his heart.

Only his brothers had access to that secret place. He'd vowed to protect them at all costs yet with a single act of youthful stupidity Stefano had managed to unleash the demon who threatened them all.

He could almost justify lashing out at his youngest brother, given the nature of the game they played and the stakes involved. It was far too easy to say Stefano had brought it on himself with his foolish actions. But in his gut he recognized the demon for what he was—a creature that derived satisfaction from administering pain to another, even his own brother.

His own mixture of guilt and regret, however, were far less troubling than the perplexing and unexpected way Stefano had reacted to the punishment. The act had brought a wash of … pleasure to his brother. The boy's body had vibrated with such sensual ecstasy that he'd been reluctant to stop, to put an end to sharing such exquisite torture. Only the presence of his men, and their collective horror at what he was doing, had imposed some semblance of sanity. He'd released his brother to his squad and left because he simply did not understand the dynamics. He'd become painfully aware that Stefano's actions that evening had left a lasting impression, had in fact changed something elemental in his make-up.

"Damn!" Antonio heaved a chair against the wall. Such introspection served no purpose other than to agitate and distract him. He needed answers.

He needed to trace the energy signature gaining strength by the hour. Grabbing his cape he strode into the cool night, sniffing like a hound on a scent and opening himself to every sensation, every energy. Convinced he was correct, he turned left and strode purposefully in the direction of the Cathedral.

****

Andreas rearranged his robes, wishing fervently for a basin of water and a cloth. He despised his unclean state, the rough wool on his aching cock, the incessant throbbing in his ankle that transmitted all the way to his hip.

He glanced at the girl lying huddled on the wooden boards. He'd covered her with the nondescript woolen blanket, though it did little to stem her shivering. Too inexperienced, she'd been barely adequate for his needs. It hadn't helped that his damn sixth sense had set off incessant alarm bells that interfered with his pleasure.

It was time to return to Cosimo's palazzo. He had a suspicion events had unfolded while he'd been otherwise occupied. Fingering the stiletto he allowed himself a moment to indulge his fantasy, then shrugged and told the girl, "Stay here until morning. The prioress will come for you."

With a smile Andreas slipped out the door and turned left, hastening toward the rear stairwell that led past Monsignor's private apartments. As he rounded the corner at the end of the corridor, he stopped, curious, all senses on high alert.

I know that energy. It belongs to the Dark One. What in God's name is he doing here—in this corridor, in the middle of the night?

The only satisfactory answer was that the Demon was seeking him. And that should not be possible. All their research indicated his powers, though impressive, should have been limited. He should not be able to track others of his kind.

Andreas blended against the dank gray stonework, wrapping himself in his shadow existence. He need not venture back to the hateful stink of the warehouse district and the docks when the object of his search so conveniently stalked the lower levels of the rectory. He would wait and see what transpired.

Better yet, perhaps he could engage in some mischief. There was no time like the present to find out whether or not he could influence the Demon's powers. And he knew exactly how to go about it.

121

Antonio slipped quietly down the long hallway, masking his persona as best he could. With the scent, the energy signature, so strong, he was hard-pressed to think rationally when everything about him threatened to collapse under the overwhelming sensations. His need for answers drove him toward the narrow wooden door on his left. Cautiously he pushed it open, his cinquedea in his right hand. He had to crouch to enter the narrow room. The candle on the small table fluttered in the breeze from the door opening before settling into a steady flame.

The small figure on the plank bed stirred and rolled over. The blanket slipped to the floor leaving the figure exposed to Antonio's horrified stare. Inexplicably his groin tightened and his cock swelled as the girl spread her legs, eyes screwed shut, her face a silent plea for mercy.

"No," he breathed, "NO!"

With more effort than he thought possible, he pulled away from the temptation, seeking the source. He had felt this from Stefano, the same unbridled desires and needs and shameless urges, though this—this siren call in the black of night—came through as a perversion. He could not, would not, yield to it. He bent down and picked up the blanket, considered laying it on her supine body, then decided against approaching her for fear he would not be strong enough to resist. He tossed the cloth to the floor and backed out the door, smacking the back of his head hard on the lintel.

"God damn it." He rubbed the back of his scalp, furious. "I know you're here," he shouted down the long hallway, "come out now."

Silence greeted him, then a slow dissipation of the energy until nothing was left but for the intense gagging clutch of his throat. His face flamed with shame at what he'd been contemplating. Disgusted with himself, disgusted with the creature that stalked him, Antonio walked blindly down the hallway seeking an exit from the hell he found himself in.

The shadow on the wall wavered, then settled as Antonio raced past, exiting finally at the door leading to the rear stairwell. The clatter of his hasty climb gradually dissipated. Andreas shook himself and emerged into the dim light of the hall.

He muttered, "That was too close." The Council would need to be informed, soon. The man's powers were strong indeed, powerful enough to negate the subliminal suggestion Andreas had implanted as soon as the man had entered the chamber.

He'd been following him, and the woman, assuming one or the other would lead him to the key. But what if the Dark One was the key itself? With powers that strong, and that precise a tracking ability, there could be no other answer.

Andreas padded softly back to the cubicle, entered, then shut the door once again.

I wonder if she knows, he mused. *Has he revealed himself to you, Veluria?*

One side benefit to his brief effort at influencing the Dark One had been a glimpse into the man's convoluted thoughts. He'd gotten snippets, mere impressions, but enough to know with certainty: someone was missing, someone he cared about deeply, someone who vexed him. There could only be one person who qualified—his idiot younger brother. And if he had gone missing, probabilities suggested the meddling operative would be involved, if not the actual instigator.

He might not understand her motives, but he had to admire her initiative.

Spreading his robe he motioned for the girl to come forward on the bed. He needed to think more on the situation. And what better way than this?

"*Succhiarmi il cazo, bambina,*" he murmured with satisfaction as the girl's mouth suckled his cock.

Chapter Fourteen

Antonio hissed, "Are you certain?" He loomed over the terrified man.

Stuttering, "Ye-ye-yes, M'Lord," the man hastened to clarify, "my informant saw with his own eyes. There was no mistaking the woman. She is, um, unique, according to my source."

Satisfied he had the truth of it, he waved to his *caporal de squadra* and said, "Well, then, Marco. Show our guest to the door."

"And the reward...?"

Terrified ... and greedy.

With a sneer he said, "Marco, will you see to Sig.Vertucci's compensation?"

Marco nodded his understanding and took the man's elbow, guiding him forcefully through the rear door onto the dock where a small craft waited to escort the man back to his domicile.

Antonio paced restlessly. The man had outlived his usefulness. It would not do to have him broadcasting to all and sundry the whereabouts of the youngest of the Medici clan and the 'unique' woman keeping him company. Marco would see that the weasel had an unfortunate accident. They would do well to deal with the so-called informant directly and cut out an avaricious middleman like Vertucci.

The stray thought that his father would thoroughly approve of this decision left a sour taste in his mouth. For all that he had railed against his family's stranglehold on all their futures, in truth he accepted, even believed, that the future of Florence and the surrounding states rested squarely on the vast clan's control over critical resources and political power. The situation with Duke

Friedrich was a veritable maze of conflicting loyalties, awash with traps to ensnare the unwary and tip unstable alliances into hasty decisions that would only benefit the French.

"What news?" Cosimo limped uncertainly into the room looking quite the worse for wear. He turned rheumy eyes to his eldest and asked, "Did you find them?"

"Yes, Papà. Sit down. You look like the devil. Can I get you some wine?"

"No. Get me my son."

"I am working on it." Antonio guided his father to a stool, settled him, then pulled a chair close to him. He clasped and unclasped his hands, a nervous gesture he'd not succumbed to since his youth. "I have a thought."

"And that is…?"

"That you allow them to escape." As Cosimo reared off the stool, Antonio reached with both hands and pressed the older man back down onto the seat. "Hear me out."

"As you wish."

"Venezia is at odds with the French. We are not. Yet you persist in placing our holdings in harm's way with your pursuit of political advantage."

Cosimo half-rose off the stool, then settled once again, with a curious expression on his face. He was unaccustomed to his eldest expressing an opinion or questioning his judgment. That his son dared to do so now indicated that the situation warranted a hearing, if nothing else. Tonio banked on the fact that Cosimo would realize it cost him nothing to at least consider his thoughts on the subject.

When Cosimo seemed receptive, he continued. "I understand the need to ally our house with the Habsburgs. I have no qualms with your choice, just with forcing Stefano into this arrangement against his will. His infatuation with the French woman may or may not be permanent. Only time will tell."

"And that is your solution? Time?"

"Yes … and no. I suggest you let them run. They have contracted passage on a ship leaving for Spagna on the morning tide tomorrow. I have arranged with the captain to make several unscheduled stops along the route. That will give us enough time to put my plan in place."

"And your plan is…?"

125

"You alert Friedrich that your youngest was enticed by one of the French courtesans to join her at court in Paris. And this happened before you were able to impart the happy news about the availability of his lovely eldest daughter. Suggest to the Duke that he should meet Stefano when they disembark and escort him back to the Tyrol where he can encounter his intended."

"And the woman?"

"Leave her to me."

"Ah, I see. So Friedrich is not the only one who will be greeting my wayward son. May I assume Nico will have a role in this as well?"

Antonio smiled, "A small part to play, but yes. He is most like Stefano, speaks his language—he understands him better than either of us."

"And why this change of heart? Just yesterday you were dead set against the union. What is different now?"

"I cannot explain, Papà, but I fear an evil influence, from that woman, perhaps from another source. There is one other player I have not yet identified. I came close tonight but failed to find him. And it vexes me."

"Yes, I have felt it also. So much so that my malady cripples me. Tell me more."

"I suspect that Veluria has powers that go beyond even my own. She can control how you feel. I think she has enraptured Stefano, bewitched him … I don't know what to call it. But I can tell you I have been the victim of its powers, both from her and from this unnamed entity."

"So you now believe that sending him to Friedrich's will insulate him from that woman's powers. Why not just steal him away yourself? You have the means to hide him. Why would you agree to this arranged marriage when you feel so strongly he will be unhappy?"

"Because he has changed, Papà, changed because of me. He no longer knows himself. I fear for him. And I cannot trust him to act in his own, or our, best interests. Placing him at the Habsburg court would be like hiding him in plain sight. I would know where he is and the Duke's residence is not so far that I cannot keep an eye on him."

126

Cosimo nodded sagely, clearly impressed with his eldest's reasoning. Though convoluted, and beginning from a premise far removed from the initial justifications, the logic remained sound and the outcome potentially favorable.

"I am still curious what you plan to do with the French woman."

"Study her."

"Ah. And perhaps bring her back home to Florence? My tasks here are nearly completed. Our cousin, Guilio, the good Cardinal, returns to the Vatican as we speak. Our shipping arrangements are in order. There is nothing more to hold me in this den of pirates."

"Then I shall return home with or without her. But I promise you this ... she will no longer influence my brother."

"Just take care, Tonio. You are strong, yes. But never underestimate the powers of a woman, especially that one."

"I understand." Antonio walked to the terrace door, swung it open and waved to his man standing on the dock below the walled gardens. "I must make additional arrangements so that their escape does not appear too easy. I assume you will see to the details with the Duke?"

"Yes, and send me Luca. Unless you have need...?"

"No, good choice. I will caution him to follow your instructions to the letter. Now, until the morrow..."

"Tonio? How are you getting to Spagna?"

Antonio grimaced. "By horseback."

"But you don't like..." Cosimo objected, but his son had already vanished into the thick night.

****

Morning eased in, stifling with cloying humidity. Veluria lifted her skirts and stepped around a mound of hemp line littering the deck. She had traded her ornate gown for a simpler travel garment of finely woven silk but without the voluminous undergarments and stays. She felt pounds lighter though the fabric held the heat and was still grossly uncomfortable. Sweat trickled down her spine and beaded on her forehead. All around deckhands chattered and moved with precision, like a well-choreographed dance troupe, as the rowers carefully guided the ship away from the dock.

She was about to enter the aft cabin when shouting from the southern portion of the dockyard caught her attention. A group of five or six men, all sporting burgundy doublets and brandishing short swords raced along the dock that paralleled the extension from which their ship moved with agonizing slowness. A quartermaster and two burley dockworkers stepped into their path. Veluria tried to move toward the rail for a better look but Stefano grasped her shoulders and pulled her toward the cabin.

"My father's men," he gasped. "Get inside and stay there."

Veluria tried to object but her lover hustled out the door, shutting and locking it from the outside. The air in the tiny cabin reeked of stale rum, urine and other noxious odors. That they would have to spend possibly weeks on the vessel made her stomach churn. Worse yet, having to entertain Stefano's increasingly unappetizing requests in and out of bed gave her further pause as to the wisdom of joining him on this insane flight from his family.

Not that I had a lot of choice in the matter.

She had the gut level feeling that she had seriously miscalculated Stefano's motivations. When he had opened to her, revealing what his Demon brother had done, how it had felt, how it had triggered a host of hidden desires, she had been appalled. She vowed to save him from the Dark One's evil influence, to protect him as best she could. Running away was only one of several options, but it had the value of buying her time to work out a more permanent solution. And for all she knew, saving Stefano might be the pivotal event that reset the timeline and saved both their worlds.

The ship rocked fore and aft as if meeting swells. They must be getting underway. She heard no more shouting other than the deckhands going about their business. Stefano knocked softly, then opened the door. He grinned at her.

"Definitely father's men. They were too late. We'll be safe now, my darling."

"But how would they know to come here?"

"This is Venezia, my love. The walls have ears." Stefano pulled her toward the narrow bunk. "Now, we have all the time in the world. I have some ideas how we can spend that. Do you want to hear…?"

Veluria cringed inwardly. No, she did not want to hear. She fervently prayed for seasickness or some malady to keep her bedridden for the extent of the voyage. The best she could do was tamp down her energies so as not to feed the young man's fantasies. Though fully schooled to indulge her partner's every proclivity, she found Stefano's fixation on pain and submission personally distasteful.

Confused and wishing for guidance, Veluria fingered the talisman hidden in her bodice—her escape route, her court of last resort. She had been in this dimension less than two months yet it seemed a lifetime and she was no closer to divining the who, the what or the how that would soon impact their worlds. She wished their statisticians were wrong, but they never were. And Reverend Mother, gifted with prognostication, had foreseen something so dire that she had taken a personal interest in the selection and training of her, their most experienced operative.

She listened to Stefano's hurried explanation, thinking ... *yes I can do that thing, just this once. If I shut my eyes and imagine...*

Her mind's eye filled with the image of a giant of a man—a dangerous, dark man—frightening in his intensity. Yet his touch was gentle, his heart fragile and welcoming. He seemed to haunt her every waking moment, her every dream, her every retreat into the safe house implanted by the sisterhood to shield her from the deprecations of her male prey. He was more than just the holder of the key. He had the potential to be the key—his violence, his energies, his connections, his family—all these things made him the nexus around which the drama would unfold. And she had left him in Venice ... or had she?

Somehow he had managed to stow away in her heart, hijacking her carefully shielded feelings and giving her surcease from the sick mind of his damaged brother. She would need to find a way to rectify her mistakes before it was too late for all of them. She knew it was already too late for her.

****

Andreas leaned against the pillar next to the dock. All of his players had scattered to the four winds. The youngest brother, and he assumed the operative, had sailed that morning. The eldest had left for the mainland on a "journey of some importance" according to a chatty oarsman. The elder Medici made plans to return to Florence. Even the Cardinal had deserted the city.

For once, Andreas felt at odds with his assignment. His entire leg ached no matter how much energy he fed it. He feared he faced surgery and an extensive period of painful rehabilitation if he could not have a real medic tend to the ankle, and soon. Though he walked in a shadow existence, whatever transpired in this world affected his physical being in his own. He no longer could afford to ignore the warning signs. He would return to his dimension and report to the Council, perhaps prevail upon them to send someone else while he healed. Whatever their decision, however uncomfortable they made him, no matter how much derision he would endure, he desperately needed to let his battered body repair itself. Otherwise he, and they, had no hope of figuring out the specific threat to their timeline. He could not fix what he could not identify. And perhaps one of the scientists would have figured out how to deal with an operative from the Sisterhood. Better yet, how to get rid of her.

Andreas slipped away from the docks. No one noticed or remarked on the odd cleric with the pronounced limp, a smallish man in a cowl, head bent in silent prayer, ghosting into the shadows.

****

"I don't like it, Tonio."

"I'm not asking you to like it, Nico. But I am out of options. The Duke's men arrived a day ahead of me. They have position and we do not. We play this my way and we have a chance to secure the prize."

"And that being…?"

"The woman."

"I still don't see how sacrificing our brother is worth the price just so you can drag this tart to hell and gone to do some experiments. If she is like us, so what?"

Antonio stared down at Nico. "More than like us, brother. Much more. There are depths to this one that must be explored."

"And what happens when you are finished with her, huh? Do you go to Tyrol and rescue Stefano, bring him home? Or is he relegated to life imprisonment just so you and father can have a new toy to play with?"

The allegation that Veluria was nothing more than a plaything stung. At one level it was true, by necessity. As long as he treated her as an object, a specimen, he avoided the adolescent pining that disrupted his nights and corrupted his days with racing thoughts and yearnings. He'd never before felt such the fool. There seemed no logic he could bring to bear to change his circumstances.

Nico asked, "Tonio, are you all right?" His voice held an edge of concern. "I'm sorry. I meant no disrespect."

Tonio acknowledged the apology with a slight nod but quickly pressed to explain why he had changed his position on Stefano being under the hegemony of the Habsburg court. It had nothing to do with Cosimo's plotting and everything to do with keeping his confused sibling safe for the time being.

"Nico, you know him, you know how he shines with all that pandering and preening at the courts. He lives for that. He will adjust to his surroundings. He always has, it is *his* special gift. Without Veluria's influence, he will once more flower as the herald of Florentine culture and sophistication."

Nico roared with laughter. "Such pretty words, spoken with eloquence. Tell me, what have you done with Tonio? Fetch me my brother for I miss him sorely."

"This isn't funny, Nico. Don't make light of what has happened to Stefano. And for that I must take the blame."

"Yes, for that you must and will. And I warned you, brother, do not hurt him again. I meant it then, I mean it now."

Nico held up his wine goblet and motioned for the innkeeper for a refill. As they waited for their wine, he probed his brother discretely. Exhausted from the trip Tonio allowed the intrusion, taking no offense. But when he probed into areas that Tonio designated off-limits, even to himself, he shut down. Nico gave him a grimace of pain—the experience would have been akin to ramming his fist into a psychic stone wall: solid and secure and opaque.

"Don't bother, Nico, you can't do that anymore. I learned this from her."

And from that stranger who dared to control my actions.

His younger brother looked surprised. "Well then, perhaps you are correct. That is a useful skill. I may have need for her myself.

131

Are we going to share the bounty or must I petition Papà for my fair share?"

"Petition away, you greedy bastard. You were always into my things."

Tonio smiled indulgently at Nico—so different in looks and coloring from the rest of the clan—that most did not immediately recognize him as a Medici. That simple accident of nature often bought him valuable time and goodwill under stressful circumstances. It also made him inordinately attractive to the ladies of the Spanish courts who favored his exotic good looks and stocky build.

The innkeeper returned with wine and plates of cheese and fruits. The brothers settled in to talk of better times when all three were boys with no worries other than getting each other into trouble. When the afternoon shadows grew long, Tonio stretched and mumbled, "Time to go, Nico."

"Yes. I will take care of the dock master. No one will interfere, no one will ask questions later. Do what you have to do and I wish you Godspeed, brother. The arrangements at the coast should meet with your approval."

Nico rose from the table, leaned forward and squeezed his brother's shoulder. A short blast of energy flashed between them. Nico shuddered and backed away unsteadily, unsure of what Tonio had just fed him.

"Dolcissimo Gesù, che cosa era quella?" he husked, "what the fuck...?"

"Now I am the one who is sorry, *mio fratello*. Now you know what I know."

Mostly, but hopefully not everything.

Some things were not to be shared no matter how close he was to his brother. In any case, Nico would need quiet time in the arms of his mistress to mull over all the chaotic images and thoughts he'd just imparted. With luck, perhaps his smarter brother could sort out the jumbled mess and come up with another plan. A plan that did not involve putting his heart at risk and his youngest brother in the clutches of conniving dukes.

Tonio watched Nico exit the inn. Already he regretted involving his brother, though he'd had little choice given the few assets at his disposal. Fingering the goblet he lost himself in introspection.

Wherever he turned his world seemed on the threshold of disintegration, decisions that once could be justified with cold logic were now riddled with hidden consequences.

Who am I? Was he the man who would betray his own brother in pursuit of some nebulous greater good? Or was that betrayal based on something baser, more self-serving? He knew many like that. He just never thought he would become one of them.

Maybe the question is: *What am I?*

Antonio threw some coins on the table and stalked out the door. The inn sat two long blocks from the harbor. His men had sighted the ship carrying Stefano and Veluria out by the point. If they were correct about the wind shifts and the tide, then he could expect them to disembark before dusk. He knew the Duke's men were stationed about the wharf.

The Reichstag pretender would leave nothing to chance. Stefano was a prize well worth extra effort. The position of Friedrich's duchy in the shifting alliances of the Reichstag rested on convincing the reluctant bridegroom to accept Teutonic hospitality and provide him with heirs. With three daughters and a proven stud of impeccable pedigree, his Duchy's future would be secure.

Tonio found a narrow alleyway running crosswise to the docks where he settled in to wait, out of sight of the Duke's men. He still had time to once more examine his motives. The reasoning, the logic was sound. The outcomes reasonably predictable.

At some point he would come to terms with the fact that it was all a lie.

Chapter Fifteen

Antonio crossed to the opposite side of the narrow passageway, still keeping out of line of sight of the Duke's men stationed at all points that bottlenecked egress from the ship. He could see the gangway clearly and kept a sharp eye as it disgorged deckhands to secure lines and see to arrangements for off-loading cargo.

To his knowledge his brother and paramour were the only passengers. Angry voices from the stern caught his attention. He recognized Stefano's irritated bark, the plaintive note prominent when he was not getting his way. Tonio was surprised that the irritation was aimed solely at the tiny figure emerging from the cabin. He could not make out the words nor could he fathom from the intonation what the argument was about. Whatever it was, it appeared to be mutual.

Stefano made one last comment, then stalked down the gangway into the waiting mass of the Duke's guard. Antonio was still too far away to hear clearly, but it appeared that the captain of the guard made a strong case for his brother to accompany the group. He was shocked to see Stefano march away with nary a backward glance at the woman now standing stranded and alone at the top of the gangway.

The small figure seemed wan, tired, her hair a tangled mass of dull black strands. She moved awkwardly, stiffly, as if she'd been ill for a long time. Her energies tracked as weak and diffuse—she looked pathetic, confused and in need of a bath and a good meal.

Veluria? What the hell—?

Antonio willed patience, keeping his senses tuned to the woman while he watched his brother and the Duke's escort squad retreat toward the town center. He couldn't risk being seen by Friedrich's men—his sheer size removed any hope of anonymity and he had no wish to explain his presence and risk upsetting his plans, such as they were. Nico's intervention and assistance rested on a confluence of luck and timing—there would be no second chance.

He also knew there were other, more compelling reasons to hesitate. For all his resolve, just seeing Veluria sent his gut into a tailspin, heat flooding his groin and making him light-headed. And that had nothing to do with her using any special siren powers ... no, he seemed quite capable of driving himself mad with lust all on his own.

He approached the gangway cautiously until time seemed suspended, divorced from the frenetic movement and incessant noise of commerce. A familiar bouquet of brine and the rank odor of decay assaulted his nostrils. The wave of dock workers swept about him, giving him wide berth. With his face set in the comfort of a scowl he lifted his eyes to stare at the deck, fully expecting the woman to have bolted for the safety of her cabin.

Instead, Veluria gazed down at him and smiled shyly. She looked neither shocked nor outraged to see him standing there. In fact, a fleeting wisp of hope and relief crossed her pale features. If he didn't know better, he would have thought she was happy to see him.

The blood left his head in a rush and it took all his strength not to bolt up the gangway and sweep her into his arms.

Veluria knew she should have been surprised at seeing the Dark One but the incessant delays, the unexpected stops, all indicated that someone had paid the captain handsomely to make the voyage last as long as possible. The days, then the weeks, had devolved into a hell-on-water for her. She'd become a virtual prisoner in the cabin, a slave to Stefano's insatiable appetites. She'd acquiesced at first, then tried making excuses only to suffer his childish whining and begging. Later he'd become ever more insistent, though the demands had been playful at first, until finally turning malicious and truly hurtful. The last night of the voyage had left her beaten and nearly broken in spirit.

Antonio, waiting anxiously for her to descend to the dock, seemed a knight come to rescue her from the depths of degradation into which she had willingly plunged in performance of her duties.

135

She knew the Sisterhood could heal her battered body, but she was not so sure about her chi, her life force. That had been corrupted and distorted as she'd sought control over Stefano's wild urges and unseemly demands. Like a dam unleashed, he'd hijacked her energy for his own and turned it against her. And with each passing day, the abomination that was Stefano became a nightmare from which she'd had no escape.

All that had kept her sane was a fairy tale, a figment of her imagination—a fantasy about a demon with the soul of an angel. The gentleness she'd sensed yet never experienced gave her a reason to live, a reason to hope.

Now he was here, waiting for her. She would have run to him if she could. Instead her body finally failed her and she sank toward the deck.

Antonio watched in horror as Veluria pitched forward. He raced up the gangway and scooped her tiny body into his arms before she even hit the deck. She weighed nothing at all. Dark circles under her eyes and fine lines about her mouth spoke of some dreadful trials she'd endured during the voyage. Unconscious, her brain had shut down so he could not read her. He would need to take her someplace where he could look after her and keep her safe.

He carried his precious burden through the narrow alleys, checking frequently to make sure they were not followed. He worried when she failed to wake up. The silence, the total absence of energy, spoke of normalcy, ordinariness and he wondered if somehow she had lost her powers.

Antonio emerged from the alleyway and hastened to the carriage waiting on the other side of the narrow street. One of his men hopped down to assist his captain with the door as Antonio carefully placed Veluria onto the cushioned seat. He climbed in and made himself as comfortable as possible in the confines of the coach. He hated these conveyances as they were fashioned for passengers much smaller than himself.

Pulling Veluria onto his lap, he rocked her like a colicky infant, all the while praying she would wake up. He had not given thought to what might happen beyond this point. He'd prepared for her sparring, the hide-and-seek tease of exploring each other's powers ...

not this absence of sensation. It made her seem dead, lifeless and he feared the worse.

Nico, I need you, Brother, to give me guidance and direction.

Unfortunately he had nothing in his experience to draw on. Fate was indeed a cruel and savage mistress for until that moment, when he held Veluria in his arms, he'd had no idea how much she completed him. She filled that void he'd protected with walls and kept all but his two brothers out.

As the swaying of the coach rocked her in his arms, he wondered what it would be like to share everything with her—all his inner demons, his unformed hopes, his yearnings. Somehow he knew she would understand and look past the ugliness that ruled him to find the man he would be ... *for her.*

He glanced out the window of the coach though there was little to see. Darkness swept across the sere landscape as the coach jounced over rutted roads no better than sheep paths, the ground rock hard and unforgiving. A warm breeze wafted past the swaying curtains, brittle dry and barren. He'd given no thought to provisioning for the trip, an oversight he was already regretting. As much as a dry throat and gnawing ache in the belly was a distraction, nothing deterred his growing concern as Veluria floated in her little death, unresponsive.

Nightscapes, shadows, and phantoms were his only companions. It had always been so.

He imagined her stirring and whispered, "You are fine, Veluria. You are safe now." Antonio stroked her hair and nuzzled her brow, still damp with heat and stress.

He would not have unwittingly put her into such a state, but could he bring her out? He'd never tried that, never needed to.

The driver and his man spoke in low tones, the sounds drifting back, disjointed against the choir of hoof beats and the grinding of wheels. Though the road was unsafe for travel this late at night, he was unconcerned as he kept his senses tuned for any pending trouble. They'd be well alerted before any brigands had a chance to pounce. If it weren't for his precious cargo he would almost welcome a fight. With no answers as to why Stefano would so cavalierly desert his paramour, or why Veluria was in such a compromised state, all he had left was anger and a need to vent it.

He took a deep breath and willed himself to concentrate. Shutting out all sound he sought the spirit that had vexed and ensnared him, imagined once more the taste of her, the fleeting hint of sweetness from which he would never drink his fill.

Veluria, come back to me…

Heart racing he watched the small twitches and hitched breaths as he drew her from whatever hidden room she'd locked herself into. *He* had an impenetrable fortress that guarded his secret self, why shouldn't she?

Veluria whispered, "I prayed you would come for me. Every day, every night, in my dreams you were there for me."

Voice thick with emotion Tonio said softly, "Sleep now. I am taking us to Portugal. On my instructions, my brother will arrange passage from there to England where we have friends who can help us."

"But what of…?"

"Hush, he has gone to Friedrich's court. My father will see that he fulfills his obligations and is safe."

"But I must tell you what has happened. You must know…"

"*Non ora la mia donna bella.* Later." He already knew or suspected far too much. His guilt would weigh heavy until he put his world to rights. For now let the shadows rule. "Close your eyes and sleep. I will wake you when we arrive."

She husked, "*Gracie, amore mio,*" and sank into oblivion once more.

He would not think on her words, yet a smiled played about his lips as he stared into the night, the echo of *amore mio* caressing his heart.

****

"I can walk. I'm feeling better now." Veluria stood with one foot on the step, both hands braced against the door jambs of the coach. She looked pathetic—her skirts were wrinkled and filthy, the usually neat braids loose with strands of lank hair plastered against her neck and face.

She glared at him, stubbornly insisting on having her way. She repeated, "I can walk. I don't need *your* help."

138

He smiled to himself. *Someone got up on the wrong side of the coach this morning.*

Tonio leaned in close and snarled, "And I can carry you. You are too weak from the voyage and..." he paused for effect, "...I haven't got all day."

The words came out a little harsher than intended. Antonio was accustomed to giving commands and to having his orders followed. While his head suggested this approach might be counter-productive, instinct told him otherwise.

Without further ado, he swept her into his arms and stalked to the inn, his man and the driver wisely choosing to busy themselves with the horses.

You aren't the only one in a mood this morning, M'lady.

The innkeeper led them up the rear stairwell to a suite of rooms, small but well-tended and very private. He pushed open the door and allowed Antonio to sweep into the sitting room still carrying the now squirming Veluria. With a smile the innkeeper gently closed the door and padded back down the stairs to see to a meal and hot water for a bath for his guests.

Antonio set his burden down on the large feather bed. A colorful quilt in a gold and green Moorish pattern lay folded at the foot of the thick mattress.

Veluria sighed as she sank into the plush softness, as well she should. Ship's bunks were hard as rocks and every lift on a swell or savage thrust into a trough rattled the joints and loosened teeth. He was not a fan of being cooped up in a cabin, seeking out, instead, a hammock below deck that would accommodate his unusual size. She would not have been accorded that option.

The urge to demand *what happened* surged strongly but now was not the time. He stood next to the bed, watching the satisfaction flit across her face, and taking enjoyment from knowing she could still find joy in simple pleasures.

Even more than learning what had transpired during the voyage he longed to hold her and coddle her—to talk with her and to plan their next moves—but knew she would want to clean up first.

At the soft knock he called out, "Come in." Two young woman carrying buckets of heated water shyly skittered past into the next chamber. The sound of water sloshing roused Veluria who looked with rapturous eyes at her captor.

139

"Is that what I think it is?" she gasped.

The young girls sidled past with one muttering, "It's filled, sir, call if you need more."

Antonio helped Veluria off the bed. She swayed slightly forcing him to steady her.

"I think you need my services one more time, Madame." With that he scooped her up and carried her into the bath chamber. The steam from the tub filled the room, releasing a subtle fragrance from the herbs sprinkled onto the surface of the water. Antonio set Veluria down and stepped away to give her privacy.

"No, wait. Please."

Curious, Antonio returned to stand close by as she spun around and patted her shoulder. "Please, the buttons. I cannot reach them myself."

He felt a frisson of excitement course through his groin. Anxiously he fumbled with the tiny buttons, his hands far too large and clumsy for the task. It seemed amazingly sensual, this simple effort, while the waiflike figure stood with her neck bent forward, as if inviting him to nuzzle and explore with his tongue. In his mind's eye he tore the offending fabric off her slim form. Instead, he took a deep breath, finished his task, then slid the sleeves down her arms, allowing a small pause to tease her fingers. Her chemise was stained and torn and he could guess his brother had had a hand in that. After he slipped the bit of fabric off to puddle on the floor in a dirty heap, he stepped back, prepared to admire the view.

What he was not prepared for was the bruising on her back and shoulders, and the fine white lines from a beating with a willow stick radiating out from her buttocks.

Furious, he grabbed her shoulders and spun her around. She stood before him, face flaming from shame, begging him to look away, but he could not take his eyes off her. That his brother would be the one to damage something so frail and beautiful went beyond his comprehension. He had sensed Stefano's descent into depravity but to see it for himself, to have it confirmed so graphically, tore him in two.

With hot fury like an anvil strike in his chest, he resisted the urge to pound his fists against something, anything. Murmuring low in his throat, he moaned, *not now, not now, not now.*

Carefully he picked Veluria up and set her into the warm water. He found a soft cloth and lye soap and gently set to cleaning her hands, then her arms and neck. Her small breasts bobbed enticingly and his mouth watered with the desire to suckle and pinch the perfect nipples. Fearing he would go too far, he stood and held out the soap and cloth.

"Don't stop. Please. I want you to do it." Veluria laid her head against the edge of the tub and sighed once more, "...please."

His heart pounding, Antonio knelt at the edge of the tub and lathered the cloth. He ordered her to stand up but had to help her as she was still too weak to do much on her own. Blanking his mind, he quickly set about his task, cleaning away weeks of grime and things he had no wish to think on.

Gently settling her back into the tub, he instructed, "Tilt your head so I can wash your hair."

Veluria sighed, "Oh thank you." Then, as if to apologize, she said, "There were no combs or brushes..."

Antonio took his time; but when he felt the water cooling, he lifted her out of the tub and wrapped her in a large woolen blanket. He rubbed her hair vigorously, attempting to dry it, but ended up making it more tangled than ever. Veluria laughed sadly and touched his hands to stop.

A lightning bolt of energy coursed up his arms, then down his torso. She felt it too—he could trace the path of the energy, first centering in her belly and spreading to her thighs, leaving her unsteady and grasping his arms as she mouthed a strangled "Oh". The vibrations set every nerve alight and threatened to bring both of them to their knees.

Antonio moaned, "I'm sorry. I didn't mean to do that."

Veluria gasped, "I will be fine. Just, please, not like that. Not yet." He had no idea what she meant. Before he could ask for an explanation, she hurried on, "I'm afraid you are right. I am still weak."

"Let me put you to bed. You need to rest." With that he lifted her easily and carried her into the bedchambers where he placed her on the bed and covered her with the quilt.

He avoided touching her as he feared sending another energy surge. It had been an unconscious act, his body reacting to hers, to the ache in his groin and the throb of his now swollen cock. That it came from him, not from her, caused him some consternation. He'd *never* had this reaction to any woman. Had he been right about her, had she touched that sacred inner core that he kept hidden from everyone, even himself?

He would need to distance himself, not so much fearing she would breach his defenses but that he could do her harm. That was something he could not bear.

He said, "Rest for now," and turned to leave.

The last thing Veluria wanted was for the man she called a demon to leave her side. Without him close she was vulnerable—from without and within.

She pleaded, "Don't leave, Tonio. Please. Lie with me. I need to be held tonight."

Veluria moved over to make room for the man who would own her heart, praying he could overcome his own deep-seated fears. To her surprise he quickly stripped his clothes and slid next to her, wrapping her in his strong arms and clutching her with a desperation borne of years of longing.

Veluria admired the restraint, the consideration, as he held her close. She knew in her bones that he struggled not to let his hands wander, keeping his needs contained so as not to inflict any more damage than her battered body had already sustained. She wished he would lose that struggle. She wanted his hands to pinch and fondle and seek out her secret places.

She could compel him, unleash her special talent as the Reverend Mother would say, but she did not want him under false pretenses. She craved authenticity, a term in currency in her timeline, as so much of her culture rested on artifice that the inner being seemed somehow hollow, a mere shadow of itself. Not unlike now, she realized with a start. It was no wonder the Sisterhood chose her for this assignment. She was the penultimate mask, a pure construct, a reflection of the world in which she existed for the briefest of moments.

Lies, deceit, and misdirection—she existed as a puppet in the service of the greater good. No different than the man of cruelty and violence cradling her with such tenderness, a man who danced to the demands of family and country, eschewing his own needs, burying them so deep it required alien powers—hers—to release the sensual man. It made their bond unique and desperately tenuous. Neither would falter in their chosen path, neither would sacrifice that which they held so dear. She understood that the Dark One's path and hers intersected at a single moment in time. He did not have her perspective, could not possibly understand the stakes, yet she knew that, for now, their futures were linked.

She and the Sisterhood had been wrong. They had set her to search for an artifact, a device, something concrete, real. She had indeed found what she sought, though she still struggled to understand the why and the how. The way forward was couched in mist, indistinct, but the man next to her was more real than anything had ever been in her shadow existence. Joined now, they hurtled toward some cataclysmic event that could disrupt both their worlds.

As she drifted into dreamless sleep she thought of castles in the sand and an in-rushing tide, and all of them powerless to stop its advance. She prayed for guidance, some hint at the future, but the only clue was that the lock on her heart had been breached.

She knew only one certainty: Antonio de' Medici was the key.

Chapter Sixteen

Antonio drew the frail form close, reveling in the warmth and clean scent, the tangle of hair soft as velvet on his chest. He trembled at the arrhythmic pulsing of her energies, and an erratic heartbeat that so mirrored his own. He wished for nothing more than to plunge into her depths, to fill her, plunder and ravage and claim her for his own. He knew how to take with violence, how to master and control yet his very core fought against his nature, cautioned him to exercise restraint. She would not be conquered or owned or manipulated. Veluria would require that which he gave to only two others: his heart and his soul. That neither seemed worthy of her he was in no doubt, but it was all he had to offer.

Filling his senses with her essence, he understood the conflict and uncertainty coursing through her mind. He shared the confusion, the sense that they existed in some time out of place, in a shadow world where reality and its reflections switched places randomly, and by some miracle he and she had ended up sharing a piece of that reality. That it would not last, that events would conspire to drive each of them back into the worlds that spawned them, on this he could wager his family's fortune. But he was not a betting man, and he was no longer willing to forego his own desires. He had finally found that missing bit to his soul, lying next to him, curled against him in sweet slumber. Tonio knew—*knew*—this would turn his world upside down and inside out. And it didn't matter. He would let his essential nature, his Demon half, do whatever was necessary to hold onto this most precious thing in his life.

He passed the long hours shrouded in mist, neither asleep nor awake, gathering his reserves. He sensed the catastrophe awaiting them, its outlines still faint. Much depended on their decisions made in the light of day, the multiple paths diverging, each leading to an uncertain destination, all fraught with peril. This was unfamiliar territory for him—this internal debate. Unlike Cosimo who seemed to relish the mental exercise of what ifs, he avoided that quagmire of plots and counter-plots by favoring a simpler approach ... but not this night.

Reluctantly he pushed the conflicting images and demands to the background. He would let matters take their own course. In the interim he would guard his woman and keep her safe. He would deal with the future if and when it emerged from the shadows.

The cool light of dawn filtered through filmy gauze curtains—accompanied by the distant sound of birdsong and activity in the courtyard below—punched through Antonio's consciousness. He had finally slept despite his best intentions. Veluria still lay curled in his arms.

"M'lady? It is time." Antonio murmured in her ear.

Veluria stretched and turned over, a smile lighting her face, her dark eyes flecked with gold and crinkled with mirth.

"M'lady? You dare to call me M'lady?" She snorted and slapped his chest, leaving a red mark that tingled and burned and fired his lust to red hot.

"I believe it is a sign of respect ... *mia donna*." Antonio leered as he fingered where her touch had lit the torch that threatened to explode in a conflagration he would not, could not, control.

"I think perhaps you show too much respect, *signore*."

He felt his face flame, half embarrassed at the banter—something he rarely engaged in, even with his brothers, most certainly never with a woman. He had no idea how to proceed. Getting it right, pleasing her, pleasuring her had taken on such import he hesitated to touch her intimately. Despite his experience he was unschooled in the niceties of lovemaking, accustomed only to relieving his itch with a minimum of fuss.

How would he compare to Stefano, assuredly the most accomplished of them all? Would she...?

With a start he realized Veluria had withdrawn from his embrace, the coverlet pulled to her chin despite the balmy breeze filtering through the narrow window. She gazed at the ceiling with a blank stare. A cold emptiness replaced the warmth of her presence. She had shut down, shut him out.

What happened? Mio dio, cosa ho? What have I done?

Veluria had more than closed an imaginary door, she'd locked herself away in a cell, leaving a residual wash of thinly veiled disgust and distaste. He prayed he was mistaken but his powers were such that he was seldom wrong. No, she had looked into his soul and found him wanting. He had feared how she would react when he revealed his more vile nature. He should have known better.

I guess the Demon got what he deserved.

Antonio slipped from the bed and gathered his clothes lying scattered about the rough wood floor. Angry at her, angry at himself, he dressed quickly and stalked to the door.

Keeping his voice carefully neutral, he said, "I will see to a light repast. When I return, we shall discuss our next steps." He did not wait for a response.

Tonio bounded down the stairs and entered the main part of the tavern. The driver and Mario lounged in a far corner looking slightly the worse for wear. While he'd been playing the adolescent with a full blown crush, they'd apparently amused themselves with the inn's wine … and likely female companionship. He'd have been better served to have joined *them* rather than give in to his foolish whims.

He slid onto the bench next to the driver, his face set in a scowl dark enough to make the men cringe. Mario was more accustomed to his moods so he simply nodded and leaned against the stuccoed wall, looking resigned to his fate. The driver opted to bolt for the door, muttering he needed to see to the horses. With an unsteady gait, the burly man made for the rear entrance to the taberna and disappeared from view.

The innkeeper approached and inquired, "What may I get for you and the lady, *senhor*?"

His temper getting shorter by the minute he growled, "I don't give a fu—" but caught himself when Mario gave him a strange look. He took a deep breath and said, "Whatever you have," then waved the man off.

With unctuous concern for his guest's comfort, the innkeeper pressed, "And for you, *senhor*?"

Tonio gritted his teeth and hissed, "Nothing." The man took the hint and turned to go.

Tonio called out, "Wait."

"*Senhor?*"

"I shall require other accommodations." He had both men's undivided attention. Hastening to clarify he said, "For myself. The *senhora* will stay in her quarters upstairs."

The innkeeper stumbled over his words, "I-I-I am sorry, *senhor*. This is but a humble establishment. We have no other..."

Tonio interrupted, "Fine, I will use," he waved in the direction of his corporal, "his space."

The innkeeper shrugged and mumbled, "As you wish," and left.

Mario stared at him in confusion for a moment, then said, "I will move to the stables. The weather suits."

Tonio was aware that the 'stables' were nothing more than a lean-to shelter, normal for these dry climes. However, Mario would not be so inconvenienced since he had an errand for the man that would take him back to Spagna and away from witnessing his further humiliation.

"I need for you to take a message to my brother, Nicolo, in the Albayzín." Mario raised his eyebrows but listened attentively. "Tell him..." he paused and thought furiously that he was about to make a monumental mistake, but rushed on, "...tell him we will not require transport to England."

"Sir?"

"See if the innkeeper can secure a mount. I need for you to make best time."

"What then, Commander?"

What then, indeed. He had no idea. From a ridiculous lovesick fantasy, he'd been cast once more into the role of safeguarding Medici interests above all else. Interests which were no longer clear.

He should have known better than to let her in. He was the biggest kind of fool. She'd seen into his black heart and been so filled with disgust, she'd ... what? Denied him? It was more than that yet he could not explain the devastation to his soul. Yes, even with all his avowal of having been born without one, the truth of the matter was that he *did* have a soul—a dark desperate entity that filled him with purpose. He wished to God it were different.

With a sigh he answered Mario's question. "Go home, Mario. Just go home." He handed the man a pouch filled with coins. "This should be sufficient to book passage on a merchant vessel back to

Roma. Father will have returned to Florence. Join him there and do his bidding as you would do mine."

"But, sir, what about you and the woman?"

"Do not concern yourself." He spoke firmly yet Mario still looked ready to protest. He clearly did not wish to leave his commander alone in a strange country without protection. One thing about his people—they were intensely loyal to him and his house.

He spoke softly, almost to himself, "We'll be fine, Corporal. There are tasks best done away from all distractions." He looked around the rustic tavern and shrugged. "This will suit for now."

Mario rose and saluted his commander with the ancient Roman fist to breast. Once more he said, "Sir," and turned to leave.

Tonio watched his man exit the taberna and murmured, "Godspeed, Mario."

The innkeeper's serving maid came to the table and waited for him to notice her. She was not terribly attractive—Nico might have used the word 'slovenly'—but her curvaceous hips and bounteous breasts reminded him that he still had an itch to scratch. Letting his eyes travel slowly over the woman, from head to toe and back again, he felt his cock thicken in anticipation. He'd been prepared to seek solace beyond prying eyes and see to his needs, but this opportunity was too good to pass up.

Pushing away from the table he rose to his full height, enjoying the small gasp and admiring stare as the wench's eyes zeroed in on his straining codpiece. She winked and indicated he should follow her. The innkeeper looked on with avarice in his eyes, no doubt tallying up a suitable charge for the additional 'services' being provided.

Following the sway of ample hips, he sighed with regret as she led him to a small copse of trees nestled in a gully behind the taberna. There would be no soft feather bed for this coupling, no satiny skin and a delicious scent of honey and lavender, no sizzle of nerves when their energies twisted and twined in a mad dance of lust. There would be no Veluria.

With a grimace, Tonio watched as the wench lifted her skirts and pirouetted for his benefit, singsonging, "*Você gosta do que vê, senhor?*" Sidling up close she bent her head back and licked her lips.

No, I don't like what I see. Dear God, I can't do this, not with this foul creature.

Before he could move away, the wench settled to her knees and quickly unbuttoned the codpiece, exposing his raging erection to her eager mouth. She tongued the tip then followed the vein to the base and back, her thick fingers squeezing his balls until he gasped.

It was too much. He needed release, his baser nature demanded it. Bracing against a tree trunk he thrust his hips, driving his thick length deep into her throat, again and again until his blood threatened to boil and he came on a roar.

Weak in the knees he allowed himself to sink to the ground next to the woman who was arranging her skirts and preparing to leave.

He grasped her arm and hissed, "No, *senhora*. I am not finished with you."

The woman grinned and slid the peasant blouse down, revealing heavy bulbous breasts. Palming a generous mound of flesh, she flicked at the thick brown nipple until it hardened. Antonio groaned as his cock responded.

How much is this going to cost me?

He knew the answer ... and convinced himself he didn't care.

****

Veluria's pulse raced at the knock on the door. She quaked with dread at seeing Antonio so soon after her retreat to her safe place. It had been sudden and unexpected ... and had nothing to do with him and everything to do with the abuse she'd suffered at the hands of his depraved younger brother. All he'd done was *think* of Stefano—it had set off a chain reaction of terror, loathing and panic that sent her fleeing in desperation away from all memory of the suffering the pervert had inflicted on her body and her mind.

The tapping came again, insistent. She realized that Antonio would not bother to politely knock so it was likely a maid servant bringing her breakfast.

She called out, "Come in."

A heavy set woman in her early thirties pushed through the door. She braced a basket with fruit, cheese and dried meats on her hip.

"*Senhora*? Where do you wish...?"

Veluria waved to a small round table in a corner of the room. "Over there, *por favor*." When the woman set the basket down, Veluria asked, "Could you assist me? The buttons..."

149

The woman nodded and made quick work of securing the bodice. When she finished she asked, "Is there anything else, *senhora*?"

"No, thank you." Before the woman could leave she said quickly, "Wait, there is one thing. Could you tell—" She was about to say Antonio's name but choked it back, not because saying it out loud cut her like a knife, but because they were in a strange country with potential enemies all about. Anonymity seemed prudent. She continued, "Please tell my gentleman friend that I do not wish to be disturbed."

The maid gave her an odd smile and mumbled, "*Sim, senhora*," and left her to deal with her troubled thoughts.

Food was the last thing on her mind but she forced herself to nibble at the fruit, the tang of the orange and the burst of sweetness enough to jump start her appetite. She couldn't remember the last time she'd eaten. She carefully removed the stiletto from its niche in her skirt and sliced bits of cheese and what looked like a savory sausage. Other than the bed and the small table there were no other pieces of furniture in the room. She gathered a handful of nibbles and sank onto the bed to mull over what she must do next.

That was almost enough to undo her again. Antonio's huge body had cradled her with such exquisite gentleness that she'd allowed his probing, knowing it to be a gift he offered her—a glimpse into the inner man. In one fell swoop, she'd violated all her training, set aside every tenet, every precept to which she'd sworn fealty.

It was impossible to know precisely how Antonio interpreted the secrets she'd shared, but she knew for a fact that he understood them to be outside of time and space as he understood the concepts. He'd cast an image of a shadow existence—his way of making sense of something that would be alien to everything he knew about his world. He recognized the potential for catastrophe without understanding the consequences. And the thing that terrified her was his awareness that their situation, their relationship, was forbidden, that they were fated to return to their own worlds. But Tonio refused to accept that fate, vowing to do whatever was necessary to keep his heart's desire. For the first time in his life the Demon wanted something for himself alone. Something he never had before—a woman to love.

Me. He wants me.

The thought filled her with elation and sorrow. They were more than simple star-crossed lovers, they were figments of each other's imaginations, living in a castle built on sand. And the inexorable incoming tide would sweep that shaky edifice out to sea, taking hearts and souls with it.

The Sisterhood would see to her cleansing and she would bury the memory and move on to serve and protect, for that was their way. Antonio de' Medici had no such safety net. He would remain in this world, a shell of a man, stripped of his humanity. There would be nothing left to temper the violence and brutality.

Have I created the monster? If Antonio is indeed the key, is my presence here the trigger that will release the hell on earth that will reverberate through all time and space?

She trembled and sobbed, "What have I done, dear Reverend Mother, what have I done?"

Chapter Seventeen

Antonio leaned against the stuccoed wall, grateful for the hint of cool against his shoulders. The heat of the day, and his exertions—he grimaced in remembrance—had left him drenched in sweat and foul of temper.

So much for relieving an itch.

"*Senhor*?" The innkeeper advanced warily, the flagon extended with unsure hands. He gave a slight gasp as Antonio ripped the jug from the terrified man's hands and drained it.

"More," Tonio growled and threw the jug against the far wall. He was deep in his cups as Nico would say and he didn't give a shit.

The taberna's resident whore gave him a wide berth as she set about preparing for serving the evening's meal. With dissatisfaction he observed her shuffling movements, her discomfort evident. He'd been merciless in his demands—on her body and his own—but nothing sated the hunger that sat heavy in his gut, a hunger that grew with every passing hour.

Idly he wondered how Veluria had spent her day while he'd fucked himself into a stupor. Why did he even care? She was nothing more than a commodity now, something he would take home to Cosimo for his father's research.

Ah, research, is that what it was? What exactly did they research, what did they wish to discover? What kind of secrets could a siren possibly hold other than a singular gift for grabbing a man by the balls and twisting until he surrendered his heart *and* his soul, burying him forever in lust and desire.

Well, no need to worry about that—she'd slammed that door in his face. But he was not without the means to self-destruct. Not at all. Now he could drown himself instead.

Well, Nico, what do you think, my brother? Do you approve of my solution? You warned me, didn't you? I should have listened.

Another flagon appeared at his elbow.

"This is a fine vintage," he announced to the empty room and tilted the vessel to admire the rich red color.

Research was it? Well, I can do research. I don't need to wait for Cosimo to work his magic. I have magic of my own. If the Frenchwoman has secrets then I damn well will be the one to dig them out of her traitorous head.

Draining the wine, he let the flask slip to the scarred wood floor where it bounced on the rushes and came to rest out of sight. Antonio pushed the heavy table away and rose awkwardly, his head swimming.

Somewhere to his right he heard, 'Senhor, are you ill?' but the words echoed and retreated so quickly he could not be sure if someone spoke or he'd imagined it.

With uncertain steps he staggered toward the door but halted as an influx of patrons barged through, chittering and laughing uproariously at something one of their party had said. The raucous noise set every nerve on high alert. With a sideways glance, the leader of the group side-stepped past him and led his friends to the rear of the small establishment.

Something about the man seemed familiar but he wasn't able to think clearly enough to remember.

With his head threatening to explode, he needed to find silence away from the din and the candlelight that sent shards of pain through his eyeballs. Mario's quarters were in the rear of the taberna but not out of earshot. He didn't relish taking refuge in the stables but his choices were limited. Unless…

"*Desculpe-me, senhor,*" the serving woman husked as she brushed past him carrying a basket with a bit of cloth hiding the contents. She reached for the door latch but he managed to get to it first.

The tang of fresh fruit and the sharp bite of cheese assaulted his nostrils. The whore'd been tasked with taking an evening repast to their guest. How convenient.

Tonio blocked the woman's way and held out his hand, secretly pleased it remained steady while all about him images and sound swirled in a dizzying dance that set his gut reeling.

"*Senhor*, I must..."

Tonio grasped her wrist with his right hand and pinched it tight until she relinquished her burden with a gasp of pain. He felt the familiar sensations wash through him ... power followed by an emptiness he could not fathom, nor explain.

This woman is not your enemy. Do not give in to what they wish to make of you. Make your own future, Tonio.

Nico's words ... or his own? What did it matter? He had the excuse he needed.

"This is for the *senhora*?" It was more a statement than a question.

The whore nodded and rubbed at her wrist absently as she backed away, her heavy breasts bobbing with each mincing backwards step. His cock seemed to appreciate the show, rising to the occasion and pressing against the codpiece with lustful insistence. The woman's eyes widened with dismay, obviously remembering when he'd said, "That will do ... for now," and slipped coins into her pudgy hands.

With a feral grin, he staggered through the door and made his way to the outer stairs leading to the second floor suite of rooms. With no memory of climbing the rickety steps, he paused on the narrow landing with the basket clutched to his waist.

What the hell am I doing here? This isn't right.

Before he could set the basket down and beat a hasty retreat, the door opened. Veluria stood framed in the backwash of candlelight, her features masked in darkness. It was like staring down a well—a bottomless chasm that would trap him for an eternity.

There was no barricade in place, no wall against which he could bash his head in a fruitless attempt to gain access. She was just standing there, soft and welcoming, ripe for the plucking. There would have been nothing to stop him had he not rendered himself impotent with his indulgence in drink ... and other things.

Feeling the fool, he thrust the basket toward the woman and muttered, "Your dinner." The words came out slurred and he was vaguely surprised she didn't turn away given the state of his foul breath and stink of sweat and sex that permeated his pores.

154

Veluria stood as if mesmerized. He said, "I-I'm s-s-sorry..." and stumbled back still clutching the parcel of food.

Rousted from her trance at the prospect of Antonio tumbling headlong down the steep flight of steps, Veluria grabbed his jerkin and pulled him through the door into the sleeping quarters. The mountain of a man lurched forward and staggered to the bed. He set the basket down and rested his head against the bedpost, his body swaying.

Muttering, "Drunk as a skunk," Veluria rushed to the bed to retrieve the basket before Tonio collapsed on top of it. She could feel the stabbing pain in his head—he was broadcasting like a vidfeed set to ear-bleeding volume in her skull. A migraine. Of earth-shattering proportions, and not the first he'd ever had, though it might be the worst. She'd had no idea he suffered from that condition.

She was also too aware of other things assaulting her senses. Keenly aware. When she'd given in to curiosity and probed for his whereabouts, she been privy to his insatiable rutting to the point where she'd nearly succumbed to an out-of-control orgasm.

She'd felt an odd mixture of jealously and awe. Jealous that he was fucking someone, not her. Awed because he had so much ... stamina. That the sex had been filled with anger and self-loathing hadn't registered right away but when it finally floated to the surface, waves of guilt and anxiety nearly consumed her. It had taken all her control to not rush out to find him, to make him stop. To make him tear *her* clothes off and impale *her*, to fill *her* with his seed. Over and over and over...

Gods above, it had been a long afternoon. An exhausting afternoon. Now this. She could barely control her reflexes as she approached the Demon.

I can't let him in. It's too dangerous for him to know what I know. He has no capacity for this knowledge, no framework to make sense of it. It would destroy him, drive him insane.

And me along with it. I am too close to this. Forgive me, Reverend Mother. I cannot use my skills. Not on this man. Not now. Not ever.

The Demon tempts me as have no others. Give me strength, Dearest Mother, for I must break my heart as well as his. I have no choice.

I love him too much.

With her nose wrinkling in disgust, she hissed, "You stink."

Antonio sneered back, "You have a gift for the obvious, M'lady."

"Why are you here?"

Tonio thought about that—confusion, guilt, and a dozen other emotions flitting across his stern features. Despite his drunken state, he apparently did not suffer from performance anxiety given the bulge in the codpiece. He glanced down at his arousal, the look of consternation almost funny had the situation—and her struggle for resolve—not been so vexing.

Bemused he gave her a pleading look then wiped his face into the characteristic scowl, eyebrows drawn into a tight line that accentuated the pulse hammering his temple.

She tapped her foot as if expecting an answer to her question. She hoped it would distract him, but from what she wasn't sure. When he simply squeezed his eyes shut against the pyrotechnics assaulting his optical nerves, she took pity on him.

"I can help you with that." He shook his head, not understanding. "The headache. I can ease the pain."

Dear Mother, that's exactly what she should *not* do! But she couldn't allow him to suffer so harshly, not when she was partially to blame.

"Antonio, please sit," she said softly, keeping her tone low and soothing. She knew all too well how the tiniest sound would take on monumental proportions, ringing like a klaxon inside the head. Ears, eyes, chest, gut—every system in the body became compromised and slave to the agony. She prayed she could get him stabilized enough to avoid the vomiting that was sure to follow. Instead of the usual swarthy complexion, his face had paled to a translucent, waxy quality.

Not for the first time she wondered how a man with such rough features could be even remotely handsome, yet he was—his dark eyes limned with heavy lashes, the severe cut to his cheekbones, the square jaw softened by the black stubble and a jagged thin scar running from his chin almost to his left ear. Straight dark brown hair hung loose about his face. She longed to brush it aside so she could observe his features more closely. She had a need to study every plane, every imperfection—to commit each one to memory.

Shaking herself free of her fanciful musings, Veluria took Antonio's arm and gently backed him to the bed, forcing him to sit. The movement caused a grunt of pain and another grimace. She was surprised he permitted her to see him so vulnerable. The Demon de' Medici she'd first met would never have allowed her such intimacy.

Tonio inhaled a sharp breath and braced his arms against the comforter. "I need to go," he hissed but made no move to do so.

She suspected he was past the point of having conscious control over his body. The migraine had him in its clutches and would not so easily be banished by sheer force of will. That he still tried was impressive enough.

"Hush. Stay where you are."

She gently nudged his thighs apart, the action causing the wool codpiece to tighten across his erection, though he seemed not to notice. She blushed to think *she* did. His arousal should be the least of her concerns yet it seemed to hold her undivided attention.

She quickly loosened the ties on the jerkin and slipped it off his shoulders. With effort he lifted one hand, then the other off the bed so she could slide the vest out of the way. The room was stuffy and warm, the upper floor still retaining the heat of the day. His brow and upper lip were beaded with sweat. She needed to cool him off.

He complained, "The light..."

"Yes, I know, but I need to see what I'm doing." She paused and pulled his shirt free and tugged it over his head. "You're too hot. This will help."

Even though he was sitting on the bed, the man was so massive he still towered over her. She gazed with admiration at the broad chest sprinkled with dark hair lightly peppered with gray. For some reason she'd never given thought to his age. Cosimo was in his sixties, though still virile. That would put Antonio in his mid-to-late thirties. In that time, no longer considered a young man. But he had the build of a Greek god with rock hard abs and bulges and grooves that begged for her tongue to explore...

Oh my dear sweet Lord.

She felt the probe before she saw the slight smile, a lopsided uptick to his lip. Through gritted teeth he asked, "Do you like what you see?"

"No." *Most definitely yes.* "Just be still and keep your eyes closed. I'm going to massage your temples, neck and shoulders."

As she worked efficiently across all his chi points, she could see him visibly relax into her hands. Without suitable pharmaceuticals, or use of her powers, the best she could do was alleviate some of the worst of the discomfort. If he could sleep without the interruption of pain, his body would take care of the rest.

Tonio gave a grunt of pain as she applied her thumbs to pressure points inflamed and ultra-sensitive to touch. She'd bypassed the bits about how much it might hurt to make it better. She was no empath but even so she could feel the tension flowing through her fingers to dissipate harmlessly through her system.

She would take it all from him if she could.

Antonio felt the first flush of relief followed by a biting sting, like someone rammed a stiletto through his eyeball, again and again.

Caro Gesù dolce, she is killing me!

Without thinking he grasped her waist and held on for dear life, fighting through the pain. Somehow, without using her powers, she drew the noxious vapors from his body into her own. How she could bear the vile stranglehold on her system, he had no idea. He knew her to be strong, but this ... this was unexpected.

Why would she do this thing for him? She knew him for the loathsome creature he was—a hideous parody of humanity, without a soul, beyond redemption. She'd taken his measure and found him wanting. Yet still, she did this act of mercy.

Would she have done this kindness had she known about his betrayal, his mindless fucking of the whore? But what was there to betray? They were not bonded, he had no claim to her, she had none to him. Not now.

With a perversion borne of his pain and the ache in his heart, he opened to her, flooding her senses with his lust as he loosed his seed countless times, replacing the image of the coarse whore with Veluria's fragile form.

She tensed and choked out, "Stop it, Tonio, stop!"

Her tiny hands gripped his neck, but were too small to circle it. Instead she pressed both thumbs against his windpipe, cutting off his air. He could have thrown her across the room, but the pressure, the denial of air to his starved lungs, made his cock tighten, so hard it turned painful. Hips thrusting he forced the rough fabric to rub seductively along its swollen length. He was close, so very close.

"Stefano, stop!" She moaned, then dropped her hands and backed away, eyes bright with tears.

Fuck fuck fuck. What have I done?

Veluria was backing to the door, confusion and despair turning her beautiful face into a picture of agony he would not soon forget. Before she could turn and bolt, he stumbled toward her, his head splitting in two. He must not allow her to leave, he had to explain his feelings, he had to say the words.

Gathering Veluria close, he murmured, "I am not Stefano. I will never hurt you." He rubbed a cheek against her blue-black hair, leaving a streak of moisture.

Dear God, what is this? Am I crying?

He'd never cried in his entire life. He had to convince her that he meant her no harm, that he would protect her with his life. He would not ask for her affections in return for he was unworthy, but she must know this one thing in his heart.

Antonio tilted Veluria's chin so that he could look into the fathomless depths of her soul, opening himself completely.

Veluria protested, "Tonio, no, don't do this! It's too dangerous."

Dangerous? She had no idea.

He held her by the shoulders in a death grip, pouring all his power into her terrified eyes, until he stood naked, completely exposed. Releasing her he backed toward the bed, leaving her fragile body to sway unsteadily.

Fists clasping and unclasping, he struggled to find the words that would send her away, that would confine him for all eternity to a shadow existence. He'd once accepted being condemned to a lifetime of being alone. That seemed a small sacrifice now. For her he would be willing to endure hell itself.

With a heavy heart he said quietly, "I love you." Turning away, he spoke the words waiting to rip him asunder, "You are free to go."

"No."

Spinning to face her, unsure he'd heard it correctly, he sputtered, "Wha—?"

Shrugging, Veluria gave him a weak smile. With blood pounding in his veins so hard he heard nothing but hope, saw nothing but desire, breathed nothing but her scent of honey and lavender.

With a whisper she sealed their fates forever, "I love you too."

159

Chapter Eighteen

Andreas twitched as the electrodes pulsed with healing energy.

"Sit still, man. You're not helping." The medic glared and returned to twiddling knobs and consulting the machine's readouts.

That was easier said than done. After the shamans pronounced him unfit for duty, he'd been confined to headquarters for 'debriefing'. More like the Spanish Inquisition, sans robes and religious fervor.

"That's all for today, Marcus." The voice came from the private elevator located at the rear of the boardroom. "Let the tissue heal of its own accord."

"But, Your Holiness..." the medic objected, but hastily reconsidered when the prelate entered the room, his face set in a harsh frown. With alacrity, he removed the electrodes—leaving sticky residue on Andreas ankle—and packed away the leads and instrument detritus.

Neither Andreas nor Matteo heard the medic leave.

"So, Andreas, are you ready to tell me about this cock-up of yours?"

"Not really," Andreas muttered, "but I guess I'm not getting a choice, am I?"

"Better me than the full Council, boy." The tall man indicated that Andreas join him at the seating area near the broad expanse of plexiglass overlooking the city. He watched his acolyte limp painfully, concern briefly replacing the scowl.

At the Reverend's 'can you manage', Andreas simply nodded and settled into the plush leather recliner with a grateful sigh. Matteo slid an ottoman close to the chair and helped Andreas lift his aching leg to settle it on a stack of pillows.

The shamans had buzzed about stress fractures and spiral this and that, all of which went over his head. What he did know was it hurt like hell and wasn't getting any better. And apparently a less-than-graceful exit through a cobbled together gateway had wreaked additional havoc on the soft tissue.

"You were lucky, you know."

"You have a gift for stating the obvious, Matt."

"The scientists have always suspected the gateway's energies might be … oh, what's the term they used?"

"In-con-fucking-gruent?"

Matteo laughed and went to a narrow sideboard bearing a decanter and heavy Murano goblets. "Can I get you anything, Andy?"

"Yeah, whatever you're having and make it a double."

"You want ice?"

"Oh fuck yes." Andreas grinned at his superior. "You have no idea what it's like back then."

"Then perhaps you will educate me?" Matteo tipped his goblet toward Andreas and sipped the amber liquid appreciatively.

Andreas considered the tall man lounging on the settee opposite him. Matteo had eschewed his cleric's garb in favor of jeans and a tight-fitting tee-shirt that showcased an impressive physique. A former cyclist with turns in the Verrano Open and the now defunct French Pyrenees Challenge, he'd retained his lean build without resorting to the asceticism preached by his cohorts.

"Well, you already know about the Sisterhood's involvement." He sipped the scotch and let the flavor explode on his tongue. The heavy amber goblet refracted light as the ice cubes bumped and jostled across the surface. He was buying time and Matteo knew it. But the man was nothing if not patient.

At the prelate's 'um' of acknowledgment he continued, "They've sent an operative, one of their … super tarts," he did air quotes, "and she's quite good."

"And does this one have a name?"

"She's called Veluria…" He hesitated at Matteo's sharp intake of breath. "Do you know her?"

"Not personally, no. But Tomas had an unfortunate encounter with this one on his last assignment."

Andreas stared at the man, open-mouthed. He'd had no idea the object of his desire was *that* operative. Tomas had had his mind scrubbed and placed in solitary for his own protection, his withdrawal so harsh he'd been on suicide watch for more than two cycles.

"Andy. Did she get to you?" Matteo sat up straight, his eyes boring into his skull like blue laser beams.

He felt the power like a slow trickle, a mere suggestion. If the prelate ever loosed his full spectrum, he'd crush him like a bug, shutting his internal organs down one at a time, maximizing the agony.

He'd seen his superior do that during an especially entertaining interrogation of one of the Sisters a few years back. It had sent the gallery rushing to the exit, retching—all except for him. He had stayed and observed. That simple act of fate, serendipity as it were, had brought him to Matteo's attention and guaranteed his position in the Brotherhood.

Under the man's guidance he had achieved clarity of purpose … amongst other things. If he admitted his culpability in succumbing to the whore's charms, he risked losing the man's trust and faith in his abilities to carry out the Order's prime directives.

Fighting the familiar tightening in his groin, he decided full disclosure would gain him not only sympathy but perchance an opportunity to make a case for returning to that timeline. Matteo understood revenge all too well.

Andreas said, "Hell, yeah, she got to me. Fuck man, it was a rush." He brandished the goblet and chuckled, "I even said a few Hail Marys as penance."

Matteo barked a laugh, "Jesus, Andy. You did not." He rose and retrieved the decanter, refilling their goblets before asking slyly, "And what else?"

"You're a bloodthirsty bastard, aren't you? How about I save the gory details for … later." Muttering, "Fuck," he twisted in the seat, trying to situate his leg to a more comfortable position.

Once settled Andreas continued, "Here's what I know…"

Two hours later, Andreas and Matteo sat glassy-eyed, having finished off the decanter. The plexiglass had automatically darkened to shield the room from the unrelenting afternoon sun.

Matteo grunted and sat back against the cushions, processing the information. Out of the blue he said, "We lost the Grand Plaza last week."

"Shit, can't the engineers...?"

Matteo shook his head 'no'. "They've tried everything. I fear we shall lose our pearl, Andy. Our world is sinking under the weight of its own folly." He sighed and rose to stand at the expanse of window overlooking the city. "Our future must be built on reinforced plasteel, like houses on stilts. Venice will never be the same."

Andreas intoned, "The Brotherhood will lead us from the sea of temptation to the light."

"From the Darkness shall we emerge," Matteo responded with a sneer, "but I fear growing gills more than I fear any darkness, my friend."

"What of the negotiations?"

"Negotiations? There are no more negotiations. All sides have retreated to their respective corners, locked and loaded. Fifty years of peace down the fucking tubes and all because something or someone altered the timeline." Matteo paced around the expansive room with long strides, fists clenching in anger. Reflexively he ran his hand over the small of his back.

"Still carrying concealed, Matt?" Andreas lifted an eyebrow. The Council would shit a collective blue brick if they knew their Head of Order flaunted one of their sacred vows.

One reason Andreas allied himself with the man was because he had a certain moral flexibility that resonated with Andreas' own beliefs.

Matteo pulled the Glock from the waistband of his jeans and set the weapon on the conference table.

"Busted." He sat at the table and tapped a manicured nail on the polished walnut surface. "So, let's review. You've got the Wicked Witch of the sisterhood sucking your dick, virtually speaking." He glared at Andreas. "It is virtual, yes?"

Andreas choked out a 'yes', the image too close for comfort.

"And you've managed to confirm what we've long suspected— that the Medicis have some genetic anomalies, Cosimo's clan in

163

particular, that give them at least a modicum of psychic abilities." He ticked off the list, "Prescience for Cosimo, a certain mathematical precociousness for Nicolo, sexual deviancy for the pup, Stefano. And for this 'key' you've ID'd?"

"Antonio, the Demon de' Medici." Andreas huffed with a mix of disdain and admiration. "He's a cold, hard bastard. You'd like him. He's as close to your gifts as anybody we've run across. He can deep-drill and core truth out of the most determined victim. I suspect he can kill psychically, and may have without realizing he's done it."

"Compared to Cosimo?"

"More powerful by an order of magnitude, but it's like comparing apples and oranges." He hesitated to bring up his real concern. "There's something else…"

"Spill it, Andy. I'm getting sober and I won't be quite so accommodating then."

"He and the Sisterhood's operative may have combined powers."

"That's not possible."

Andreas agreed in principle but he'd seen, and felt, the reality of their powers when they danced and blended outside the strict genetic encoding imposed by the scientists and mathematicians. For all the Brotherhood had enlightened their world with carefully applied scientific dogma, they still fell short when it came to understanding human emotions.

"Possible or not, I felt it. Veluria is assuredly aware of the implications, the Demon … I doubt it." His heart ached with her betrayal of his sacred trust. He could still feel the phantom fingers of her energies wafting through his system, like a drug that gave him a perpetual high.

"So you think this coupling is the event that does … what exactly?"

"Matt, I wish the fuck I knew. All I do understand is that it's not normal, that she's fighting it." He carefully placed his leg on the floor and eased himself to a standing position. The pain wasn't nearly as bad. Limping to the table he spoke with such intensity that the prelate ceased breathing for a moment. "Whatever has caused the change in our reality, our hegemony over the peace process, is a direct result of something that *will* happen."

Irritated, Matteo growled, "But what?"

"I. Don't. Know." Andreas stared out the darkened glass with sightless eyes, hating to admit he had absolutely no clue what would be the final trigger to set their worlds askew.

"So let's think this through. She's run off with the youngest Medici but Antonio's in hot pursuit. Veluria's not the prize. The son is. He's the glue to cement Florence's position in the upcoming political transformation. They'll make sure the pup fulfills his destiny, leaving the Demon to return the woman to Cosimo."

"But why to him?" Andreas could barely contain the grip of despair clutching his heart. If they hurt her, they would answer to him, personally.

Matteo shrugged. "She's a curiosity if for no other reason. They'll recognize a kindred spirit. Cosimo's too smart to let an asset like that get away."

"But she can leave any time she wants," Andreas objected.

"Well, they don't know that, do they?"

Andreas felt suddenly very foolish. Here he was, a world removed, and the woman still commanded his heart ... hell, she consumed his entire being. If Matteo ever guessed, a mind-wipe would be the least of his worries.

Matteo continued, his voice barely masking his concern, "Andy, we both know mucking with time has unintended consequences. Damn, just having two operatives in the same time-space might be the exact reason why all of our current efforts have disappeared down a giant political black hole."

"And if either Veluria or Antonio de' Medici somehow do *something*...?" He didn't bother finishing the thought. The probabilities ranged from n minus one to infinity with more solutions than even *he* could fathom.

"I don't think it's an 'either or' situation, son. My gut's telling me we're going to have to neutralize both of them."

"Then send me back. I know where they are. I'll take care of it."

"Not until you are at full capacity. You can barely think straight when you're in so much pain. How do you think you'll get around?" He smirked at the small man. "I didn't think you were fond of horses."

Andreas felt the whine build in his throat. He wanted to get back ... to her. God, he longed for the promise of having her twist in ecstasy under him. With a start he realized Matteo had taken him by the arm and was guiding him toward the elevator.

"Patience, boy. With them in Spain, or whatever the fuck they call the peninsula, no one's going anywhere fast." He tapped at the button on the wall and squeezed Andreas' shoulder. "Remember, for once, time's on *your* side."

"Can I at least talk with the statisticians?"

"Later. Let's go to our quarters and get lunch. Saul promised to prepare your favorites."

Andreas wrapped his robes about his small frame and limped after his superior into the elevator. They rode to the living quarters' floor in companionable silence. Matteo led them to his suite and keyed in his code.

Andreas sighed with satisfaction. The smell of tomato sauce simmering on the stove filled the room with a fragrance he loved.

Matteo asked, "Are you hungry?"

"I can wait." A thrill of anticipation shimmied down his spine, hot blood flooding his loins.

"Good. I thought as much." Matteo slipped Andreas' robe off his shoulders and moved in close to nuzzle his neck. "God damn, I've missed you, boy."

Andreas whispered, "How much time do I have?"

"A month, my love. And I plan to make every minute worthwhile."

Matteo lowered his head to plunder Andreas' mouth, commanding every fiber of his being.

Andreas pulled away and gazed coyly at the older man. "When shall I tell you about … you know. Before or after?"

Matteo laughed out loud. "You tease. You know I can't wait." He led Andreas into the bedroom and roughly shoved him on top of the feather quilt. "All right. I want details. Now."

Andreas grinned and launched into his tale, "She was a filthy piece, almost made me gag, but…"

Chapter Nineteen

Tonio stretched and scratched at his tousled mop of hair absently. The air in the room was stuffy, thick with humidity, leaving his skin clammy and prickly with unease. He had no idea where he was or how he'd gotten there.

I can't remember my own name. Goddamn that hurt.

His scalp felt bruised, like he'd been whaled on by a squad of corsairs wielding battering rams. Prodding at the multiple lumps, his fingers came away sticky with blood.

I can't have been in here long if it's still fresh. Where the hell am I?

Pushing himself off the dirt floor he staggered to the heavy wooden door and listened carefully. Distant voices echoed as down a cavern but he couldn't quite make out the words. The shuffling of boots alerted him to his captor's approach.

Backing toward the far wall, he realized with dismay that he was completely naked. And he ached for good reason. Whoever held him captive had pleasured themselves with fists and who knew what devices. Not a stretch of skin lacked ugly greenish yellow bruises, the dull hues indicating he'd been subjected to such punishment over days, not hours, the colors showing healing. Only his weeping scalp indicated recent activity.

Why can't I remember?

He sank to the floor and waited as his captors, and it seemed an invading army's worth, jostled about outside the dank cell. What light entered came from a narrow slit situated high on the wall against which he braced himself. Even with his imposing stature, the window was too high to see out.

That left out dungeons, a small comfort.

Three swarthy men crowded into the narrow space effectively blocking his exit. Bracing, he rocked on his haunches, thighs screaming in agony as his sore muscles protested.

The man to his left smirked and said, "So the demon is finally awake." The other two tittered appreciatively.

Antonio watched the three through slitted eyes, waiting for one of them to make a wrong move, but in truth he doubted he could move fast enough to overpower them, even if given the chance. Ribs ground in protest as he attempted to snatch a breath and stabbing shards of pain rent through his gut. The small movements were a symphony of agony leaving him light headed and disoriented. Parched lips and thick tongue spoke to days without water or sustenance.

What do they want with me?

The leader growled, "Bring him," and backed away so his burley cohorts could advance toward the crouching figure. As Tonio's muscles twitched with the effort to hold himself steady, the man said, "Don't try it, *senyor*."

The man relayed rapid instructions to his men who quickly bound and blindfolded Antonio before he could react. The accent seemed familiar, tantalizingly so.

Roughly his captors shoved and pulled him through what seemed an interminably long corridor—he knew this from his frequent collisions against the rough stone walls—until releasing him to fall in a heap on a smooth stone floor that felt blessed cool against his fevered, battered body.

He took what small measure of comfort he could from the sweet contact, knowing the surcease from pain would not last long.

To his right, a high-pitched voice giggled with glee. "Suspend him. Let's see if his memory improves when we start to peel layers off his back."

Two, maybe three, men jerked him off the floor and attached manacles to his wrists—not for the first time judging from how his flesh screamed in protest as the burred metal scrapped and tore through scabs and lacerations.

With a howl of pain, he twisted violently against the inexorable pull on his shoulders, yanking the joints to within their breaking point.

168

With the first bite of the lash, he moaned, "Why...?" then bit down on his tongue, the words choked back until only agony and blood and the first thrill of fear consumed him.

The last thing he remembered was a faint voice admonishing him, "Tell us what your brother plans at court ... and we will end this."

****

Veluria hissed in dismay as Antonio slid bonelessly to the floor, a silly smile on his face, as he dragged her with him.

With a slur he murmured, "You love me?"

She'd regretted the words as soon as they left her mouth, knowing she'd condemned them both, but the truth of it was undeniable. The giant had flung himself across the room, pinning her against the door.

That had been his undoing, the migraine and wine finally taking their toll. She wanted to rail at him, call him a stupid ass, but instead she gently brushed his lips and disentangled herself from the unconscious man.

"Well, you big oaf, what do I do with you now?"

She should leave him to snore fitfully on the hard floor or try to lift him to the bed—an impossible task for one his size and weight. She tried tugging on his legs and barely managed to move them away from the door.

"All right. Think. Maybe the innkeeper can help me get him on the bed." Why she needed to see to the idiot's comfort was beyond her. He was the one who'd spent the entire afternoon banging the bitch downstairs. Then he went and got himself shitfaced on top of that.

"Then he tells me he *loves* me? Sweet Mother, tell me he isn't the one." But he was and her lips twitched at the memory of his tongue tangling with hers, and the scent of a man in full rut, claiming his prize.

She stared at the expanse of chest, and pictured how those hard muscles would bunch as he thrust...

Blushing, she debated her options. Let him stay on the unforgiving floor and wake up stiff ... *oh dear, yes* ... or try to make

169

him comfortable enough to sleep off the effects of the migraine and his exertions of the day.

"Damn it, bed it is."

She kicked at his legs to make more space so she could exit the room, her skirts catching on a rough bit of wood. Annoyed, she heard the fabric tear. She was going to look like a vagrant if she didn't find new clothes. Her laughable undergarments could stand in a corner as it was. If she could trade places with Tonio, she wouldn't touch *her* without a power wash with industrial grade soap.

When the Demon had opened to her, he'd tapped into almost everything she was. He might not understand the full extent of his new knowledge but he would, given sufficient time. She felt strangely free to express her thoughts as if she were in her own time, a liberating and imminently stupid lapse of judgment. She could not presume that Tonio was the only adept in this time and place. She had more to protect than just herself now.

She had to find a way to shield the man who had stolen her heart. Skipping down the uneven steps, she found her way through the weak light cast through the taberna's leaded glass windows. Raucous laughter and singing greeted her as she pushed through the door. The party toward the rear of the small room did not take note of her progress to the archway at the rear that led to the kitchen.

She peered around the door jamb, hoping to spy the innkeeper. The man seemed to be nowhere about, nor was the slovenly whore. Another narrow door led to the back of the taberna. She smelled the rank odor of manure and rotting bedding. Wishing for a candle or a lantern, she cautiously edged past the paddock, wondering what she might be stepping in.

For some reason she felt the need to be cautious. Something seemed out of place and she couldn't put her finger on it. Whispering, "*Senhor*," her heart nearly stopped when a hand gripped her arm and yanked her into a lean-to of some sort.

"Ssssh, *signora*, be quiet."

"Paulo, is that you?" Paulo was Antonio's driver. He was a wizened elf of a man, not much taller than herself.

"Yes, *signora*." He leaned in close and kept his voice to a harsh whisper. "We have trouble."

"Trouble?"

The man was beside himself, his body trembling uncontrollably, muttering in a dialect she didn't understand. She risked a scan but managed only detecting abject terror and the fact that the innkeeper and his serving woman had fled the premises, temporarily.

"Those men mean him harm," Paulo hissed, "and we must warn my master."

"Who are they?" She felt rather than saw the small man's shrug. "Paulo?"

There was no point pressing him. He had little intelligence beyond having heard the men boasting of their exploits—and the fact that the whore had happened to mention that an Italian gentleman of means resided at the taberna.

She had a good idea they might be from the Catalan resistance, though why they would be sequestering a cell so close to the coast escaped her. She was familiar with Italian politics and the incessant squabbling of the city-states, but the fractured enmities of the peninsula had been only rough-sketched during her tutorials.

What interest they might have in Antonio wasn't clear. They did not seem to know about *her*. She was sure she hadn't been noticed when she'd walked through the inn. That gave her an advantage. She would skirt around the outside of the building and make her way to their rooms.

"Listen to me, you must harness the horses. Work quickly. I will alert Antonio and bring him here." Paulo pulled away before she could finish. Hissing, "Hurry," after his retreating figure, she gathered her skirts and made her way toward the building.

Her eyes had adjusted to the ambient light making passage to the stairs easier. As she reached the edge of the building light flooded the packed dirt in front of the building—the sound of booted feet moving quickly and with purpose brought her up short. Before she could bolt for the stairs the group ascended stealthily and slammed the door open so violently she could feel the impact against the wall.

Damn it! Tonio! Wake up, wake up, wake up!

Nothing but a solid wall met her silent scream as she poured all her powers into rousting him. But it was too late—her cries echoed hollowly as Antonio's essence faded from her control.

****

Nicolo strode to the door, his annoyance at being interrupted yet again with the petty concerns of the court toadies overriding his natural caution. He yanked the heavy door open and glared at two disheveled travelers, their cloaks stained and matted with mud and other detritus.

At first he did not recognize the small man trembling with anxiety. He gave the tiny woman at his side only a cursory glance as he muttered, "Paulo? Wha—?"

"Please, *signore*, please…"

Nico looked beyond the bedraggled couple seeking his brother's tall frame. His gut told him something was horribly wrong.

The woman placed a calming hand on the old man's arm and spoke huskily, the words coming with difficulty. "We've come about Antonio. We … he needs your help."

Gathering his wits, Nico pulled the door completely open and called for his manservant. "Ferran! Ferran!" The sound of running feet on the ceramic tiles, followed by concerned chatter, seemed to agitate the old man even more.

"Come in, Paulo, *signora*?" He tenderly grasped the old man's arm and guided him into the foyer leaving the woman to follow unsteadily.

He fired rapid instructions to his staff to bring food and drink. Settling Paulo on a settee he turned to the diminutive woman and guided her to a stool where she could sit comfortably. Her dark eyes looked dull and lifeless, like all hope had been drained from her, leaving just a shell. He thought he recognized her but from her haggard appearance it was difficult to say.

His manservant brought a tray laden with goblets of water, wine and plates of cheese and dried meats. The woman drank her water gratefully but Paulo waved his away. Nico glanced at the woman who nodded at him. Obviously she was as concerned about the old man as he was.

"Ferran, take Paulo to our guest quarters."

Paulo protested, "No, *signore*…" but Nico insisted. Once Paulo had left the room, he sank to the settee and said, "Now, madam, tell me who you are and why you are here about my brother."

The woman spoke slowly, fighting for each word as exhaustion threatened to claim her. Nico detected a faint energy signature, the memory of it a niggling irritation.

172

Why can't I place you?

The woman hesitated, yet he sensed her agitation and confusion, as if she feared revealing too much.

What the hell is going on?

Nico disliked using his secret abilities on strangers but he knew he must risk it. Fear for Antonio beat like a drum in his skull. He sent out a probe, only to be met with a sense of welcoming relief.

Shit. This was the Frenchwoman! What was her name again?

"It's Veluria."

"Veluria. I must know. Will you allow…?"

She held up a hand and bit her bottom lip, then nodded assent. Too weary to shield herself, the woman held nothing back, every thought, every feeling flooded his senses.

Sweet Jesus. Antonio in love? That's not possible!

The woman, Veluria, frowned and said, "Believe it. But that is not the issue. Tonio has been taken by separatists who plan to hold him for ransom, torture him … oh *signore*, I don't know what they plan to do!"

Nico rose abruptly and left the room, his fury and fear so strong he knew he would swamp the woman with his out-of-control powers. Ferran met him in the antechamber.

"Call the captain of my guard. Ask him to meet me in one hour with his full complement."

Ferran nodded and hastened to do his master's bidding. Nico paced the small room, desperate to get his anger and worry under control. What he'd gleaned from the woman made no sense although every feeling, every sensation rang true.

He had to set aside that which he did not understand and instead focus on the immediate threat. He could only imagine what the separatists hoped to accomplish by detaining Tonio. His brother had little direct contact with the halls of power, operating instead in the shadows doing their father's bidding. But a Medici was a prize that could be parlayed into a sizable ransom payment since Cosimo's fondness for his sons was well-known.

If they were indeed in hiding at the coast, then the question was: who would they contact first? Him … or Cosimo? Everyone knew he attended to matters in Carlos' court, brokering deals and seeing to his family's interests. He would be the logical choice. However, given the fact that the deed was spur-of-the-moment, his ability to predict their next steps was severely hampered.

The other concern was that without a solid plan in place, the perpetrators of the kidnapping might not be disposed to treat his brother with kindness and consideration. And given Antonio's demeanor and reputation, it was likely he'd be subjected to the worst kind of torture.

They would not care if their captive was just mostly alive so long as they got their payment in full.

Shit shit shit.

"*Signore?*"

Nico spun to face Veluria. She gazed at him, her dark eyes pleading. With a wash of guilt he realized he was being an ass, treating the woman without consideration for the trials she'd been through. The trip, and her despair over Antonio, had drained her reserves so that she could barely function.

He said, kindly, "Forgive me, madam. I will take you to a guestroom. You may take your rest and freshen up." He took her arm to guide her to the rear of the hacienda.

"No, please."

"Madam, you must rest. Let me see to this…"

"Nico … may I call you Nico?" He nodded *yes* so she continued, "You don't understand. I can help you find him."

"I appreciate your offer, but leave this to me." He was not about to explain his and Tonio's link. He would feel his brother's essence, even from a distance. He just needed to get close enough.

The woman said quietly, "It won't be enough. He is hurt, Nico. He does not know himself. He won't know *you.*"

Angrily he growled, "And you know this how?"

Weakly she replied, "Because I am like you … but more." She stared at him, willing him to believe.

"All right. I will accept what you say, for now. But you will rest. We have a hard journey ahead of us and I will not be slowed down by a…" He was about to say 'a weak woman' but thought better of it when she glared at him with a thunderous expression.

"Can you ride, madam?"

"Well enough."

"Then I shall procure suitable attire. Your skirts will not suit for this travel."

He pointed down the hall and said, "First door on your right. I shall send Marie to tend to your needs." He turned away but she grabbed his arm and turned him toward her.

"We *will* find him, Nico."

He gave her a dark look, his face set in rigid determination. "We will indeed. Veluria."

He left her weaving uncertainly down the hall and strode quickly to meet with his captain. They would need to travel fast and light, keeping provisioning to a minimum.

He had a bad feeling they were quickly running out of time.

Don't you fucking die on me, Tonio. Don't give up. I'm coming for you.

Chapter Twenty

Friedrich examined his prospective son-in-law with interest. The reports had not done the young man justice. He carried a prettiness about him—a fey quality—yet there was something rough-edged too, as if the boy-to-man transition had taken an unexpected turn. He sensed that there might be interesting depths to plumb beyond the surface naiveté.

"Does he meet with your satisfaction?" The leer in the man's voice was unmistakable. He was used to it.

Ignoring his secretary, Friedrich moved to the other side of the narrow viewing slit, tiptoeing on the ledge to get a better perspective on the room below. His quarry passed in and out of his view as he paced about the antechamber, not so much nervous as bored.

Boredom was good. He had entertainments enough to satisfying the most discriminating tastes. With a grimace he backed down the ladder, taking care with foot placement lest he appear clumsy. His secretary had been with him for years but still … it did nothing for his image to land in a heap on the stone floor.

The man continued, "Have you decided which of your daughters to present for his pleasure?" He dipped a quill in an inkwell, pausing to look up, the droplets settling about the edge of the pot. "I will need a name for the contract, sire."

"Name? Oh yes. Um, I had thought of bringing each one forward for the Medici's inspection."

He suspected that was not a particularly good move, given his daughters' wildly differing sensibilities. His secretary confirmed his doubts with a vigorous shake of his head.

"Well, Gustav, you seem to have some strong opinions on this matter. Perhaps you would care to enlighten me with your ... erudition?" Friedrich's voice oozed with menace as he moved to tower over the seated figure. The quill quivered in the man's fingers, leaving splotches of ink to fall on the stone floor. Most times he indulged his man's sometimes bold nature. Today he wasn't disposed to be as accommodating.

Not when so much rested on making the right choice.

Gustav stuttered, "S-s-sire, f-forgive me, but I think, perchance, Wiltrud would be the proper bride for your purposes."

Interesting, she hadn't been his first choice but he was curious to hear the man's assessment. Withdrawing far enough to allow the quaking man some breathing room, he said, "Go on."

"Rumor has it, your eldest, Marie, *may* have the special attention of Duke Willem." At Friedrich's raised eyebrow the man hastened to continue, "A most unsuitable match, to be sure, given the man's age and circumstances." Before Friedrich could comment, he held up a finger and said, "The Duke's territories would be a useful buffer against Vladislav's ambitions."

Friedrich mumbled, "Fair enough," pausing to think on that option. Marie was the least clever and least attractive of his three daughters. Placing her with a man in his dotage would preclude her producing grandchildren for his benefit, but there were worst fates to be sure. And covering his ass with an ally on his eastern boundary had become an imperative given the posturing and bald-faced aggression from some of the neighboring duchies.

Curious now, he asked, "And why is this just coming to my attention?" He didn't care for surprises, not when it came to matters of state.

Gustav swallowed and gripped the edge of the writing desk, staring hard at the tapestries lining the walls as if to draw inspiration for the expected explanation. Sweat beaded his brow but he decided to skirt around his failure to alert his sire to the rumors floating about the court, trivial as they seemed.

Visibly garnering his resolve, Gustav said, "Margaret is still young and unformed. She would be unsuitable for Stefano de' Medici given his reputation and experience..." he lowered his eyes and murmured, "...and proven potency."

Rigid with irritation he glared at his secretary but the man's eyes remained pinned to his inkwell. What vaguely amused him was his secretary taking *him* to task about any potential impropriety rather than concerning himself with why his master had made that particular selection in the first place.

However, Gustav had a point about the girl being not much more than a child, despite the fact he had based his decision on other considerations. He snarled, "She is fourteen, soon to be fifteen. That's old enough."

Margaret was his favorite, flighty but full of fun. She tasked him daily with her antics. By bringing the Medici lad to his court he'd hoped to keep his youngest close and under his direct supervision. He didn't like when someone cast doubt on his decisions, yet the man did, on occasion, keep him from making a fool of himself.

Staring at Gustav, he said, "Wiltrud," with distaste. She'd been an unlikeable child, dull and obstinate to a fault and she'd grown into a cantankerous young woman with an unappealing demeanor. She was not unpleasing to the eye, but her strident tones and incessant whining taxed all who served her.

His secretary was all too aware of Wiltrud's shortcomings. Why would he think she'd be the more suitable candidate?

"Sire, the Medici boy will most certainly fulfill his duties admirably and produce an heir in short order." As if sensing he walked on uncertain ground, the man hastily qualified his statement. "With any daughter *you* so choose."

"But…?" Friedrich could guess what was coming. His secretary had been the unfortunate recipient of Wiltrud's particular deprecations more times than he could count, her hatred for the man almost palpable. Gustav had no reason to defend his daughter, and every reason to see that she be placed in an uncompromising situation.

Yes, indeed. If Gustav's hint that the willful brat could hold up to certain … punishments, then perhaps the idea did have merit.

Clearly uncomfortable, his secretary spoke hesitantly. "The, um, guard who returned Stefano de' Medici to our safekeeping relayed certain, uh, observations about the boy's proclivities."

Friedrich kept his face impassive. He had also been privy to the rumor and innuendo. That much explained Gustav's recommendation. Although he disliked the roundabout way his

178

secretary arrived at his suggestion, the logic behind it had a certain appeal.

Friedrich said, "I see your point about Margaret being too young," and too innocent, though he avoided voicing that concern.

He'd have preferred delaying the final decision, perhaps manipulating the courtship period, but in truth time was his enemy with events across the continent proceeding apace. He'd demanded the immediate presence of the suitor and Cosimo had been more than accommodating in allowing him to dispatch his own men to see that his wishes were met.

Friedrich understood and appreciated Cosimo's motives in agreeing to the union of their houses. Whether or not the young man was on board with their plans was another matter entirely. It would be best to proceed with alacrity.

He approached the lectern and tapped on the parchment. "Wiltrud it is. Well done, Gustav, well done indeed."

Before the man could puff up with pride, Friedrich gave him a feral grin and purred, "We'll see to your reward ... later."

The man's face drained of all color but he bent his head to the task. Friedrich rather liked stoics when he was in the mood for a bit of relaxed sport.

With a quick brush of his tunic, he advanced to the door and said mostly to himself, "Well, let's take the measure of Cosimo's pup, shall we?"

With a flourish he stalked into the antechamber to greet his guest.

****

Stefano fidgeted under the intense scrutiny of the Duke and his court toadies. The trip had been a nightmare of sleepless nights and long, hot canters over rough terrain through the Swiss territories. Friedrich's Guards had been willing enough companions; but tasked as they were to bring him to the castle in the shortest time possible, that left him little opportunity for the pleasantries he so enjoyed. Upon his arrival he'd been primped and polished and dandied up to suit the Duke's peculiar fashion tastes. Now he stood on display, fully aware of his responsibilities and the expectations of his family.

As Friedrich introduced his intended, he noted without interest her plain features—horse-faced he and his drinking companions would have dubbed her—but her build was satisfying, plump in all the right places. Unfortunately she displayed a haughty demeanor, brow set in what looked to be a perpetual frown, and the glint in her eye gave her a less-than-welcoming presence.

Stefano had hoped for an undemanding consort, one content to manage her clutch of children, tending to her needlework and whatever other duties the Habsburg spawn used to fill their days, leaving him free to find his pleasures elsewhere.

He had a feeling that even Antonio would have turned tail and run from the arrogant martinet paraded for his approval.

As if I have a fucking choice.

As he engaged in the polite salutations and feigned a vague display of interest in the young woman whose name grated on his nerves, Stefano let his mind wander, thinking back to the last time he'd seen *her*.

He still felt the sting of Veluria's rejection, her harsh words even now ringing in his ears, shutting out the incessant background droning about plans presented as if he had a say in the matters of state. He knew *that* to be a falsehood. He was here as his father's puppet. Nico had made that clear during their brief encounter in Spagna—before Friedrich's Guards had whisked him away to an uncertain destiny.

Why am I not surprised to see you here, Nico? Still Father's errand boy? Are you going to make sure I don't embarrass the family again?

Nico ignored the insult as he always did. There seemed nothing he could do or say to rattle the man, something he ached to do for he hated the closeness—the bond—that Nico and Tonio had had since they were children. He was ever the odd one out, though both doted on him, spoiling him at every opportunity. Somehow it was never enough.

He'd listened with half an ear as his brother explained what he called 'the facts of life' and assured him of the rightness of decisions made on his behalf, for the good of the family and ultimately for his own good. And without a backward glance he'd strode off, leaving him with the Guards and his damned destiny.

180

Well, he would serve the family's interests for now. But when the time suited, he would chose a path more aligned with his developing needs and desires.

Friedrich waved off his disapproving daughter and her panicked handmaidens—who knew full well that their mistress' displeasure would come with a cost— and bade his entourage to leave them alone. Once the room cleared, he approached the young man and took his elbow.

"*Kommst mit mir*, Stefano." Friedrich noted the boy's puzzled expression, then smiled slyly and switched to his heavily accented Italian. "Come, please. We can talk and I have a few things that might interest you. Things to make your stay perhaps more pleasant."

Friedrich smiled to himself. The reports from his informant had hinted at activities on board the ship that bode well for developing a very particular relationship with his soon-to-be new son-in-law.

As he steered the young man toward his private chambers, Friedrich asked, "How old are you, boy?"

Stefano looked puzzled at the question but quickly replied, "I am approaching one-and-twenty, sire."

The older man chuckled and said, "Just Friedrich when we are alone, my boy. There is no reason to stand on formalities now that we shall be so *intimately* aligned."

His curiosity obviously peaked, Stefano followed him obediently through the bedchambers and down a steep staircase that led, level after level, into the lower reaches of the castle. Friedrich guided him into a chamber from which the door could be locked from the inside for privacy, but which he left propped open, causing the torches to flare and waver, casting strange shadows on the walls.

Despite the enclosed, windowless space, the room was not stuffy. Fresh rushes had been recently applied to the smooth stone floor and the walls were dry and hung with muted tapestries in deep burgundy and blue shades. It had the feel of a drawing room, albeit on the chill side since the large fireplace at the rear of the long, narrow space sparked with dying embers.

Friedrich placed a few logs and kindling onto the smoldering coals and prodded at the logs until the dry wood caught with a satisfying hiss. He ignored his young guest, allowing him to view the room's accouterments at his leisure. He shivered at the prospect of explaining some of the finer points about the various devices arrayed about the space. Some would be familiar, others less obvious.

The Duke turned away from the blaze and watched his young— dare he call him apprentice?—with admiration. The boy was tall and not too muscular, with well-shaped thighs and strong hands. Friedrich loved strong hands. And he loved the air of innocence so cleverly masking what he sensed was an adventurous and discerning nature—one that would appreciate and embrace the unexpected.

He padded silently toward the young man, until he stood close enough to whisper in his ear, "Well...?"

Stefano hesitated, unsure, still scanning the space, but as understanding dawned he smiled and nodded to his host.

"Do you like what you see, my boy?"

Stefano sighed with pleasure, "*Sì, mio signore,* I like it very much, indeed."

"Then, perhaps if you are not too weary from your journey...?"

Stefano turned, his eyes smoldering with lust and anticipation. He husked, "I'm not tired at all, *signore*, not at all."

Friedrich grinned and said, "Excellent. Gustav," he paused at Stefano's questioning look, "my secretary, shall join us later. But for now we have all this for our own enjoyment."

"Join us?"

"Gustav recommended Wiltrud be your intended. A most excellent suggestion, do you not agree?" The boy clearly did not so he added quickly, "Which is why I wish to reward my faithful servant for his initiative."

Stefano kept his face carefully blank but the small uptick at the corner of his mouth indicated he understood.

"Good, I see you are in agreement. Then let us begin, shall we?"

Friedrich felt his gut twist with excitement as he paced to the door and shut it securely, lowering the cross-beam to keep interlopers out. When he turned around, his new cohort was already fondling a willow stick.

Chapter Twenty-One

Nico sank wearily to the ground. He'd lost two of his complement to mishaps from their precipitous charge through the Mesata Central, relying on local knowledge to bypass known strongholds whose occupants were not sympathetic to Carlos. The tracks had been rough, laming horses and challenging even the toughest of his men, pushing all to their limits.

He watched Veluria approach from the direction of the Rio Tagus. She'd said nothing earlier that day but the plea in her eyes had finally convinced him to stop and rest. While his men saw to the animals and set to finding sufficient deadfall for a small campfire, he did guard duty. Not that his men were inclined to partake of a beautiful woman bathing in the moonlight—all were bone weary and exhausted beyond measure.

Lunging to his feet, he gathered his cape and flung it around the tiny woman's shoulders. They'd said little to each other for days, each guarding secrets that few would comprehend. She nodded her thanks and shivered as the chill air caressed her damp skin.

"Come M'lady, the fire will dry you off in good time."

He guided the woman to a spot opposite where his captain snored softly, the other two men walking the perimeter. He knew he should sleep before taking his turn but suspected, like all the other nights, he would remain in a half-waking state. Fear for his brother, the nagging sense that he could reach out and touch him if only he tried harder… Instead, distressing thoughts from alien images and ideas crowded his mind, distracting him from focusing his search.

"Thank you, Nico." She tucked her legs under the cape, her slim body still quaking.

Nico murmured, "Come here," and drew her onto his lap so he could cradle her in what little warmth his body could provide. They needed to talk. He was sure she would not want to hear what he had to say.

"I'm losing him." He didn't bother keeping the misery out of his voice. "Each day, he grows weaker. I fear we shall not be in time."

He felt Veluria shake her head against his chest, the words muffled and indistinct, mirroring his growing despair. She pushed away and stared up at him, her damp hair cascading about her thin face and narrow shoulders. She seemed to have shrunk into nothingness, worry and care consuming her as it did him.

Angrily she brushed the strands away and hissed, "But we must, Nico. We seem so close. I can feel him also."

There seemed nothing more he could add to her admonition, so he murmured, "Let me do something about that," and before she could protest he spun her about to sit perched on his knees. The black strands fell in wild disarray down her back, knotted and still caked with the dust and dirt thrown up by hooves. The muddy river had done little but deposit more silt and grit. If she were like his Isabella, it was probably a good thing she could not determine the state of her tresses.

When he pulled his fingers through Veluria's hair, separating the strands and peeling away the worst of the grit, she sighed with pleasure, much the way Isabella did…

She said, "Tell me about her."

Disconcerted that she could so easily read his thoughts, he asked, "What do you wish to know, M'lady?"

"You love her." It seemed an odd statement, though the truth of it must be evident to her senses, so he waited for her to continue. "But … you are not…" she struggled to make sense of her perceptions, "…not together?"

Nico smoothed the silky strands and separated them into thick clumps, taking his time, using the activity to help him frame his answer such that she would not see or feel the pain and anger that gnawed at his gut every day of his life. Pressing on Veluria's upper back, he said, "Lean forward," and began to expertly braid the thick hair into a tight strand.

Veluria had more patience than he would have credited any woman, allowing him to determine what and how much to tell. He rarely spoke of his feelings, not even to Tonio with whom he often shared his most intimate thoughts. But not about *this*.

Sadly she said, "She is not yours to have."

Curtly he stated, "No," hoping that would be the end of the discussion. He was not going to be so fortunate.

"Does she know? How *you* feel, I mean?"

Nico finished plaiting, tying off the end with loose strands as Isabella had taught him. He wasn't sure he had an answer for Veluria's perceptive question. He'd often felt the adolescent suitor, lusting after his first crush. In too many ways it was true. The boy she'd seduced had showered her with assurances of his undying affection, the man he'd become had hardened and withdrawn, punishing them both for a situation neither could control.

His brother suspected but had yet to press him. It was a good thing. Were he to reveal his agony he feared Tonio's solution would destroy the fragile hold he had on Isabella. He had given her the one thing she desired above all else. The fates had had other plans for her, for them.

Veluria patted the long braid appreciatively, then spun to face him, the wavering flames from the campfire illuminating her features. He had little room in his life for sympathy and regrets but the compassion on the woman's face touched his heart.

She stroked his face, her fingers scraping against the hard bristles. He had no reason to trust this creature but she had insinuated herself into their lives. That she loved his brother more than life itself he had no doubt. With all he cared about hanging in the balance, perhaps it was time to confront his deepest fears.

Inhaling, he shut his eyes and opened his soul...

Veluria was unprepared for the wash of emotions, not so much the volume but the intensity, white hot, the burden of his feelings consuming the man from the inside out. As for all of them, the ugliness of his world had corrupted and darkened his spirit, yet he clung to one thing, and one thing only, his love for a woman who'd eschewed his devotion, yet pleasured them both on an altar of false hope and lies.

She cradled his face with her hands and whispered the question he feared most, "Why? Why does she turn away?"

When the answer came, she gasped and wrapped her arms about her belly in shock, the scene playing out in hideous detail, every nuance, every accusation, every bitter phrase etched into her soul.

Nico spoke softly, face twisted in a rictus of pain, "We've been lovers for what seems most of my life. I was fifteen, she was twenty-three." He moved to prod the dying embers with a branch, adding more twigs, then returned to sit next to her side-by-side so she could only see his face in profile.

Jaw twitching, he continued, "The Count was, is, impotent and cannot have children. We were virgins and learned from each other. I knew if I waited long enough, was patient enough, her husband would surely die. I prayed nightly." He hissed, "I am not proud of that but I had little recourse at the time."

"How often did you see her?"

He shrugged, "Two or three times a year only. It wasn't until Father sent me to Carlos' court that I was able to finally spend more time with Isabella. We were very discrete, not even my household was aware of our trysts." Nico rubbed his scalp mindlessly and stared into the flames. "It's my fault. I should have been more … careful. But it was so seldom that I forgot myself, and … and…"

"She was pregnant."

"Yes. Isabella was overjoyed. I was not. I knew it was a mistake for which we would pay a terrible price. I had no idea how high that price would be."

"What about the Count?"

"He knew, of course. Oh, not that I was the one who cuckolded him, but that Isabella had been unfaithful, of that there was no doubt."

"What happened?" Veluria could piece it together from the fractured images she'd gleaned but Nico's pain had been bottled up too long. This *thing* he carried with him was like a cancer eating his soul.

"The man was no fool. He claimed the child for his own." Nico nervously wrung his hands, the silence deepening between them until she was sure he'd go no further. When he did speak, the sounds came out flat and brittle.

"Cosimo recalled me to Florence on other matters. I was away during her confinement. Only Tonio knew of my distress, though not the reason. He kept me sane and occupied. When I returned to court,

I had a beautiful daughter, a child I determined to claim for my own. I named her Theresa in honor of my mother, but of course, that was my child's secret identity, one I would reveal in good time."

Veluria asked, "What did you do next?"

He laughed but the sound came out like a harsh bark of anger. "Do? What I seem to do best. I prowled the back corridors, making deals, keeping secrets. I played my part, handling negotiations, ever visible yet hiding in the shadows. I wanted my child but I desired Isabella above all else, my lust, my love more than I could bear."

Nico paused for the final time. She braced for what was coming, praying she had the strength to offer him solace, knowing he would deny it for himself.

"I, we, decided to meet. I remember," his voice took on a dreamlike quality, "it was high summer, so hot the air felt thick and heavy. We'd ridden to an abandoned hovel, not wanting to risk being discovered. She was … different. More rounded, her belly so softly bulging I wanted nothing more than to stroke it and follow the curves with my fingers, and imagined planting new life in her womb. Isabella's breasts were heavy with milk, creamy white, the tips dark … she was the most beautiful creature I had ever seen and I knew I would love her for all eternity."

The man buried his face in his hands. Lost to her. Lost to a private hell he would never escape.

"It was not 'til next morn, the sky just barely lightening, when we were finally sated. We agreed to separate, I to my quarters, she to the hacienda. For all that I claimed to love my child, it never occurred to me to ask about her. To inquire as to her well-being. I assumed a nursemaid had been employed to see to her security that night. I was wrong."

Nico turned and looked at her, tears streaming down his face. "She'd gotten tangled in the bedding, my sweet daughter, and suffocated. There were none to hear her cries."

Veluria suppressed the urge to gather the man in her arms, fearful still that his anguish could turn to fury in a heartbeat. She understood why but caution stayed her.

The pain in his voice cut like a knife. "She blamed me for luring her away, for so tempting her, for appealing to her baser nature. She said it was my fault our daughter was dead, that I was not to attend mass or the burial, nor could I mourn my child in public."

"Nico, no…"

"She was right. It was my fault. All of it." He brushed at his eyes with his sleeve and lunged to his feet. "Get some sleep. I shall stand guard. My men are weary and I will not close my eyes this night."

Veluria wanted to find some words of comfort but there seemed little she could say. He needed someone to tell him to move on, that Isabella was unworthy of his love. She could voice the sentiments, but as a stranger to the man, they would offer neither comfort nor would they carry weight. She fervently hoped that since he had finally unburdened himself, perhaps the healing could begin.

Her heart heavy, she watched the tall man stride into the darkness, shoulders rigid with grief.

She whispered into the still air, "We'll find Tonio, I promise. I will not allow you to lose one more thing that you love."

Sweet Reverend Mother, please help me bear the weight of this sorrow, for I fear for both our souls.

****

"Come, my lady. It is time to go." Nico had sent his man, Luca, to find her.

She'd been up since first light pacing the river bank, using the water's energy to focus her abilities. Not for the first time she rued having left her few talismans behind at Nico's hacienda. But her exhaustion and the need for haste had overcome other considerations. All she had was her stiletto concealed in her boot. When the time came, it would have to do.

For now she must rely on her own resources. Antonio was close. But … in which direction?

"M'lady?"

"Yes, I'm coming, Luca." She waved him off and returned to the slippery bank.

Where are you, Tonio? Speak to me.

It all flows downhill, the water flows down—

If you die, you bastard, I swear on the Holy Mother…

"Veluria?" She nearly jumped out of her skin as a large hand landed like a dead weight on her shoulder, nearly bearing her to the ground.

"Nico! You startled me."

188

"I found him. I know where he is." Nico spun her around and gripped her arms hard enough to leave a mark. His face was haggard from lack of sleep and anxiety but his sapphire blue eyes glinted with hope. "Don't worry, M'lady, my brother's too big a bastard to die. God doesn't want him anymore than the devil does."

Veluria pointed downriver, then swept her arm to the south and west. "There's a hollow with some kind of a feeder stream to this river. I think he is there."

Nico grinned. "I think you may be right. Come. There is a town nearby. I think it is time for us to join forces, madam, don't you agree?"

It's about fucking time...

"I heard that."

For the first time in weeks Veluria laughed out loud. As she trotted to keep up with the tall man's stride, she allowed a small kernel of hope to take seed. It wasn't much but it was all she had left.

Luca had her mount saddled and ready. Nico lifted her effortlessly into the saddle and settled her boot in the stirrup. With a flourish he bowed from the waist and said. "Would madam care to instruct us as to the day's activities?"

Nico's men stared at him and then at her, open-mouthed. She urged her horse forward until she came even with the small group of horsemen. They were a ragged troupe, near the end of their endurance, yet their tired faces lit with anticipation, awaiting her command.

"I believe, gentlemen, that today will be a fine day to go ... demon hunting."

One-by-one they nodded and moved into formation behind her. Nico came alongside, his face set in a stern line, every fiber of his being prepared to do battle. She had no doubt that by the end of the day blood would be spilled.

And when Nico's done with them, I want to cut their balls off with a dull blade and make those sons-of-bitches eat them raw, she thought.

Your wish is my command, M'lady...

Veluria kicked her horse into a canter and called out, "I heard that, Nico!"

Chapter Twenty-Two

Nico felt the weariness bleed away, every sense on high alert. Tonio's signature had weakened to the point where it was but a memory, a faint stirring in his chest, heartbeats once synched but no longer.

The hollow lay below his position. Little of the hacienda was visible from his vantage point. Instead he gazed upon a poorly tended orchard, trees branched helter-skelter forming a thick, impenetrable mat that could hide his men's approach.

But he needed to find a way down to the flats without resorting to the rough path on the rocky slope opposite his position. Either that or simply march up the road and knock on the door. With the town so close, almost within viewing distance of the compound, a weary traveler excuse would not suffice and would leave him and his men exposed to potential lookouts.

That he detected no guards along the ridge was not surprising. Veluria recalled there being six or seven men in total, their presence at the inn sheltering her and his brother pure happenstance. They'd taken Antonio only after someone had recognized him, either by reputation or from having had an unfortunate encounter with his brother's unorthodox methods of interrogation. However, whenever, they'd recognized the value of their acquisition, the truth was they'd had him long enough to grow lax in their diligence. Especially if Tonio had become weak enough to no longer require constant surveillance.

The hour grew late, the sun already below the ridge, casting long shadows and obscuring details. It would be foolish to attempt negotiating the steep descent, the loose rock and soil, in full sunlight, never mind in the dark with no moon to offer even a hint of light.

He could see better than most in the dark, given his unique senses, but his men could not. Backing away, he ran at a crouch, keeping low, his joints protesting at the unnatural gait. He and Paulo had left their ragged group a half mile distant in a parallel gully to avoid chance meetings with townsfolk.

Still light enough to see, he met Paulo, waiting at the narrow entrance to the gully.

"What did you find?" he asked, keeping his tone low though the rough terrain dampened sound.

"I went to the ridge opposite. You were right, Commander. The track's too steep, too loose for safe passage."

Nico cursed silently. The abductors had chosen the site well. Likely they'd chanced on a long-held stronghold for the separatists. This spot was ideal, far enough away from the court to avoid routine sweeps by Carlos' Guard, yet close to the Rio Tagus and convenient egress into more accommodating territories. The town provided provisioning, entertainment, and eyes and ears tuned to strangers.

Desperation crept with long icy fingers up his spine. The darkness was both enemy and friend. How could they use it to their advantage?

"Come, let us confer with the others. We must decide now for a plan of action." Nico didn't say what he knew to be true … his brother would likely not last the night.

Paulo chirped a high-pitched whistle, alerting the others to their arrival. Off to his right, Veluria approached with an armful of branches, staggering under the unruly weight. She gave him a wan smile and carefully laid her burden near a growing pile of deadfall.

Curious, Nico glanced at Paulo who shrugged.

Veluria explained, "Maso is building an enclosure for the horses. He said whatever happens, he has no wish to walk home."

Nico chuckled. His men lived and died at his command, their loyalty beyond question. Fortunate for him he'd also chosen men with intelligence and initiative. It would do them well for what lay ahead.

He instructed Paulo to bring Maso and Christo to the small spring near the southern edge of the gully. They'd set up a makeshift camp but could not risk a fire. They would have to make do as night fell, leaving the warmth of day to succumb to a pool of chill air settling into the basin. Maso had already cordoned off a section, allowing the animals access to water. There was little forage for the hungry beasts but at least they had the weak stream to sustain them until…

Nico knew it was more an *if* than *until* with the odds stacked so solidly against them. Trying not to think about the woman and how he could protect her while trying to rescue his brother, he motioned his men forward and bade them to huddle close so he could speak without his voice carrying in the still air.

Veluria propped against his leg, leaning close so as not to miss a word. It was an intimacy that raised eyebrows on his men but he ignored it as best he could. The warmth of her touch, and the rise and fall of her chest causing her breast to rub provocatively against his arm, was a distraction he could not afford. That she did it unconsciously did not negate the strong stirrings in his loins.

Nico stretched a leg and pushed away, positioning himself so he faced his four stalwart companions, their faces hidden in shadow. He'd never been one to foolishly commit either himself or his men to a course of action that was nothing more than suicide, preferring retreat over valor any day. If he could talk his way out of conflict, he did, usually successfully. When he had to fight he waited until the odds on his side were irrefutable.

Neither situation seemed to pertain, except…

He stared hard at Veluria's pinched face and silently asked, *'Will he last 'til daybreak, milady?'*

Veluria rubbed her temples, her thin features a mask of concentration. When she hissed an audible breath, his men turned as one to hear her pronouncement. If they had misgivings about the silent communication between himself and the woman, they kept it carefully hidden.

"I-I can't tell. I want to say yes but in my heart I don't think so."

"Commander," Paulo spoke quietly, "we risk perhaps too much trying to take them in the dark, despite the element of surprise. They have position." Maso grunted agreement as Paulo continued, "And they have knowledge of the hacienda that we do not. Should we manage to infiltrate the building, we do not know where your brother is being held, how many are inside and what weapons they bring to bear."

Christo added, "They could also kill him before we could get to him. Cut their losses."

"We only assume they wish to hold him for ransom, Commander. They may have ... other motivations." Paulo spoke the truth that had Nico's gut in a knot. The thought that Tonio might be simply a plaything for some sick perverts instead of a political tool hadn't escaped his attention.

Again, they had no way of knowing. They'd left long before a ransom demand could arrive on his doorstep, and too little time had elapsed for Cosimo to become involved.

Had he locked them into a maze with no exit?

"I'd considered approaching as an envoy of Cosimo's, come to offer a fair ransom, perhaps buy us time and information about the hacienda. Demand to see Antonio before the exchange takes place." He and Veluria had mapped out that strategy as one among many options. His shoulders sagged in resignation. "Unfortunately we have no wagon, no conveyance of any sort that would maintain that artifice long enough for us to effect a rescue."

"We are too few in any case. Under normal circumstances a full complement would have accompanied such treasure." Paulo waved at their group and sighed, "We do not qualify, I fear."

Nico grimaced and took Veluria's hand. They had to join, to see what, if any, essence of Antonio remained. Her small hand squeezed his as palm-to-palm they shared their gifts, opening to their joint fears. The link only confirmed what each had determined on their own.

Releasing Veluria's hand he said, "My brother is fading and will not survive this night. I am going in." He stood and faced his men, "I will not ask this of you. You have each proven your bravery ... and your worth. No more is necessary. I relieve you of your obligations to me."

He pulled Veluria to her feet and said, "Go with Paulo. He will take you wherever you wish."

If we live through this, I promise I will bring him to you, M'lady, wherever you are.

He turned away and stalked into the night.

Veluria stood transfixed, unable to move let alone breathe. The man was foolhardy ... and magnificent. And more than the others she understood that should he find Antonio so terribly compromised that living would be a burden, he would do the unthinkable. And then he would wreak a terrible vengeance.

If you live, Nicolo, only if you live...

One-by-one, Nico's men rose and gathered their belongings, adjusting swords and quickly setting the brush in a rough semi-circle around the grazing horses.

Paulo came behind her and whispered, "It would be best if you stayed here, Madam."

Shrugging, she reached for the short sword that Maso extended toward her. She nodded, though she was sure Paulo could not see the movement. Murmuring, "Yes, that would be best," she trotted after the men, their long strides covering the ground between them and their commander.

Nico had taken the long route, aiming for the mouth of the gully in which they sheltered. She knew without asking that the man intended to try for a full frontal assault on the compound. He would rely on his strength and his ability to penetrate the minds of his opponents. She doubted even one so strong as he could handle more than one opponent at a time. It would be their job to provide a sufficient distraction to allow Nico to find his older brother before his captors decided to summarily execute him.

Pulling alongside Nico, she huffed shallow breaths in an effort to stay even with the man.

He hissed, "You should not be here."

"You need me." He gave her a dismissive wave of his hand. "I can ... offer a distraction." Nico hissed, "No," but she continued, "It is my job. It's what I do, Nico. Allow me to use my gifts."

Waves of displeasure and something more rolled off the tall man but he did not argue with her.

Paulo moved to take point, the other two fanning out to the right and left, slightly behind her and Nico. A click brought them to an immediate halt. Nico had her arm in a vice grip as he moved to shield her with his huge body. Someone was coming toward them. As one the small group melted against the rock wall forming the east face of the hollow, small brush and a few straggly trees providing the only shelter.

Nico sank onto his haunches, pulling her down to his level. Tapping his index finger twice on her arm, he let her know two men approached—but whether from the town or the hacienda was difficult to tell. The sounds of shuffling feet seemed to emanate from their left which would indicate the hacienda.

Had they lucked out? Perhaps the men were bound for the pleasures of the town, leaving two fewer at the compound.

The strangers were speaking in low tones, not bothering to mask their passage. They seemed at ease and strode with a casualness that indicated there was no urgency to whatever their plans for the evening might be.

When they finally passed close enough for her to make out the words, she was able to catch only a word here and there, the rest an incomprehensible dialect.

When the men had disappeared into the night Nico pulled her up and moved to speak with his group.

Paulo hissed, "Catalanese.

"I agree, separatists for certain." Nico turned to her and asked, "Are you sure of the number you saw at the inn?"

"Yes, there were at least six, probably seven. I was trying to be inconspicuous and at the time had no idea as to their intentions. But yes, at least that many."

"Let's assume seven. With those two gone, that will leave five."

Christo said, "Two to patrol the grounds."

Paulo interjected, "Perhaps only one. They seemed unconcerned. This is not the first time they have gone into town for an evening's entertainments."

Nico agreed, "They've gotten lazy. But let's assume two outside." He touched Christo's arm and said, "You and Maso, front and rear, quietly. You know what to do."

The two men melted into the night. Veluria asked, "What do we do?"

"We wait, M'lady."

Nico had learned patience at the knee of his formidable father. Being the scholar of the three sons of Cosimo de' Medici had awarded him the private tutoring and insights into the matters of state that so consumed the older man's interests. It had been Antonio who'd instructed him in matters of warfare and self-defense.

His father he accorded the utmost respect and veneration for his knowledge and political acumen, but it was Tonio who commanded

195

his allegiance. They could have been twins but for the five year difference in their ages. Ever mindful of their similarities, as boys they'd come to an unspoken agreement to go their own way, separate and equal, neither relying on their shared gifts to gain advantage.

He long ago accepted Tonio's devotion and love for their youngest brother, in fact shared it, though with Tonio it approached an obsessive need to protect Stefano from the vagaries of their world—and the gifts both he and Tonio considered curses. It had made Tonio's abuse of Stefano all the more shocking.

If they survived this hell they'd fallen into, he and Tonio would need to talk, seriously talk, about what had transpired that night. He'd been deadly serious when he'd warned his older brother that he would not tolerate such behavior. How far he would go to protect Stefano was not something he wished to think on.

I can kill you later, Antonio. If you do that ever again … I can and I will.

"Nico?" Veluria's voice had a shrill, uncertain quality.

"I'm sorry, M'lady," he whispered. "It's nothing." Damn the woman for reading his thoughts.

It's not nothing, Nico. I know what he did. And he will suffer for it 'til the end of his days.

This is not the time…

Maso appeared out of the gloom, wiping his blade on his tunic. He slipped the knife into the sheath and asked, "Where's Christo?"

Paulo answered, "Not back yet."

"He was right behind me. We saw only the one guard patrolling along the perimeter by the olive grove." Patting the blade he said, "I took care of it."

Nico muttered, "Shit. Paulo, stay with Veluria. Guard her with your life." Unsheathing his sword he growled, "Maso, you're with me."

Since nightfall, he'd been shielding himself from Antonio, deliberately cutting off all awareness so as not to distract his mind from the task at hand. But he couldn't continue to hide his gifts. He needed to find out where Christo—and most likely the other guard—were located before an altercation alerted the house to their presence. Tonio was ever in his thoughts, no matter the distance. For others, he had to be close, sometimes almost touching, before his senses kicked in and permitted his invasion of another's being.

196

Being with Veluria had somehow accentuated his abilities, though he'd had little opportunity to test that theory. Now was as good a time as any to see if he was right.

With one hand on Maso's shoulder he pulled the man to a halt and whispered, "Hold." Extending his senses, he scanned the still night. Not a sound—not insect or night creature—interfered, the beat of his heart the only accompaniment to his labored breathing. With effort he took shallow breaths, stilling his pulse. Tonio's essence wafted past, too weak to pinpoint.

But you live, my brother. Just a little longer...

He was about to give up when the faintest sound caught his attention. A chink of steel, gagging choked off, shuffling...

Releasing Maso's shoulder he ran silently in the direction of a stand of carob trees, the outline clear against the night sky. They'd yet to round the curve of the hollow to where the hacienda would afford pale light through the many windows. As it was still early in the evening, it was best to assume no one in the household slept.

Christo struggled to hold a small man squirming in his grasp, forearms locked about the man's throat but failing to gain sufficient purchase to finish the task. Nico idly wondered why Christo hadn't just cut the man's throat. The answer lay on the ground—Christo's blade had landed some distance away.

He pressed the tip of his sword against the man's cheekbone and whispered to Christo, "Do you need help?" He thought he heard Christo mutter, "Fuck you," but couldn't be sure. Smiling he said, "Free him."

Christo complied, though not without some reluctance. He pushed the man off and rolled to the side, grunting in pain. Nico saw that his jerkin and sleeve were covered in blood. He'd received a severe cut on his upper right arm—it looked deep and nasty—that must have hurt like hell when he applied pressure on it.

Slipping the blade to the assailant's throat he drove the tip into the man's windpipe, just enough to let him know he was deadly serious.

There was no time for verbal niceties so he slipped directly into the man's mind and demanded, *How many are in the house?*

The squirming stopped, replaced by abject terror. Unlike Antonio who could sift through the strong emotions with impunity, he was often stymied by his victim's fears and misgivings, needing to expend time and energy he simply did not have.

I will make it quick ... and painless.

"Th-th-thr—" It came out a choked-off gurgle as Nico drove the blade clean through the man's throat.

Christo staggered to his weapon and bent down to pick it up, his fingers grasping the hilt but unable to grip it sufficiently to lift it off the ground. With a groan, he used his left hand and hoisted the heavy sword awkwardly.

"You are of no use to us now, Christo. Go back to Paulo and take his place. Guard the woman as best you can."

As Christo moved unsteadily to do his bidding, he and Maso stepped cautiously toward the house, mindful they might be spotted at any time given the lack of sheltering vegetation. Maso tapped his arm and bore right toward the hillside. A small wooden outbuilding that reeked of urine and worse lay behind the rear porch with a flagged stoned path leading to it.

Candlelight flickered and wavered in the still air, throwing uncertain shadows onto the ground outside. The building had an air of neglect. Several window panes were missing and others were cracked; the porch at one time had been tiled but now lay littered with broken ceramic bits and dried vegetation.

Whatever occupied the residents did not require wasting beeswax in the rear rooms. Though small the hacienda was likely laid out in typical fashion with a central courtyard surrounded by a colonnaded archway with rooms leading off from it.

Paulo joined them, ghosting to a halt beside him. With a nod he acknowledged he understood when he motioned his men to the right and left of the house.

But before he could take a step, a piercing scream rent the night.

Chapter Twenty-Three

Veluria sliced at the hem of her shirt, making a strip long enough to bind Christo's arm. The fabric was filthy from their travels but she had nothing better with which to tend to the man's wound. The slice was deep, nearly to the bone, severing muscle and blood vessels. The bleeding was less than expected given the nature of the injury, but she feared infection without the ability to cleanse the cut of dirt and debris. Even if the man managed to avoid complications, she doubted he would ever have full use of that arm again.

Christo muttered, "That's fine, madam," and pulled away with irritation. Clearly he was unhappy about being relegated to sitting on the sidelines seeing to her safety. She had to agree.

The piercing scream was like a dagger to her heart, reverbing down the walls of the gully. As one their heads snapped around, following the source of the sound. Christo groaned and struggled to pick up his sword.

She cried out, "No," but the man was beyond listening to her. Even in the dark she could see the bloom of fresh blood on his tattered shirt.

Shifting the heavy weapon to his left hand, he growled, "Stay here," and moved away, each step labored.

Veluria hastened to Christo's side and wrapped her arm about his waist, taking as much of his weight as she could. He grunted, "M'lady," and gratefully accepted her help. They moved slowly but steadily through the now silent night.

Are you there, Tonio? Can you hear me? We're coming for you.

Only the sounds of their labored breathing and the soft scuffling of boots on loose gravel and packed earth measured their progress.

Veluria desperately hoped that the pain and misery of that single sound had come from some unfortunate creature of the night, prey in the grips of a predator. But she knew it came from Antonio and it was the final thing that snapped his control and forced him to vent his agony.

The bastards had finally broken his body. She feared they'd broken his mind and his spirit as well. A flash of fury such as she'd never known or felt before blazed through her mind—Nico.

Nico froze in place, allowing the echo of his brother's scream to wash through his senses in a cleansing flood of pitiless revenge. Veluria's terror had threatened to consume him. He needed to shut everything out, to allow the madness to take him, for nothing and no one mattered now. He knew what they'd done to his brother, every heinous act, every violation of body and spirit—the pain ripping through him with deft strokes, filling his throat with bile so thick he wanted to choke on it.

It was the knowing that nearly did him in, the realization that they'd stripped Tonio of his reason for living, the warrior broken of will, weak and defenseless.

Even now he felt *them* ... the cruel delight in breaking a man's spirit, the bloodlust and perversion, the evil that permeated their souls.

And he felt Antonio, awakening to memory—of who he was, of what he had been. Too late.

Too late, too late, too late...

Nico drew his blade and gestured toward the house, "He's in the courtyard." That he knew with certainty. But the rest was still a guess. He reached out, siphoning though confusing images, letting reason help him work through the possibilities. Finally he said, "There are two with him, the third must be occupied elsewhere."

Antonio moaning, *No, no, no...*

He was missing something but his men grew restless, waiting for his command. If he were seeking divine guidance he would not find it this night. He knew what lay on the other side of the walls. And for that a lifetime of penance would never be enough.

Maso pointed to a broken window and muttered, "Through there?"

Nico nodded agreement and took off at a run, calling back, "Paulo, with me."

Circling swiftly around the rear of the hacienda, Nico and Paulo searched for the door that would lead to the kitchens. Nico smelled the stink of stale wine and rotting food off to his right. Their third man was crouched in the dim light from the partially open door, his head back, flask tipped. Blood red droplets sloshed over the rim to drip into the parched earth. The man's tongue reached for the liquid, eyes closed against the night.

Nico took a fistful of greasy black hair and yanked back. The man's eyes popped open, staring upward in disbelief, then down at the blade slicing slowly across his jugular, the acrid stench of iron replacing the vinegary sweetness as the man exhaled his last breath. Nico settled the body face down and looked for Paulo.

His man had taken position at the door, sword at the ready. With a nod at his commander he slipped through the opening and disappeared into the maw of the kitchen. Nico continued around the corner of the building looking for another doorway but finding none. He would have to resort to the front door.

Feeling time slipping away, he angled away from the building, and from the weak light filtering through the windows. He relied on his men's training and discipline to wait for his sign. All about him the night had come alive, sounds magnified, drowning out the drumming of his heart and the painful raspy gasps as he stutter-stepped to avoid broken bits of stonework.

A lantern illuminated a small patch of porch and weed-strewn yard. It hung suspended on an ornate wrought iron hanger, swaying in an invisible breeze. Tempted to extinguish the candle, he decided instead to allow his eyes to adjust to the light. Once he entered the house he would need all his faculties. He couldn't risk being even temporarily blinded. That thought brought him up short.

He could feel his men, their patience wearing thin. It was time to confront what he most feared … having to free his brother into a hell no man deserved, let alone one who commanded his love and respect. Would he take the coward's way out, did he secretly wish that the choice would be conveniently removed?

Only now was he coming to the full realization that rescuing Antonio might mean releasing him into God's grace.

Whispering, "Sweet Mother of God, give me strength," he opened the heavy oak door, his promise to Veluria weighing heavy on his soul for he feared he would keep it and earn his brother's everlasting hate.

You will mistake pity for love and that which has not destroyed him this night will surely do so when kindness and caring become the torture he can no longer bear.

Sliding through the opening he moved his blade to his left hand, the metal warm to the touch, and replaced it with his sword. No amount of blood would feed his voracious need for revenge. Blackness invaded his soul and he welcomed the void, knowing what he was now was nothing compared to what he would become.

Nico raced through the foyer, no longer caring if they heard him, saw him. Out of the corner of his eye he glimpsed Maso rushing off to his right to engage in a blur of metal and incomprehensible shouts.

Paulo? Where was Paulo?

He knew Tonio writhed against his restraints but he refused to look. Not yet. The sight would transfix, distract. He couldn't afford that.

From the bowels of the surrounding rooms men poured, some still rubbing eyes heavy with wine and sleep, cursing in a language Nico didn't understand.

Dear sweet Jesus, they faced an army of armed men. Why did I not feel this?

Paulo bellowed in anger and dismay, his alert coming too little too late. There were too many for Nico to focus on anything but his brother's anger and agony. The hairs on the back of his neck stood up in warning. He spun in time to avoid being gutted, going down on one knee and angling the sword upward. His attacker's momentum carried him forward. Eyes wide, arms pinwheeling, the man sought to halt his precipitous advance only to land impaled on Nico's sword.

Switching his blade to his right hand, Nico rolled past shuffling feet, slicing neatly through Achilles tendons before coming to a stop on his hands and knees. With a lunge, he raced back to grab his sword, seeking Maso and Paulo. Both men were pinned, backs to the wall, Paulo bleeding from a slice to his cheek and Maso splattered with blood and gore. Nico couldn't tell if it was Maso's or his opponents.

His men fought well but visibly tired under the onslaught. Nico waded in, his blood boiling, forgetting technique in favor of blunt force assault, the ring of steel-on-steel music to his ears.

Tonio called to him. He tried to shut him out but the voice in his head was insistent.

Use me...

Dammit. His brother offered what little power remained to him. Nico shuddered at what it cost Tonio but accepted the gift and added the weak life force lingering in his brother's soul.

The one called Tomas. Save him for me...

I'll save him for both of us.

Veluria gasped when Christo crumbled to his knees, weakness, pain and loss of blood finally draining the man of all stamina.

"A moment, madam," he husked, voice wracked with dismay that he showed such weakness.

There was a moment when time suspended, when Veluria imagined the gateway appearing, Reverend Mother on the other side beckoning her home. With all her heart she wished for nothing more than the safety of her world, relief from the unrelenting violence, the harsh reality of a time so alien she quaked at the otherness and feared what it might do to her psyche.

I don't want to love him. Not like this.

But who, what did she love? The charming man-child who amused and delighted her senses, who'd become a vicious pervert with his universe turned inside out until only pain begot pleasure? She felt responsible for Stefano, inextricably so.

But her heart beat for the man who had been stolen from her before she had a chance to explore what her feelings meant, before understanding the depth of the Demon's commitment, his bond so formidable, so compelling, she nearly drowned in the power he offered her. Without reservation, he'd bared his innermost secrets—a man without mercy, without compassion, who believed himself forever damned. *That* demon gave her his heart to do with what she will. Yet to allow him to love her would be his death, for he would not survive the loss to come and that was a stain on her soul she'd carry to her grave.

She'd allowed Antonio to *need* her, an unacceptable error.

Perhaps it would be best for him to die this day, my child. You would save him the pain of your betrayal.

But what of me, Reverend Mother, what of me?

There is no you, dearest Veluria. You are but a construct, a tool. You are your Sisters, the One. You will return to your home when this is finished ... and forget.

Veluria quailed at the thought of abandoning the people she'd grown to care for. Even Nico, strong, intelligent, savage in his devotion...

Damaged goods. Damaged heart. I have the power to heal it.

Be careful, child. There are many types of betrayal. Do not confuse compassion with love.

Veluria bent to adjust the makeshift bandage on Christo's arm when the night air split with shouts and the unmistakable ring of metal on metal, the gurgling screams of men dying, gagging on blood and bile. The terrible sound of retribution.

Christo barked, "Help me to my fe—" but the words choked off mid-sentence.

Veluria watched in horror as the man she would have called friend pitched forward, blood pooling by his severed neck, the head rolling off into the darkness. Blanching, she turned to face her attackers, recognizing at once that the men staring at her with interest were the two they'd seen heading into the village.

She couldn't understand the rapid exchange but from their leers she knew they'd determined her sex and were already congratulating themselves on coming upon such an unexpected prize. They seemed unconcerned about the din and screams coming from the house. When the tall one leaned close she realized why—his breath, his body, stank of ale and garlic and sex. Drunk. Perhaps too drunk to register the sounds of slaughter.

But who? Who screamed their last breath? Panic danced in her chest, sending flutters of fear into her throat, her ears hammering dull staccato beats. Icy tendrils skittered up and down her spine, the fleeting registers of chaos and cruelty staking a claim to her

204

consciousness, edging close. She was being buried alive in terror that only imagination could claim.

Weaving slightly, the taller of the two pinched her upper arm painfully and dragged her toward the house. Her sword lay on the ground next to Christo's body, useless. All she had left was the blade stuck in her boot. She would use it, on herself if necessary. She had no illusions about surviving this intact.

The smell was throat-gagging strong, the air laden with gore, dust and blood, trapped inside the enclosed space, an arena of death and destruction. Veluria slipped on something slick and nearly went down, her mind closing against the possibilities. Her captor jerked her up and thrust her forward into a sea of bodies—men who had once been whole but now lay shattered on a killing field, no longer recognizable as human.

Veluria's mind blanked at the sight—Antonio strung up like a carcass, twisting weakly, kicking out as Nico pressed his two attackers back, his sword arm bleeding freely. Tonio managed to connect with one, causing the man to stumble. It was all Nico needed to gut him.

Feeling the madness grip her she screamed at Nico but her words were lost in clang of metal and the roaring of madmen locked in mortal combat. The man holding her dropped her arm briefly so he could draw his sword.

It was all she needed. The blade lay nestled in her boot, so near, yet so far. He was quicker than she would have given him credit for, the sword brandished with drunken glee. But she was faster and nimbler. Dropping to a crouch, she gripped the hilt and yanked the blade free, nicking her calf in the process. The slice stung but was shallow.

The man reached down and yanked her long braid, dragging her off the ground and shaking her like a dog with a bone. Scalp screaming in protest, she bit her lip and waited until he set her down, backhanding her cheek so hard she saw stars. She stumbled back, whimpering, her head ducking as she clutched her cheek with her left hand, the right fingering the blade until she had a firm grip. When he approached to deliver another blow, she bobbed away, and feigned a stumble, coming in low, below his fist, and buried the blade to the hilt in his groin.

The bellow of rage and pain was lost to the bedlam around her. The blade slid reluctantly out of the soft flesh with a satisfying pop. He had yet to release her so she sliced the wrist holding the sword, the blood spurting to coat her face as the weapon slipped from his grasp. With cold-blooded precision she grasped the heavy sword and drove it deep into the soft belly tissue.

The man staggered for a heartbeat, then dropped like a rock to lie writhing at her feet. Time stilled once more as she contemplated what she'd done. Her first kill. She knew with certainty, on this night, it wouldn't be her last.

Grimly Veluria turned to confront the horror that would haunt her to the end of days.

Chapter Twenty-Four

Do not look, M'lady." Paulo gripped her arm, tugging gently. "This is not for your eyes."

Is this what our world becomes, Reverend Mother, this insanity? Beasts released to ravage all we've built? Have we learned nothing?

No, my child. For history is never our savior and ever our weakness, and the peace we safeguard is as dust in the wind.

Then why am I here?

To salvage what we can…

Salvage? Is there no hope?

Find the other, Veluria. We shall need both of you now.

"M'lady, please…"

"No, Paulo. I am strong."

"Strong enough for…" he waved his hand at the carnage, "…this?"

Veluria's voice cracked, "Not for this. No."

With trembling fingers she gripped Paulo's wrist until he grunted in pain. They watched Nico cut his brother down, the hemp yielding ungracefully, thick ochre fibers splaying out in ragged clumps, the sword edge dulled to near uselessness. Tenderly he wrapped his arms about Tonio's waist and lowered the shattered body to the blood-soaked earth.

Paulo pleaded with eyes clouded in pain, "I must help him."

Reluctantly she freed the man and followed slowly as they staggered, single file, through a hellish landscape, the air already thick with the stench of death, cloying at the back of her throat. She listened for a moment, insects buzzing fitfully, the horde yet to descend, savoring what little peace remained before the internal screaming shut all her senses down.

What shall I do if he lives?
Hope that he does not, child.

Nico murmured something to Paulo, his man carefully averting his eyes from the wreckage that was once his brother. Sound echoed hollowly as Paulo moved away to do his commander's bidding. She followed the man with sightless eyes, unwilling to look down, mind blanked, denying the acceptance that would free her, free him.

Nico sank to his knees and pulled his brother into his arms, knowing full well that every touch was agony, that not a spare inch of flesh remained undamaged, the violation so cruel she had no idea how her Demon had survived so long.

Veluria crouched low, finally willing her eyes to see, to comprehend the atrocity she could no longer deny. She whispered, "Dear God, how does he live?"

Nico stared at her, eyes dry and hardened to pinpricks of hate. Slowly, carefully, he pivoted Antonio's body for her to see the true horror, leaving her to gasp for air. Falling to the ground, she scrabbled away, fighting the nausea. The stone pillar gave her something to brace against as she retched her agony into the barren blood-soaked soil.

Please don't let him live, not like this, robbed of all his senses, his very manhood. No man should suffer so.

Would Nico have the strength? What would his conscience dictate? His love for Antonio was a palpable thing, his pain and suffering so profound her mind paled at the depths of his despair.

Paulo approached with a handful of clean cloths and handed them gingerly to Nico, taking care not to touch his commander. It was not out of fear, but out of respect. The two brothers were joined in ways neither she nor Paulo could ever understand, and every fiber of her being dictated she turn away from what was to come.

Tentatively she probed, seeking that last essence of the soul Antonio had revealed, the promise of his love … the love she did not

208

want and did not deserve. Instead she found a wall shutting her out, closing off the inner being, the man who would be demon and lover and protector now locked with the one who knew him best. It was as it should be. She had no place in this world; she was alien to this time, both a shadow and a lie.

Paulo spoke softly, though his voice intruded like a shout, grating and unexpected, "Sire, what do you wish me to do?"

Nico hissed a breath, glancing first at her, then at his man. "Find Cristo and Maso. We shall not leave them in this place without paying our final respects."

"Sir." Paulo turned to attend to the grisly task of recovering the remains of his brothers-in-arms, but stopped and asked quietly, "How many?"

Veluria was uncertain what he meant until Nico replied grimly, "Three." At that point she knew her prayers would be answered and the beginning of her search for absolution would commence.

"M'lady, leave us. Please."

"No, I cannot." She said it with as much resolve as she could muster. What he asked next nearly derailed her.

"Did you love him?"

Did she love him? Veluria noted the use of past tense, as if her feelings could be so shallow that they'd not survive when confronted with a mere shell of a man, all he'd been, all he could be hacked off like hunks of meat. Butchery so complete she wondered if he could still be called a man.

She cared, deeply. She understood the gift he'd offered, the promise he made although even he could not fully appreciate the depths of his own yearnings. That it had been for naught, an unrealized, unconsummated passion—did that make it less real, less authentic?

She loved, for that was her reason for existence, part and parcel of her training. She was a master of the physical and emotional, cursed to wield her abilities in the service of a greater good. What she'd never realized until she'd met Antonio was that her spiritual being had lain dormant, untouched by all. Antonio believed he had no soul, yet he offered her that phantom gift and in so doing it became real ... and hers alone.

209

Did she love him? She'd asked herself that question dozens of times. She thought, she hoped, there was an answer, but now she would never know.

Nico deserved the truth. It was all the comfort she could offer to either of them.

"Yes, I could have loved him."

He nodded in understanding, then rose onto his knees and gently positioned Antonio on his back, grimacing at the sight splayed out in mute testimony to courage and self-sacrifice. With tenderness he pressed the cloths onto his brother's ruined face, his mouth set in a grim line. Antonio weakly grasped Nico's wrist with his left hand, leaving it there in silent supplication.

Veluria knelt by the men and placed a trembling hand on top of Nico's.

"Does he know I'm here?"

"No, M'lady. I will not allow that. Even he is not strong enough to bear your witnessing this."

Together they waited until Antonio's life force dissipated into the waiting night, the hand that had gripped Nico's wrist falling softly to earth, lying in repose. The huge man seemed somehow diminished, smaller in death than his fearsome presence in life had been, in the end just a man. Not a demon nor a devil.

Veluria said, "His suffering is over." She made no effort to mask the relief she felt.

"I fear, M'lady, that his suffering is just begun."

Veluria looked at him with surprise and stuttered, "Wha—?"

Nico carefully crossed his brother's arms over the massive chest, then stood with difficulty. Veluria followed suit and moved to stand next to the grieving man.

He asked, "Do you believe?"

"Believe?"

"In your world. Do you have hell?"

Veluria wasn't sure how to answer, yet she knew he needed the assurance. "Yes, we had this," she pointed to the courtyard and continued, "but on a scale that not even you could imagine." With a shudder she growled, "We brought hell to the living."

"Then nothing changes."

"No, Nico, nothing changes. That's why I am here."

Nico shrugged and said, "We will leave that discussion for another day, for when we find comfort in each other's arms. For now, we must pay our respects."

Veluria gaped as Nico bent and gathered his brother's body into his arms, as if he weighed nothing.

Are you strong enough for that?
Yes, M'lady, I am strong enough for this.
He was the key.
No, M'lady. You are wrong.

Nico carried his burden to the rear of the building, exiting through the kitchens. She trailed behind him, pondering his words.

Antonio's death refused to register. Her training and analytic mind took over, sparing her the burden of dealing with her errant emotions. She should be grateful for the automaton she'd always been, yet this family, these men and the violence of their time had somehow corrupted her control and left her caring. They'd breeched her once impenetrable defenses. Would the Sisterhood be able to repair the damage or would she be cast adrift to spend the rest of her days in loneliness and despair?

What if she could not fulfill her mission? That had always been a possibility—that she could and would be collateral damage. Yet the bigger question remained—how much of the horror of this day lay at the feet of her and her kind? Had she so compromised the timeline by her actions as to render the coming cataclysm inevitable? Was their deity exacting retribution for their folly and hubris in manipulating time and space? They meddled with history, paying obeisance to ancient principles, yet vindicating the endgame with false justifications and an unerring belief in the righteousness of science.

Veluria stood under the shelter of an olive tree and watched Nico and Paulo dig shallow graves in the soft earth of a weed-strewn garden. The men worked silently, sweat streaking bloody faces, arms and chests, with only the chink of metal on stone to disturb the frail pallor of grief. She wondered if any amount of washing would cleanse their bodies of the layers of hate and rage. It was far easier to clutch the hard kernel of anger, to hold it close, to nurture it like a

211

lover. Gentleness and caring sloughed too easily away, replaced by an ugliness that was a cancer consuming the soul.

She turned away as the men lowered the bodies into the shared grave, Maso first, then Cristo and finally Antonio. Nico looked up expectantly, eyes questioning. She gathered a handful of dirt and approached, one foot in front of the other, her shadow-self leading a solemn procession of all whose fates rested on this moment in time.

Never taking her eyes off Nico's face, she tossed the dirt onto the remains and murmured, "*Requiem in pace*," and touched her lips, brow and heart in order while the two men made the sign of the cross. When the men shoveled the first mounds of earth into the grave, she backed away and walked quickly to the other side of the house, her heart threatening to burst.

Nico found her much later and held her head as she dry heaved onto parched soil. With regret he informed her, "It is not over yet."

Nico lifted her easily and settled her against the tree trunk, keeping his massive hands braced on her narrow shoulders. She shook her head to indicate she didn't understand.

"We found one still living. He is the one…"

She gasped, "The one who did … that to-to…" The words trailed off as she fought against the memory.

"Yes." There was a frightening terseness, almost an eager anticipation to that single word.

"Why are you telling me this, Nico? Let it be over. Please. Let's just leave this wretched place to the vultures."

Nico tipped her head up and stared into her eyes. She didn't like what she saw.

"You said you would cut their balls off and make them eat them raw." Darkness descended over his ragged features, cruelty etching fine lines about his lips and eyes. "And I said you could do that after I was done with them."

She whispered, "And are you done with him?"

"I have yet to start." With that he spun and marched back to the house, disappearing through the door into the dim reaches of the foyer. She heard the footfalls on tile, then nothing.

Nico had made her an offer, a chance to exact revenge. Why? What did that prove? Did he doubt her feelings for his brother? Was he punishing her for the equivocation, having expected a more impassioned avowal of her feelings?

212

Somehow that seemed wrong, too out of synch with what she knew of the man. The Demon had proven his cruel, unforgiving nature but what of his brother? Rumor had it they shared abilities though Nico never exercised the level of power and control and sheer dominance of his brother. Tonio had been the merciless assassin.

So what manner of man was Nicolo de' Medici? Beyond the power broker image, he was the man who loved unreservedly, only to be cast aside and swept away with grief over his daughter's death—a death for which he held the blame tight to his heart. He was a man who loved his brothers and his family above all others, who would willingly die to protect them.

Were all who felt the unbridled passions of love and lust the same as those who found solace in ruthlessness and spite? She'd seen no spark of that divine madness that allowed retribution using the most heinous acts. There'd been nothing but a glacial determination in his eyes. And unless she stopped him, he would slip into a hell beyond even his imagining.

She knew in her gut Nico no longer cared about his own soul. But she did. And that was a path forbidden to her kind. Her own hell beckoned as she teetered on the brink of choices made in the heat of the moment rather than cold, hard analytics.

Massaging her temples, she tried to recall something he'd said, something that should have raised a flag but did not at the time. His peculiar statement, '...when we find comfort in each other's arms,' had a ring of truth. And a promise that sent shivers up her spine, whether in fear or something else she couldn't say. But there was more...

He'd said she was wrong. Antonio was not the key. Then who or what was? And how did Nico even know that? She'd risked all by opening herself to Antonio. Then she'd invited Nico in, just far enough to share powers, to find Tonio. That was it. Had he slipped in using Tonio's link? Was that even possible?

If what she suspected were true, then Nicolo had knowledge he was not meant to possess. Tonio had shared that knowledge yet he cared little for the particulars, intent only on the passion he felt. Nico on the other hand, knew and understood her mission—she was sure of it.

What he intended to do about it remained to be seen.

At the first scream, she raced into the house, ignoring all but the tragedy repeating itself in front of her eyes.

"Nico, stop!" Ears ringing with the echoes of agony, she pleaded, "Nico, you are better than this. Please, please don't be like them..."

Nico turned and scowled down at her, his face contorted in a nightmarish mix of pleasure and pain. His brother had been a demon, but this man was more, far more—*he* was the weapon that would destroy them all.

Sneering, Nico spat, "Madam, you don't understand."

"Understand what?" She already knew the answer but needed to keep him talking, focused on her and not the evil threatening to pervade his being.

"Today I am exactly like them."

"And what of tomorrow, who will you be then?" He kept his face blank but she caught a tremor in his lower lip as he warred with his need for revenge and the exacting price it would cost his immortal soul.

To Paulo he said, "You are free to go," and watched as his man nodded his understanding.

They waited a heartbeat, two, then Veluria said with conviction, "You are the key, aren't you? You shared energies, masquerading one for the other, indistinguishable." It was so clear now that only one of the pair remained. She wondered if the Brotherhood operative realized their error. If he did not, then there might still be hope.

Nico laughed, the sound oddly grating amidst the silence of death and the man whimpering as he hung suspended, awaiting his execution.

"I admire your dedication, M'lady." The hint of sarcasm stung but she deserved it. "But as I said before, this is a conversation for another time..." He allowed the final thought to linger unspoken.

Veluria blushed, vexed that he could twist her emotions so easily. She spat out, "Finish it."

"Do you still wish to ... participate?"

Her throat tight, she came to a decision. She'd made her first kill this vile day. She knew it would not be the last.

Handing her a sword, Nico stepped away and gave her room to advance. The man's eyes were squeezed shut in silent prayer as his body twisted against what was to come.

Heat—boiling, hot enough to curdle her blood—sent a wave of nausea through her gut. She lifted the weapon and angled sideways. The man whimpered once and pleaded in a language she couldn't understand, though she could taste his terror.

Nico whispered, "You loved him."

"Yes."

"Then I shall end it."

But only if I prove myself to you. Why, Nico, why?
Because we are one now.
I'm not strong enough for this.
But I am. Together. For Antonio. For the man we both loved.

Paulo gazed wide-eyed as two swords rose as one, then quietly melted into the dusk. Pausing at the grave he said softly, "It is done." For the second time, he'd been released from his obligations. He was free to go.

With his back to a tree he patiently waited for his commander and his lady.

Chapter Twenty-Five

Andreas let his eyes sweep the dais. It was one of the few liberties permitted when faced with the full Council in regal attendance. The fact that all fifteen members chose that day to put in an appearance indicated the seriousness of the current situation.

Matteo sat to the far right, studiously ignoring him as was their way. The man paid rigid attention to forms, insulating his people from the vagaries of fanaticism through ritual and a keen understanding of mathematics.

"Hand me my cassock, boy."

Andreas moved to comply. Matteo stood in front of a full-length mirror, frowning at the reflection.

"You have not worn formal choir vestments in years, Matt." He slid the sleeves of the garment up his prelate's arms and adjusted the tight-fitting shoulder seams over the fine-weave tunic. "I'm surprised it still fits."

Matteo gave him a rude gesture and smiled grimly. "Are you worried?"

"Should I be?" It was a valid question. Although Matteo had assured him that the convocation was a briefing only, he couldn't get past feeling that he was headed to the woodshed for a good stropping. Or last rites.

"I told you before, if there's punishment to mete out, the old men take volunteers. Few have the stomach for it anymore." The man carefully buttoned the ankle length robe, fumbling with the ornate wooden toggles.

"Here, let me." Andreas moved in front of his lover, crouching to reach the lowest set, and finished the task. Smoothing the fine fabric over Matteo's slim form, he turned to the valet to retrieve the lacy rochet. "Lean down, you're too tall for me to reach."

Matteo muttered, "Shrimp," as he lowered his head to receive the overgarment. The narrow fit of the cassock allowed the flowing sleeves of the rochet to settle elegantly about his wrists. Not bothering to hide the complaint he said, "I feel like a fucking fop."

"It's tradition…"

"Don't start." Matteo grimaced. "I can't stand that ancient tune."

Andreas bit his lip, choking back the urge to hum the melody. Normally such teasing would have the man chuckling, but this day he sheltered behind his ceremonial garb, sober to the point of glumness. What did he know that he wasn't sharing?

"Which cape, Your Holiness?"

Matteo chose to ignore the sarcasm and said, "Just the mozzetta today, Andy." He sighed with displeasure, "And the zucchetto." He set the small red cap on his slicked-back greying curls and surveyed the effect.

Andreas stared with awe. The man was magnificent. He moved to stand side-by-side with his lover and superior, not bothering to hide his admiration for the man who'd chosen him above all others.

Matteo's features softened incrementally as he scanned the small figure standing beside him. He fingered the rough woolen robe and said, "I'm sorry for the discomfort. I had the costumers scrape the inner fibers to remove some of the coarser bits. But we had to leave it mostly as is."

Andreas nodded he understood. His comfort hardly mattered in the big scheme of things. The wool fabric irritated his skin in a satisfying way, a constant reminder of his mission and his resolve. His small stature, while unusual in his own time, allowed him to fit in easily, to become truly invisible to the masses going about their daily lives.

What he couldn't understand was why Matteo, of all men, would choose him as consort. He was nothing, no one…

"I know what you're thinking, boy, and you're wrong. How often do I have to tell you…" he let the words trail off and pulled Andreas to stand in front of him.

217

When Matteo gripped his arms and leaned in to nuzzle his ear, Andreas groaned, "Don't, Matt, you'll get the vestments dirty."

"You're right. The Three would have my ass in a sling if I showed up less than pristine." He backed away marginally and said, "It's time."

Andreas murmured, "Yes," but remained rooted to the spot, struggling to find the words that eluded him. Finally he said, "I feel like…"

"…we'll never see each other again," Matteo finished the thought. The tall man's eyes grew soft with longing and regret. "We know the risks."

"It doesn't make it any easier."

"That's why we have faith, Andy."

Andreas had no answer to that. What he had was more—and less—than simple faith. And it waited for him on the other side. But that was not something he would willingly share with the man who'd given him his heart. He had no qualms about breaking with his faith but he would suffer grievously if he ever lost Matteo's regard.

That his lust continued to be a real and present danger was something he agonized over nearly every minute of every day. There would be opportunity. There would be a choice. He would own his betrayal when the time came.

He followed his superior down the hall leading to a set of antechambers. Matteo ushered him into an austere room, no more than ten by ten, with a single mahogany bench set against a cream stuccoed wall.

When Andreas settled onto the seat, Matteo leaned over him and lightly brushed his mouth, running his tongue along the bottom lip, savoring the taste.

Cupping his chin, the man said intently, "Pay careful attention, Andreas. The playing field has changed dramatically."

"I ask you again. Do I need to worry?"

"Yes, my love. You do." He stood, head bent, and made the sign of the cross over Andreas. "I fear this time … we both do."

Matteo paused at the door and said, so quietly Andreas' strained to hear the words, "If you take her, will you love her?" Without waiting for a reply he disappeared into the Council's chambers and shut the door with an audible snick.

Andreas fingered the stiletto, tempted to seek a distraction in the carefully applied cuts, his emotions seething with the wish to say no but his body already responding to the implied promise.

He *needed* the prelate. He *craved* the woman. Time and distance had done nothing to alleviate the constant yearning in his soul.

If it comes down to it, which will you choose?

A voice intruded, "Father, if you'll come with me, please?"

Andreas rose reluctantly and followed the cleric into Council Hall.

The mathematician scribbled on an antique whiteboard, leaving streaks of oily silicone polymer where the side of his hand brushed the slick surface. Residual solvent flavored the air with memories of youth and foolish choices. Andreas wrinkled his nose with pleasure. Before the day was out he'd be immersed in the stink of antiquity in a way none of the Council or their scientists could imagine.

The man completed transcribing the formulas, then stood back and surveyed the information with a mixture of pleasure and dismay. The probabilities, the portents, were so compelling that they had the ring of inevitability. It was their gift and their curse, this ability to predict within a narrow margin of error, a margin so small it practically reeked of being error-free. But that was a hubris the council carefully avoided for it would negate plausible deniability and undermine their authority.

The Council embraced a certain level of fallibility, allowing for Fate and divine intervention when the situation suited. Fear of the unknown no longer functioned to keep the narrow-minded cabals in line. Self-serving rationality and the pursuit of reason provided sufficient purpose and meaning to maintain the peace.

Or it had until everything changed…

Matteo rose and thanked the cadre of scientists, then bid them leave. When the room had cleared, he scanned the upturned faces of his fellow members, waiting for acknowledgement to proceed. Andreas realized he was going to hear analysis suitable for one far above his pay grade, as the lab techs would joke.

Kneeling at the lectern, Andreas bowed his head and waited.

Matteo stepped down from the dais and approached the whiteboard, considering the complex computations before launching into a summary of what they'd inferred from the perturbations in the timeline.

"We've all had time to examine the extrapolations. There are now four antagonists, three prepared to go nuclear, and one prepared for mop-up duty." A Council member chuckled. "Yes, Lucas, that would be *us*. However, it's not in our best interests to reside over yet another nuclear winter. One was enough."

The Council murmured their agreement.

Andreas looked up with interest. He'd no idea any of the cabals had access to weapons of mass destruction. That alone gave added import to halting the degradation of the timeline.

Ruefully, Matteo continued, "As good as our analytics are, we cannot predict with certainty who or what in the distant past interferes with or precipitates these catastrophic events."

Matteo picked up a marker and circled the final equation. He waved Andreas to come forward.

"This probability boils down to two branches." He tapped at the sigma sign and raised an eyebrow. "Unfortunately the outcomes appear diametrically opposed."

Andreas asked, "How so?" as he struggled to comprehend the intricate zero sum calculations. His grasp on the fundamentals was intuitive and that made it useful in the field. But in a laboratory, or in this situation, he was at a loss.

Matteo paced before the dais, one hand kneading his temple, the other clenching and unclenching his phantom beads. Ceremonial garb precluded the comfort of their tora as the clacking noise was deemed too invasive for Council proceedings. That his lover exhibited that weakness in front of his peers was a measure of the seriousness of their position ... and the urgency for his own intervention.

"Holy Father," Andreas employed the formal term of respect to refocus the tall man on the task at hand: to bring him up to speed on events that had unfolded while he'd rehabbed and regained his strength. From an almost infinite number of possible outcomes to only two indicated a radical paradigm shift. What in god's name could have happened to warrant such a collapse?

"Yes ... yes, forgive me." Matteo pointed to a heavy-set, swarthy figure and said, "Salvatore, if you please...?"

The man cleared his throat and spoke with the authority of a university lecturer, his voice booming through the narrow chamber. "We have had some unexpected developments. When you left, all the principals were positioned," he fingered a universal remote, aimed at a screen suspended toward the rear of the room that displayed a map of the Mediterranean region, "here, here … and here."

Andreas took a proffered laser pointer and flicked it quickly over Florence, then the Iberian Peninsula. He knew Tonio pursued his younger brother and the Sisterhood operative. He also surmised Tonio would employ his doppelganger brother Nicolo in whatever scheme they'd devise to secure the woman and return her to Cosimo. Reasonably sure of the outcome of that confrontation, he'd predicted that all but Nicolo would return to Florence where he could reengage with Veluria, using her to run point while he figured out how to neutralize the key: Antonio de' Medici.

Salvatore nodded his agreement and said, "And under normal circumstances you would have been correct. However," he tapped the desk with irritation, "apparently your Sisterhood operative managed to join her powers with the Demon de' Medici." He paused at a hiss from one of The Three and nodded agreement, "And, no, none of us believed that to be even remotely possible."

Andreas exchanged a glance with Matteo. Even living a daily existence with the impossible did not preclude having a few surprises thrown into the mix. He hadn't been wrong. For once he'd have preferred it otherwise.

He listened with interest, and increasing dismay, while the stocky prelate related the reconstruction of events, ending with the death of the Demon. While they could never know exactly what had transpired, the one thing they knew for a certainty was that the man they'd all regarded as 'the key' was no longer a player on history's stage.

Removing the zucchetto, Matteo slapped the cap against his cassock. "We have two possibilities, gentlemen. One, Antonio de' Medici was the key and his death sets off a series of events that have yet to occur. Or two, we were wrong and he is not the key."

One of The Three interjected, "If that man wasn't the key, then who the hell is?"

Salvatore offered, "Cosimo? He has the gift. He is, and always has been, the kingmaker."

Matteo shook his head vigorously against that assessment. "The man has never once taken the direct path. His is the power behind…"

Andreas interrupted, his brain doing the rapid calculations. He could almost taste the potential. "It will take place at the Habsburg court. Friedrich stands to become a member of the Reichstag, bringing as he does the goodwill of Florence—and undoubtedly Venice—along with a guaranteed Papàl blessing. Leo owes his position to his cousin. He'd consecrate a union with the devil himself if it fit Cosimo de' Medici's purposes."

Picking up the thread, Matteo continued, "I agree. My gut tells me that whatever the precipitating factor, it has yet to happen. We still have time. Cosimo will not risk his house with a personal visit to Friedrich's duchy. He's sent his son to act as his eyes and ears."

"So this boy is the key?" A disembodied voice from the far end of the dais quavered with age but the prelate's eyes had a hard, bold look.

Both Andreas and Matteo answered as one, "No!"

Andreas ducked his head quickly and murmured, "…Your Holiness." He'd almost forgotten himself, a fact his lover had reminded him of with a quick pinch to his butt. The pinch became a caress before Matteo moved away to address The Three in the center.

"We have two possibilities. We have validated that the Sisterhood's operative, this woman called Veluria, joined her powers with the Demon. It's possible she may have taken on some of the Medici's gifts. While our geneticists assure us that such transference is not only unlikely but close to the realm of unthinkable, I for one am not willing to forego any potential consequences of such a bonding. On the other hand, we do have some compelling evidence to indicate that Nicolo may have assumed his brother's fate based on field observations." He indicated Andreas should continue.

"I followed the man I thought to be Antonio de' Medici to the docks and watched him board the ship that would take him back to Iberia. His signature energy, the way he moved and carried himself—everything spoke to me of the Demon. There was no one more vexed than I to discover that it was his brother, Nicolo. No one,

222

including myself, had believed the rumors to be true. But I assure you, I do not make mistakes." He stared at each of The Three in turn. "Not about this."

Salvatore spoke quietly, "Do you have a way forward, young man?"

"Yes, Holiness. I need to know what Cosimo knows. All information passes through his house. I can use my contact with the Monsignor to pave the way. Between him and the elder Medici I will have the excuse I need to enter Friedrich's court legitimately. And from there, I will await developments."

Matteo agreed, "This is a reasonable plan and well within mission parameters. I suggest we move on this immediately." He turned to Andreas and spoke softly, "Go to the chapel and begin your meditations. I will join you shortly."

As Andreas proceeded down the aisle toward the rear door, he heard one of The Three say, "I hope to hell you know what you're doing, Matt."

"So do I, Tom. But right now we've got three sets of guns to our collective heads. Whatever we do isn't likely to make matters any worse than they already are."

Andreas slipped into the hall and padded silently to the chapel. After carefully locking the outer door he knelt at the altar and began his prayers, readying mind and body for the difficult journey ahead. The only thing that made traversing dimensions tolerable was knowing what awaited on the other side.

That, and the man approaching from the secluded sacristy to his left. He smiled when a rough hand stroked his neck and whispered, "Come back to me in one piece, Andy, or by God..." Matteo lifted him up and led him to the small room where vestments and sacred vessels had once been stored but now contained only a narrow cot and bedside table.

Andreas sank onto the mattress and sighed with contentment. He would leave the clacking beads and monotonous repetitions of meaningless words to the true believers. Unlike them, Matteo understood his needs.

Slipping his woolen robe, he murmured his passion as his lover prepared his body to ease through the gateway on a sigh of pleasure.

Chapter Twenty-Six

Veluria paced uncertainly about the small cabin. Movement had been ill-advised for hours as she lay prostrate, braced against the violent yawing of the vessel as they raced on a downhill slide toward Roma. Nico had used his considerable resources to secure a craft, compensating the captain for lack of cargo at usurious rates. The thought of another ship, another time and place, had her quaking in her boots but she'd numbly acquiesced, knowing full well they had few options.

Time seemed irrelevant now. She had little memory of its passage, only that they flew at a punishing pace to the coast, her mind blank to all but her grief. She was not the only one to retreat into a shell. Nico rarely spoke and when he did it was to address Paulo, commands issued tersely and always just out of range of her hearing.

His man had tended to her needs, little as they were. Now he was gone, tasked to safeguard his commander's position at Carlos' court, to offer the explanations and assurances that might forestall the inevitable questions and opportunism of men tuned to the misfortune of others.

Each retreating behind their barricades, they avoided close contact though she was ever aware of the man's presence as he moved about the vessel, joining the crew in the mundane tasks of piloting a ship through shallow, dangerous waters. It was a phantom presence, unsatisfying in ways she could never explain, as if they'd been conjoined twins, now severed, the parts diminished and so much less than the whole.

The larger questions of who and what they'd become seemed irrelevant. It was the trivial iotas of living she missed now. She no longer recalled the flavors and odors of food, eating mechanically, if at all. She missed taking a bath, soaking in steaming hot water, relaxing away the cares of the day. Would she ever again know that exquisite pleasure of feeling clean, scrubbed free of doubt and self-recrimination? Would she never again know her true purpose, the fulfillment of her fate, her service to the greater good?

I have lost my way, Reverend Mother.
It is the ennui, child. The beginning of the Little Death.
Then bring me home.
It is not yet time.
I grieve. Why do I suffer so?
Who is it you grieve for, child?
I ... don't know.

The light tapping on the cabin door broke her reverie. She wanted to ignore it, preferring to stay cocooned in her despair, out of sight of the man fate had dictated as the savior or destroyer of them all. With Tonio she'd been convinced of the rightness of that choice—that his destiny and hers would unite to do what Reverend Mother decreed: salvage enough to save both worlds.

The man who waited outside the door was both a stranger and a collaborator, a man she feared like no other.

"Madam?" Nico's voice was tight, insistent. Waves of displeasure, anger, confusion assaulted her senses. Pummeling her with power.

Dear Holy Mother, what manner of demon had they unleashed that night?

Veluria backed against the bunk, calling out, "I wish to be alone," yet her voice quavered, broadcasting her fears. She sat heavily on the cot, curling reflexively in a ball, the rough clothing stretched across raw open wounds as the willow stick flicked with precision. Air curdling with a sensuous whoosh, time slowed, skin stretched taut to receive the offering. Edge brittle and slick with blood, slicing like a sword tip, stripping each layer to reveal the woman beneath the mask. Enduring. Her gifts perverted. Powerless.

She opened her mouth in silent supplication.

For me, Reverend Mother, I grieve for me…

****

Nico rubbed his scalp with frustration. He understood the woman's need to be alone, he shared that, as he shared far too many things with her. But he had questions and they would soon be home, with Cosimo, bearing news no father should ever hear. Only this woman could help him make sense of the images and thoughts that consumed his being now. It was a waking nightmare, his head filled with Tonio and the woman's combined knowledge, dangerous and inexplicable. He'd been led down the path of madness his brother followed, with regret to be sure, yet that seemed of little consequence given the threats to their worlds.

Worlds.

How was he to wrap his mind around such a heretical thought? He'd been raised on two realities: heaven and hell. This life, this shadow existence, was a mere stepping stone to another, authentic reality. Realities bartered, bought and sold on the whims of men whose concerns had little to do with the hereafter, and everything to do with securing advantage in the now.

That he believed in neither mattered little. That he could believe in a reality that mirrored his own, with a life force, a history, inextricably linked to events in the here and now … *that* defied his understanding, yet he accepted it as truth. What truly troubled him was why he cared about either future.

And the one person with whom he could explore the hidden messages buried in the confusion lay dead in a shallow grave, dead by his own hand. What he'd done was out of love, not mercy, for he had none in his soul. If he were to employ his skills in the service of history, mercy would play no part.

He would do what he must and if that meant selling his soul to a devil he did not acknowledge, then it was a small price to pay to exact revenge. And to save the one thing he and his brother should never have shared, the one thing he'd foresworn he'd never do again … give his heart to a woman.

Feeling ten kinds of foolish, he approached the cabin door and tapped softly, hoping against hope she'd be asleep and would not answer.

Dammit, I can't continue on this way. I need to see her. Now.

"Madam." The single word came out harsher than he intended, the formality feeling strange on his tongue. Before he could soften his tone and try again she confirmed what he already knew and he quailed at the distress he heard. She suffered as did he, yet he needed to know why and how it was so.

She said she *could* love his brother. He needed to know what that meant, for reasons that he would surely regret. He felt her grief like a living thing, felt his own need and hers, felt a kernel of hope blossom when it had no place in his soul.

The silent scream split his skull, reverberating and echoing, a long drawn-out susurration that left him staggering. He bolted through the door only to stop abruptly when his eyes found the source of the mental din. Waves of pain and terror boiled and bubbled around the tiny figure curled on the bunk, knees drawn to her chest, arms wrapped about her head. She lay still, deathly still, eyes squeezed shut and mouth open in an 'O' but no sound emerged. It was as if she'd turned to stone, forever damned to an eternity of denial and fortitude, yet all about her the air danced in fevered vortices.

In that instant he understood who and what she was, and he cursed the Order who'd taken such a thing of beauty and corrupted it into a vessel to use as they pleased. They'd filled her with purpose and convinced her of its moral rightness. They'd taught her love, then denied her the means, convincing her that the divide between could and would was unfathomable, with no promise of a hereafter to console and sooth the harsh reality. At least in his world, men of faith offered lies and empty promises. His world was cruel, ruthless … but hers? It spoke to a brutality he failed to comprehend.

Now they both walked in the shadow of history, condemned to repeat its mistakes. Nothing changed. Nothing ever would. Not unless *he* did something about it. She and his father had called him 'the key'. He hoped to hell they were right.

Sitting on the bunk, he lifted Veluria into his arms, gently cradling the still form, rocking her as he would have done with the daughter denied him for all time. She lived, though barely, the breaths coming shallow, slowing imperceptibly and he feared she willed her life force away.

"Veluria, don't leave me, please," he whispered into her tangled mass of hair, one hand stroking her cheek, the other pressed against her back.

With a start he realized the fabric was sticky and when he pulled his hand away it was slick with blood.

"Sweet Jesus, what is this?"

Turning Veluria over, he stared tight-lipped at the streaks of blood imprinted on the thin blouse. With trembling fingers he took his blade and sliced through the fabric, revealing pale ridges of welts in a pattern he recognized. She'd been whipped, though not recently. These were old wounds, healed over, yet now some split and opened afresh, spilling her heart's blood.

Willing power into her frail form, he crushed her to his chest and made a deal with deities he did not quite believe in. Throat tight, he hummed a lullaby he'd crooned to his daughter, the infant he'd held close—in his mind and in his heart but never in his arms, kept away from his child through spite and hatred and vindictiveness.

He'd vowed never to shed another tear, yet as darkness fell and the woman barely clinging to life continue to slip from his grasp, all he had left were his tears. Pulling a worn blanket about her, he determined to stave off the icy tendrils of death welcoming them both.

"I'll do it. Whatever it takes. Just tell me what to do, Veluria," his voice cracked with emotion. Begging he cried, "Please. Don't leave me. I don't want to be alone anymore."

****

Veluria registered soft murmurings, a voice echoing down a long, dark tunnel, then the sharp sting and burn, igniting her back in blazing heat. Groaning, she cried out, "Stop! What the hell are you doing?"

"Cleaning your wounds, sweetheart. Be still. I know it hurts."

Hurt? 'Hurt' didn't touch it. She squirmed but Nico had her in a vice grip and wasn't letting go. What the hell had happened? He was obviously treating wounds of some kind. Had she fallen? She couldn't remember…

"This will feel better." The man didn't sound as sure as she would have liked given the extent of discomfort she suffered.

My back, what's the matter with my back?

"Nico…?"

"I'm sorry, love. I can't put you out like Tonio could. I don't know how." The effort to speak his brother's name took an obvious toll as he paused for several heartbeats before saying, "Give the tallow some time to work."

She yelped in surprise as the hot wax coated her raw flesh, his fingers carefully spreading the cooling makeshift salve with a gentleness that surprised and impressed her.

"Is that better?"

She mumbled a string of curses into the rough cloth of his jerkin then stopped when he hissed a breath and went still. He carefully lifted her up and set her down on the bunk, then rose and stood over her, a peculiar expression on his face. She allowed her eye to travel down his long torso, confirming what she suspected.

The tall man picked up the bowl and soiled cloths and set them on the small table. She thought he might withdraw but instead he came to kneel next to her, lightly stroking her hair.

"Rest now."

"Nico, what happened?"

"I'm not sure. You have old wounds that opened. Almost as if they were new."

Dear Holy Mother. Stefano. The willow stick. How could she have forgotten? What was happening to her?

"Something's wrong, Nico. None of this is right." She rose to her elbows with difficulty, the tallow cracking and sloughing off but the pain had lessened to where she hardly noticed it.

The man's face was a terrible thing to observe. Anger and dismay and a thousand other emotions played across his features.

"My brother did this." The man's eyes turned dark with killing rage. He spat out, "*Both* of them."

Sputtering, "No, don't ," her throat caught as she struggled to say the man's name, "don't blame Antonio."

She sat up with an effort, all too aware she bared her breasts to his hungry gaze. He reached down and pulled the blue-black tresses forward, arranging the long strands carefully to cover her nakedness. His fingers grazed the soft flesh, sending a chill up her spine, heat pooling between her legs. It was an unexpected consideration, an unexpected … pleasure.

"Forgive me, M'lady, I ruined your garment. I will find something else for you to wear." He spoke stiffly and she worried he had reason to be angry with her though she couldn't figure out why.

"No, M'lady. My anger is for Antonio who unleashed the corruption in Stefano."

She'd forgotten he could read her thoughts when her defenses were down. Everything she'd been taught, all that had come automatically, a result of training and discipline, flew in the face of the man's superior power. In the deepest recesses of her mind, the one place she still controlled, she wondered if this man, the key, was more powerful than all of them.

The man's face remained grimly stretched tight over sharp-edged cheek bones, dark stubble adding danger and allure in equal measure. Fine lines radiated from wide-set blue-grey eyes, the brows coming together in a stern expression. With his thin lips set in a straight line he looked like a man who faced life with a dour austerity, yet she'd seen him relaxed and at ease with his men, laughing and joking. She'd liked that man. *This* one she wasn't as sure about.

"It wasn't his fault, Nico. The darkness in Stefano was always there. It would have come out no matter what." She grimaced, remembering the subtle signs that she'd used to her advantage to bind the young man to her. Of them all, she'd been the most culpable. She'd awakened the beast. Antonio had simply opened the door.

Reverend Mother, I should not be here. Bring me home before I lose myself.
When the time is right, my child. Only then.

Nico stared at her oddly, as if he could almost hear that particular conversation, one designed to be a closely guarded secret. But that wasn't possible. Even linked, he should not be privy to those most covert thoughts.

His mouth curled upward in a cruel parody of a smile. He said softly, "There is blame enough to go around, M'lady."

She was growing weary of the formality, the incessant use of 'M'lady' in an effort to distance himself from his desire. Every instinct dictated that she unleash her wiles, force him to acknowledge and move on his lust. At least then she would be on familiar footing, and not engaged in a cat-and-mouse game of reluctant seduction.

"Be careful what you wish for, Veluria." He stood over her and stared, his blue eyes crystalline and sharp, hard as diamonds. At that moment in time he looked like he hated and loved her in equal measure. When he finally spoke, the threat pierced her like an icicle through the heart. "You won't like me that way."

"You said 'when we find comfort in each other's arms'. Do you remember?"

"Yes, I remember. But today is not that day." He turned and left the cabin so quickly she barely registered his leaving.

****

Damn his foolish heart. The woman vexed him, tempted him beyond a man's endurance. He was beginning to appreciate why both his brothers had fallen under her spell. But he was not them.

He knew a thing they had not. Veluria was destined to be his … but on his terms, not hers. And nothing, no one, would stand in his way. He planned to possess her and keep her safe, even if he had to destroy both their worlds to make it so. When she'd nearly slipped away, he'd been shocked and dismayed at the level of his despair. Whatever happened, losing her was not an option, but he wasn't foolish enough to think he controlled his own destiny.

What do I need to do to convince you to stay with me?

She'd been sent to safeguard *her* world. *His* destiny lay on a different path. He must vouchsafe his house and his lineage, and Veluria was the means to accomplish that. Cosimo understood that better than any of them, his gift of prescience shared the night before he'd embarked for Spagna. Yet, as with all things, there was a murkiness to the prognostication that left far too much room for interpretation and misguided judgments.

She thought them all naïve and unschooled, unable to understand the particulars—and in some ways she was correct. But the more time he spent with her, the more he penetrated her powers, the easier it was to adjust to a new mindset.

The captain of the vessel interrupted his thoughts. "We'll be making port by morning, sir. Is there anything you need before then?"

"Um, yes. Do you happen to have any women's clothing on board?"

The captain gave him a sly smile and nodded yes.

"Well then, bring what you have. My lady desires clean clothes before disembarking." He motioned to the cabin and said, "Leave them by the door. I will see that she gets them."

The captain tipped the brim of his cap and turned away.

Nico continued to stare at the rolling waves, the weather still unsettled, causing the ship to pitch uncomfortably. He was hungry, his belly growling, but the hunger extended far beyond that.

Yes, I remember, M'lady. But I want more than comfort, more than simple sexual release. I don't want your false promises.

What I want is a sacrifice I do not deserve. I want you to choose.

I want you to choose ... me.

Chapter Twenty-Seven

The Monsignor looked displeased enough to give even Andreas pause. Much resided on the man's ambitions, and connections, to ease his path. If he withdrew his patronage, Andreas would be forced to secure other means to insinuate himself into the Habsburg stronghold.

The sense of urgency, of time speeding up, had engulfed him with an almost physical presence when he'd exited the gateway, wiping away the satisfaction of his lover's embrace. It was a rude reminder that the games he played had consequences—and he'd been removed from the chessboard long enough that he was now at a disadvantage.

"It's been weeks. I hope you have something worth my time, Andreas."

"Your Holiness, please forgive me, but..." he parted his robe to expose the still weeping wound on his leg, "...I was injured in my travels and was forced to seek shelter until I healed enough to return to Venice." Silently he thanked Matteo who had come up with the excuse, and his scientists with their clever devices.

"Return to Venice?" The Monsignor raised an eyebrow in interest.

"I had intelligence from a reliable source that the Demon had pursued his younger brother to Spagna in order to bring him back to the fold." He gave the prelate a quizzical glance, not sure how much the man knew about Cosimo's plans for the pup.

"Explain."

Andreas launched into what he knew about the flight, filling in details where necessary but leaving it vague enough that should the man hear the real story he could lay any misinformation at the feet of unreliable rumor.

"By the time I had healed sufficiently and managed to reach Castile, it was too late to determine what actually happened. All I knew was that the Demon was headed west, toward the Portuguese border. I decided to follow that lead as per your instructions." He sighed with regret, "I fear I do not know the fate of the youngest Medici."

"Cosimo's youngest is now firmly entrenched at Friedrich's court." The man did not look happy at that state of affairs. With Florence and the Papàl States all currying favor with the nominal rulers of half the continent, the Monsignor's understanding with Siena looked to be on shaky ground. With Habsburg backing, the Famiglia Medici stood to make Tuscany a major economic and political power in the region.

Andreas merely said, "Ah," and continued with his report. While the scribe diligently recorded pertinent details, the Monsignor looked bored and inattentive. That changed abruptly when Andreas said, "The Demon is dead, your Holiness."

"Antonio de' Medici? Dead?" He leaned forward, palms splayed on the mahogany desk, and growled, "Are you quite sure about that?"

"Yes."

"And you know this … how?"

Andreas paused before continuing. The Order had nothing substantial he could use to explain how and why the Demon had died, just that he had—and the location. He knew all too well that the devil was truly in the details and that plausibility rested solidly on perception. The Monsignor was canny *and* perceptive. For that only the truth would suffice.

"Only by rumor, Holiness." He moved toward the desk, glancing furtively left, then right. Whispering so that only the prelate could hear, he said, "The young one's brother was part of it. She had no reason to deceive me for how could she possibly discern my interest?"

With a wave of his hand, the Monsignor dismissed the scribe. When they were able to talk freely, the Monsignor asked, "Do you have any details?"

"Regretfully, no. It seemed enough to establish the veracity of the claim without pressing for unnecessary details." He gave the man a sly grin. "I was, after all, occupied with other pursuits."

The Monsignor laughed out loud. "So your ... appetites continue to stand you in good stead. Well done, Father." He stood and moved toward his quarters but before exiting the chamber he asked, "Have you done sufficient penance, my son?"

Heat pooled in Andreas' groin, his cock responding to the implied promise. He lowered his head and sighed, "No, Sire, I fear no penance shall ever be enough."

"Well then, retire to your quarters and rest. You shall join me on the morrow. We make haste to Friedrich's court."

"You, Holiness?"

"Hmm, yes. I was fortunate enough to secure the Papàl Legate's charge to extend best wishes on the happy union of those houses. Friedrich stands to gain some importance now that Cosimo has singled him out for Florence's special attentions." His tone turned sharp. "Our interests, and those of Venice, must be seen to."

Andreas muttered, "I understand," and turned to leave.

As he limped to the door, the Monsignor called out, "Father? Should I send someone to assist you with your meditations?"

Without turning around, he simply nodded assent, a grin splitting his features. With any luck his meditations would include the young novitiate. For all her inexperience, he'd rather enjoyed that encounter.

In the meantime, he would use the seclusion to concentrate on finding the whereabouts of Veluria. Her presence was a palpable thing, yet he knew she was not in the city, a fact that distressed him and taxed his patience.

The Sisterhood's operative would have come to the same conclusion as the Council. Whatever was about to happen was centered on the Habsburg court. *She* would be there. He counted himself fortunate that he understood the power of anticipation— something Matt had taught him. Once he sorted out the major players and determined the sequence of events, he would decide how best to secure the prize ... Veluria.

He'd almost dozed off when a tap on the door roused him from the near slumber. The same girl stood transfixed in the doorway, eyes lowered demurely, but when he took her hand he sensed an eagerness that had been lacking before.

He gently removed the cape, pleased to find she'd been allowed to grow her hair back, the dark brown curls a short cap on her lovely head. Pressing her to her knees he parted his robe and fondled the silky strands as her clever tongue explored with bold strokes.

He would not be returning to this wretched time and place. There would be none to care about a young sinner who succumbed to the joys of the flesh. He fingered his stiletto, willing patience. The night was long and there was no need to rush.

****

Nico lowered himself from the carriage, surprised at how stiff and sore he felt. He didn't like to admit it, but he wasn't the man he used to be. He turned to assist Veluria, helping her gather the folds of the rich gown to keep the hem from scraping on the wet stones.

She seemed marginally better, the wounds finally healing after he'd insisted she see a surgeon in Rome. The Pope had sent his personal aide once Nico explained the need for discretion. He'd not planned on revealing Antonio's death to anyone but Cosimo, but circumstances dictated otherwise. Leo was his father's right hand, and owed his position as pope solely to his family connections. Of the few people in the world he trusted, his father's cousin was one of them.

In a way, telling Leo had taken the hard edge of pain away, not making the telling any easier but at least it gave him a template to use once he confronted Cosimo. His father would demand details and there would be no way to hide his final solution. The man's powers would never allow such a deception.

Are you worried?
No … yes. I'm not looking forward to this.
Do you wish me to be there when you tell him?
No, sweetheart. This is best done without you being there.

He chuckled and felt a wave of relief when Veluria flashed him an answering smile. The silent communication suited them, building a layer of trust, one day at a time. Unfortunately their link was often

236

unreliable, a fact that irritated him more than Veluria. She seemed to find his ability to penetrate her thoughts disconcerting at best.

What would she think if she knew of his power to access that most secret of places ... her link with the woman she called Reverend Mother?

"You need to rest. The journey was not easy and I am concerned that you still suffer those ... episodes." Nico understood all too well what was happening to his woman and he felt powerless to stop it. He hoped his father—if he could get past his grief—would be able to shed some light on how to deal with it.

"All right but we'll need to talk, all of us together. Soon." She pinched her mouth shut, the tension closing her eyes to dark slits.

"I understand the need for haste. But we must have a plan. It serves none of our ends to rush in without understanding all that has transpired." He waved his manservant forward. "Take my lady to my quarters and see to her comfort, Tomas."

The man looked mildly surprised but recovered quickly and took Veluria's arm, leading her into the palazzo and disappearing from view. Nico took a deep breath and waited outside for his father's summons, muted bird song and the distant sounds of gardeners tending to the estate's grounds helped settle his racing heart.

"Sir?"

Nico startled but gathered himself and followed Cosimo's secretary into his father's private suite.

He looked around with interest, as if viewing the space for the first time. While his own taste favored a certain level of austerity, Cosimo preferred the ornate flourishes so unique to the Florentine elite. In truth, it had been years since he'd seen his ancestral home. Much of his adult life had been spent in the service of rulers like Carlos, or prowling the halls of power in Rome and Venice. As his father's personal envoy, he represented his homeland, yet he was as rootless and adrift as any vagrant. It took the grief of his child's death, and the potential of the woman waiting for him in his quarters, to underscore how much he'd missed in his life. Like all of them, he felt the press of time.

A large window overlooked the small gardens to the rear of the palazzo. In the distance, clouds boiled over the rolling hills, dark and ominous, a fitting tribute to his mood.

"Nicolo." Cosimo's voice had an edge to it.

Nico waited for his father to join him, delaying the inevitable. The man already knew but he would need to hear the words.

"Father, I-I..."

Cosimo took his arm and led him to a bench seat near the fireplace, bidding him to sit. He'd rather pace the room but his father would want to look directly into his eyes, to assure himself that his son was not trying to hide the truth. The elder settled himself stiffly and glared dry-eyed for a long moment.

Nico opened to the probing, laying bare all he knew, all he understood. He spoke quietly and succinctly about that day, about his older brother's final breath and what had passed between them. Holding back nothing he shared his pain, the animal rage and the final act of revenge.

Before he could continue, trying to make sense of the impossible for his father's benefit, Cosimo interrupted.

"Is she worthy, boy?"

"Yes, father, she is worthy."

Cosimo rose and wandered back to the window, now streaked with rain coming down in torrents.

"You see, my son, the heavens shed tears for us."

Nico joined him, the two men staring sightless, lost in their own thoughts.

Cosimo said, "He's not really gone, you know." He touched a hand to his heart, then reached over and pressed the palm against his son's tunic. "He lives in you, he always has."

"Sometimes, Papà, I wish it were not so."

"We seldom get what we wish, boy. Now tell me what you know before the pain takes me to my bed. My time on this earth grows short and there is still much to do."

Nico quickly recapped the dangers and opportunities as he understood them, then waited while Cosimo processed the new information.

"I will not lie to you, boy. I am distressed about Stefano and I fear for his immortal soul if we leave him in Friedrich's hands."

"You knew the rumors, father. Why did you send him in the first place? Surely there were other options."

"Yes ... and no. You know how rumors operate, little lies and half-truths, sometimes more but often less than the reality. I had no

238

proof, no indication that my boy would be..." he choked on the words, "...a willing accomplice." Cosimo rubbed a hand across his eyes.

Nico asked, "What do you wish me to do?"

"You will go to Friedrich's and bring Stefano home."

"And if he does not wish to come?"

Cosimo grinned and said, "You are a negotiator. Convince him."

"And what about...?"

"Not today, my boy. I wish to retire. You will bring me the Frenchwoman in the morning..." He held up a hand and muttered, "Yes, yes, I know she's not French, but allow me that small anchor. What you bring to me is an improbability, something for which we could all burn at the stake."

Nico escorted his father to his bedchambers and bid him good evening but before he left Cosimo said, "You do believe her, don't you." It was more a statement than a question.

"Yes, Papà, I do."

"Then the danger is real."

"Very real. But I shall make sure our family is safe. You have my sacred trust, Papà."

Nico hurried through the darkening house. An odor of simmering stew wafted from the kitchens, reminding him they hadn't eaten since morning. Though his stomach rumbled at the tempting aromas, he hastened up the stairs. He needed to speak with Veluria, to prepare her for her meeting with Cosimo. He trusted her but his father did not. She would have to earn his consideration, otherwise the man would hold her hostage, even in the face of a disaster he'd envisioned in nightmares.

Nightmares made manifest by the appearance of beings out of time and place, like avenging angels, ready to wreak vengeance on the folly of those who sought to harness history to their own ends.

No stranger to retreat, he knew this time it was not an option. Be that as it may, he had no intention of letting history gain the upper hand.

****

Veluria indulged in the luxury of a bath, soaking away the grit and grime of travel over rough roads. Her subconscious followed the interplay of energies between Nico and his father, using her abilities to interpret emotion, intent, desire, if not actual words. That was an intimacy she enjoyed only with Nico, albeit at the whim of a very erratic gift.

Drying herself with plush cloths, she slipped into a silk robe left for her by one of the maids. She chuckled to herself. Even in a time when both men and women were far shorter than people in her time, she was still diminutive even by those distant standards. Bunching the robe about her waist, she tied it off with a soft cord to keep the hem from tripping her as she glided across the ceramic tiled floor.

Nico's quarters were simple and elegant. A large bed commanded one end of the long, narrow room, a wardrobe and chest on the west facing wall and a writing desk and chair by the tall bank of windows that let in the morning sun.

Someone had come in while she bathed and lit candles, their flickering shadows on the stark white walls giving the room an ominous air, though the intricate wooden paneling on the ceiling softened the effect. As in Venice, thick oriental rugs gave the space warmth and character. It was very much a man's room, lacking any feminine touches.

Nico entered the chamber in a rush, but paused long enough to take in her still damp hair hanging in clumps about her shoulders. She felt suddenly frumpish and awkward, why she wasn't sure.

She was about to ask him how his meeting with Cosimo had gone but the man brushed past her and began to disrobe. She watched with interest, her belly aflutter with possibilities. Though not nearly as tall as Antonio, he was still an imposing figure at close to six feet, well-muscled, his chest peppered with sandy brown curls.

When he approached, she bowed her head and asked, "Is this the time? Will you finally find comfort in my arms?"

Nico pulled at the cord, loosening the robe and slipping it off her shoulders. He ran his fingers through the damp tresses, separating strands until they lay straight down her back.

He tilted her head up with a single finger and solemnly said, "No, madam. Not today."

A surge of disappointment and dismay flooded her veins but before she could voice the question … the complaint … he scooped her in his arms and carried her to the bed.

There was no mistaking his interest, the feral look in his eyes—the blue of the Aegean replaced by darkening pools of lust—and a hunger so intense it threatened to consume her. For all her training and experience, she knew that this time would be her first for he would command her body and own her soul and she would willingly submit.

He hissed, "Look at me."

As if she could take her eyes off him ... yet she hesitated, the frisson of fear at what she was about to do sent a thrill of anticipation down her spine. He touched her cheek, the intimacy and gentleness so profound she could have cried from the sheer joy of it. Leaning in he brushed her lips, tenderly at first, then demanding as his tongue explored her essence, probing with punishing force until she gasped and fought for a breath.

He hissed, "Do you understand now?"

Slowly he lowered his huge frame over her, nudging her legs apart, his cock pressing on tender flesh as he teased and withdrew. She thrust her hips, seeking him, yet he denied her, a smile playing on his lips. She had no idea what she was supposed to understand, and she didn't care.

"It's not comfort I want now."

"What do you want?"

"This…" He slid inside her, her body in tremors as it stretched to accommodate his thick length. "I want this."

Lifting her hips, he thrust, driving deep, again and again, until she moaned as the spasms gripped her in waves of pleasure. She wrapped her legs around his waist and rocked until he roared his release, spilling his hot seed deep into her womb.

Nico lay back on the pillows and drew her close, nestling her head on his shoulder. He murmured something but she couldn't make out the words. Eventually his light snoring was all she needed to drift to sleep.

When next she woke the candles burned low. The rain had stopped sometime during the night. She turned over, prepared to settle back against the man who would rock her world only to find him staring at her with a devilish grin on his face.

He traced the planes of her face with his lips, exploring every inch of flesh, with such exquisite gentleness her body practically vibrated from the sensation.

Nibbling at her ear lobe he husked, "Tell me what you want."

Want? What did she want? No one had ever asked her that. Not ever. And it was not a simple question. She knew what he asked. But would she be able to live with the consequences of her answer?

Are you strong enough, M'lady?
Yes, Nico. I am strong enough for this.
Then tell me, what do you want?

You, Nico. I want you.

Chapter Twenty-Eight

Nico cursed under his breath. "Damn it, woman, hold still."

"Why don't you call for your housekeeper?" She grunted as the stays tightened about her ribcage. "Do you even know how to do that?"

Brushing his lips along her shoulder, he murmured, "I know how to do many things..." He spun her about and stared admiringly at the soft mounds of flesh. With his thumbs he traced the edge of the corset, eyes growing dark with passion.

Veluria knew they kept Cosimo waiting, she could feel the twinge of irritation. It would not do to make yet another bad impression. Their first meeting had been ... perhaps inconclusive was the correct term, not quite the sparring match she'd anticipated. However, everything had changed since that fateful day in Venice. She needed her wits about her, otherwise she and Cosimo would act at cross-purposes.

Yet she found it nearly impossible to concentrate with Nico's lips and hands stroking and prodding with devilish insistence.

A knock on the door left Nico sputtering, "What!"

"Sir? It's Paulo."

Her lover's face split in a huge grin. They'd not seen nor heard from his man since he'd been dispatched to court. Nico grabbed her robe off the bed and hastily placed it around her shoulders. In two strides he reached the massive door and yanked it open, pulling his friend into a bear hug.

Before Paulo could extricate himself Veluria wrapped her arms about his waist. The man's ears turned red from embarrassment.

Stuttering, Paulo said, "Um, s-sir… May I have a word?" He looked from her to Nico and backed out of the suite.

Nico raised his eyebrows at her but she nodded and waved him off. The door shut quietly leaving her to wonder what was going on. It had nothing to do with Cosimo, of that she was sure. The urge to eavesdrop was strong but she would no longer risk violating Nico's privacy. The playing field had changed dramatically, though her lover would not recognize that term. When she made her decision, when she gave this man her heart, she could only guess at the consequences.

That the Sisterhood would disapprove was a given but what they would do about it was unclear. There were simply no precedents. She mentally keyed onto the word 'salvage' as her guideline. It indicated that not everything was cast in stone and that alternate outcomes might be possible if she made the correct choices—and whatever those choices might be they included Nicolo de' Medici.

As Nico came into the bedroom he instructed Paulo, "Find as many good swordsmen in town as you can. We leave tomorrow, first light."

"Yes, *signore*." Bowing he gave her a quick smile and turned to leave.

"And Captain," Nico's voice was thick with emotion, "thank you. For everything."

Paulo stiffened, pride and embarrassment warring across his grizzled features. He muttered, "Sir," and beat a hasty retreat.

Nico came into the room holding a bundle of clothing. "Paulo brought this back from my hacienda in Madrid." He handed the crumpled clothing over. "He thought you might need it."

Veluria took the soiled dress and laid it carefully on the bed, her anxiety and need to examine the hidden pockets ramping up until her brow beaded with sweat. She'd been certain she would never see her precious talisman again.

Was now the time for full disclosure? She'd given this man her heart. Was she also prepared to reveal all of her secrets?

Nico wrapped his arms about her and whispered in her ear, "You won't find them there." He laid a hand, palm up, onto the fabric, her stiletto looking small in his huge hand. "A beautiful, elegant weapon for a beautiful, elegant woman."

Them, he said 'them'. He knew.

"Yes, I know everything, my love."

He unfisted his left hand. On it lay the device in the shape of a cross embedded with tiny gems, each one part of the encoding, the technology, that would take her, take them ... home.

When he laid the crucifix on the bed, her hand reached reflexively for it but she stopped, fingers hovering over the device. She thought she'd made her choice—it had seemed so easy when she'd been convinced there were no other options. Giving her heart was one thing, giving up her life's work, her purpose, was something else entirely.

This was not the right time to confront that choice. She feared it would leave her open to error. Every decision, every perturbation, pushed them down a path that shut out all other probabilities. She could change history, she could not change fate.

Nico said, his voice harsh and unyielding, "Know this. Whatever happens, you are mine." He pinched her arms once, hard, then released her and hissed, "Get dressed. Cosimo awaits and I have much to prepare."

Terrified Veluria cried out, "Nico?" but he advanced to the door and left without a backward glance.

Her body quaked with fear and loathing. By leaving the possibility open that she could and would return to her own time and place, she'd hurt him grievously. He knew better than she that he had no place in her world, that his very existence would be anathema.

Swiping at the tears pooling on her cheeks, she dressed and prepared to meet the one man who could derail everything.

****

Cosimo said, "Come in, my dear." He waved to the bench, "Please. Be seated."

The man was smaller than she remembered, somehow diminished in stature, the burden of his son's death and the events to come weighing heavily. The lines about his rheumy eyes spoke to pain, yet she never doubted his fierce resolve to protect what was his.

She folded her hands in her lap and waited while he poured a goblet of wine and attended to the polite forms. She gratefully accepted the wine and sipped it while allowing her gaze to sweep the room, taking the measure of the man through the treasures displayed so casually about the space.

She said, "Nico…"

"…will join us shortly." He sat in a chair opposite and gave her a calculating look. "My son has told me what *he* knows." She blanched at the implication of that emphasis on 'he'. Cosimo continued, assured of her undivided attention. "Now, my dear, it is time to tell me what *you* know."

A thousand warning bells went off all at once, her head splitting at the deep drilling, the unmitigated brutality of the assault, far worse than what she'd experienced so many weeks ago in the tunnel by the canal. The goblet fell from her hand, the red wine pooling like blood about the hem of her skirt. Fingernails gouging into her palm, piercing the skin, releasing thin streams of viscous blood to drip on her skirt, she was helpless to gainsay the man's powers.

Like Nico he demanded but unlike his son, who had gently peeled away each layer, taking the time to understand and assimilate the knowledge, Cosimo rampaged through her senses like an angry bull, smashing her barriers apart like so much fragile glass.

Dear Reverend Mother, stop this!
Allow it, child.
No! It hurts, it hurts so much…
Be strong, my child. Your trials have yet to come.

An eternity, or an instant in time, passed—she could not be sure. Then it was over. She expected to feel ravaged—raped, violated—but nothing quite described the turmoil, like angry seas tossing a small craft after a wicked storm. Her gut bubbled and boiled and she feared she would vomit from the bile rising to her throat.

Cosimo cradled her head and crooned soft words she could not understand. If he were attempting to comfort her, he failed miserably. Her soul yearned for Nico's touch, his love—only that could calm her battered spirit.

Have I destroyed that too, as I've destroyed everything I've touched in this world? Stefano, Antonio… Lost to me, to the ones who love them.

She did not hear Nico enter the room. He tore his father's hands away from her head and drove the older man back until he landed with an audible thud on the ornate seat. She couldn't see her lover's face but his voice was thunderous.

"What have you done?"

"What I had to, boy." The old man's voice wavered slightly but he stared up at his son with resolve.

"If you've hurt her…"

Cosimo glared at her with a mixture of fear and awe. Even Nico was surprised at the man's expression. With a pleading note, his father said, "Let go of me."

Nico complied and moved to stand behind her. She still could not see Nico's face, nor could she read whatever passed between father and son, a communication so private, so intimate, she had no means to interpret what it meant.

The hands that gripped her shoulders with punishing intensity promised violence, the man so out-of-control she believed him capable of anything at that moment.

She grew lightheaded, the silence, the total absence of sound amidst a cacophony of emotion, stretched her resources thin. Nico's groin pressed against her back. He would not feel the slick weeping as her flesh ripped to the sweet sting, Stefano's hiss of pleasure amidst the damning words of comfort.

With an effort she pulled back, forcing her concentration on the here and now. Time warped and wavered and her senses told her they no longer had the luxury of engaging in such sport.

Talking, always talking, never doing… The other awaited her.
It was time.
Time.

The tunnel echoed with the unspoken words.

She is mine.
Do what you must.
I will not leave her.
Protect…

The willow stick whistled, such a sweet melody, slippery, slick, the taste of iron thick on her tongue, soothing her parched throat…

247

Thrusting, driving, his sobs rend her soul, possessing her, devouring her.

She is mine.
No Tonio, she was never yours. She never will be.

****

The dim light in the room told her evening quickly advanced. She'd been out for hours. She lifted her head to find Nico staring with anxious eyes.

"How do you feel, sweetheart?" Nico gathered her close and stroked her hair.

She mumbled into his chest. "What happened?"

"You had another episode. My father put you out," he shrugged, "if that's the correct term."

Veluria said, "We call it stasis."

While grateful for the older man's intervention, for she was sure she had needed it, she wasn't happy about how both men seemed able to exercise so much control over her body and her senses.

Cradling her breast, his thumb flicking the nipple until it stood taut, Nico gazed with hooded eyes, his breath ragged with need. Lazily tracing his fingers over the soft rise of her belly, he probed her moist folds, his lips purring against her throat like a great jungle cat.

Playing her body like an instrument, his mouth wandered at will until she lost focus and gave in to the man's power and dominance. She arched her hips as he pleasured her beyond her endurance. With a cry she answered his silent plea...

Yes, Nico, I am yours.

****

Cosimo watched the carriage drive away. The retinue was smaller than he would have preferred but it would do on short notice. Paulo had done a good job of securing some of the city's better swordsmen, if not the most savory. Of their loyalty to Florence there was little doubt. Paulo and his son would see to it that they acquitted themselves well in service to the family.

He'd slept little, partially because not even their thick walls could muffle the telltale sounds of his son's impressive stamina. But mostly he'd fretted over the confusing mountain of information that the woman had reluctantly offered under his unrelenting attack. He understood little of the particulars but the broad outlines were clear. Each world existed as a shadow of the other. It mattered not how. He was willing to leave that conundrum to men of letters who would spend lifetimes analyzing and arguing and coming to false conclusions.

He regretted inflicting so much pain, but it was a necessary consequence to justify learning what he could. Time was never on anyone's side and he'd learned early on not to rely on it. Cosimo disliked causing his son dismay, and to his surprise he realized he also felt compassion for the woman and the difficult choices she would face. What those choices would mean to his son.

He understood their current precarious situation, swords at every throat, the fate of the continent teetering on shaky alliances, ill-begotten marriages and the insatiable hunger for power.

All he wanted was peace and an opportunity to build a legacy of prosperity for Tuscany and the Famiglia Medici. What he foresaw was war and the disintegration of his direct line, but not the house. That would survive. But only if Nico and the strangers averted events that still lurked in the shadows.

He wondered if he would ever see any of them again.

"Sire? I brought your meal." Tomas set the tray on the bench and joined him at the window.

Cosimo said quietly, "It feels unsettled, does it not?" He looked up at the clear sky and shrugged. The coming storm he sensed had nothing to do with the weather. Turning to his secretary, he smiled grimly and spoke with a voice filled with remorse, "Sometimes it is better not to know."

Tomas looked confused for a moment, wondering if that were a question he was expected to answer. When Cosimo returned to gazing out the window, he asked instead, "Shall I have Stefano's quarters prepared, sire?"

Cosimo ignored the question and moved to sit on the bench. He surveyed the food on the tray, lost in thought.

"Sire?"

"Take this away. I'm not hungry."

Tomas picked up the tray and said again, "Stefano's quarters, sire."

Irritated at the man's persistence, he barked, "No," then apologized quickly and said, "Not yet, Tomas."

The man quickly retired, leaving Cosimo alone once more. He wandered back to the window and gazed at the wind rustling the trees.

With a sigh, he muttered, "Not yet."

Chapter Twenty-Nine

Andreas prowled the narrow halls with increasing frustration. Veluria's presence was everywhere and nowhere, yet so far he'd failed to penetrate the barriers she'd so cleverly erected. He'd not detected that kind of power when first he'd become aware of her presence and he puzzled over its source.

The few times he'd managed to caress her senses he'd found they opened like petals on a rose, the scent sweet and intoxicating, yielding as she was trained, as if she'd been created solely for him.

"Father, a word." The Monsignor grabbed his arm and propelled him quickly to a small alcove where they could speak privately.

One thing they'd learned early on, the walls had eyes and ears. Little escaped the voyeuristic Duke and his lackeys. It had taken his considerable skills to determine the few places where he and the prelate could talk undisturbed.

As the Monsignor chattered on about packing up their entourage and heading back to Venice, he raced through all the possible reasons he could bring to bear to convince the man to stay.

"Your Holiness." Desperation gave his voice an edge that caught the prelate's attention. The man looked down at him curiously.

"Well?"

"The Medici son is here for a reason."

The Monsignor sneered, "Of course he is. He and his father, that *merchant*..." he spat the word with distaste, "...are simply currying favor with a man who stands to gain a position in the Reichstag."

"But..."

"Cosimo's no fool. He's not going to rely on that idiot pup, Stefano, to see to his plans being carried out. The boy's use is to provide heirs," he snorted and leered at Andreas as if he were somehow to blame, then continued, "but from what we've seen and heard, that won't be happening anytime soon."

Andreas sputtered, "But Cosimo can't possibly know…"

"Oh don't be so naïve, boy. Of course he knows. *Everybody* knows. Why do you think he dragged Nicolo from Carlos' court? He needs to make sure Friedrich doesn't go off and make alliances with undesirable elements in the Reichstag." He chuckled, "Not everyone is on board with Maximillian's grandson as heir apparent."

"But, Holiness, you cannot know that for a fact. There may be other reasons, and if we leave precipitously, there will be no way to know or to safeguard your and Venice's interests." He stood to his full five-feet-eight and stared at the prelate, prepared to use his last trump card. "The Papacy goes whichever way Florence goes. If Friedrich is as unreliable as you suggest, then would it not be in your best interest to have an ear in the court so that you may be alerted ahead of time."

The Monsignor considered Andreas words and said, "That idea has merit. But I still plan to leave, tomorrow if possible. The seasons turn and travel will be difficult, if not impossible soon."

Andreas' gut churned. He hadn't received the dispensation he needed to justify remaining behind. He wasn't so foolish as to think the Duke stupid enough not to recognize a blatant spy when he saw one. Right now he wandered the halls unremarked because he'd been billed a simple-minded monk of no consequence. As part of the Monsignor's group he was invisible. Alone he would stick out like a sore thumb and come under the very watchful eyes of the Duke's enthusiastic guard.

He also did not wish to be singled out for the Friedrich's special attentions. Though he hadn't seen the infamous 'parlor' himself, he could well imagine what delights it might hold. He appreciated a man with eclectic tastes, having his own particular interests, but he had no intention of being on the receiving end of perverted sexual torture under the guise of religious fanaticism.

He might not have been the best student Matteo ever had when it came to history, but the Inquisition would seem tame compared to what the fair Duke considered righteous retribution.

Andreas called down the hallway to the Monsignor's retreating back, "Holiness, wha—?"

"I will think on it, Father. See me on the morrow."

Frowning, Andreas spun in the opposite direction. There was little to be gained from fretting over things he couldn't control. It would be better to gather more information while he had the opportunity. He had no intention of returning with the prelate to Venice.

For now he needed to figure out why no one had seen the Medici pup for over a week. The Duke's daughter, Wiltrud, was known to spend her evenings in meditation in the chapel. She was most likely praying for divine intervention to relieve her of the burden of a loveless marriage or thanking her deity for having the foresight to provide her father with a new toy and leaving her, and her sisters, to go about their lives relatively free of parental intervention.

If he were a betting man, he'd go with door number two.

****

Veluria wriggled on the uncomfortable bench, the stays cutting into her ribcage and precluding any thought of actually enjoying the generous repast set out by the Duke's kitchens. A hunter by avocation, the man's passion provided an astonishing array of table fare: wild boar, venison, pheasant, rabbit and small birds that she assumed were quail.

The keep that housed the banquet hall was part of the original ancient structure with thick walls, a perpetually dim interior and the dank musty smell of too many unwashed bodies intermingled with wet dogs and stale urine.

Surprisingly, she was the only female in attendance, the duke's daughters feigning illness or disinterest in affairs of state. In any other court it would have been construed as rudeness of the highest order but the Duke seemed content with the arrangement, and none remarked on the oddity.

If Nico was concerned, he made no show of it, entering into easy banter with Friedrich, trading hunting stories and court gossip. Her lover was a natural in the ways of the court, just as his younger brother was.

As for Stefano, they had yet to meet with him. Friedrich apologized effusively for the inconvenience. He'd had no idea they would arrive so soon and had sent the young man on a 'mission of some importance'.

253

The fact of the matter was he shouldn't have had a clue that the castle was their destination. They'd driven hard and fast, making sure any layovers did not include potential spies who could alert the Duke to unwanted visitors.

Their initial audience had been a long drawn-out affair, tedious in the extreme but it had given her an opportunity to observe Friedrich's two remaining daughters, the eldest having been recently sloughed off to a neighboring duchy.

The youngest, Margaret, was perky and given to a quick smile. She was attractive in an adolescent unformed way, flat-chested, narrow-hipped, but with wide-set eyes and clear complexion she gave the impression she might someday grow into a reasonably attractive young woman. Hopefully not like the older sister, Wiltrud, Stefano's new wife.

Calling her 'plain' was being generous. She carried a perpetual scowl that spoke to a difficult disposition and a sharp tongue. If Stefano had had a choice, he would have chosen the immature Margaret in a flash.

Idly she wondered if the woman's scowl had anything to do with her new husband's very particular tastes. Despite the rumors about Friedrich, the castle staff had been singularly tight-lipped. Neither Nico nor she had been able to glean any useful information about what actually transpired in the lower reaches of the castle.

Paulo had had more luck in the town located near the river winding through the foothills. He and his men spent their evenings there, building rapport with the merchants and innkeepers with their generous patronage. Drink loosened tongues enough that Paulo could piece together a picture of fear and loathing for the man who provided protection for the region. That protection came with a steep price. Nearly every family had lost a member, or knew of someone who'd succumbed to the Church's vigilance and the Duke's insatiable 'appetites'.

Nico had presented Friedrich with a few 'trinkets'—an array of baubles and silver that would have amounted to a king's ransom. Cosimo had casually thrust the chest into Paulo's hands before they'd left Florence. Had she known what the chest contained she might have insisted that their ten man retinue was hardly sufficient for the rigors and dangers of the trip.

The elder Medici had chosen the gifts well. Friedrich was a peacock, sporting an elaborate brocade tunic edged with fur over a shirt of exceptional quality, the weave so tight she could have sworn it was silk. His new jewelry—an ornate ring and gold necklace—were remarked upon often during the course of the evening.

Feigning weariness, she excused herself and left the men to the serious drinking. Instead of heading to their quarters, she turned left and followed a hall that she guessed might lead to Stefano and Wiltrud's quarters. The stairs circled down to a lower level. She took them cautiously mindful of her skirts and the potential for a nasty fall.

The entire day she'd been uneasy, with little to occupy her thoughts while Nico was out and about with Friedrich. She practiced maintaining her shields, using Nico's additional power to buttress her own diminished capacity. Though erratic, the 'episodes' as Nico called them, still plagued her, leaving her temporarily weakened.

It had been Nico who'd discovered the Brotherhood operative lurking about the castle. He'd recognized the man from Veluria's description and had set one of his men to keep an eye on the cleric.

The man's presence validated her assessment that time and history approached a confluence in this place. He had arrived before them, part of a group from Venice claiming Papàl indulgence for the newlyweds. Nico doubted Leo was aware of or had sanctioned the visit. But he simply made note of the fact and dismissed it. The party was due to leave the next day. Fewer players on the stage made it easier to narrow the list.

I just wish I knew for what...

Low voices emanated from behind plain wood doors on which a cross had been inscribed. She assumed this was the chapel but it seemed late in the evening for services. She paused, straining to hear the words. Two voices, a man and a woman. From the accent she recognized Wiltrud's strident tones. The man was unknown to her but when she heard him say his name, Andreas, a sense of recognition washed over her.

Putting herself at risk did nothing to help them resolve the dilemma they all faced. She turned and huffed up the stairs, the stays and her skirts making progress difficult. Retracing her steps she eventually found their quarters and gave a sigh of relief. It turned out to be premature. When she opened the door Nico stood by the bed, his face set in a grim line. He looked ready to murder something … or someone.

"Where the hell have you been?" He rubbed his hands through his tousled curls and glared at her. "I've been searching everywhere."

He reeked of wine, sweat and panic. She wasn't sure whether she wanted to throw a bucket of water on him or jump into his arms. He saved her the effort. He was on her in a single stride, crushing her to his chest and devouring her with hungry kisses.

Growling, "Turn around," he tore at the laces, releasing the cumbersome device to fall to the stone floor.

"Nico, we have to talk…"

Ignoring her, Nico carried her to the bed and dropped her unceremoniously onto the brocaded coverlet. Stripping quickly, he mounted her slight form, ready to plunder and dominate.

Veluria turned away from his probing tongue and hissed, "I don't like you this way."

The air sizzled, cracking into a million bits, thin slices oozing fluids, yellow pus-filled maws opening to the bone.

She twisted, stilled, knowing the worst was yet to come—the violation so profound she cowered in abject terror.

There was nowhere to hide. No one to protect her. No one to care.

Alone. So alone.

Rocking her in his arms, Nico moaned, "Oh, my dear sweet Jesus, please … please forgive me." She was only dimly aware of the man's tears pooling against her cheek.

Somehow the pain had been different, less real, more of a foreshadowing of something worse—or better—to come. She'd been both repelled and attracted, each episode offering an embellishment as if the experience remained incomplete, unfulfilled.

Why? Why her and why that singular incident, repeated endlessly in a purgatory of pain chasing pleasure.

Wailing, "Please, make it stop," she sobbed into Nico's chest, clinging to the last shreds of her sanity.

Nico whispered, "I will, I promise. Even if I have to kill him myself."

****

Andreas leaned against the cold stone wall, immensely satisfied with his evening's activities. The pup's bride had been surprisingly adept at satisfying his needs, her sharp teeth a delightful accompaniment to her equally sharp tongue. And she'd been more than willing to supply him with the information he sought once he'd properly motivated her.

Now he had the excuse he required to stay in the duchy. The horse-faced bitch would petition daddy for him to become her personal confessor. As such he would have access to every part of the castle, including the enticing 'parlor'.

The only down side might be the drain on his stamina, something for which he must guard against with the denouement of their dilemma approaching at breakneck speed. However, it was a sacrifice he was willing to make. While he'd felt it wise this night not to inquire about Stefano, he would need to press the woman on their next meeting. The players must all be present: Stefano, Friedrich, Nicolo de' Medici. Somehow, one or more of those three men held the key.

The Sisterhood and the Council both toiled to save their worlds from a coming apocalypse. Given a choice, he would prefer salvation come from rational mathematicians than the meddling matriarchal geneticists.

Palming his blade, he glided across the rough stone floor, feet bare, his cowl pulled over his head—just a monk reciting matins, the liturgy rolling with practiced ease off his tongue.

The Medici's tail had gone off with his fellows to the town, whether or not with his commander's blessing mattered little. Lacking anything new to occupy his mind, he allowed a rare moment of introspection. Usually Matteo, ever the theorist, asked the unanswerable, but on this propitious evening, with his lusts sated, he was ready to explore the anomalies he sensed.

His timeline skewed in his own world, the impossible made manifest with weapons and factions deployed in a dizzying array, the onslaught so sudden and terrifying it held them all hostage to fear. *Her* timeline manifested in the here and now, corrupting and altering events. *He* was the audience watching events unfold, *she* was the actress on the stage.

Matteo would work it out, using complex mathematical functions. He had only his gut instincts to guide him. The woman who consumed his thoughts and commanded his desires, existed here as a physical entity. He was but a shadow, an avatar. Yet both of them bore the consequences of this wretched time and place. If the world was truly a stage, when had it become improvisational, directionless?

The Sisterhood bred and trained their novitiates for the difficult transitions between shadow worlds. The Council more wisely used constructs to achieve the same ends, assuring control and suitable outcomes for mission parameters.

Changing history might be unacceptable but he saw no recourse. There was a cancer spreading in a time and place about which they knew too little. The alliances, subtle shifts in power, who lived, who died—such tiny details formed the weft and weave of fate gone awry.

That the woman was here, now, gave him the assurance he needed that he'd whittled the possibilities to three. If it proved to be Nicolo de' Medici, it would be his greatest pleasure to console her, transferring her allegiance to its rightful recipient.

As he approached his quarters, Andreas detected the first hint of burn, a tingle of pain as his neural net registered agony of uncompromising intensity. With a groan he sank to the floor, his back to the wall, rocking back and forth, his head connecting with the unforgiving stone, each crack an echo of her flesh splitting, tearing apart.

Their worlds ripping asunder, shadows in full retreat.
None should suffer so.
I will stop it even if I have to kill him myself.

With trembling hand, he drew the blade across his thigh, slicing deep, following the line of the vein, so close, so temptingly close. The stiletto fell from his stiff fingers, bouncing soundlessly on his blood-slicked robe.

Tomorrow. It will be over tomorrow.

It was time. Matteo would not approve … but he would understand. That was why they chose him over all others.

Chapter Thirty

Andreas watched Stefano dismount in the courtyard below. The narrow enclosure was crowded with the Monsignor's retinue preparing for departure. The prelate exchanged a few words with the Medici pup, then turned away to continue directing his men to carry the chests to the waiting wagons outside the inner walls. Even from his great height he could see the men's breaths misting in the chill morning air.

Wiltrud demanded, "Come back to bed," her voice petulant, needy.

"Hmm, in a minute." Andreas licked the blood off his lower lip, already swollen and tender. He been sorely tempted to respond in kind but he still had need of the woman's services.

He turned and stared at her. Mumbling, "The apple didn't fall far from the tree," he girded himself for round two, not sure he'd gotten the best of this particular bargain.

"Your husband has returned."

Wiltrud shrugged, clearly not caring one way or the other. He needed information and had little time left for games. Unfortunately, this one was not as stupid as she looked. He needed to play her correctly or he would lose what little advantage he had.

"Will he come here," he waved a hand to encompass the small bedroom, "or will he report immediately to your father?"

The woman snorted, "Here? Not likely." She glanced at him with a sly look. "Why do you ask?"

Giving her his best smoldering stare, he said, "Because I have something special planned for our meditations this morning. It would be best if we were not disturbed."

She smiled in a way that made his blood run cold. "Father plans to meet with *my husband*," her voice dripped with venom, "later this morning. I assure you, they will be *occupied* for much of the day."

Relieved he would not be under *that* kind of pressure he approached the bed, assessing the woman's demeanor and calculating just how far he could push her before she started screaming in earnest. She would soon learn her sharp teeth were no match for his … creativity.

Grabbing a hank of hair, he twisted viciously, yanking her forward until she yelped in pain. Her hands beat at his fist as he hissed, "Turn over." When she failed to comply, he kneed her into position, pressing with his full weight on the small of her back. She groaned, her body vibrating with anticipation.

"Do you require penance, my child?" He brought his palm down on her ass, hard, leaving an angry red mark. With his left hand he irritably shifted the bedding out of the way until he connected with her breast, his fingers seeking and finding the taut nipple. With thumb and forefinger he pinched and pulled until she cried out, her voice muffled in the bedding.

Grimly he cupped her chin, squeezing the corners of her mouth. "Say it."

She let loose with a jumble of words in her native tongue, none of which he understood. Squaring his shoulders he prepared to deliver another blow, muttering, "I'll take that as a yes."

Grimacing, he wondered why, with their worlds running out of time, there was time enough for *this*.

Andreas cradled the woman in his arms. He'd managed to stem the sobbing with soothing promises of her everlasting salvation, trading her kind of hell for one that only he could deliver. Fighting the urge to end the charade, he imagined Matteo counseling patience, knowing the answers lay in the quivering mass of flesh under his control.

"Tell me about Stefano." He struggled to remain neutral but annoyance tinged the command.

Wiltrud stuttered, "Wh-wha—?" Her voice echoed fear and confusion, but still she moved closer into Andreas' embrace as if seeking shelter from whatever demons stalked her. She mumbled into his chest, "What do you wish to know?"

"Where did he go?"

"To Corinthia. Leopold and some of the Dukes were to meet in secret to discuss my father's ascension to the Reichstag."

"Friedrich already has Cosimo's blessing. His election is a formality. Why a secret meeting?"

Wiltrud rolled away but he squeezed her arm hard enough to make her flinch. She gave him a calculating look, her plain features turning sharp with distrust.

He purred, "I can make it worth your while," as he probed her swollen folds.

"My father has an understanding…"

"Yes?" He withdrew his busy fingers and waited.

"Don't stop, please." The strident tones of a woman used to getting her way were replaced with the whining that told him he was close to getting what he wanted.

"Tell me," he wheedled, "and I will give you everything you want." He cupped her soft mound and waited.

"I-I don't know exactly. That's why he sent that pig to meet with the others. He was to report back with their final decision."

Satisfied, Andreas rose from the bed and slipped into his robe. Bemused, he wondered at the woman calling Stefano a 'pig' given her own rather draconian tastes. He would have thought it a match made in heaven based on the rumors about the youngest Medici.

He motioned for the woman to get out of bed and barked, "Get dressed."

"But…"

"You are going to show me your secret passage. I need to know exactly what information Stefano has to relay to Friedrich." When she showed signs of balking he said, "Afterwards I have something very special planned for you."

Palming the stiletto hidden in the folds of the rough cloth, he thought, *very special indeed.*

****

Nico slapped Paulo on the back and chuckled loud enough to be heard in the far reaches of the courtyard. His men lounged with careless disregard for the activity about them. The Monsignor and his retinue had departed, leaving Friedrich's people to go about their daily activities unencumbered by *those* demanding guests. As he suspected, Andreas had remained behind.

Paulo muttered, too low to be heard by anyone but him, "Your brother returned early this morning. I was told he retired but will meet with Friedrich for the midday meal."

"Is he with his wife?"

"No, sire. Marco followed the Monk. *He* is with the duke's daughter."

"Ah." Nico wasn't sure what to think about that. There'd be a good reason for the man's interest in Stefano's wife but what that was he couldn't fathom. For the moment he had other pressing concerns.

"The carriage is ready, Commander, but may I make a suggestion?" Paulo laughed at something one of his men said and leaned in to have a word with the man. When he turned back to Nico he whispered, "I think it best to go mounted and leave the carriage behind."

Nico had to agree, but with reservations. What concerned him was that Veluria was their weak link, fragile from the blood loss and pain from the episode the night before. He had no idea if she was strong enough to ride, but restricting her to the slow carriage would guarantee they'd not get far. Not with a mounted guard at the Duke's disposal.

He'd bade Veluria to stay in the room to recover while he arranged to secure his brother for the trip home. It mattered little whether or not Stefano would agree to the summons to return to Florence. If the rumors Paulo had accumulated were even remotely true, it was all too possible he'd lost his youngest brother to the worst sort of corruption imaginable. However, leaving him here was not an option.

Paulo looked at each of his men in turn, and with a subtle nod signaled them to go about their assigned tasks. When next they saw them, they would be heavily armed and ready to defend their retreat.

"I wish we could do this under cover of night, Paulo."

"So do I sire, but the road is treacherous. It's best if we make it to the river crossing and the safety of the forest during daylight. Once there, we can take a stand if necessary."

"Let's hope it's not."

Paulo nodded toward the keep. "Here comes Marco. Perhaps he has news."

The man approached, alarm and irritation warring with his features. He said, "The monk and the woman called Wiltrud? They disappeared into a corridor and I lost them."

Nico had a bad feeling about that. He asked, "Can you take me there?"

Marco nodded yes. "It's in the Duke's wing, sire." He paused, looking uncomfortable.

Paulo hissed, "What is it?" and listened as Marco whispered in his ear. With raised eyebrows he waited until the man had finished, then dismissed him.

Nico grunted, "Tell me."

"It, um, seems the monk and the Duke's daughter are on ... intimate terms."

Nico cursed under his breath. He had no idea what games Andreas played or what any of this meant. Let the man keep to his agenda. He needed to see to his own world—to get his brother out of the clutches of a madman and to get Veluria to a safe place until he could figure out how to stop whatever was tearing her apart, literally, inch by inch.

The question remained: could the monk, acting on his own, stop whatever was driving their shadow worlds apart? If he took Stefano away, would it change the course of history enough? He doubted it. He, the cleric and his brother ... the Duke, Veluria ... all were linked. He needed to sever that link but who, what and how?

"Dammit. Paulo, prepare yourself and the men. I'm going to find out what the hell's going on."

****

Andreas crouched next to the still figure and carefully wiped his blade on the hem of Wiltrud's skirts. He'd heard enough to understand the full extent of the disaster awaiting both this world and his own. Plots, counterplots, assassinations—with Stefano assigned the task of murdering Carlos before he ascended to the throne, denying him the mantle of Holy Roman Emperor, and leaving it open to one of the Austrian pretenders. That would leave the continent ripe for the machinations of the minor duchies, placing

263

them all between the greed of Françoise and the sleeping bears to their far east, the Khanates and the Ottoman Empire.

Not even the meddling French could come up with such a bold scheme.

Without Carlos, the continent would be thrust into a catastrophic series of wars that could send the region back to the Dark Ages and permanently remove the stabilizing influence of the Holy See. *That* world, the one on which the Brotherhood, the Council—even the Sisterhood—rested would no longer safeguard what passed for civilization in their post-apocalyptic world.

The way was clear, but he would need help. Stefano had been charged to leave within the week for Castile. How convenient for Friedrich that Nico had played into his hands by coming to the castle and removing himself from Carlos' court. Without Nicolo de' Medici to say otherwise, Carlos would have no reason not to trust the younger brother.

Dammit, Matteo, you should have prepared me better.

He was ill-equipped to deal with seasoned warriors, and even if he managed to effect a way to stop Friedrich and Stefano, he would be stranded in hostile territory with no way back to his own world. Home was Venice—and Matteo, a shadow within a shadow. But how to get there?

He needed an army. And he knew exactly where to find one.

****

Veluria's stomach rumbled, a good sign for it meant that something in her battered body was normal. Suspecting Nico had instructed Friedrich's staff not to disturb her, she decided to head for the kitchens. Surely not everything had been consumed from last night's dinner.

Had it been less than a day? She was lost in time, in more ways than one—unsure about her mission, conflicted about her feelings for the man who would own her heart, fearful for her own life as time cycled violently about a vortex with her at the center.

It was not to have played out this way. Never had she or her kind encountered such a…

Cluster fuck, my child?
Reverend Mother!
I must be brief. We are no longer secure. Listen carefully. The
Brotherhood agree. You and the one called Andreas must dispose of
the problem.
The Brotherhood?
Hush, child. Do you have the talisman?
Yes, Mother.
Use it when the time is right.
The problem ... who, what...? Reverend Mother?

"Are you lost, M'lady?" Friedrich loomed in her space, driving
her back against the rough wall. Reverend Mother's communique
had so disoriented her she'd lost sense of where she'd wandered.

"I, uh, was looking for the kitchens, Your Grace." She squeezed
past the man's lean body and gave a quick curtsy. Tendrils of fear
tickled her spine, her senses on high alert. Something about the man
made her physically ill, as if true evil was a living, breathing entity.
He had the look of a deadly predator, one who liked to play with his
prey, drawing out the agony as long as possible. The bones of his
face pressed close to the flesh, leaving harsh planes and hollowed
black eyes from which he assessed her with interest.

He literally made her skin crawl.

But he was also the reason she and the Brotherhood operative
were here. It was time to tap her training and finally get answers.

Glancing boldly at the duke, she purred, "Perhaps, *monsieur*,
you would care to join me in a light repast?"

The man's eyes glistened with flecks of gold, the prominent vein
in his temple pulsing, throbbing, as she accessed pheromones
designed to accentuate her natural allure. The man's tunic covered
his groin but she knew without looking that she had his attention. He
nodded and gave her a feral grin, his teeth an unexpected white
against the pallor of his skin.

"Follow me, M'lady."

"Please, call me Veluria."

"As you wish, my dear."

Without looking back he led them down a stairwell to a landing
where a torch in a wall sconce caused the yellow light from the
flames to dance eerily on the grey stone walls. She couldn't be sure

265

but it seemed they were in the original part of the ancient edifice. It reeked of age and mildew, the damp condensing on a millennia of sorrow and suffering.

Friedrich held the torch high, though the illumination it cast barely dented the oppressive darkness.

"Careful, my dear. I fear it grows steep. I do not wish for you to injure yourself from an untimely misstep."

"Is this the way to the kitchens?"

"Um, no. We'll breakfast in my *private* quarters."

Not unaware of the danger she faced, in hindsight she should have taken note of his emphasis on 'private', but by that time it was already too late. She had the man's undivided attention and the promise of sport. The best she could hope for was to glean sufficient information so that either Nico or Andreas could finally put an end to the threat.

Her job was to provide the Duke with sufficient entertainment without having him resort to more extreme activities. She'd failed with Stefano. She did not intend to fail with Friedrich.

A landing opened to a short hallway that ended at a sturdy door reinforced with wrought iron. The Duke strode into the room, bidding her to wait a moment while he lit the candles. Nervously she wondered how Nico would ever find her in the bowels of the castle. She'd been relying on his knowing, sensing, her whereabouts but realized too late her foolishness. Hadn't he said last night that he'd looked all over for her and couldn't find her? Yes, he'd been drunk, and she'd assumed that had prevented him from using his faculties.

What if he could *not* sense her?

It doesn't matter. I can't go on with this pain. I have to put an end to this. My world, my time, my Sisterhood are counting on me.

I have suffered enough.

I have nothing more to lose. I will end this … now.

"Come in, my dear." The Duke took her hand and led her into the long narrow room. She heard the door whoosh shut and the bolt snick into place.

Placing a hand on her shoulder, he propelled her further into the space. Smiling with anticipation he placed his lips close to her ear and husked, "Do you see anything you like?"

266

She'd thought she'd had nothing more to lose.
She'd been wrong, dead wrong.

Chapter Thirty-One

Time stilled. The satisfaction he'd felt drifted away, remembered pleasures distilling to unease, then outright fear. It was a pressure, delicious at first, an indulgence he craved until recognition flooded his senses and he understood he no longer controlled their destiny.

Madness—and the sharp tang of terror—pierced his senses. It was the sound of death meted out with an agonizing promise.

Andreas withdrew the stiletto and slashed the palm of his left hand with a vicious short stroke, his fist clenching reflexively against the sharp pain. Watching the blood drip onto the cold stone, he willed an end to his desperate yearnings but knew it was not to be.

She would ever be his heart's desire, forever just out of reach, not of his time—denied to him in this one. Was it better to let her pass into history, to be absorbed quietly into the bowels of legend, than to exist forever as his personal Holy Grail, unattainable, forever a judgment and test of his worth?

What was his future worth without her?

Nothing.

Without her there was no future. For any of them.

Racing down the narrow corridor he called out for Nico, praying the warrior was close enough to hear.

****

Nico sensed his men fanning out in a wedge, mere steps behind him. Contrary to his orders, Paulo had gathered his most trusted swordsmen and pursued him into the dark reaches of the fearsome structure. Of them all his captain was more aware of their peril and the stakes on which they gambled his family's future.

He'd searched frantically for some sign of his brother, or even the Duke, but failed as the corridors snaked in a dizzying array about the keep. What started as a vague disquiet blossomed into an anxiety so profound he feared his lungs would collapse under the intense pressure. Trapped in a purgatory of phantom pain and desperate pleas, he could little discern from which direction danger lurked.

He motioned Paulo forward but before he could issue an order his captain hissed, "Commander, there is evil here. Shall I dispense Arturo to secure your lady from your rooms?" He flexed his wrist, the movement causing a flash of light as flames reflected off the metal shaft of his long sword.

Nico growled, "It is already too late. He will not find her there."

"Sire?"

"I can't expla—"

Paulo gripped his arm and pulled him toward the wall, moving forward to block the slight figure advancing at a run from the direction of the banquet hall and Friedrich's private quarters.

Nico pushed Paulo aside, cautioning him to stay his hand. The slap of bare feet on stone and the heavy breathing of a man laboring under a thin veil of panic resounded through the corridor.

He stepped into the path of the small cleric, his eyes noting the disheveled robe, streaked with blood, and the wild-eyed glare reflecting a terror he felt in his bones.

The man called Andreas skidded to a halt and collapsed against the wall, his breath ragged as he sucked in great gulps of air. Gasping, "He has her!" he gripped Nico's arm to steady himself.

Paulo demanded, "Who—" but Nico interrupted and barked, "Tell me where. Now."

Andreas huffed, "In the old dungeons in the keep."

"Do you know the way?"

"No."

"Then can we follow her ... essence?" Paulo looked at him curiously, unsure what they were talking about. Nico ignored him and glared at the cleric. "You can sense her. Better than I, is that not true?"

Andreas nodded but choked out, "It will take too long."

"Then tell me a better way, fool, or I will gut you here and to hell with your mission and your world."

Nico gripped the cleric's throat and squeezed until the man's eyes bulged. The satisfaction of crushing the man's throat paled against the sense of otherness he detected, an awareness of a kindred spirit, of one who shared the curse that had plagued him, and Tonio, all their lives. It gave him pause but he had little choice than to go with his instincts. He needed the man and his ungodly abilities … for now.

Cursing, he released Andreas to drop to the floor. The man looked up at him with hooded eyes, a mixture of fear, respect and uncertainty flashing across his narrow face. Staggering to his feet he rasped, "Your brother knows the way."

Nico turned to Paulo and said, "Go to his quarters and…" but stopped when Andreas interrupted, "No! He is not there."

The air turned sullen with a chill that cut to the bone. Nico looked at Andreas, the man's face mirroring his own agony.

Andreas stumbled back the way he had come. Nico hesitated an instant then followed, his men taking up position behind him. In his head he heard echoes of despair, but whether it came from the man in front of him, or from the distant reaches of the castle he could not be sure. He no longer had a clear sense of himself, tangled as he was with realities that defied everything he knew and believed.

When he drew even with Andreas, he asked, "Where is Stefano?"

"I saw him in the banquet hall. He was to join Friedrich later." Andreas glanced over his shoulder, then back at Nico. "There's a complication."

Nico ignored the man and strode ahead, all rational thought driven away by the clamoring in his skull. The clatter of well-armed men, their booted feet lock-stepping on the hard floor, should have raised a warning but he barreled forward, heedless of all but the driving need to find his brother and his woman.

"Nico! Wait! Friedrich's guards are in the banquet hall…" Andreas' words vanished in a din of metal and muttered curses as the men behind him shoved forward, swords drawn in readiness, leaving the small man to cower in the corridor.

****

Nico wasn't sure what to expect when he finally met his younger brother. He and Stefano had been close, yet nowhere near as bonded as he'd been with Tonio. Both older brothers had tormented and

270

teased the boy mercilessly, yet protected him with a fierceness borne out of love and the respect due one of the blood.

Though it had been months since he'd last talked with the young man, that conversation still rang loud and clear in his head. He'd been pitiless in his apparent disregard for the boy's wishes, reminding him of family duty above all things. That he hadn't believed a word of it meant nothing now. What he'd done was in the interest of saving him from Antonio's wrath and from his father's stern retribution. At the time how could he have known he was driving the final nail into a coffin of Stefano's own design?

Praying he could change the sneer of hostility into one of relief, he approached the table and slid onto the bench, only vaguely aware of his men taking defensive positions about the small hall.

Without preamble he spoke in a low voice, pitched so that only Stefano could hear, "Sit quietly and don't speak." Stefano gave him a blank stare as if he did not recognize him. "I am here to take you home." He noted his brother's hand twitching toward the short sword on his hip, but reached across the table and pinned it to the rough wood. "Listen to me, carefully. This is a mistake. You do not belong here."

Stefano glanced at the ballet of men circling for position, the tension ratcheting all about them, yet over the two men glaring at each other, a pall of silence hung heavy with accusation and unspoken threat.

His younger brother's voice dripped with sarcasm, "You have no idea where I belong."

"It's not here. Whatever he's done to you, I will make it right. You have my word."

Stefano leaned across the table and hissed, "You're too late, Brother. I finally know who and what I am. Taking me home will change nothing." He locked eyes with Nico and said, "You wanted me to have purpose? You and Tonio. Well, I'm pleased to inform you that you have finally succeeded."

He sat back and crossed his arms over his chest, his face no longer a reflection of youthful naiveté and charm. Instead, his eyes bore testament to depths of depravity and savagery Nico could barely imagine, yet knew he must confront.

Time pressed uncertainly, his awareness that he needed his brother's co-operation but was unlikely to secure it without lengthy

271

debate, if at all, warred with his roiling gut and the sensation that all this talking was for naught with Veluria in the hands of a madman.

He was out of time and out of patience. Pushing away from the table, he advanced on Stefano and gripped his arm, yanking him unceremoniously from the bench. Hissing, "Come with me. I have need of your services."

Stefano jerked away and shouted, "I'm not going home with you!"

"I don't recall giving you a choice, boy." The deadly silence of a room full of heavily armed men waiting for a signal settled like a pall.

"You and father ... and Tonio ... you can all go to hell."

Nico set his lips in a grim line and spat, "Tonio's dead."

Stefano collapsed on the bench, his face a twisted mask of pain and disbelief. As Nico counted off the precious seconds, hoping that would shock his brother into changing his mind, he finally became aware of movement behind him. The chink of swords and shuffling feet alerted him to the danger his rash action had put them all in. He needed to get his brother out of the hall and away from the guards.

If he thought Stefano would see the light he was sorely mistaken. The young man said, "That changes nothing. Leave, Nicolo. There is nothing for you here."

"Wrong answer, little brother. You *are* coming with me."

Once more he grabbed Stefano's arm and pulled him up. With a nod at Paulo, he hauled the struggling boy toward the door, taking care to keep his brother's hand away from the sword sheathed at his waist. His men formed a wall about them, creating a narrow passage of bodies through which he dragged his squirming, cursing brother.

Paulo shouted, "We'll hold them, sire," and turned into the fray.

Andreas met them at the door, his brow creased with concern. "It took you long enough. We must hurry."

Stefano continued to hurl invective on his brother, landing blow after blow until Nico was forced to pause to catch his breath.

"Listen, you goddam fool. Friedrich has Veluria!"

"Wha—? Veluria? Here?" He stared at Nico, then Andreas, who nodded assent.

The cleric moaned and braced his hand against the wall. "He's hurting her..."

Stefano stuttered, "Why does he...? Where?"

"You would know that better than us. We need to find him and get Veluria before he hurts her," he choked out the word, "...more."

"I-I ... uh, I know where he is."

"Take us." Nico pleaded, "You cared for her once. Please, Stefano, don't let him do this to her." Holding his breath he waited a heartbeat for his brother to decide his loyalties. He would do whatever was necessary to force the boy to comply. He and his conscience would wrestle with those consequences later, if he lived long enough.

Stefano weighed his options and said, "Follow me."

"Will there be guards?" Nico had to shout the words, the din from the hall echoing through the corridor.

Stefano laughed without mirth and pointed to the battle in the banquet hall, "There will be."

****

Andreas held up a hand and listened intently. Faint shouts came from behind a doorway to their left. In front of them a corridor led to the newer section of the castle.

Stefano muttered, "Those are the Duke's private rooms. There's a passage from there that leads to the interrogation chamber." He shrugged. "There will be an army headed to protect Friedrich now."

With all the duke's guards milling about, none of them could see any clear way to access the chamber without fighting their way to it.

Nico murmured, "I'm not leaving her," and moved into the hallway. Andreas gripped his arm and pulled him back as Stefano muttered, "Wait." Irritated he waved his sword toward the tall man, unable to bear the intense pain crushing his chest any longer. Nico nodded his understanding, his expression indicating he was not immune to the suffering either.

Crouching low, Stefano moved quickly toward a plain wood door hidden in an alcove in the opposite direction of the milling guards. Depressing the latch, he eased it open and motioned them to follow. Barely shoulder-width the corridor ran the length of the Duke's chambers, the few narrow slits admitting weak light to filter through, leaving streaks of pale color on the dank grey stone floor.

Nervously, Andreas wondered if anyone had found the Duke's daughter. He'd left her body in a similar access tunnel. From the hubbub both in and out of the duke's chamber, he suspected his dirty little secret was a secret no more.

He hoped to hell the Stefano brat knew where he was going. Veluria's essence faded in and out the longer they trolled the godforsaken halls of the castle. Whether or not they'd be in time to avert permanent damage was problematic. That she would still be alive was not the issue. The pervert would extend his pleasure as long as possible, days if necessary.

Everything rested on Nicolo de' Medici neutralizing the Duke. The young brother was an annoying complication and one he would have preferred not to deal with. All he could hope for was to salvage as much of the timeline as possible. Without the Duke, he could not predict what young Stefano would do. Assuming they all lived, would he return with Nico to Florence, or would he exercise his rights as bereaved consort and take the remaining daughter as his bride? He wouldn't put it past the pup to jump on such an opportunity. He was, after all, a Medici.

They exited from the confined passage onto a landing that led down a steep flight, disappearing into the gloom. Echoes of movement, an occasional shout, indicated they would not be alone once they reached the infamous chamber. Friedrich's guards would ensure their master was undisturbed while he indulged his passions.

Once they reached the lowest level, Nico took point and moved soundlessly toward an open area from which the murmuring of voices could be heard. Peering around the corner he held up four fingers, his body tensed, ready to spring. Stefano drew him back and hissed, "Nico, wait..."

The tall man paused while Stefano asked him, "Can you fight, Father?" That caught Nico's attention.

Andreas' answered, "Well enough," but looked with regret at his tattered robes and bare feet and knew in his heart he would not acquit himself well on a field of battle. That was not his training or inclination. Nico looked like he agreed.

He whispered to Stefano, "Is the Duke's so-called prowess with a sword accurate?"

Nico's brother only nodded, leaving Andreas' stomach to flutter with anxiety. There was no way he could handle the Duke, even motivated as he was to save the Sisterhood's damn operative. He did none of them any service by getting himself killed, least of all Matteo who he feared would act rashly should he so carelessly lose his life. That was not something his conscience, such as it was, was comfortable carrying into the next life.

Stefano said, "Go, Nico. I can handle him…" he flicked his head in the direction of the locked door. "He'll let me in. I am, after all, expected."

Nico looked like he wasn't sure he could trust his brother—and God knew *he* certainly wasn't convinced the boy had changed his allegiance so suddenly. The tall man asked the question Andreas was about to voice, "That locks from the inside. If something happens to you…?"

Stefano said, "There's another entrance," he waved off to the left toward a dark alcove at the far end of the hallway. "Inside you will find an opening covered with a tapestry. It's a tight fit." He looked at Andreas with a measured stare. "*You* will fit. I am not sure about my brother."

Nico risked a look at Andreas and shrugged. It had been quiet for too long now, the absence of Veluria's pain almost worse than the unrelenting agony they'd been suffering for what seemed like hours. They had few choices remaining. Nico said, simply, "Go," and moved aside to allow Stefano to move into the corridor.

Nico whispered, "Go to the passage and see if what my brother says is true."

Andreas breathed a yes while they listened to Stefano announce his presence to the guards. For long, agonizing moments they waited while Stefano directed two of the armed men to check out the stairwell and keep watch for any of the Medici entourage. That left two behind. Nico and Andreas exchanged a glance.

The duke greeted the young man with pleasure, his words cut off when the door shut with a resounding thud. Even from their remote location they could hear the interior bolts being thrown.

Andreas muttered, "There better damn well be another entrance." He turned to Nico and asked, "What are you going to do?"

Nico gave him a feral grin and said, "Even the odds."

Chapter Thirty-Two

Nico would have preferred not to have his targets split, the two men guarding the door, the other two off on a stairwell he couldn't see from his vantage point. While he appreciated Stefano's effort, in truth the boy had never been much of a tactician when it came to fighting. He'd been more likely to charm an opponent into joining him at a tavern than defeating him in a show of strength.

Measuring the heft of his sword, he appreciated the fine balance and honed edge. Counting off the seconds, he gave the cleric enough time to scurry out of sight. Sheathing his weapon, he boldly strode around the corner and casually approached the startled men.

Imperiously he walked to the door and raised a fist as if to pound on the wood, only to have a guard move between him and the reinforced door.

The man barked, "Hold."

Nico heard a sword being unsheathed behind him. To the man blocking his path he growled, "Do you know who I am?"

The guard nodded and gave a quick glance to his henchman. The Duke's men were not known for being simple-minded. It wouldn't take long for them to err on the side of their orders which were to protect the Duke's privacy at all costs.

He kept his left hand at his side, the stiletto palmed with the blade shielded by the sleeve of his tunic.

"I was told my brother visits the Duke." He waved his right hand in the direction of the stairwell. "I was directed to this location."

The guard grunted but refused to move. He stared up at Nico suspiciously.

"I have a matter of some urgency to discuss with my brother." He pressed close to the man, towering over him, using his size to intimidate him into moving. It didn't work. He felt the prick of a blade against the back of his neck.

The man in front of him grinned and said, "The Duke does not wish to be disturbed."

Nico raised his right hand and backed away, the point of the sword still knicking at his flesh. He muttered, "Well then," and allowed the hilt to slip across his palm. "When you see my brother, will you give him a message—?"

Dropping to a knee, he flipped the stiletto to his right hand and rammed it down through the guard's instep, then rolled, narrowly avoiding the broadsword arcing past his shoulder blade. Continuing the roll, he came to an abrupt stop against the wall, his knee impacting the cold stone with a painful crack.

The din in his head threatened to disorient him, the distraction of men shouting an alarm, racing feet, screams of panic, the fierce stab of pain, blood trickling in warm rivulets. Bracing against the wall, he pushed himself upright and drew his sword.

The one guard bellowed his distress. The other advanced with a look of anticipation, the promise of sport overriding what should have been caution.

Nico shut down the competing sensations and focused on the man circling to his left, effectively splitting his attention between the cursing guard struggling to extract the blade from his foot and the unwieldy weapon pointed at his throat.

Unlike Tonio, he could not take control, could not shut down the mind of an opponent, but he *could* use their thoughts to anticipate next moves. For that he needed clarity, not the cacophony of sensations swamping him. On instinct he dodged to the right barely avoiding the metal connecting with stone, showering the dimly lit area with sparks.

Damn it. That was close.

He was boxed between the two guards with little room for maneuvering and in the recesses of his mind he knew more would join them shortly. He needed to end this now.

****

Andreas pressed an ear to the opening but the heavy tapestry muffled sound from the two men situated at the end of the room farthest from his location. From what he could hear, it was not a pleasant conversation. Risking detection he moved the material away from the wall and peered into darkness.

Extending his senses he detected a large device partially blocking the opening. If he were lucky he could shelter behind the object until opportunity presented itself. Wriggling through the gap he crawled to the right and crouched, fighting to keep his breathing under control. Whimpering off to his left nearly drove him insane. Veluria was awake … and in pain.

Did he dare attempt penetration into her fractured psyche? The urge to sooth her fears—to ease the agony—was almost too much to resist, yet he knew in his gut that was an unacceptable risk. She could interpret his invasion of her core as yet more torture and alert the Duke and Stefano to his presence with damning words.

The Duke spoke in his native tongue but Stefano answered, "Yes, that is *my work* as you put it." His voice held a strange mix of pride and regret.

"Most impressive, my boy." There was a shuffling noise followed by a strangled moan. It sounded like the Duke had gagged Veluria to keep her from crying out.

What in God's name did the madman plan to do?

"They are lovely, are they not?" Stefano grunted non-committally. "These are banned, you know. Pity. I find them oddly … arousing." He laughed, the tone pitched high like a girl's giggle.

Andreas shivered. He suspected the Duke was planning to adorn Veluria's body with illicit piercings, something that even in his day was viewed with distaste and carefully regulated. Such ornamentation in the brotherhood was anathema to their vows of austerity. He had no objections one way or the other if one of his brethren chose to flaunt themselves in that manner. But he did object to wanton disfigurement of the work of art that was Veluria.

Muted sounds of scuffling and shouting pierced the air. Andreas stood and peered around the edge of the device, the size of a small wardrobe, just large enough to contain … a body. His gut clenched at the thought. He couldn't see Veluria but the Duke and Stefano were in his line of sight, both men glancing at the door with curiosity.

The Duke kept his eyes trained on the door but said to Stefano, "So you brought your friends."

"Friends...?"

"Do you think me a fool, boy? Your brother, your former mistress. An armed escort. This bears your meddling father's touch." The man stalked toward Stefano, driving the young man toward the far wall.

Stepping awkwardly away, Stefano drew his blade, his face set in a grim line as the Duke advanced, sword in hand, thrusting with controlled, precise movements. Flicking his wrist with practiced ease, the older man scored first blood, the slice shallow along the young man's ribcage.

Stefano hissed a breath and rolled his shoulder, shaking off the sting. Blood blossomed on his tunic, a thin red line. He continued to retreat under the Duke's unrelenting attack, the echo of steel-on-steel reverberating throughout the room, punctuated by the more distant clash of weapons beyond the thick walls.

Stefano tripped and stumbled, unable to find his footing amidst the clutter of instruments and devices littering the room. Only youth and quickness saved him from being skewered against a wooden platform, though his opponent connected with a deep gash to his sword arm, severe enough that Andreas feared the young man's arm had been rendered useless.

Friedrich surveyed the damage and chuckled, "Cosimo should know better than to send a boy to do a man's job."

Andreas could do little more than watch. His instincts told him to free Veluria while the combatants were engaged, yet they remained too close to wherever the Duke had secured her—probably strapped to a platform of some type. If he exposed his presence, the Duke would surely lop his head off in one fell swoop. Dead he did none of them any good.

The war beyond the walls ebbed and flowed with no end in sight. At least the boy's older brother had sufficient skills to keep the guard occupied and ignorant of the drama unfolding in the room— not that the Duke required assistance.

Andreas cared little if Friedrich dispatched the boy—he was willing to delegate *that* responsibility to one far more skilled than he. However, in that event, that left him and Veluria at the Duke's tender mercies. That outcome was not one he wished to contemplate.

He needed to get to the door, unbolt it and allow Nico access. Without his help, all was lost.

Bare feet slapping the packed dirt floor, he bolted toward the door only to be brought up short at the vision of Veluria strapped to a table, her body in obscene display as she twisted weakly against leather bonds slicing through tender flesh. Fascinated he watched blood pool and dribble off the table to fall with desultory ease onto the floor, the reddish-brown stain instantly absorbed.

Eyes wild with panic, she followed the two men sparring just within her field of vision, mouth grimly wrapped about the gag. He backed toward the door, willing her to see him, to know he was there. Turning to be sure he was headed in the right direction, he lost sight of her momentarily. When he turned back, he found her staring at him, the recognition lining her face with hope.

When she opened to him he nearly lost himself in the sensuous caress of all that she was. Precious moments passed as he sought to reassure her but she turned away to watch the Duke toying with her former lover.

Stefano struggled gallantly but the Duke would soon tire of the game and dispatch the young man, either killing him outright or disabling him enough that he would provide additional entertainments later.

The evil of the man's essence poured off him in waves. Andreas had never believed in a devil … or hell.

Until now.

Racing to the barricade, he threw the bolts and yanked the heavy door open to a world awash in carnage such as he'd never dreamt possible.

****

Staggering to the right, Nico yanked his stiletto from the guard's foot and shoved him out of the way. Tensing, he sensed the air shift and dropped his shoulder as he launched his body against the swordsman, burying the stiletto to the hilt in the man's gut. Though not a killing blow, it dropped the man in his tracks. Hands sticky with blood he grappled with the sword and swung it in a high arc— the sharp edge making a clean slice. Grimacing as the metal impacted hard stone, he gasped and steadied himself for the next wave.

As he suspected, the guards from the stairwell had come to see what the fracas was about. With little room to maneuver, and the stone slippery with blood and other bodily fluids, he was hemmed in and outmanned.

More shouts, the clash of swords...

Nico weighed his options. The newest arrivals moved cautiously but steadily on his position. With his back to the wall, he had no place left to go. Injured, bleeding copiously from wounds to his torso and thigh, he was no match for fresh troops. If he surrendered, he could live to another day, perhaps barter his freedom in exchange for concessions from his father.

But I'm not the only one to consider. If I surrender that still leaves Veluria in the hands of a pervert. I am worth a ransom but she has no value other than a plaything.

Hands trembling, Nico lowered the heavy sword and bowed his head in a posture of surrender. He edged toward the door, stepping over the prone form of the decapitated guard, keeping his mind blank as he booted the head away to roll past his newest antagonists.

Flicking his eyes from one to the other, he waited for them to make their move. In the distance, echoes of more fighting gave him a frisson of hope that his men might be advancing to his position. He need only hold these two off long enough.

A flash of steel to his left, the trajectory froze in his peripheral vision, offering a choice. He swiveled to take the blow on his shoulder blade, using the downward turn to hack through the gauntlet protecting his opponent's wrist to his right. Sword and severed hand fell away as he reeled from the ice penetrating the muscles of his back.

More men poured into the hallway, some advancing with weapons raised, others backing in, the clatter too loud in the confined space to make sense of who fought whom. Paulo had brought the battle to him.

Inside and outside the walls, all he detected was anger, panic, and senseless death. He needed to get inside but he was rapidly losing his strength.

A blow knocked him against the barricade, setting his head ablaze with pain. Something gripped his jerkin and yanked him backwards.

Nico fell through the open door and landed on the dirt floor in a daze.

****

Andreas hissed, "Get up. Get up, damn you!"

The man was a dead weight as he tried to haul him to his feet. Once upright he staggered drunkenly using Andreas' body to hold himself steady.

"Can you fight, man?"

Nico nodded wearily but Andreas wasn't sure he had enough left to handle a skilled swordsman like Friedrich. Grunting, he spun Nico's huge form around and said, "She's alive but not for long."

The room settled into a profound silence, not even the racket from the battle outside the walls seemed to penetrate the barrier of evil cocooning the scene playing out before their eyes.

Friedrich held a blade to Veluria's throat, the whisper of a thin slice across her windpipe leaving a fresh trail of blood to trickle in meandering streams across pale flesh. The hands holding the blade were obscenely delicate, long-fingered and elegant. The Duke placed a hand on her blue-black hair and stroked the tangled strands, quieting her frantic motion as her eyes took in the tableau: Andreas propping her injured lover, the man's sword hanging uselessly at his side, the Duke to her right, looming, enjoying the moment.

Stefano lay in a crumpled heap behind the Duke, his life force pooling darkly under his torso. There was no indication that the boy lived or died. At that moment it mattered little.

Nico visibly relaxed, his senses opening to Andreas.

Remove the bonds. You must get her out of here.
But...
My men are outside. They will see you to your destination.
I cannot take her with me.
But you will see her safe.
Yes.
Then prepare yourself.

Friedrich must not live.
I know.
Are you strong enough...?
I am strong enough for this.

Hissing as he stepped aside, taking his weight on his injured leg, the tall man hefted his sword and angled away from the table on which Veluria lay.

Nico challenged the Duke, his voice resolute, "Let us finish this."

Friedrich sneered, "As you wish." He followed Nico to the center of the room, his sword held easily in his right hand. "It will give me great pleasure to send my condolences to Cosimo. Such a tragedy to lose two sons on the same day."

Whatever Nico said was lost in the clang of steel and the clatter of bits of wood hitting walls and floor. Andreas ran to the table on which Veluria lay and tore at the unyielding straps. He pulled his stiletto from the folds of his robe and hacked madly at the restraints, moaning "I'm sorry, I'm sorry," as he connected with soft tissue on her wrists. When her hands were free, he pulled the gag out of her mouth and set to work on her legs. After helping her to sit up, he searched for something to cloth her battered body.

Veluria nodded at a nearby chair and croaked, "My dress." He slipped it over her head, carefully smoothing the soiled fabric along her petite frame.

She pointed to an ornate ladies' stiletto lying by Stefano's body. He shook his head and said, "Leave it. We must hurry." Taking her hand he guided her toward the tapestry and the escape opening.

This was not how he imagined that first touch, that loving burst of sensuous pleasure, fingers entwining in wicked warmth, exploring. Instead all he felt was bile rising in his throat as he fought against the anger threatening to consume him. None of them was worthy of her. Even damaged she was more precious than gold.

He'd set in motion what needed to be done. His last task in this world was to save the only thing worth salvaging, even if he never touched or saw her again.

This was the truest test of his worth.

He would not let her down.

****

Nico was only barely aware that Andreas and Veluria had made their escape. The Duke continued to taunt and tease him, inflicting minor damage, weakening him until he had no recourse but commit a fatal error.

He gasped, "What did you hope to gain, you bastard?" Advancing, he pressed Friedrich toward a pile of debris on the floor behind him but the man cleverly sidestepped to a clear area.

Chuckling, the man refused to engage, preferring to let his sword speak on his behalf. It was a debate that for once Nico was not going to win. Too late to dodge, his reflexes lost to pain and weariness, he felt the blade slide in, aware only of a comforting warmth, not even sure what part of his body bore the blunt trauma.

Sinking to his knees he swung wildly, the weight a burden he could no longer bear. Stars danced in his eyes as he awaited the final blow. He hoped Tonio would greet him with forgiveness in his heart. For Stefano, he simply prayed that God would show mercy for a misguided young man.

Locking eyes with the devil himself, Nico lifted his sword to parry the blow one last time. Friedrich's dark eyes turned smoky, savoring the pleasure, lips parted in anticipation, pink foam speckling his cruel mouth as he sighed his last breath.

Stefano released the stiletto jammed into the duke's throat and let the man slide boneless to the floor. Sinking to his knees, he stared into his brother's eyes and murmured, "Tell Papà I died well, Nico. Don't let him know…"

Nico caught his brother as he pitched forward. When Paulo and his men burst into the chamber, he sat cradling Stefano's body, staring dry-eyed at the wreckage of his life.

His last thought before slipping into oblivion was, *I did what you wanted. I hope to hell your world is worth it.*

Chapter Thirty-Three

Andreas nervously fingered the braided wool cincture loosely resting on his hips.

"Hold still, boy." Matteo fiddled with the amice, wrapping it around Andreas' neck and shoulders. He smoothed the fabric over the long linen garment, murmuring, "…helmet of salvation…"

Turning to face Matteo, Andreas intoned, "…may I deserve nevertheless eternal joy," as his superior adjusted the long thin vestment over his narrow shoulders. The words stuck in his throat. 'Eternal damnation' seemed more appropriate to his situation.

Matteo muttered, "Where did I put the maniple?" as he searched through the pile of vestments on the cot. "Ah, found it." He turned to stare solemnly at Andreas but pride flecked his eyes with gold.

"Dammit, can you help me with this?" Andreas tightened the rope holding the vestments in place.

Laughing Matteo said, "Don't forget the words."

"Yeah, yeah, continence…" he grimaced, "and what was that other thing?"

"Chastity."

"Right."

He ducked his head as the older man settled the heavy chasuble over his shoulders. Matteo smoothed his unruly hair back behind his ears and said softly, "It's just a traditional saying, Andy." Concern creased Matteo's face.

Andreas knew he'd been distant, moody, using the excuse that he needed meditation after the trials of his mission. Although his injured ankle was largely mended, the medics had recommended removing the pins and subjecting him to the machinations of their torture devices to strengthen the bones. He had welcomed the discomfort and painful rehabilitation.

Matteo leaned down and brushed his lips, his hand cupping his chin gently. It was all he could do to not cringe in revulsion. The last thing he deserved was this man's affection in light of his monumental failures … and the secrets he now harbored in his soul.

Secrets he must carry to his grave.

"Are you ready?"

He wasn't but he followed Matteo into the corridor prepared to lie through his teeth. But about what he wasn't sure.

****

The Three were the last to take their seats. Andreas knelt on the hard marble dais, head bowed in respect. Once more he faced the full Council, something few operatives ever encountered in their short working careers, let alone twice in succession.

He had no idea why he merited such attention. The debriefing had been, at best, perfunctory, the half-truths he'd spewed sufficient to allay concerns about his lack of detail. He'd had what the scribes called 'continuity issues' but he managed to gloss over the more glaring holes in his recitation, alluding to the rigors of the flight from the Habsburg territories and concerns over the failing health of the Sisterhood's operative.

Matteo rose and said, "Please take a seat, Father."

He moved to comply, carefully arranging his vestments. The chasuble lay heavy on his shoulders and he longed to remove the unwieldy garment. Sweat pooled on his brow and ran in rivulets down his back. The maniple lay across his lap. He briefly considered using it for its intended purpose, to wipe away sweat, but decided against giving them the satisfaction.

He glanced at his superior but the man was in quiet conversation with two of his colleagues. There was nothing about Matteo's demeanor to give him pause, yet an undercurrent of suspicion lay like a pall over the proceedings. As usual he listened with only half an ear while the scribe reviewed the documents, reading his statement in measured tones—a mere formality as the fifteen members would have fine-tooth combed every phrase, searching for inconsistencies.

He'd allowed for a sufficient number to give his story credibility. What he could not account for were outcomes.

That's why he was here.

"Can you please tell us…"
"…and what happened after…"
"How can you be sure…"

With flat tones he fielded each question, keeping his face blank, preparing for the summary statement. Matteo would not be accorded that privilege, given their acknowledged relationship. He'd gone into the proceedings aware of that fact, yet it left him with a feeling of disquiet. These men were masters of innuendo. Matteo's special spin might have been all he needed to lay this matter to rest once and for all.

His stomach sank when the head of The Three rose and walked behind the row of chairs on the dais, circling the bench and approaching his position. He quickly bent his head to mask his dismay.

Instead of stopping in front of Andreas, the stocky prelate walked over to a projection table where a tech stood ready with a remote.

"I'll take that…" The prelate reached for the remote, then turned and waved Andreas to join him.

Somewhere off to his left a voice instructed the attendants to clear the room. For a moment he could swear everyone held their collective breaths until the final soft swoosh as the chamber doors sealed.

The prelate said, "Well then," and clicked the remote.

The image danced and wavered, too pixelated for clarity. The prelate cursed and adjusted the gain, but the projection stayed out of focus.

"Does anybody know how to use this damn thing?"

Matteo jumped down from the dais and took the device away from the frustrated man. With deft fingers he altered the settings, then handed the device back to his superior. The prelate grunted his thanks and waved Matteo back to his seat. His superior moved past him, a hand lovingly brushing his back. The small gesture gave him a measure of comfort.

It was immediately dispelled when he turned to the holographic image. Blood drained from his face, leaving him light-headed and nauseous. He doubted he was the only one.

The head of The Three nodded respectfully and said, "Reverend Mother. Kind of you to join us today."

The woman smiled warmly and replied, "My pleasure, Jules. It's been too long."

'Jules'? To his knowledge no one, absolutely no one, had ever spoken with, let alone seen the Church's head. Apparently he'd been wrong. He risked a backward glance at the rest of the Council members. Only the remaining two members of The Three were not in a state of shock—everyone else sat with mouths agape.

Andreas fought the urge to step behind the prelate, out of line of sight. Flight was not an option, though it crossed his mind.

The man he now knew as 'Jules' continued the exchange of pleasantries, directing the woman's attention to each member of the Council. She nodded to each in turn, then said firmly, "I understand you have good news and bad news for me."

"Um, yes." He gripped Andreas arm, anchoring him in place. "We've secured an accord with the competing factions, each allowing oversight." That was clearly the good news.

"But not disarmament...?" The woman looked both displeased and resigned with the state of affairs. Jules looked like he agreed with the woman's assessment.

Regretfully, the man answered, "Yes, Madam, but under the circumstances, perhaps the most logical outcome."

The woman asked Jules, "Is this the one?" and focused her attention on Andreas.

The man called Jules released Andreas' arm and backed away, leaving him to face his judge, jury and executioner alone.

"Tell me..."

****

The morning air still held the bite of autumn, Andreas' breath hanging in a soft grey mist as he panted from the exertion of carrying Veluria through the dense forest.

They'd run the horses to exhaustion, finally resorting to staggering through the woods on foot. Andreas' bare feet ached from the cuts and bruises but he knew his discomfort was nothing compared to the pain that Veluria silently endured. He'd been aghast at the amount of blood she'd lost, the back of her dress sodden. Not for the first time he wished he'd stayed and killed the bastard who'd violated her rather than delegating that task to Nicolo de' Medici.

He needed to find shelter and food, yet the district remained devoid of human habitat, not even a stray sheep herding cabin to offer respite from the elements.

Tenderly he laid the frail form on a nest of pine needles. She shivered, still unconscious, and he sensed her life force draining away.

An opening to his right gave promise to a break in the endless tract of pine and rocky soil. They'd been on a downhill slope for hours. He prayed he'd find a village, a stream, something that would offer up a smattering of hope.

****

"But you are certain that the assassination was carried out?"

"Yes, Madam. As I said, I procured transport and continued on to Tuscany." He paused, trying to recall the exact sequence of events.

"And…?"

"The woman, Veluria, was … damaged. Beyond my capacity to help." He allowed tears to moisten his cheeks. "She was brave to the end, Madam. You and the Sisterhood can be proud of her contribution."

Reverend Mother gave him a strange look, a mixture of sadness and regret. Shuffling on the dais reminded him he needed to continue.

"I stopped at an inn close to Florence. The news had already arrived. The death of the Duke, the de'Medici boy. Of Nicolo I had no information other than lack thereof, so I assume he still lives."

Lived. His head ached and his ankle still throbbed. Somehow he suspected the woman was not buying any of it.

Jules interjected, "That would be consistent with our current situation."

Reverend Mother ignored him and went on, "What I do not understand, gentlemen, is why we still have perturbations. With

Carlos' path to Holy Roman Emperor unchecked, we should have seen a reversal in the oscillations..." she stared pointedly at Jules and demurred, "…unless, of course, your mathematicians were wrong?"

Shrugging the man said, "It is still an inexact science."

"Hmm, yes, I suppose it is." To Andreas she spoke so softly he strained to hear the words, "Thank you. At least she was not alone at the end," but the look she leveled at him chilled him to the marrow.

Jules barely had a chance to mutter, "Madam…" before the image faded. Andreas knew the collective sigh of relief was not imagined.

****

"We destroyed the avatar as you requested." Matteo sounded relieved, for good reason. For him, it was an insurance policy that Andreas could not return to that time and place. With a sigh he asked, "Are you sure about this, Andy?"

Matteo pulled him into an embrace but he shrugged the man away, the thought of his superior extending any kindness turning his blood cold. He zipped the small valise and slung it over his right shoulder.

He and his conscience had a journey of discovery ahead of them.

"I'll be here when you want me, boy." The pain and sadness in the man's voice cut like a knife.

Andreas shouldered his way through the door without a backward glance. The whispered, *I love you*, trailed behind him, a ghostly shadow of the passion he'd once felt but would never experience again.

Take this, Andreas. Keep it safe.
What is it?
The way home.

He fingered the strange device, the workmanship exquisite, each jewel in the crucifix cut to perfection.

Are you sure?
Yes.

He choked back the words. She could never know the depth of his despair. Instead he asked, *Are you strong enough?*

Yes, Andreas, I am strong enough for this.

The ancient Amalfi coast stretched with torturous curves to his left and right, the villages climbing the cliffs with wanton disregard for gravity and the passage of time. He leaned over the abutment and wondered at his fate and the fate of his world. If he cast this stone, would the ripples extend beyond his own time and space, to crash with unknown force against some distant shore? Or would he and all he knew fade into shadows, forever ephemeral, insubstantial...

In his heart he realized he cared little for the fate of a world that had already eaten itself alive with hatred. History would play out directionless, immune to the petty concerns of such like him and the others.

She had placed the ultimate test into his hands and bade him do with it as he willed.

Mounting the scooter he glanced to the south, the narrow road beckoning. Hesitating, he palmed the crucifix, the metal burning red hot into his rough palm, and made the sign of the cross, then threw the device into the waiting ocean below.

****

"Boy, it's good to see you."

Nico tried to hide his dismay. Cosimo lay on the large bed, his body wasting away with age and infirmity and grief. The news had arrived long before Nico'd been well enough to travel. Paulo had managed to spirit him to a neighboring duchy, one friendlier to the Medici family, where they had wintered and he'd regained his strength.

"I came as soon as I could, Papà." He sat on the edge of the bed and held his father's hand, the skin parchment thin and brittle to the touch. As brittle and cold as his heart.

The old man's eyes held a world of sorrow and regret. They spoke quietly of nothing in particular until Cosimo's lids lowered and he appeared to drift into sleep. Nico tucked the quilt about his father and rose to leave.

Huskily, Cosimo said, "Wait."

"Yes, Papà?"

291

His father's eyes darted to the window, the light growing dim with the setting sun. "I want you to tell the gardener to bring in fresh herbs for dinner."

"I'll tell Tomas to…"

"No, you, my son." He shot Nico an imperious look. "Now."

Shrugging, Nico mumbled "All right," and left the bedroom. He took the stairs leading to the rear of the villa and exited through the kitchens. The well-tended gardens looked the same, though he had trouble recalling where on the estate the vegetables might be located.

The slight downhill slope taxed his injured leg. He would probably walk with a limp for the rest of his days, though he could still sit a horse well enough. His fighting days, such as they'd been, were clearly over. Feeling as old as Cosimo looked, he wandered about the grounds, enjoying the late evening breeze.

In the shadow at the base of a hill he saw a small figure bent over a mass of greenery. Not wishing to proceed further he shouted, "Excuse me. My father wishes herbs brought in for dinner." Feeling foolish, he realized Cosimo hadn't said what kind so he hastened to add, "He didn't say what."

The woman rose and pushed a long dark braid off her shoulder. With her face still in shadow, she brushed her hands on her skirts but made no indication she understood the request.

Moving closer, he said with more irritation than he intended, "Did you hear me…?" but stopped abruptly, his heart pounding in his chest.

She was the same, yet different, painfully thin, her pale skin stretched over prominent cheekbones, dark shadows lining her eyes with emotions he couldn't begin to describe. She'd pulled her glorious mane into a tight braid, accentuating the planes of her face and giving her an austere, almost untouchable demeanor.

Watching him limp forward, he could see the hope and fear race across her face, unsure of her reception, of his feelings after all that had happened.

He had refused this fantasy, skillfully locking it away, content to remain an empty shell. Yet she had defied fate, making a choice, a sacrifice he would never understand but would spend the rest of his life proving that she had not chosen in vain.

He scooped her into his arms, crushing her to his chest.

She whispered, "Are you strong enough…?"

"Yes," he husked, his heart in his throat, "I will be strong enough," then paused to inhale the scent of honey and lavender that was uniquely Veluria before murmuring, "…if you tell me what you want."

"You, Nicolo de' Medici. I want you…"

~The End~

About the Author

Nya Rawlyns has lived in the country and on a sailboat on the Chesapeake Bay. When she isn't tending to her garden or the horses, the cats, or three pervert parakeets, she can be found day dreaming and listening to the voices in her head.

Website: http://the-men-of-crow-creek.weebly.com/
Blog: http://loveslastrefuge.com/
Website: http://www.romancingwords.com/index.html

Her published works include:

THE CROW CREEK SERIES: Ash & Oak, Pulling Leather, Strapping Ash, Sorting Will, Flankman
The Crow Creek Collection, Vol. I

THE HOLIDAY TOAST SERIES
The Christmas Toast
The Valentine Toast

The Shadow of This World
The Wrong Side of Right
Cajun Gothic (Blood Haven)
The Strigoi Chronicles: Penance, Fane, Michel, Dreu
Acid Jazz Singer (Hunger Hurts)
Finish Line (novella)
Dance Macabre (short story)
Skin
The Guardians of the Portals
Sculpting David (Red Sage, novella)
Hunter's Crossing (Red Sage)

29194194R00181

Made in the USA
Charleston, SC
03 May 2014